The Masks
Our Origins

To Mom

My friend, my role model, my support system, my hero.

The Masks
Our Origins

Payton Balog
Copyright © 2024 by Payton Balog

Prologue

SCATTERED WHISPERS ECHOED THROUGHOUT the crowd. Men, women, even children stood shoulder to shoulder, eyes locked on the two most famous women in Height City as they battled once again.

Red and blue lights flashed across the buildings. Every shop and office within a two block radius had their doors locked and their shutters closed. The owners were either in hiding or somewhere in the crowd, probably on the edge of their seats. Police officers kept people from getting too close. Civilians recorded everything with their phones. Some were live on Instagram and other social media platforms, who knows how many followers were tuning in. News vans from every major channel were parked on either side of the road. Hundreds of reporters shoved their way to the front, desperate to narrate each detail of the fight.

Alice stomped her foot, trying to see over everyone's shoulders. It was useless. She could only see the sparks. She had to get closer, but how? Could she push her way through? Would anyone step aside to let her pass? An idea popped into her head. It wasn't practical but it'd work, hopefully.

She zipped up her ragged, olive-green sweatshirt and pulled the hood over her head. She crept by Savanna Ann, a reporter for Channel Six; Savanna Ann, at the moment, was describing the scene and listing the most popular battles between Glisin and Destroyer. There were a lot.

Focused on getting closer to the fight, Alice dove between two men. One was sturdy and muscular like a wrestler while the other one was skinny. They didn't notice her but she heard them taking bets on whether or not Glisin would land the next punch. How could that even be a question?

Her hands and knees barely grazed the ground as she scurried toward the action. She didn't want to miss anything.

Alice, the determined twelve-year-old, wasn't supposed to be there. It was dangerous. Being near Destroyer could mean death. She'd proven several times to the public that she was ruthless and heartless. She'd often raid thriving businesses with her gang. They took what they liked - money, jewels, expensive weapons, knickknacks, accessories, artifacts, food, appliances - and destroyed the things that bored them.

Destroyer struck fear in the hearts of those who couldn't defend themselves. On more than one occasion, she was reported to have murdered the city's inhabitants. She didn't have boundaries or limits. She smiled as her victims screamed, and when they begged for their lives, she laughed.

But Alice couldn't help it. This was too exciting. Too important.

Her parents didn't know she snuck out. She didn't plan it. It all happened so fast. She'd been wanting to witness Glisin in action for months. Years, even. This was her chance.

As soon as her family finished dinner - her mom made a casserole - Alice went to her bedroom. She debated doing homework, then decided to try calling her best friend, Jess. An alert popped up on her phone: DESTROYER SPOTTED AT CITY HALL. CONFIRMED: CITY COUNCIL MEMBERS TAKEN HOSTAGE. MAYOR PORTER IS ALREADY DEAD. GLISIN IS ON HER WAY TO SAVE THE DAY.

Glisin, Height City's superhero, was going to battle her archenemy. The woman who made Height City tremble with her cruel smile, rainbow curls, and a pair of red, leather gloves. When the gloves came off, things were rumored to crumble.

Alice heard about Destroyer's powers but she'd never seen them in action.

Before a single rational thought could enter her mind, Alice climbed out her bedroom window and ran down the sidewalk, away from her house.

Alice finally managed to crawl ahead to the front row of the crowd. While trying to get back on her feet, she stumbled on the uneven curb but quickly steadied herself. She smiled. She couldn't believe it. Glisin in action. She could hardly keep herself from jumping up and down.

The hero and the villain were stuck in a perfect rhythm, each able to see ten steps ahead, punching and kicking, swinging, and dodging, twirling and cartwheeling. It was majestic. Destroyer moved like a rageful lion determined to rip apart her prey while Glisin's movements were fast and calculated like nothing Alice had ever seen.

Glisin dodged Destroyer's heel and stumbled backward. She caught herself, adjusted her footing, and shoved her hand out in front of her. Navy blue lightning sparked from the center of her palm blasting Destroyer into the air. The lightning's heat left a big, charred mark on the pavement.

A few people cheered. Others waited in silence, eager to see what would happen next. One guy shouted, "That's right, no mercy!"

Destroyer wasn't down for long. She hopped to her feet shaking the dust off. Her rainbow curls were stuck to her face, sweaty and tangled. Her eyes burned with hatred. Her face twisted in anger. She pulled off her gloves and hooked them to her belt. The stakes were raised and she wasn't backing down.

She lunged at her enemy.

Glisin ducked, twirled, and kicked Destroyer in the stomach. The villain came back more determined than ever. She screamed like a rabid banshee, attacking Glisin with everything she had. The women locked onto each other in a chaotic whirl of anger and frustration. They'd been battling for years and still neither of them had really won the war. Nobody knew what started their feud but Height City had always been their battlefield.

Alice held her breath. Glisin had won - or at least tied - every fight she ever fought. This one wouldn't be any different. She'd win again. Still, Alice's palms were starting to sweat. She reminded herself to breathe.

"Come on," she whispered. "You can do this."

Neither woman could land a single punch. They dodged one another's attacks until their movements started to slow. Destroyer swung her arm but Glisin flipped backward, hand flat on the road, as her legs went above her head and she landed in a crouch.

She stood up. Lightning glistened in her eyes and over her body. Navy blue electricity danced across her skin. She lifted her hand, ready to blast Destroyer again, but the villain was too quick. She grabbed Glisin's wrist.

No! This isn't happening. It can't be real.

The hero's body crumbled. Every finger, limb and skin cell became ash. The only thing left of Glisin was a black mask.

A blood-curdling scream vibrated against Alice's throat. Fog stuffed her mind. All the people, all the noises, everything faded, distant and blurred, a million miles away. Her knees buckled. She knelt on the sidewalk, hands trembling, as she bent forward. Hot, salty tears stung her eyes. A sharp ache seized her chest and she started to hyperventilate.

Silence swept over the crowd and consumed the city. Nobody could move or speak. They stood in complete shock as Destroyer took a victorious bow and left them all to stare at the pile of ashes.

Destroyer succeeded. She killed Height City's savior. She killed Alice's mom.

Chapter 1

Alice

Alice jolted upright in her bed, panting, as sweat dripped from her forehead and tiny, white lightning bolts flickered between her fingers. Her body trembled with the faded horror of her usual, torturous nightmare. Why was her mind so obsessed with this torture? Every night, every time she closed her eyes, her mom's death replayed and skipped like a scratched DVD.

The worst moment of Alice's life.

She took a deep breath, mentally counting down from ten over and over until the lightning stopped. Her heartbeat calmed. She stretched her hands and clutched the green and purple striped comforter, trying to steady her panic.

Her mattress was a hand-me-down from her old babysitter.

A first-edition Glisin poster hung above the bed. Loosening her grip on the comforter, Alice studied Glisin's signature turquoise suit, black boots, the matching belt, and her mask. The navy blue thunderbolt stamped on her chest was a symbol of hope and safety.

She stood as if she was invincible. She always stood like that, even when she wasn't in uniform. Ironic. At home, instead of Kevlar, Susan usually wore a T-shirt and leggings or her favorite ruffled apron.

Alice could still picture her wearing it. She'd be folding dough or mixing batter in the kitchen and either flour or sauce or both would be splattered all over the fabric.

She was a great baker. Alice used to be her taste tester.

Alice's tired eyes drifted from the poster to the nightstand. Next to the alarm clock was a family photo featuring Alice at seven years old. She looked innocent and carefree while Mason and Susan were so obviously in love and happy, if not a little tired.

How were people blind to the fact that Susan Johnson and Glisin were the same person? It didn't make any sense. Maybe because they didn't know the person behind the mask. They just knew the mask.

Height City built their hero into a demi-god. A powerful protector who never let them down. At least, until two years ago.

"Damn it," Alice sighed when she saw the time. She shoved herself out of bed and hurried to the small closet. A full-size, black-framed mirror hung on the door. Mason had painted little daisies on it but they were faded now. Her reflection was dim and out of focus.

She slid on a pair of yoga pants. She wore Susan's old T-shirt as a pajama top, which hung past her knees and was loose around her torso.

Alice used to be the spitting image of her mother which Mason always said made her lucky. As she got older her own individual traits set in. Her dad still called her beautiful. But her hair stayed identical to Susan's, so after Susan died, Alice dyed her hair purple.

As usual, she twisted her tangled, purple strands into a ponytail.

One wall of her bedroom was devoted to photos she had taken. Most of the photos were of random people, strangers on the street, smiling, kissing, laughing with their children, walking their pets, drinking coffee, skateboarding, doing art, or playing music.

Alice liked to notice people. They were fascinating.

Her photos were also of nature and animals she'd seen in Moon Park; flowers, bees, birds, chipmunks but her favorite photos were of Height City; City Hall where Alice found herself going more often than she liked; the little independent record shop her dad used to love. A white, cement building with a flickering, neon sign; the abstract statue outside Vance Technologies. A glass building with over a hundred floors; Key Hotel with its beautiful, rounded stone archway and marble floors. The photos starred many other buildings too.

Some of the photos were doctored like the one of City Hall. Alice made the photo so it'd be dark and haunting like an old black-and-white horror movie. Her favorite doctored photos were of the people she loved. One was of her parents standing in the kitchen; Mason was kissing Susan's cheek while she made breakfast. Alice made the photo all different colors, bright, vibrant, and lively. The love on their faces when they looked at each other made Alice smile. Another was of Jess, her best friend, hugging a stack of books. Pink roses were faded into the image and Alice made it look vintage and worn.

She grabbed her favorite ragged, olive-green sweatshirt, stuffed her textbooks in her backpack, and grabbed her camera from a leather messenger bag. An eleventh birthday present from Susan's mom.

"Dad?" Her voice echoed through the empty living room.

The seventies-styled couch - Susan picked it out - faced a flat-screen TV. Two side tables were on either side, each decorated with Susan's old pottery, including some vases, a bowl, and a plate with Alice's fossilized handprint from when she was a baby.

The coffee table was bruised and chipped. Alice vaguely remembered knocking her head against it when she was nine. It still had the old, half ripped Bugs Bunny and Daffy Duck stickers she stuck to the corners when she was four. Magazines and new, hollow beer bottles lay underneath it.

No answer, no surprise. Mason was never home. He was either at work or drinking at his favorite bar. He fell off the wagon two years ago. The same night of Glisin's funeral.

Alice passed a shelf dedicated to her athletic rewards. Trophies and team photos. At seven, she joined swimming, at nine, she started track and cross country. She also used to play soccer, basketball, and tennis.

She grabbed her sneakers, which were old, dirty, and falling apart but she loved them because her dad bought them for her. She'd wear them until the soles broke.

Creaky, wooden steps led to the cracked, uneven sidewalk outside her house.

A chihuahua stood in her neighbor's window barking furiously at the construction crew tearing up the old pavement. The men shouted jokes over an angry drill. One man waved to Alice with his yellow helmet. Another man carried a two-by-four on his shoulder, and as he turned, the wood swung toward the man who waved. It was going to smack him in the head.

Alice's powers bubbled under her skin and vibrations crept up her arms, making her fingertips tingle. The chaos around her slowed and the chihuahua's barking drifted farther away. She was hesitating.

She closed her eyes and counted to ten. It took all her concentration to drown her powers. They were an instinct she kept denying. Her body wanted so badly to let the energy soar but she hadn't, consciously, used her powers since her mom died.

When she opened her eyes, she saw the two-by-four swing over the man's head when he bent down to pick up a penny. Alice sighed, a little relieved, and headed away from the construction site.

Small businesses were grouped on the next two blocks; several boutiques that sold vintage clothing and knickknacks, some restaurants, a snow globe shop, and a music store. People drifted in and out of doorways, chatting, laughing, living their lives as always. Ever since Destroyer killed Glisin, things had been quiet. Nobody understood why Height City's notorious villain stopped her violent raids but people had settled into the tranquility.

Alice jogged the last four blocks until she stood in front of a three-story, brick building with a flat roof. A tall, metal fence surrounded the back parking lot and an American flag waved above the front steps. The limestone sign next to the sidewalk had the words MORGAN HIGH elegantly carved into it.

Alice ran up the stone staircase and shouldered open the first set of front doors. The second set was locked. *Seriously?* Was she really that late? And on the last day of freshman year, damn it.

She pressed the buzzer and the receptionist remotely unlocked the doors. Alice ran down the hall but the bell rang as soon as she reached her first class. *So close.* She stepped aside and the other students poured into the hall. Their overlapping voices were like white noise and static. Nobody paid her any attention as they headed to their lockers and collided with all the other students from the other classrooms.

The teacher sat at his desk wearing a gray suit with suede elbow patches and an orange and yellow polka dot bowtie. His dusty beige hair had gray streaks but he looked young, maybe her dad's age.

"Miss Johnson," he said.

"Mister Scotts," she frowned. Usually, he called his students by their first names. When he didn't, it was a cause for concern.

"You're late again." His tone was kind. He didn't seem angry or upset. That was a good sign, right?

"I'm sorry," she said. "I overslept."

"I understand your family is going through a difficult time," he sighed, sympathetic. "But next year, you can't be late or skip homework, and you have to participate in class."

For the entirety of freshman year, Alice walked or took the city bus to school. She sat at the back of the room and kept her hood above her head in hopes she'd be forgotten. Instead of homework, she'd sleep or take photos. She didn't care about her education anymore, neither did Mason.

"My dad doesn't drive me," she whispered, slightly embarrassed about the lack of interest her father had in her well-being. It wasn't a secret. Mason missed every student-teacher meeting and he never answered the principal's calls.

She pushed a strand of loose hair behind her ear. "My dad doesn't drive me and I don't always have money for the bus, so I walk or I run," she shrugged. "I don't really live close."

"You don't have anyone else who could give you a ride?" Mister Scotts asked. "Since your father isn't able to do it."

Alice swore she heard pity in his voice. She tore her gaze from the floor. "Not really."

"I see." Mister Scotts grabbed a Post-it off his desk and wrote on it. He used the blue pen he graded papers with, why didn't he use red? "Here."

She took it. It was his phone number. "I don't understand."

"My son and I have to leave early because I have to be here at the same time as the rest of the faculty. He always complains about it, he'd rather sleep in," he rolled his eyes, humorful. "And you two would have to share the radio," Mister Scotts chuckled. His smile made his face wrinkle in a light-hearted, wise way. "But if you want, we could come pick you up and give you a ride."

Alice wasn't sure what to think about the offer. It was nice but was it weird? She liked Mister Scotts. He was a good teacher. Alice could tell he loved his job. He was so passionate about his lessons, he was patient with his students, and never made anyone feel embarrassed or ashamed for asking questions.

Alice liked that he wore fancy bowties every day. It was dorky but cute. But giving her a ride seemed like such a big favor. He shouldn't have to go out of his way. Then again, Alice didn't have another option.

"I'll see, maybe. Thanks, Mister Scotts."

"Have a good summer, Alice," he said. "And remember, next year, you need to step it up."

She nodded. She'd keep that in mind.

She pulled a textbook from her backpack and handed it to him. He put it on the pile, then went back to work. And she left the classroom.

Tons of students were walking the halls. Overwhelming, excited chatter filled the air as the other kids discussed their summer plans.

Jess met Alice by the door. "Is everything okay? What did Mister Scotts say?"

"Everything's fine," Alice shrugged. "He said that I need to clean up my act, which I guess is true. My grades aren't the best."

"I could tutor you next year."

"I don't know. Maybe."

They walked side by side, avoiding collisions with the other students. The random snippets of conversation were enough to give Alice a headache. Most of the football team, in their yellow and blue letterman jackets, stood by the wall, talking about the huge party they were going to throw. The Honeycombers' end-of-school-year party was a tradition that started around the sixth grade.

Alice was a Nester. It meant she lived in the Nests. The large section of the city between the Burrows and the Honeycombs. The Honeycombs were considered the rich side and the Burrows were the poor side. You were either one of the three or an out-of-towner.

Jess wore a polo shirt and khakis. Her long, well-brushed, brown hair had pink streaks. She dyed it the same time Alice did hers.

They stopped at Alice's locker. She opened it.

Jess adjusted the perfectly organized pile of notebooks in her arms. She was the one person who stuck by Alice through her grief. Although, Jess didn't know the truth. Everyone thought Susan left in the middle of the night. A lie Mason created because his wife died as Glisin. There wasn't a body to identify, so it worked, her identity was safe.

Alice wasn't sure how she felt about the lie. She knew it was so none of Glisin's enemies would come after her or Mason, and Height City gave Glisin a beautiful, respectful funeral but Susan never got one. Alice wasn't allowed to openly grieve her mother's death.

She hated lying to Jess. She hated throwing Susan's reputation under the bus to save her alter ego but what else were they supposed to do? Everyone thought Susan abandoned her family, the neighbors still whispered about it, but at least Glisin was honored and adored, right?

After it happened, Alice shut down. She folded into anger, grief, and despair. She didn't have an interest in anything. Her friends from her middle school basketball team and the swim team moved on. Jess stayed, probably because she needed Alice as much as Alice needed her.

Jess's mother was difficult. Jess spent every spare second she had at Alice's house. She'd been by Alice's side ever since they met; when Jess, at six years old, walked up to Alice's sandcastle and suggested a way to make the drawbridge open and close.

Alice shoved her backpack into her locker. "So, how was Brittany's birthday party?"

"It was good," Jess smiled. "A little dramatic. She and Tony argued very publicly. I'm not sure what exactly happened but Jake and I had fun."

"Jake? The same Jake your mom loves?" she grabbed her books and closed her locker.

They headed down the hall.

"Yes, him. Unfortunately for her, he and I are just friends."

"Really?" Alice chuckled. "I'd thought she'd be planning the wedding by now."

"It's ridiculous," Jess said. "She'd love it if we were promised to each other already."

"Well, he is from a Honeycomber family like you. Good breeding and all that." Alice couldn't imagine having rich-people problems. "I'm glad you had fun."

"You could have come with, you're always invited."

"Invited by you. Not the thrower of the party or anyone else," Alice said. "Besides, I like hanging out with you. Only you." She hadn't been much of a people person since her mom died. She was too wrapped up in her nightmarish memories. Jess, unlike everyone else who believed the lies about Susan, didn't bad mouth or gossip about Alice's family. Jess loved Susan too.

"Okay, but you're my best friend," she said. "If you want to come, ever, then you can. Brittany and Cindy will have to deal with it."

Alice bobbed her head in response. They had talked about this before. It was always the same conversation. Alice appreciated the invitation but she doubted she'd have a good time. She didn't belong at a party. She wasn't sure she belonged anywhere.

"So, anyway." Jess chuckled. "My mom pulled some strings and got me an interview at her law firm. It's for a summer internship."

Alice smiled. "Wow, that's huge. When is it?"

"After school. The internship would start in a week. If I get it, I'll be busy."

"That's so great, Jess. Is it with your mom?"

"No," she shook her head. "It's with one of my parents' co-workers, Fred Willin. He's the best there is, so I can't screw up. My mom wrote talking points on some note cards and told me to memorize them. I've been reading them every night. And my dad helped me practice my handshake and I've already chosen an appropriate outfit. I feel ready... ish."

"It sounds to me like you're prepared." Alice admired Jess's preparation and religious study habits. She wasn't sure if it came from pressure or passion. Jess's fingertips were peeled. Picking her cuticles was one of her nervous habits. The first time Alice noticed it was when they were in the second grade, right before a spelling test, Jess picked her cuticles so hard that her fingers started bleeding.

"There's nothing to worry about," Alice said. "You'll do great."

"Your supportive positivity is appreciated but unhelpful."

"As always."

"Oh, God. I'm so sorry," Jess frowned as if she'd said the worst possible sentence in the world. "I mean, thank you so much for your support."

"It's okay," Alice tried to keep a light-hearted smile on her face. She didn't want Jess to think she was mad. "You're nervous."

"Take my mind off it. What are your plans after school?"

"The usual. Linda's Diner. I'm gonna take photos."

"Cool," Jess paused, hesitating to ask her next question. "And your dad? How is he?"

"He wasn't home when I got up."

"Again? I'm sorry."

"I'm used to it and at least, I know where he is," Alice said. She needed to change the subject. "What about Layla and Bennett? Where are they going for their anniversary this summer?"

"Mom wants to go to a villa in France," Jess said. "And Dad wants to stay home. He doesn't really feel like traveling, I guess."

"Is he winning the argument?"

"So far but Mom's a closer."

"Yeah, they're going to France."

"Most likely."

"Are they letting you go this year?" Alice asked.

Jess's parents didn't take her on trips, personal or otherwise, but maybe they'd start now that she was older. "Never in a million years," she said.

Leo spun in front of them, walking backward as they walked forward. He wore a gray beanie, a T-shirt with a list of font types, and jeans. His short, messy hair was a dusty beige color. His smile seemed to hint that he had something fantastic to say.

"What?" Alice asked.

He chuckled. "Brittany and Tony broke up."

"What?!" Jess's jaw dropped. "How-"

"Guess he cheated on her at her birthday party."

"Oh my God," Jess said. "Is she okay?"

"Don't know," he shrugged. "I'm just the messenger. There was a big screaming match in the west hall. She broke up with him in front of a huge group of us and told everybody what he did."

"That's embarrassing for him," Alice said.

Leo nodded. "Right?"

"Poor Brittany." Jess's phone beeped. She took it from her backpack. "Post-break-up-slumber party. Do you want to go?" She RSVPed.

"I'm not invited," Alice said. "It's okay. They're your friends."

"Save me a biscuit," Leo smiled.

Jess gave a half-humorous, half-annoyed squint and put her phone away.

Alice looked at him. "You need a hobby."

"That's the consensus," he saluted them. "See you guys next year."

The girls waved as Leo pushed through the crowd and darted clumsily around the corner. Leo was a floater. He knew everyone but they didn't know him. Alice liked him. He was nice. She wondered what music he liked since if she took Mister Scotts's offer, she'd be sharing the radio with him.

"I'm surprised Brittany and Tony broke up," she said. "They've been dating since grade school."

"I know," Jess said. "Brit must be heartbroken."

"That's why you're going to her slumber party," Alice said. "She'll tell you all about it and you guys will do whatever it is you do at those things."

"Are you sure you don't want to come?" Jess asked. "I know they're not your friends but they could be if you guys gave each other a chance."

"They're... Um... I'm not-"

"A Honeycomber? You know that doesn't matter to me, right?"

"I know it doesn't. It does to them. I'm a Nester and I'm cool with it."

"Fine. Okay. See you at lunch?"

"Definitely," Alice nodded.

Jess smiled. She hurried around the corner and headed to her locker.

Alice's classmates became distant. A faded dream. She used to be part of the group. A jock-type on almost every team. Now she was nothing. No one ever spoke to her, not that she wanted them to. Her eyes lazily combed the crowd. She wanted the bell to ring. She wanted this day to be over.

Bobby Jones, a girl in her class, knocked into her shoulder. Alice stumbled sideways but steadied herself against the wall.

Bobby tripped after the collision and slammed, chin-first, onto the floor. Laying flat on her stomach, she groaned. A few Honeycomber girls laughed. Bobby jumped to her feet, brushed herself off, and went to lean against some lockers.

Bobby was a Burrower. People said she was a huge slut. The girl wore tons of mascara, shiny lip gloss, jewelry, and weird, sparkly outfits like she was starring in a Madonna video. She definitely stood out.

Alice would never want that much attention. Most of the time, she wanted to melt away and never come back. Maybe then, she'd feel better.

***

Bobby

Bobby wore her favorite four-inch heels, a black tutu covered in sequins, and a colorfully beaded top with a low, squared back.

The cold lockers made her skirt itch.

Mini disco balls dangled from her ears, swinging playfully, as she bobbed her head. Shiny bracelets were bunched on her wrist. Her hair was short and curly, cut above her shoulders, the top was red and the bottom was orange, blending in the middle like a sunset.

She dyed it herself.

Johnny walked up and she smiled. He was so handsome. He had a buzz cut and wore a simple, baggy T-shirt and ripped cargo pants. With a blank expression, he ignored her and opened his locker. Did he see her at all?

"So, what are you doing after school?" she asked.

He shrugged. "Don't know. Might hang out with some of the guys or something."

"Well, we could do something. Maybe a movie?"

"Maybe. I'll let you know." He didn't look in her direction or acknowledge her presence, other than talking to her like she was a gnat buzzing in his ear.

He's probably tired, she thought. That had to be it, exhaustion, and possibly hunger. Her smile drooped into a frown. "Johnny?"

"Just chill, okay? Geez," he snapped. "I'll text you."

His rigid tone made Bobby flinch. What did she do wrong? She fought the urge to cry. Her voice stayed steady but she spoke quickly, afraid she might show too much emotion. "Okay, yeah, totally."

She stared at the floor. Johnny let out a long, drawn-out sigh. He hooked his hand on her hip and pulled her against him. He kissed her. Hard. She wrapped her arms around his neck. She had to stand on the tips of her toes to be semi-level with him. Why'd she have to be so short?

After a few more, deep, rough kisses, he pulled away and gave her an Eskimo kiss. She smiled. She loved when he did that. It was their thing. His smile was wicked and beautiful but his eyes were dark and mysterious. He unhooked his hand and dropped her. She stumbled into the lockers.

She watched him leave, then went in the other direction.

Bobby could feel everyone's judgmental stares, disgusted by her existence. She knew the rumors and what people thought. She'd often catch them talking behind her back or making up stories as if her feelings didn't matter.

Brittany Mikes spread the horrible rumors at the beginning of the year. Those rumors became Bobby's reputation: slut, whore, loser, cheat, stupid, friendless. None of them were true. She got a mixture of Cs and Ds. As in math every time. She always tried her best. Johnny was her first and only boyfriend to whom she was faithful.

"Burrows' trash," Brittany crossed her arms. "Is your boyfriend bored with you already?"

She and Cindy Cohen were in their cheer uniforms: pleated skorts and long-sleeved shirts. The school colors were bright yellow and dark blue. Their posture was queen-like. They were gorgeous, which wasn't fair. To make herself feel less intimidated, Bobby always imagined them with warts and green skin. She kept her back toward them.

"I can't decide if she's dressed like a prostitute," Cindy said. "Or a toddler."

"He must be using her," Brittany said. "I mean, who'd want to date a gothic clown?"

Bobby turned. She opened her mouth to say something, anything, but nothing came out. The words stabbed at her dry throat and stayed there.

They laughed.

Tears stung her eyes but she wouldn't let them see her cry.

Bobby ran into the girls' bathroom and locked the door. Her heels slipped on the tile and she used the sink to steady herself. She looked in the mirror. Tears, glitter, and mascara smothered her cheeks. She dabbed the trickling black water with a brown paper towel.

Sometimes, she wished Brittany and Cindy would turn into fleas, so she could smash them under her heel, or maybe they could both get lost in a ditch, either option would do.

Bobby slapped her panda-shaped purse on the counter. She took out her phone - safely framed by a sparkly DIY case - and pressed one. Speed dial took control.

"If this is about Johnny, I'm gonna hang up," Casey said. "What's up?"

"You have to give him a chance." Bobby's tone was more defensive than she meant it to be. Her best friend's hatred of her boyfriend was ridiculous. They couldn't be in the same room without Casey trying to rip Johnny's head off. "He has a rough exterior and commitment issues," Bobby said. "I mean, his dad completely screwed him up. He acts like a jerk but he really loves me."

"Sure he does," Casey scoffed. Bobby could hear the eye roll. "He's a jackass. He's worse than that guy in *Pretty in Pink*, you know, uh... Steff, something. I forget who played him."

"Steff Mcgee and he is not! Stop that," Bobby wiped the mascara from her hair. "Look, I just... Brittany is being a bitch and, I, I'm so glad it's our last day. Summer vacation is a dream come true. After today, I can hang out with Johnny and you... Well, when you're not working. By the way, are you working?"

"I'm headed to Sally's," Casey said. "I don't go to The Arena until midnight."

"Sally's," Bobby repeated, excitement fizzling in her chest like a shaken soda. "Are you meeting Tommy? Are you guys gonna have the talk? I have ship names ready!"

"T and I are…" she clicked her tongue. "Whatever we are. Why does there have to be a label?"

"'Cause you guys have been acting weird for months," Bobby said. "You're the one that kissed him, remember? You started this."

She found out about the kiss because Casey started acting weird after it and got annoyed when Bobby wouldn't stop hounding her about why she was acting weird. Bobby, Cole, and Dave had watched the potential couple's awkward dance for months. Couldn't they see they were meant to be together?

"I remember," Casey said. "Hey, I want veto power on whatever ship name you've got."

"Commy," Bobby chuckled. "Ta-da!"

"God, no. Pick another one and while you're at it, break up with Johnny."

"Johnny and I love each other," she said. "He's not what you think. Okay? I swear, he's funny and fun and I, I really love him and you need to get on board and… I mean, relationships are complicated, okay?" She switched subjects. "So, did you hear about Scarlett Gorden's new fashion line?"

Her words were an understandable babble, spilling out from her mouth with no control or filter. It happened when she wasn't sure what to say next or when there was too much to say in one moment. She hated doing it but no matter how hard she tried to stop, she couldn't.

"Does it involve pants and shirts?" Casey asked.

Bobby rolled her eyes. "Yes."

"Wow, well, it should be a hit. Are we still on for Linda's later?"

"Duh. And when we meet up, you can tell me all about how you defined your relationship with Tommy and you're now," Bobby smiled. "Officially, his girlfriend."

"And you can tell me how you found some self-respect and broke up with Johnny."

"Stop insulting my relationship and define yours."

"Stop letting him treat you like a lapdog."

"He does not!" Bobby shouted. A pause. "So, Linda's?"

"See you there." Casey hung up.

***

Casey

She put her phone in her pocket.

Blue, neon letters in the glass doorway spelled out SALLY'S PLACE.

The big, open-concept room was separated into two areas by a glass shelf filled with colorful liquor bottles. A redwood bar and rugged, leather stools stood behind it. A wide staircase went from it to the pit-like dance floor surrounded by a railing. Several staircases led to the various booths built into the walls. Scattered chairs and tables were by the front door.

The owner stood at the bar. Her hair was long, wavy, and black. Her skin a silky brown. She wore a black tank top, khaki shorts, and gold hoop earrings. She was probably middle-aged, maybe younger. She favored her right arm and had a scar, possibly from a blade, on her left palm.

"Is the crew meeting you here?" Sally asked. "I'm not giving you any drinks."

"Just Thomas," Casey sat down. She yanked off her boots - black, leather, knee-high, heels - and dropped them on the floor. She scrunched her toes.

People in the Burrows knew her and Tommy by their street names. She was Cece and he was Thomas. They were famous.

Sally pointed to the boots. "Are those mine?"

"I may have found them in your closet."

"You went upstairs, which is off-limits, and stole my boots."

"Yep. Cool apartment, by the way."

20

Sally rolled her eyes. She poured soda into a glass and slid it to Casey. "Take any more of my stuff and you won't get a drop even when you're twenty-one. Got it?" Sally shook her head, smiled - to show she wasn't going to use her shotgun like she usually did when she was angry - and continued wiping the counter.

"That threat only works with Dave," Casey held up the glass. "Thanks."

She looked at her bubbly reflection in the carbonation. Her eyes were piercing green. Her hair was sky-blue, straight, shoulder-length, and messily brushed. She wore a black, leather jacket over a white, cropped T-shirt and ripped jeans. The thin chain around her neck held a silver, angel wing charm.

Tommy gave her the necklace on her fifteenth birthday. When he did, without thinking, she kissed him on the ledge of their favorite rooftop. The city lights were bright, shimmering all around them while car horns were faint, whispering below them. He kissed her back, no more surprised than she was. Afterward, they got stuck in some sort of awkward limbo but she never took the necklace off, not since she put it on.

The door squeaked and Tommy walked in. His hair was short, messy, and brown. It didn't curl. He wore whitewash jeans, hiking boots, and his favorite gray, pullover hoodie. A leather laptop bag was slung over his shoulder.

Casey hid her smile.

He sat next to her. "Hey, Sally."

"Thomas," she poured him a soda, glanced between them, and flipped the rag on her shoulder. She winked and walked away.

Casey clicked her tongue. *Subtle.* She nodded toward the bag. "New toys from Betty?"

"Yeah. She wants me to meet the buyer in, like, an hour," Tommy opened it to reveal scraps of different high-tech devices and wires. He dropped it on the floor.

"How much?" she asked.

"Hobbs said a couple million."

"Good deal. What's the tech?"

"Do you really care?"

Casey shook her head. Technology wasn't in her wheelhouse. She cleared her throat. Why did she feel nervous? She was never nervous. "So, B is coming up with ship names for us."

"A ship name?" he asked. "We aren't... Even... we're um.."

"Exactly, yeah but she wants us to define each other or whatever we are but she's in love with Johnny," Casey said. "So, her judgment's questionable."

"You have to let her deal with her own stuff. You can't protect her from herself."

"No, but I can make Johnny disappear or bash his grill in," she smirked. "Find out if B likes making out with a toothless guy."

"Maybe try punching a bag first," Tommy sipped his soda. "What's the first ship name?"

"Commy."

"Ooh... huh."

"Yeah."

He smiled. "What about Tasey?"

She laughed. Was he serious? Did he want a ship name? Did he want to be a couple or was this a joke? Casey didn't know which option made her panic more. "You're not helping," she chuckled, trying to play it cool. At least her face didn't feel warm, so she wasn't blushing. *Good.*

Tommy nodded. "It's a difficult job. B's got her work cut out for her." His face, handsome and reserved, didn't indicate what he was feeling. "Any plans today?"

"Cake and pie at Linda's with B," she said. "Wanna come?"

"Can't. I've got plans with the guys. We could all meet up later."

"We'll see," she shrugged. "Hey, since when do Cole and Dave count as guys?"

"Hilarious," he said. "Dave says the same thing about you being a girl."

"It's almost cute, him cracking a joke without a sense of humor," she said. "Like Cole trying to be normal."

"They're your friends too."

"I know."

He stared at her. What was he thinking about behind his perfect brown eyes? She held his gaze and took a deep breath. Her pounding heart threatened to break open her chest. She was weirdly aware of it. Only around Tommy did Casey lose her shields.

She resisted the nervous urge to fiddle with her necklace.

Tommy looked at the bar and the urge broke. "Are you ready for your fight tonight?" he frowned, letting his concern for her break through his emotional walls. "You got pretty banged up at the last one."

"I'm like a cat, I've got nine lives," she put a hand on her hip. "I'll win. Always do."

"You do know you're not invincible, right?" he asked.

She smiled. "That theory hasn't been proven."

It was nice to have someone worry about her. She worried about him too. Their line of work was dangerous but they could take care of themselves. They'd been watching each other's backs since they were kids. Betty Beater's Unstoppable Team.

"Betty wants me to hack some Swiss bank accounts," he said. "I'm not sure why but it seems serious."

"Isn't it always? She wants me to threaten a lawyer."

"Who?"

"Fred Willin. He isn't listening. I'm supposed to scare him into obedience but hey, I've got some time to kill," Casey said. "You said you've got an hour?"

"Yep."

"War?" she suggested.

Tommy grabbed the cards from behind the bar. They sat in the corner booth. It had a perfect view of the entire club except for the back hall where the bathrooms, storage room, cellar, and the staircase to Sally's apartment were.

"Too bad B isn't here to shuffle," Casey said.

"She's a shark," he smiled. "I'm glad we stopped playing poker with her."

He started mixing the cards, making the deck blur and mesh until each suit was unreadable.

Maybe Bobby was right, they needed to say out loud what they were to each other. They needed to talk about it. How did you even start that type of conversation?

Casey fiddled with her necklace.

Tommy dealt the cards. "You're up first."

"T..." she stopped herself. Was she sure about this? Something in her expression must've given her away or maybe he could read her mind because the next thing she knew, he kissed her, deep and wanting, loving. She sunk into the moment immediately like it was the most natural thing in the world to have his lips locked with hers.

She held his hoodie and pulled him closer. Their heartbeats seemed to sync together as his hands drifted into her hair and gently cupped her face. His fingers were warm, rough, and calloused from the way he held his guns. The kiss didn't last long but it felt like forever. This changed everything. They pulled apart and looked at each other. If she wasn't blushing before, she was now.

Casey chuckled. "Guess we're gonna need a ship name."

"We already have a really good option."

"Tasey isn't an option."

"I think it is," Tommy said. She kissed him. He grinned against her lips.

***

Jess

Jess packed up her locker, went to the girls' bathroom, and changed her clothes. She smoothed out her black, turtleneck dress and adjusted the gray blazer.

She tried five different outfits before she chose this specific one, so it had to help her make a good impression. She whispered Layla's talking points as she tied her hair into a side ponytail and grabbed her bags. She headed down the hall.

Jess seemed to be the only person in the entire school who was stressed, instead of thrilled. It wasn't uncommon. She was also the only person who knew the answer to every question any of the teachers asked. She always raised her hand.

This interview could change her life. She couldn't fail. Even thinking about failure brought terror to her bones but it was normal. Her mom had high expectations.

Alice, wearing simple jeans and her olive-green hoodie, stuffed pencils and crinkled papers into her backpack. She looked tired. She always looked tired. "Hey."

"What do you think?" Jess gestured to her outfit.

She glanced it over and nodded. "Very professional. Pretty too."

Neither one of them was fashion-conscious. It would've been a better question for Brittany or Cindy since they kept up on all the latest sales and bought the newest, hottest items but they weren't around. Besides, Jess trusted Alice's opinion the most.

"Really?" she asked. "Are you sure?"

"Yeah," Alice said. "I'm sure."

"Okay, good. It's just... My mom says my hair, the pink streaks are going to limit my chances. I'm not sure if that's true," Jess sighed. "Because I know she hates that I dyed it but-"

"She hates that you did it without her permission," Alice swung her bag on her shoulder and closed her locker.

Jess pointed at it. "Aren't you going to wipe out your locker?"

"What?"

"Well, after a year, the lockers get dirty and it's rude to leave them like that all summer."

"Jess, did you wipe down your locker?"

"Twice."

The hall was decorated with yellow and blue posters and streamers. Gold sports trophies were in wooden china cabinets along the walls. Each classroom had a number and a teacher's name. The floor was cheap tile. Everything smelled like Windex and sweat.

Tony O'Hare passed by them wearing a letterman jacket and expensive jeans. Mousse made his black hair shine. His eyes floated over Jess's body and he smiled, "Looking good, Jessica."

Did he check her out?

Alice scoffed. "Guess he isn't wasting any time."

"If he thinks I'm going to betray Brittany like that, he's a neanderthal." She played with her ponytail, trying not to pick her cuticles. What if her pink streaks ruined her chances? If she didn't get this internship her mom would be disappointed. Why didn't she get Layla's permission before she dyed it? "Maybe it was a sign. Maybe this outfit isn't professional, maybe it's-"

"It's gonna be fine," Alice's calm, comforting tone helped lessen Jess's fears. "You'll do great."

"How are you so sure?"

Alice locked their arms. "I just am."

Jess smiled, thankful for her best friend. She wished she believed in herself as much as Alice believed in her. They pushed open the glass doors and stopped on the top step. Her dad's silver Range Rover was parked on the curb. Thank God, it wasn't Layla.

Bennett opened the window and waved. He was always fond of Alice. He told Jess, once, that they were lifers. She asked him how he could tell. He only smiled.

"Hi, Mister Peace," Alice waved.

Jess took a deep, shaky breath. "Wish me luck?"

"You don't need it but good luck."

"Thanks." Jess hurried to the car. She sat in the passenger seat, closed the door, and dropped her bags in the back. She strapped herself in. *Safety first.*

Bennett quickly kissed her on the forehead and they drove away.

"Is that the fourth outfit?" he asked. "Very professional."

"If I don't ace this, what do you think Mom will say?" Jess picked her cuticles. "I know she'll be disappointed, but..."

"She will be," he admitted. "But we both believe in you and even if you don't get the internship, I'll be proud. I'm always proud of you."

The comforting words hurt. Her gaze dropped. "But mom isn't."

Bennett's silence gave her the answer. He focused on the road. They shared several features. Her favorite was the caramel-colored eyes but she inherited her good cheekbones from Layla. Was it too much to ask that Layla be proud of her no matter what? Apparently. Her mom was a tough woman to please. She wanted what she believed was best for Jess. The plan was clear. All Jess needed to do was succeed. Failure wouldn't be tolerated.

She picked her cuticles more harshly.

They drove to a white and red paneled building. Tall glass windows lined every floor. It could've been mistaken for a skyscraper. Intimidating, terrifying, and important. The Adler Building. Several businesses were inside, including Peace and O'Hare Law Firm. Layla was a partner and Bennett came from a long line of highly respected lawyers. The best in the courtroom, which was a difficult reputation to live up to.

He parked in the garage across the street in a space reserved specifically for him. Jess got out of the car, checked her outfit, and took a deep breath. Maybe she should've brought a bag to puke in, in case her nerves won.

People in suits filled the lobby. Serious, well-educated businessmen and women who radiated perfection. The marble floors were polished and crystal vases lined the walls. An antique Egyptian rug lay under a gold plaque that listed the businesses on each floor.

Bennett led Jess to the elevators and pressed the button. He put a reassuring hand on her shoulder but it didn't work. She was still completely freaked out. Her fingers started bleeding. *Crap.*

The doors opened, and a girl with sky-blue hair appeared. She met Jess's gaze. Her green eyes were fierce and chilling. An icy devil. Why was a Burrower here?

She tucked a knife into her leather jacket. Another poked out from her boot. Why did she have those? Who was she? What floor did she come from? She smirked and walked away, through the lobby, and toward the front doors, confident and threatening.

Bennett led Jess into the elevator.

***

Alice

Alice took her bags home. No Mason. His absence and drunken misery were a tradition at this point. The disappointment she felt was paired with relentless loneliness and a broken heart. The feeling hadn't changed in two years.

Her hood covered her head and her hair lay on each shoulder. The leather messenger bag bumped her knee as she walked, the torn strap laying across her body. Earbuds blasted classic rock in her ears.

It turned off the world and made everything disappear. She, alone, existed. Alice and her camera as she took pictures of people. Did they feel this way too? Broken. Maybe it was just her. She couldn't tell from their facial expressions. Some people looked happy or excited, others looked focused or confused or sad or angry.

She stopped at Linda's Diner. Its cement walls were blue. Red awnings hung above two rectangular windows on either side of the front, double glass doors. There weren't flowers, bushes, or anything to make it cute. It just was.

Inside, the floors were black and white checkers. The booths were red and white. The yellow counter and its blue stools were in front of the kitchen window. Vinyl records hung above a colorful jukebox. A small hall led to the bathroom, an office, and the storage room.

An old, wrinkly man with saggy eyelids and a drooping mouth was framed in the right window. He ate pancakes and chatted with the owner; Linda wore a cute, yellow dress with a white collar and adorable red buttons. Some pens and a decorative notepad were tucked inside her apron. Its strings were tied in a perfect bow. Her thick southern accent could almost seep through the walls. It was that powerful.

Alice lifted her camera and framed the shot. A girl passed behind her.

A nearly invisible tug pulled her pocket. She thought nothing of it until she realized her wallet's weight was gone. The girl had sky-blue hair and wore a leather, biker jacket. She held the wallet.

"Hey!" Alice shouted. "That's mine!"

The girl turned. "What's yours?"

Her eyes were piercing green. Underneath her cropped T-shirt were scars all over her belly, which was flat and solid. Were those abs? Alice had never seen a girl with a six-pack before. Impressive. But what were the scars from?

"The wallet you stole," Alice put her camera in her bag. "Give it back."

"You must be seeing things, plum head. I didn't take anything."

Alice scoffed. *Plum head? Are you kidding?*

The girl turned to the door and grabbed the knob as Alice came to the steps. She wanted her damn wallet back.

SCREEEEEE. Tires against pavement.

Alice turned, only to see a car speeding toward a ten-year-old boy in a jean jacket. He stood frozen in the road. The car was going to hit him.

Alice's heart hammered, faster and faster, adrenaline pumped through her veins. Shock and worry clouded her mind as an overwhelming buzz slapped her ears. She couldn't feel her body anymore.

Just electricity.

***

Casey

Casey heard the tires screech. She turned. A boy in a jean jacket stood in the road as a car bulleted toward him. Why couldn't it stop? The people on the sidewalk gawked like dumbass pigeons. They were about to watch a ten-year-old die.

Could she get to him in time? Probably. The problem was they wouldn't be able to get away. The car would kill them both.

Sparks flew off the girl with the purple hair. Tiny lightning bolts flickered over her body, wildly glistening against her skin. Her body burst. Light flashed and Casey had to cover her eyes.

Twirling bolts of white lightning sped around each other, creating one giant bolt. It consumed the boy and he vanished, almost like the girl had. The car crashed against the lightning, making it shatter, and it became billions of tiny tangled shimmers like a spider web of pure light.

Everyone stared, shocked and amazed. Some stumbled, a few stiffened. Others took out their phones and tried to record it. Nobody seemed to believe it. Was it real?

Incredible. Casey was reminded of the way Glisin's powers used to look but this was different. Indescribable.

The car skidded through the web and came out partly charred. The driver was fine. His wide eyes darted around, checking to be sure what happened wasn't a dream or a hallucination, and his hands shook on the wheel. His panic made Casey chuckle.

She refocused on the lightning.

It put itself back together and flashed, temporarily blinding everyone on the street. Casey adjusted her eyes in time to see the boy safe on the sidewalk. He seemed a little disoriented but he was alive, and probably as shocked as everyone else.

The girl with the purple hair stood exactly where she'd been before, fingers flickering.

Casey's jaw dropped. "Holy hell."

***

Alice

Alice felt her body again. She stumbled forward and patted herself down. Was everything in the right place? Her clothes were there, her bag, her camera, her hair. Considering she didn't feel like a kidney was where her lung should be, she assumed her organs and skeleton were fine too.

Oh, wow. Her powers were incredible. She forgot how amazing they were. A euphoria that couldn't happen with anything else.

She laughed. Her first time saving someone's life. It was an entirely new feeling; pride, bewilderment, strength. Amazing. Who knew?

"Holy hell." The girl with the blue hair stared at her, amazed.

Alice's stomach flipped. What did she just do?

"Oh my God." She used her powers in public. She didn't mean to. Instinct and adrenaline took over. There was nothing she could do to control or fight it. How could she be so reckless? So stupid? Now a stranger knew her secret and could expose her abilities. Susan's identity. It'd put Mason and their extended family in danger. This one mistake, in one moment, was going to ruin everything.

"You're Glisin's kid," the girl said. "Aren't you?"

Powered people weren't uncommon. Nobody knew how certain people in the world got their abilities or in what generation it started. A few years ago, Cruise Industries did research on powered people. In one study, they learned powers were somewhat hereditary.

Alice couldn't speak. Guilt and fear suffocated her.

The girl opened the wallet and took out the school ID. "Alice Johnson."

What Susan would say or Mason before he started drinking? She couldn't imagine the anger level. It would be so many notches above the time she accidentally broke the kitchen window with a baseball. Maybe it would be above the time she deleted Mason's work files to make room for a video game she loved. Her dad spent the entire night redoing them, so he wouldn't get fired.

Alice dry-heaved. "I think I'm gonna throw up."

"Not on the boots," the girl stepped back. She was calm, too calm, and interested in what she saw. What if she told people? It'd be all over the city. Destroyer would hear the news for sure.

"Did anybody else see me?" If other people saw Alice transform they would've appeared by now. They'd be asking questions or calling the police or something.

"They saw freaky lightning save that kid," the girl said. "Not you."

"Okay... okay..." Alice gathered her thoughts. She shoved down her panic. The words unclogged themselves from her throat and she met the girl's gaze. "Please. *Please*, don't tell anyone. I will do anything, I swear to God, but you can't tell people. You have to keep my powers a secret," she begged. "Nobody can know, ever."

"So, you are Glisin's kid, right?" the girl asked. Did this person hear anything said to her?

"Uh, yeah. I'm... it's..." Alice shook her head. "You can't tell anyone, okay? I'll do anything, I'll pay you, or, or wash your car, or-"

"Relax," she chuckled, shrugging. "I won't blackmail you but I could. If I felt like it," she smirked. The smirk seemed bold like she was saying *I'm awesome* without speaking. "I do, however, reserve the right to change my mind."

Alice figured that was a threat. She'd have this sword hanging over her head forever. "So, you're not gonna tell anyone? Really? 'Cause this can't get out, it can't happen."

"I can keep a secret." The girl took her phone from her jacket. It must've buzzed. The screen was broken. "And she's bailing on me. That's fan-freaking-tastic."

"What?" Alice asked without thinking.

"My friend. I was meeting her here but she's bailing to go to some concert with her boyfriend."

"Oh." Alice paused. "Sorry."

"I changed my mind, my silence isn't free," she put her phone back. Alice's nerves tightened. What did she mean she changed her mind? "Buy me some cake and my lips are sealed."

"What?" Alice didn't understand. Shouldn't this random person be more frantic? She should have a billion questions and be acting insane but this girl was calm. She was using knowledge of this huge secret to get herself a free dessert. Not what Alice would've expected. Was it a trick?

Alice's phone beeped. She grabbed it from her bag. Jess's contact photo was a picture of her laughing, face hidden behind a book. The text said: I GOT THE INTERNSHIP! I'M GOING TO CELEBRATE WITH BRITTANY AND THE OTHERS. YOU'RE INVITED.

Alice congratulated her but declined the invitation. Her pride and excitement for her best friend were paired with the realization that Jess was moving on. Alice was in the same place she'd been two years ago. Maybe a worse place.

She looked at the girl with the blue hair. "If I buy you a piece of cake, you won't tell anyone my secret?"

"Can't talk if my mouth's full," she said.

"What about when it's not full?"

"Guess you'll have to wait and see," she said. She seemed to be enjoying this.

Alice didn't like that answer. She frowned. She didn't have a choice. She had to trust the girl with the blue hair. And if this girl told her secret, Alice would have to deal with it. "You, uh, kind of stole my wallet."

"Right." The girl gave it back but she kept the school ID. Alice didn't stop her. What would be the point?

"Okay, um," Alice said. "I'll buy you a piece of cake. What's your name?"

"Cece. The name's Cece."

They went into the diner. They both waved to Linda and sat in the booth by the left window. Cece on the right. Alice on the left. They sat in silence for an awkward three minutes while Linda refilled ketchup bottles at the counter.

"Why is there a knife in your boot?" Alice asked.

Cece clicked her tongue. She leaned forward and folded her arms on the table. "I'll show you mine if you show me yours."

"Meaning?"

"Tell me your story and I'll tell you mine," Cece said. Was she serious?

Alice hesitated. Was it a good idea to share anything more about herself? Of course, Cece already knew everything important. Alice wouldn't have to lie, she could tell Cece things she couldn't tell anyone else. She could talk about her mom, both versions of her.

"Deal," Alice said.

Chapter 2

Casey

CASEY STARED AT HER cracked reflection in the shattered mirror. Her leather jacket was on the coat rack beside the locked door and her boots were sitting on the cold, cement floor. These were flat and had thick, long laces with silver buckles in the center. Each one had six pockets. A knife in every one.

Sally took her boots back.

An endless ocean of chants called Casey's name. "Cece! Cece! Cece!"

They begged to see Betty Beater's champion, which wasn't new. She'd been the champion for years, since she plunged her fingers into a grown man's eye sockets and he screamed. He screamed until he died, and his blood drenched her body. She lived. That's what counted.

A few months ago, she met Glisin's daughter. They talked about a ton. Alice was excited and relieved to have someone to talk to about everything; her powers, her dad, her mom. She ordered pie. Why pie? Cake was better.

They exchanged numbers and met at the diner whenever they both had time. Shockingly, Casey enjoyed Alice's company. She couldn't believe it. She didn't tell Alice her real name - and some other things - she tried to stay vague about her life, so she'd feel safer. Guarded.

Betty would love to know Glisin had a daughter. Why didn't Casey tell her? Why didn't she blackmail Alice? She still could if she wanted to but she didn't. Alice was a good person. She probably didn't deserve whatever violent, torturous things Betty would do to her.

And she didn't have anything Casey wanted.

"You ready?" Dave knocked, shouting over the echoing cheers. "They're getting restless!"

"Be out in a minute!" Casey wore a loose, white tank top over a fitted, black one, stretchy leggings, and stained socks. She tucked her necklace under her shirts and opened the door.

The Arena was a rundown lobby with broken, boarded windows and soundproof walls. The cage was in the center of the room. Bright lights made a spotlight. The floor was covered in dry blood. The bars were steel twine weaved to make a basket. Barbed wire framed a door on either side.

Burrowers were piled on top of each other. Cockroaches in a tin bucket. They screamed and cheered when Casey revealed herself. Warm bodies created an aisle to the cage. She cracked her knuckles and psyched herself up.

Dave opened and closed the door for her. He locked it from the outside. In the cage, she was alone. The spotlight washed out the crowd, making the people into shadows.

"Everybody shut your yappers!" Dave screamed into the microphone. They obeyed. He was the bookie. They used to bet on who'd win, now they bet on how long it'd take Cece to knock her opponent to the floor.

"You've made your bets!" Dave climbed the cage wall, hanging from it with one hand and one foot, he looked out at the crowd. "Who's ready to see Cece take down another one of Betty Beater's Most Wanted!"

They roared. Their hot, collected breath squeezed her body. It stank of raw fish, copper, and thrill. She was the Crime Queen's prodigy. Everyone knew who she was and who she worked for. Betty Beater held Height City hostage under her elegant, iron thumb.

"Our loser!" Dave laughed. "Nah. Our challenger! He stole cash from Betty's lower command! And what's the rule?"

He held the microphone to the air. The crowd screeched, "nobody betrays Betty Beater!"

"Exactly! And the punishment for his crime is a cage match!" He hopped down.

The crowd screamed.

The other door opened and a man walked in. He was muscular under his tank top and baggy shorts. Casey was less than half his size. He clutched a knife. Opponents were allowed a weapon to add a little extra pizazz because it entertained the crowd.

Dave lowered the microphone and leaned forward. "Yo, Cece."

She faced him through the bars.

He nodded to the challenger. "You got this, right? 'Cause if you die, I won't get my money."

"What's the time most bet?" she was annoyed with him already.

He glanced at his bare wrist as if he had a timer set. "Ten seconds. You got this?"

"Shut up."

"How Tommy kisses you, I'll never know."

Her opponent was right handed but favored his left foot. Prior injury to the right? He could be trying to trick her but it wasn't likely. He looked stupid. If he stole from Betty's lower command it meant he was from the streets, possibly trying to get into one of the lower gangs. A stupid newbie.

"I got this." She took her stance.

He readied himself, shaking. Afraid to lose?

Casey smirked.

Dave had to go to the back of the room and behind a desk built into the floor. She waited for him to pull the cord. The siren blared and the crowd shut up, all eyes on the fight. Their stares weighed her down like a heavy chain hanging around her neck.

Her opponent launched forward and swung the knife. She ducked, turned and he stumbled past her. He caught himself. He looked mad, which made her laugh. His deep breath was a desperate growl. He jumped, aiming to tackle her. His body smacked against her foot like a cinder block.

She kept steady, unwavering.

He staggered back.

Casey cartwheeled, launching off her hands into a backflip. The crowd screamed as she rolled through the air, 'oohing' and 'ahhing' as if it were the first time. She landed perfectly as always and dove into a somersault before her opponent could cut her cheek. She grabbed his arm and took the knife. He tried to punch with his free hand but she caught it, twisting his wrist. CRACK.

He screamed.

Dave's anxious finger tapping was silenced by the blurred cheers. He did it during every fight. She memorized the sound. A ticking clock. His payday relied on her victory.

She dug the blade into her opponent's throat.

Knives were her favorite weapon. Maybe because of the cold steel or the personal touch to the kill. She could feel everything. His skin's resistance and the muscle. It didn't protest long. The jolt of his heart. Its slowed beats. The panicked yet calm sobs begging to live.

Blood splattered on her shirt. It seeped down her fingers, hand, and arm. He was choking on it, on the same blade he brought to protect himself. The smell of old pennies comforted her.

Did these grown men ever feel embarrassed before they died? After all, their murderer was a fifteen-year-old girl. She used to count her wins and kills. Eventually, the number got too high. She remembered the first man's face. She was eleven at the time.

The fight was a challenge. Her initiation. A chance to prove she was Betty's diamond in the rough. Desperation to live wasn't a new feeling. Terror was tradition at the orphanage. Somehow, she survived.

The current man's eyes were shocked. The same look all her victims had but in his, there was disappointment. He shouldn't have expected to win.

Casey pulled the knife from his throat and stepped away. His blood gushed down his torso like a red waterfall. He dropped.

"Eight seconds!" Dave yelled into the microphone. The crowd roared.

Casey's arm automatically shot into the air. The knife was her trophy and blood was her uniform, drenching her hair, body, and clothes, as a single drop trickled down her cheek.

"Cece! Cece! Cece! Cece!"

***

Tommy

Techno music blasted from the speakers. Colored lights flashed above the pit. Drunk, all-aged adults and teenagers danced, losing themselves in the crowd. Sally could spot a fake ID from a mile away. She gave minors mocktails or sodas but never alcohol. They tried to sneak it in but she'd bust them, so Tommy never bothered.

"What are you doing?" he asked.

Cole stirred five different sodas together. They sat in the corner booth. Cans, bottles, carbonation, and crazy straws covered the table. "Cole's Sensational Soda," he said like it was obvious.

Tommy smiled. "Is this gonna be like your Christmas drink?" he asked. He remembered Cole's Christmas drink as a cross between eggnog, chocolate milk, and mustard. "'Cause B threw up for a week after she had that."

"Hopefully maybe?" Cole kept mixing.

Tommy shook his head and laughed. His friends were the best. Fantastic and unique. He loved them, even if Dave did drive him crazy most days.

People danced and drank. One woman hopped on the bar and did a jig. Lights flashed across their familiar faces and bodies.

As Betty Beater's tech support, Tommy did business with tons of Burrowers. He was lucky. He didn't get bloodier jobs anymore. He was trained for it, of course, and he had killed for Betty before. The first time he tortured someone, he puked twice. The blood, the bruises, the screaming, he hated every second of it, he hated himself for causing the irreversible pain. He decided to stick to computers from then on.

The people he didn't know were mostly Nesters. Some were Honeycombers. He didn't pay much attention to them because he didn't need to watch his back when they were around.

Johnny and Bobby were hidden in the crowd. She wore a sparkly, fitted gold dress and moved easily in her four-inch heels. Every time she turned, Johnny danced with another girl. She didn't seem to mind that he had a date. Bobby was Casey's first friend outside the orphanage, then Tommy met her. He introduced her to Dave, and eventually, she introduced them both to Bobby and Cole.

They'd all been best friends ever since.

The couple danced against each other, intertwined. Bobby swung her hair and hips with a giant, carefree smile spread across her face. Was that a bruise on her forehead? Did Johnny hurt her?

"Hey. Who introduced B to that guy? Johnny," Tommy asked.

"Dave," Cole glanced at the couple. "They're in the same line of work."

Dave was many things. The Arena's bookie, an amateur fence, a mechanic, and a drug dealer under Betty's umbrella. It was good money. None of them did drugs but Dave found no problem in selling cocaine, pharmaceuticals, and other things.

"Of course they are." Tommy clenched his fist, nails digging into his skin.

Johnny was a Markinson. If that wasn't bad enough, he had a reputation for being unstable, for being violent and mean. One rumor said that before Johnny started working for Markinson, he tried to win Mick the Menace's favor in hopes of becoming one of his professional assassins but for some reason, Mick never accepted him.

Cole finished the soda concoction. He tasted it and spit it out. He wiped his lips. "That's pretty good."

"If it's good, why'd you spit it out?"

"Spit take."

"Let me," Tommy said. Cole handed him a glass. He sipped it and nodded, "Hm. Not bad."

"Told you," Cole said. "Where'd B go?"

Tommy searched the crowd for Bobby's fiery hair. His stomach tightened when he couldn't find her. Did she leave? Where would Johnny have taken her? He needed to make sure she was okay.

***

Bobby

Bobby spent her summer with Johnny. She argued with Casey the whole time. Why couldn't her best friend approve of her boyfriend? She constantly defended him whether he deserved it or not, which was exhausting. She was sick of screaming, so she stopped talking to Casey altogether.

Worst decision ever.

Johnny put his mouth to her ear, hot breath tickling her skin. His arms kept her pressed against him. Sweat leaked through his shirt and kept it tight on his torso. She could feel his muscles, his strength, which both impressed her and scared her. She liked to dance with him, even if it was while some bitch flirted with him. Bobby ignored her.

"Come on." He led her through the crowd. A bachelorette party danced and waved light-up bubble wands. Laughing uncontrollably, they wore fluffy boas,

41

plastic crowns, and matching tank tops. The bride-to-be was two drinks away from puking.

The couple scooted into a booth. The table was sticky. A broken bottle was underneath it. Johnny wrapped his arm around Bobby and held up a plastic baggie filled with white powder.

He flashed his wicked yet beautiful smile. "Want some?"

He did worse drugs than her. Sometimes, they made him act unstable or mean. He always apologized after he came down from the high. He'd say it wasn't really him and that he didn't mean it. He loved her. She loved him.

Bobby took a joint from her purse. "I'll stick to this."

She put it in her mouth. His lighter clicked. The flame danced near her lips, beautiful and deadly, threatening to burn her if it got too close, then it disappeared. Johnny put his lighter back in his pocket and snorted a line of cocaine.

Smoke clouded the booth. The music thumped against her bones like drums in her belly. The lights spiraled like pieces of falling glass, sharp and lonely. Johnny kissed her temple. His hot breath stung her face. His fingers got tangled in her hair as he pulled her head back slightly and kissed her neck, lips rough and slow, each kiss made her feel stiff, unsure.

It was impossible to remember a moment without distortion. She'd always been the wrong version of a broken-hearted little girl. It's why she dyed her hair. Whatever innocence she used to have died alongside her dad. She was twelve when it happened.

She used to have an early morning paper route that she'd do before school and she swept up at a grocery store after hours. The owner gave her free groceries and paid her under the table.

She had to try and pay her dad's medical bills somehow.

The grief overwhelmed her. It made her chest empty. Her thoughts would crumble into chaos as if she'd lose her mind. Johnny showed her how to lose the pain. He helped her escape. It felt good.

His lips moved slowly on her skin, wanting, desperate. His touch sent shivers down her spine. His hand moved up her thigh but she blocked it, keeping his fingers near her knee. She didn't do drugs because she wanted to stay aware. Her mind was crystal clear. Nothing between them ever went too far, she wouldn't let it.

"Hey," Tommy stood at the edge of the table.

"Tom- Thomas," she corrected herself. She pushed Johnny away. "Hey, wanna sit with us?"

Johnny grunted his disapproval. He wiped his nose and leaned back, looking at Tommy like he was a piece of trash that belonged in the gutter. His hand rested on Bobby's neck, gentle but in control, ready to strike.

"No. I can't. Cole's over there," Tommy nodded toward the corner booth. He stared at her, intent and caring, protective. "I wanted to make sure you're okay. You're okay, right?"

"She's fine." Johnny's hand tensed on her throat. His fingers traced the birthmark on the back of her neck, warning her, telling her what to do.

She stayed still.

"I wasn't talking to you. B?" Tommy wouldn't go until he heard it from her. He was her brother in everything but blood, he'd protect her no matter what. She knew that. She needed that.

Bobby cleared her throat. "I'm fine."

"Okay..." he wasn't convinced. "Well, if you're not okay or safe, call me. I'll be there."

Johnny barely squeezed her neck but the slight pressure made her flinch. Did he know his own strength or was he doing this on purpose? She couldn't always tell. He was telling her to wrap it up, he wanted "Thomas" to leave.

"I'll remember that but I'm okay right now," she hesitated. "I promise."

Tommy stood solid. He eyed Johnny with disgust and suspicion. He looked like he wanted to strangle Johnny with his hoodie but he refrained. He nodded, accepting Bobby's answer, then walked away. He went back to the corner booth. Part of Bobby wanted to go sit with him and Cole.

Johnny sat up and strapped his arm over Bobby's chest, trapping her, making sure she couldn't escape.

She leaned against his shoulder and smiled. "So-"

"Betty's tech support?"

"What?" Panic hovered around her heart but she didn't let it show.

"I didn't know you were friends with him," he said. "I knew about Cece but-"

"Oh. Yeah," she smiled, nervous. "Guess I forgot to mention it."

Johnny worked for Markinson. The second most feared crime boss in Height City. He and Betty hated each other. There was a fragile balance that if broken could lead to an all-out war. Casey and Tommy's association with Betty and their reputations as Cece and Thomas protected Bobby. People knew they cared about her, so they left her alone.

She kissed Johnny, deep and flirty, trying to distract him. He leaned into the kiss, into her, and yanked her against him, hands wrapped around her waist. Her distraction worked.

"So," he chuckled, eyes half closed. "I hear you play poker."

"A little." She smashed the joint against the table. Bobby was an incredible poker player. She could cheat without anyone realizing it. Vincent, her dad, taught her all the tricks and she learned some from her own experiences. She always won.

"There's a poker game in a bit," Johnny said. "It's a few blocks from here and I'd love to see you in action. Card shark, right?"

"I mean... I don't know," she wasn't sure what to say. Was it a good idea? "I play here all the time but not in... it's probably not the same type of game you're talking about it."

The poker games at Sally's Place were on equal ground, no weapons were permitted. No one broke Sally's rules, which was why Bobby didn't have a problem playing there. Sally wouldn't let her get hurt.

"Well, if you win," Johnny gently stroked her cheek. "We can split the prize. Fifty/fifty."

"Prize? How much?" She could use the money. She had debts to pay, bills, and such.

Before he could answer, Sally slapped a broom against the table and scooped his drugs into a trash can. Another one of her rules, no cocaine allowed. She glared at Johnny with rigid suspicion but her gaze softened on Bobby. Was it pity or concern? Hard to tell. "Get the hell out of my club and if you come back, don't bring the party favors, capiche?"

"Who are you again?" Johnny asked. His tone was respectful but cocky. He knew who she was, everyone in the Burrows knew who she was. She was Sally. *Doy.*

"The owner," Sally said. Her tone signaled a threat. "Markinson boy, yeah?"

"Yeah."

"Mm-hmm," she nodded, unsurprised.

"Come on. Let's go to that poker game." Bobby yanked Johnny out of the booth. She needed to get him away from Sally as soon as possible before either of them did something violent. He grabbed Bobby's hand, fingers locked together.

Sally held the broom as a readied weapon. Almost as intimidating as her narrowed glare. "So, you're the boyfriend?"

Johnny chuckled. "Sure."

Tommy and Cole were watching from their booth. Each boy looked curious and ready to back up Sally if something happened. They both knew where she kept her shotgun, so if need be, they'd go grab it for her.

Bobby waved to them both but only Cole waved back. His smile, sweet and goofy, made her worries fade.

Sally dropped the trash can in Tommy's lap. "Dump it."

"Yes, ma'am," he saluted.

Bobby hid her laugh. She followed Johnny to the door and they stumbled out of the club. She squeezed his hand to keep herself from tripping.

He shouted at the sky, "and graceful, they exit!"

"Shush," Bobby pulled him forward. "Alright, where's this poker game?"

He yanked her closer. She held his torso and walked backward, letting him guide her down the sidewalk in the direction they needed to go. He gave her an Eskimo kiss and smiled as if she were a prize he craved. His pupils were dilated and he smelled like whiskey. White powder dusted the edges of his nose. "You smell good."

Bobby giggled at the compliment. "Yeah?"

***

Jess

A thousand lights illuminated the pitch black valley of skyscrapers. They blurred the sky and drowned out the stars. A sea of headlights crowded the roads below.

Jess loved the law firm's view. It made the early morning coffee runs and organizing case files even better. Fred Willin was a great boss. She learned so much from him. Layla's pride was a bonus.

Jess spent her summer working and at slumber parties with Brittany. She texted Alice every evening, detailing her favorite parts of the day.

The glass conference room contained several lawyers sitting in leather, swivel chairs around a large, oval table. Files labeled with different colors, loose-leaf paper with lists and seemingly random information, pencils, pens, million dollar briefcases, and research were spread across it.

She handed out coffee.

The entire floor was open concept. Private glass offices and polished, light wood floors. Carpets marked the waiting areas. The chairs were cushioned. Outdated magazines were piled on the tables.

Jess wore a gray pantsuit and a white, ruffled top. Her ballet flats had little flowers on the toes. Her loose bun was stylish and classy. She watched, at least, a hundred YouTube videos to get it perfect. Her pink streaks were gone, faded over the summer. Layla was thrilled but Jess wasn't. She liked the streaks and the color but she didn't want to disappoint her mom again.

Fred sipped his espresso. "This is good coffee."

"That place across the street is the best," Bennett smiled. "Thanks, honey."

"You're welcome." She gave Layla a long macchiato.

Layla sipped it and paused, a long, deafening pause that made Jess sweat. She picked her cuticles. Did she screw up? Was the coffee bad? Was there too much milk?

"Very good," Layla said.

Jess sighed. The tension in her muscles eased and she felt instant relief. She didn't fail. She pleased her mother. She memorized each lawyer's usual order but still took a list, which she always triple-checked. She didn't want to ruin their work or their focus.

Bennett smiled and winked, trying to comfort her in his usual quiet way. It made her feel a little better. Once she checked that the other lawyers didn't need anything else, Jess headed to the door. She had a few more tasks to finish before she left for the night.

She glanced at Fred's papers. A name was highlighted in yellow. "Ted Marson?"

He quickly covered it. "That's confidential. You shouldn't snoop."

"This is the case to release a prisoner from Steel Prison," Jess said. "Isn't it?"

"Yes," Bennett answered absently, stirring his coffee.

Layla cleared her throat. It meant *Shut up*. He glanced at her, eyebrows raised. He didn't seem to realize he'd defied her or he didn't care. He sipped his drink. Were they ever happy together?

"Jessica, go do your work," Layla commanded. "If you don't have anything to do, I have plenty of extra work. I could assign you something."

Jess stepped forward slowly. She glanced at the table. A plan started to form in her head but she wasn't sure it was a good idea. "Mom, Ted Marson is a known arsonist, he murdered his wife, there was eyewitness testimony, how could you-"

"*Enough,*" Layla scowled. Her tone meant *I'm always right and you need to accept it.* Paired with her confident, iron gaze, it'd knock a stampede down from miles away. Terrifyingly effective in a courtroom. "When you graduate from Zak City Law, you'll understand."

"Layla, enough." Bennett's tone told her to stop talking. She side-eyed him.

Jess's entire existence suddenly felt wrong. "Sorry," she looked at the floor and folded her hands behind her back, picking her cuticles. She still wanted to know what they were hiding.

She bumped the table with her knee, hard, and the lawyers' coffees spilled all over their papers. Fred cursed under his breath. He, Bennett, Layla, and the others quickly started trying to clean it up, frantic and distracted. Jess slipped the page she saw off the table and backed out of the office. "I'll go get some paper towels."

"Good, yes! Go!" Fred shouted, wiping the coffee with the sleeve of his million-dollar suit.

Jess hurried to the break room. Her heart was racing. Did she really do that? She couldn't believe it. She'd need to have her head examined or maybe she lost it. She did as she promised, she grabbed the roll of paper towels but she didn't bring them to the conference room, she used them to dry the paper she took. She read it twice. "New evidence?"

Apparently, there was new evidence that proved Ted Marson didn't commit the crimes he was arrested for, which was impossible. He was on the news for weeks, the trial was huge. He murdered his wife.

"This doesn't make any sense," Jess whispered. Why would her parents want to help release a known murderer from prison? Especially when they helped put him there.

"Did you get those paper towels?" Bennett asked. He must've come to see what was taking her so long. He paused when he saw the paper in her hand. He frowned, glanced back at the conference room, and sighed. His shoulders slumped and he reached out his hand. "Fred's right, you shouldn't snoop."

"Dad, please don't tell Mom," Jess begged. "I wasn't, I didn't-"

He took the paper and patted her head. Her mom liked to pat her head too, she hated it. "I won't tell her," Bennett promised. "But you should listen to her, this case is complicated."

What did he mean by complicated? She didn't understand. She thought she'd proven herself. Fred let her sit in on his meetings and take notes, he took her to the courthouse too. He let her help with other cases, why not this one? Why was it complicated? Jess kept her questions to herself. She hated not knowing things.

She followed her dad back to the conference room. She handed Fred the paper towels. She didn't mean to make such a mess. The coffee spilled on everything.

"Why don't you take the rest of the night off, Jessica?" Fred said, focused on cleaning up. No doubt he wanted her gone, so she wouldn't ruin anything else. "You've done wonderful work today. You're a great intern, one of my best."

"I'll give you a ride home," Bennett said. He spoke to his daughter with warmth and pride.

She shook her head. "No, that's okay. I'll call a friend."

"Are you sure?" he asked. "I'm happy to do it."

"I'm sure. I'll see you at home." She headed to the elevators. Could she be wrong? When Ted Marson was convicted his face was in every newspaper and on every news channel for weeks. He was an arsonist. A murderer. Why did her parents want to release him? Could it be a mistake? Maybe she was wrong.

She stepped into the elevator and the doors slid shut. Alice didn't own a car, so Jess dialed Brittany.

Another girl answered. "Jessica!"

"Cindy?"

"Duh," she laughed. "Where are you? We're having an end-of-summer slumber party and you have to be here. Please!"

"I'm at the office," Jess said. She never thought she could sound so adult. It was pretty cool. "Can Brittany pick me up?"

"Hold on. Brittany!" Cindy screamed. "Jessica needs a ride! Are you sober enough to give her a lift?"

A pause.

At most of their slumber parties, they'd get the key to Missus Mikes's liquor cabinet. The woman loved a mid-morning wine bottle. Jess never drank as much as the other girls did. If Layla ever smelled alcohol on Jess's breath or clothes, she would not be happy.

"She said 'yeah'," Cindy said. "She'll be there in five. See you soon."

Jess hung up and leaned on the railing. She loved their sleepovers. They'd binge-watch tons of movies. Jess liked romantic comedies and Cindy loved horror. Brittany preferred musicals. Once, they built a fort out of sleeping bags, pillows, cushions, and blankets, basically anything they could find but it collapsed when Cindy kicked it in her sleep.

Another time, Brittany's little sister, Stacy, invented her own ice cream sundae. They ate it and made fun of a horrible action movie.

Jess waited in the lobby until a pink Corvette parked on the curb. Brittany's dad bought it for her. It was a beautiful car and well taken care of with rainbow lights blinking on the hub caps and expensive, leather seats.

Jess put her seat belt on. "Thanks for this."

"I can't believe you called me," Brittany laughed. "I lost my permit, remember?"

"Oh my God! That's right. You hit that fire hydrant." Jess wasn't in the car when it happened but Brittany told her about how she drove off the road while she was checking her phone and accidentally crashed into a fire hydrant. No one was hurt and the damage was minimal but her dad was forced to suspend her permit. "I forgot," Jess said. "Wait, you shouldn't be driving. We could get in serious trouble."

"I doubt it. Your parents are awesome lawyers and my dad's the mayor," Brittany said. "Besides, I couldn't leave you hanging. You need a ride."

She slammed her foot on the pedal. The car jerked forward and raced down the road. Jess laughed without thinking. Sometimes, Brittany was reckless or oblivious. She didn't account for certain things or people, and she took advantage of her father's job more often than she'd admit.

Brittany's reddish-blonde hair was in a French braid. She wore a dark blue sweater over kitten-themed pajama pants and a loose tank top. Her nails were long and well-cut, thanks to a standing appointment at her favorite spa, Eden's Oasis. "I've decided something. I love being single."

"Oh yeah?" Jess asked. "Well, I'm glad you're over the breakup."

"Me too." Brittany spent most of their summer sleepovers complaining about Tony. She called him names, stalked him on social media, and rolled her eyes at the fact he was dating again. "And hey, you are totally one step closer to getting into that college you want. Zak City Law, right? You are gonna be an amazing lawyer," she pointed to Jess's outfit. "You already look the part."

Everything was going according to plan. Jess was a fantastic intern. She learned about the job, the rules, the cases, the criminals, and more. Layla was happy. Jess had a bright future, so why'd it feel stale? Pride and calm centered by a comforting loneliness. "Can we drive around before we go back to your place? I kind of want to soak it up, you know?"

"Soak what up?" Brittany asked.

Jess shrugged. "I'm not completely sure."

"Alright. I'm in," Brittany chuckled. "But we have to get back soon because Cindy is making margaritas and if I'm not there, our kitchen is gonna be a crazy mess."

"I can't believe you didn't bring her with you," Jess said. "Leaving her unsupervised is a hazard."

"She's drunk!" she laughed. "I don't want her to throw up in my car!"

They drove past Key Hotel where Brittany and her family lived. The penthouse was beautiful, one of Jess's favorite places. The concierge knew her name and always told her to go right up. She never had to wait for permission. She'd known the Mikes family for almost her entire life. Brittany and Jess had been in the same class since kindergarten, and their families attended the same parties and social events.

Brittany opened all four windows allowing cold wind to slap their faces. She screamed, punching her fists into the air, as she drove with her knees.

Jess laughed. "You're insane!"

"Try it. Come on!"

Jess hesitated. She took a deep breath and screamed at the top of her lungs but it was drowned out by the wind's rapid whistle and car engines. It felt good. She couldn't believe she did it. She couldn't believe a lot of things tonight.

They shared a smile.

***

Alice

Alice lay sprawled out on her couch, one leg over the back, another hanging off the edge, and both her hands were clasped together on her belly. The cushions were deflated but comfortable and they smelled like beer. Mason must've come home long enough to have another six-pack.

A three-year-old tennis match played on the TV while classic rock blasted from her earbuds. For dinner, she heated frozen fries in the toaster oven and dipped them in ranch.

This was her summer. Boring nights and whatever she found in the fridge. She often met Cece at the diner and texted Jess whenever she could. Alice liked her home but she hated its sad, peaceful quiet. Being alone sucked. She missed listening to her parents talk about their days, whisper about how much they loved each other, or discuss important topics such as Susan's heroics.

She pulled a blanket over her legs. A Christmas gift from Susan's mom. Alice didn't know her grandmother. Susan didn't speak to her. Mason's parents were dead.

Alice turned the music off and listened to a toothpaste commercial. Why were there so many brands? Didn't they all do the same thing? The question faded as she closed her eyes. Images started to spiral and dance; the sidewalk, the crowd, the street. Destroyer's rainbow hair. Susan's turquoise suit. Their strong, fluid movements were perfect, as familiar as old friends.

Alice gasped when the ashes fell. Panting, she sat up. She'd never get used to that nightmare, it was horrible, reliving her mom's death. She took deep, steady breaths to calm herself and the lightning flickering between her fingers.

Her phone started ringing. The screen flashed Mason's number.

She grabbed it. "Dad?"

"Afraid not."

"Eddie?" she recognized the voice. The old man owned Mason's favorite bar. He was a family friend and a stable presence in Alice's life. She loved listening to his war stories.

"Did your dad come home?" he asked.

She slid off the couch. She went upstairs, a small area with two bedrooms and a bathroom. Her parents' room was bigger than hers but not by much. The queen-size bed was untouched. Mason didn't like to sleep in it without his wife but sometimes, he'd stumble into it, drunk and unaware of what he was doing. Two square tables stood on either side. The lamps matched. An antique jewelry box sat on the dark wood dresser. It still held all of Susan's favorite earrings and necklaces.

The doorframe was marked with Alice's heights and ages from every year since she was three.

"No." Fear rattled her spine. "Why?"

"He was here for a while but he left. I didn't see him or I would have stopped him," Eddie said. "He was pretty drunk and I have no idea where he could have gone."

"Did anyone else see him leave?" she asked. "Maybe one of the guys who play pool late?"

"He was the last one to leave," he said. "Tell me what you need me to do."

Nausea almost knocked her down. Tears threatened to burst from her eyes. She wanted to cry but it wouldn't solve anything. This couldn't be happening, this couldn't be real. Was her dad missing? Was he hurt? Or worse. She hated this. She hated not knowing if he was okay or not. "Could... Could you look near you? I'll look around here. Please."

"I'm already locking the doors," Eddie said. "Listen. It's gonna be alright, okay? We'll find him. Do you want to stay on the phone?"

"No. Just... just text me." She grabbed her sweatshirt and put on Susan's old sandals, which almost fit her feet. She ran out her front door and down the sidewalk.

The night was warm with a slight breeze, which blew against her face, distracting her from her fears.

Every townhouse was identical. Brick with stone columns and different colored front doors. Some were white, others were yellow or brown. One still had July Fourth decorations in the windows. A few cars were parked on the street but not many.

Late-night wanderers hailed cabs or walked to wherever they were headed.

Alice texted Cece. It couldn't hurt to have another person help her search. She would've texted Jess but she was probably still at the law firm. Alice didn't want to bother her.

She looked everywhere she could think of; alleys near her house, neighbors' houses, unlocked cars, truck beds, dumpsters, the bus stop. After thirty minutes, Alice went into full panic mode.

Tears spilled from her eyes and her hands shook. The sidewalk started to spin. She couldn't stay balanced. If she lost another parent, she might lose her mind. Not that she had him now but he was alive, at least.

Her parents used to be so in love. They were happy. Their inside jokes, their kisses good morning, and good night. They'd share proud glances every time Alice did something adorable or good, as simple as getting an A on a quiz or making a basket in one of her games. They didn't know she noticed.

Mason looked at Susan like she was the most amazing woman in the universe. She'd assure him that she'd come home. He and their daughter were the reason she fought. She loved them more than anything.

Alice wiped her tears with the sleeves of her sweatshirt. She checked her phone. Neither Eddie nor Cece had found him. She needed to think. Where would he go? He had a car, so he could be anywhere. *He could be wrapped around a telephone pole.*

Her phone rang. She answered. "Did you find him?"

"No," Cece said. "He hasn't come home?"

"No, I went back there." Alice tried to keep her tone steady. She tried to keep herself from panicking but she couldn't. Her mind jumped from one horrible scenario to another. "He could be dead, Cece. I... I can't... I can't do this, I can't lose him. I can't-"

"What about your mom?"

Alice wiped snot on her sleeve. "What?"

"There's a giant memorial for Glisin in Liberty Cemetery. What if he went there by instinct or something," Cece said. "It's worth a shot."

"Meet me there." Why didn't she think of that before? She took off running, sandals popping against the sidewalk. One of the soles must've broken.

Her powers bubbled like boiling water alongside her anxiety. Her fingertips tingling, she felt her worries and fears crackling in her head, pushing against her skull, making it ache. She drowned the electricity that surfaced beneath her skin. This wasn't the time to use her powers. It would be too reckless, too open. She couldn't panic. She had to stay calm.

How she ran six blocks so fast, she'd never know. Liberty Cemetery was framed by a tall, arched gate and a gothic, metal fence with stained glass lamps built into each pike. Mournful light tried not to wake the dead.

Mowed grass and gravel paths crunched underfoot. The headstones were all different. Some were squared or circular or pointed, some had flowers or empty vases near them and others were plain. Some dated back to the seventeen-hundreds.

Alice wondered about these people's lives. Who had they loved? What did they do for a living? What did their houses look like? What were their hobbies? What or who killed them?

In the very back of Liberty Cemetery was an old mausoleum with Roman-like columns and an arched rooftop. Chubby, stone cherubs framed the double doorway. Each cherub was posed in some sort of prayer, ready to protect or bless the heroine inside.

It sat empty for years. No one claimed it, so when the city's superhero died, Mayor Mikes declared it a historical landmark and they put a stone casket inside, which held ash and a black mask. Turquoise streamers decorated the oak trees nearby. Stuffed animals and melted candles were piled on the mausoleum's steps. Thank-you letters were plastered on the walls, each one was from someone who loved and mourned Glisin. Height City missed her too.

"Why didn't you choose us!" Mason screamed. His voice was exhausted and heartbroken. His words were slurred. He flung a whiskey bottle at the locked door, and as its shattered pieces showered the grass, he stood still. Was he waiting for Susan to come out and answer his question?

Alice hugged herself. Her dad was in pain. Usually, it was a quiet burden they didn't acknowledge or talk about. Witnessing it made her cry.

He knelt down. His distant sobs made her chest ache. He sounded how she felt. She couldn't hear the questions he asked but she wondered what they were, probably the same ones she'd been asking for years. Why'd Susan have to go face Destroyer that night? Why didn't she say goodbye? Why'd she choose to wear the mask when she knew how it could end?

"Al," a voice spoke behind her. Cece wore a black tank top under a white one and leggings. Her arms and fingers were stained in blood. Who's blood? Her angel wing necklace shone in the shattered light of the crescent moon. She didn't move. She didn't come closer or try to comfort Alice. She stood still, unsure of what to do.

Alice used her sleeves to dry her tears. She wanted to be strong but it was hard. She hated life without her mother. Her family was broken. She was broken. "I'm fine."

Chapter 3

Alice

"He hasn't mentioned it at all?" Cece asked, hands tucked in her jacket pockets. "It's been two weeks. Maybe he was too drunk to remember."

Alice shrugged. She hated thinking about that night at Liberty Cemetery. After Cece got there, the girls helped Mason to his feet despite his drunken stumbles and slurred sobs. They hauled Mason into Eddie's car and the old man drove them all home. He helped Alice get her dad to bed and he slept on the couch. He didn't want Alice to be alone. She couldn't sleep though, instead, she sat outside her parents' bedroom, listening to her dad breathe.

"He's been home every night, so I guess that's good. Maybe we don't have to talk about it. We never talk about anything that has to do with Mom."

"Yeah, keep it bottled up," Cece nodded once. "That'll help a lot."

Alice learned that Cece's main setting was sarcasm, which she found entertaining. Alice liked her. She loved hanging out at Linda's Diner with her. Cece liked to tease Alice about ordering pie when there were several different types of cake on the menu. They had light-hearted arguments about it but mostly Alice loved the fact that Cece listened to her stories.

They were comfortable together.

"Maybe my dad and I aren't meant to have a relationship." Alice wasn't ready to accept it. She decided to change the subject. "You don't have to walk me to school, you know? Mister Scotts can give me a ride."

"I still don't get why he drives you to school," Cece said. "You guys have a weird relationship."

"He's my only option. Dad's either hungover, drunk, or gone," Alice sighed. It hurt to say out loud. "And if I wanna make it to junior year, then I can't be late again and I have to get at least Cs and Bs."

Eddie told Alice to take Mister Scotts's offer. When she told him she was afraid of being a burden, he said she wasn't. She deserved help. Her mom wouldn't want her to give up on herself. Susan would want her daughter to be happy, to heal.

"School," Cece smiled. "Making child labor legal."

"Jess is tutoring me."

"Your Honeycomber bestie?" Cece wasn't a fan of Honeycombers. Whenever Alice talked about Jess, Cece would crack jokes, all in good humor, but Alice could sense the tension in her voice. "What grades did you use to get?"

"Ds or incompletes. Have you talked to your best friend? Uh, Bobby, is her name, right? Bobby Jones?" The connection was baffling. Alice never would've guessed Bobby was friends with Cece.

"Radio silence. Apparently, she's been spending all her time with the boyfriend," Cece said. "She wants me to approve of him and I don't, so we're not talking." She didn't talk much about Bobby's boyfriend, whenever she did, she'd cringe. Mentioning him seemed to leave a bad taste in her mouth. But when she talked or mentioned Bobby, it was like she was describing color or sunshine, then she'd remember they weren't speaking, and she'd deflate. It was obvious how much she missed her. Their bond sounded a lot like the one Alice had with Jess.

"Johnny, right?" Alice asked. "Is Bobby's boyfriend?"

"Yep." Cece made a face.

"We're getting better at this, remembering the names of people in each other's lives. I'm a little proud."

"Don't be too proud," Cece said. "It took us three months."

"Well, we have a lot of people in our lives," Alice smiled.

They stopped at the limestone sign. MORGAN HIGH. Parents dropped off their teenagers who hurried up the steps. Honeycombers were dressed in name-brand clothing and pretty jewelry while Burrowers wore ripped jeans and spikes on their boots. Nesters had simpler clothes, less noticeable. Everyone drifted into their own groups, chatting and chuckling. School buses weaved in and out of the back parking lot, engines making an ugly sound.

"Off to prison you go," Cece said. She stood behind the limestone sign, slightly out of sight.

"School."

"Same thing."

"Wow, okay," Alice chuckled. "There's a window in the first floor girls' bathroom. If you ever wanna make a conjugal visit."

"Maybe I'll bring a cake with a file in it. Do me a favor?"

"Sure. What's up?"

"If you see Bobby, text me a picture," Cece's protective glare lunged at the building. "I have to know if she's comatose or not."

"I will. Thanks for walking me."

"I get bored easily. Call me later." She walked away.

Alice ran up the steps and through the doorway. She was glad she wasn't late and she had all her homework done. This year was going to be different. It needed to be.

She avoided people. She hated when her shoulders touched someone else's. They barely paid attention to her, nobody seemed to realize she was there, but she didn't mind. She didn't need an invite to the next big party or to chat with anyone between classes. She had her camera. She'd take pictures if she needed something to do.

She went to her locker. Leo appeared by her side.

She looked at him. "Hi?"

His eyes darted around the crowds. He leaned against the lockers and relaxed his torso but his shoulders were tense. Was he waiting for someone to attack him? Why was he so paranoid?

"Sorry. I'm avoiding that jerk, Tony O'Hare, and the football players," he said. "And nobody really knows you exist, no offense."

"None taken," Alice grabbed her books. "Why are they bothering you?"

"We have an unsaid feud going on, don't ask." He watched the other students, fascinated. "Look at these people, suddenly we're divided."

"What do you mean?"

He shrugged. "Well, take you and Jess- it's okay I called her that, right? 'Cause the teachers call her Jessica and-"

"That's her name but yeah, you'd have to ask her." She gestured to her classmates. Their faces were tired and groggy. Their movements were sluggish and bored. They were practically knocking into one another. Did everyone just wake up?

"Okay, so," Leo continued. "You guys were inseparable in grade school. She was the teacher's pet and you were a sports star. You did homework together, she went to almost all your games and meets and you had a secret handshake-"

"We were eight." Alice remembered creating their handshake. They sat on her bed, laughing and giggling at the different ones they came up with, practicing over and over until they finally memorized it.

She crinkled her eyebrows. "How do you know all this?"

"We've been in the same class forever and I pay attention," he shrugged. "Like I know now she's hanging out with Brittany Mikes and Cindy Cohen. And everyone in this school calls you Ally."

She closed her locker and leaned next to him. It was true. People didn't know her name. Why would they? She was barely there. She liked flying under the radar. Besides, Ally was a pretty name.

She tilted her head back against the lockers.

Leo was right, she and Jess weren't together as much. Were they drifting apart? If they were, she knew the reason. She was pulling away because she couldn't tell Jess the truth about Susan. Lying to Jess was terrible. She felt the guilt like a bag of bricks lying on her chest.

"Jess is my best friend," Alice said. "She's allowed to have other ones."

"Just an observation." His voice was relaxed and sweet as if he had never been rude in his life. She'd known Leo for a while but they bonded during their recent trips to school. Leo was Mister Scotts's son. He had dorky taste in music and usually, he was doing his homework in the backseat when they picked her up. Sometimes, Mister Scotts would buy them both breakfast sandwiches.

"I remember your mom," Leo said. "She always brought snacks for the whole team and your dad bragged about you."

Susan used to search for healthy snack recipes on Pinterest. She was determined to make them for the team. Alice figured she liked having a part. She didn't always get to come to the games and be included in certain things. Being a housewife slash superhero was a full-time job.

Mason worked a lot but he came to every game or meet that he could. Alice remembered seeing him in the bleachers with a proud, excited expression. He clapped the loudest and always looked happy.

"Thanks, Leo," she smiled.

He nudged her shoulder. "Sure, Alice. See? I know your name."

They both chuckled.

Brittany and Jess walked up, arms locked as they laughed about something amongst themselves. Brittany wore her cheer uniform, which was a yellow, long-sleeved top and a matching skirt with shorts underneath. The Morgan High falcon - with its dark blue feathers and threatening stare - was stamped on her chest. Her bun was held by a dark brown spider-clip and her white sneakers were double laced.

She was really pretty, Alice noticed.

Jess wore a white polo shirt, a long, jean skirt, ballet flats, and little pearl earrings but something was missing from her figure. Did she change her hair?

"I'll see you after school," Jess said.

"Okay. Bye, Ally. Leon." Brittany waved to them, trying to be polite, then left.

"Sorry. She tends to get people mixed up," Jess cleared her throat. She opened her locker, which was right next to Alice's. It was clean and organized. It would've seemed freakish to anyone who didn't grow up with her. Her books were organized in order of her classes, a whiteboard calendar hung on the door and a magnetic shelf held extra supplies like pencils, scissors, paper clips, highlighters, markers, and several other things.

"There's no Leon in this school." Leo pointed inside Jess's locker at the three-hole punch. "You know, every teacher has a three-hole punch, right?"

Jess shut the door. "It's just in case."

Alice realized why Jess looked different. "Your pink streaks are gone."

Jess brushed her fingers through her hair. "Oh, yeah, uh," she didn't meet Alice's gaze, instead she looked down at the floor. "They faded over the summer and I haven't redyed them. I'm not sure I will."

"You loved them," Alice said. "You were so excited about them. It took you two whole hours to choose the perfect shade of pink."

"Two hours to pick *what*?" Leo was baffled. The girls looked at him, then refocused on each other. He stood still, shifting on his feet, as he waited to see who'd speak next.

Alice frowned. "What happened?"

She remembered when they went to the hair salon to get the dye. Alice was tired of looking in the mirror and being reminded of Susan. She wasn't sure why she chose purple. Maybe because it looked cool? Maybe because it complimented her blue eyes.

Jess decided to join in at the last minute. Pink was her favorite color but she had to choose the right shade. She looked at every box, going back and forth about whether or not she should actually dye her hair. She ended up getting really excited.

Jess hesitated, uncertainty seized her features. The same expression she had every time she let Layla make a decision for her, even when she wanted something different. Jess always gave in. Alice hated it.

"My mom. She likes my hair better without them and she's a force of nature, you know? I don't want to upset her," Jess said. "I'm sorry."

"Don't apologize. It's your choice." Alice heard the slight anger in her tone and felt horrible.

Jess looked at the floor. A silent apology. Why did she always do this? Why was she always sorry?

"Let me get this straight," Leo said, not sensing the tension. "You let your mom control you?"

"I don't let her control me!" Jess shouted, then lowered her voice, "who are you?"

"Leo Scotts. We've been in the same class since second grade except middle school," he said. "Remember? For career day in second grade, you dressed up as a veterinarian."

"How do you remember that?" she asked. "I don't... I'm sorry but I, I don't recall you at all."

"It's okay, I didn't exactly stand out. I still don't. I dressed up as an astronaut," he chuckled at the memory, then paused. He cleared his throat. "Uh, never mind. Can I ask you a question?"

"Sure."

"Do I call you Jessica or Jess?"

"Jess. It's a nickname. I prefer it."

"Cool," he leaned a little closer to her. "Jess."

Alice glanced between them, hiding a smile. The three stood beside a chaotic crowd of their classmates. The many conversations weren't understandable. Everyone smelled like sweat, bad cologne, and floral perfume. A freshman, wearing a yellow dress and sneakers, tried to find her way, as she carried a pile of textbooks bigger than her. She almost tripped when Cindy went running past her.

"Jessica!" Cindy shoved through a group of Burrowers and cringed. They looked as disgusted with her as she did with them. She ran up to Jess, ignoring Alice and Leo. "You have to come to the gym."

"What for?" Jess asked.

She laughed. "What for? Oh my God! Cheerleader tryouts, duh."

Alice and Leo shared a look. They knew they weren't part of this. Did Cindy even know they existed? Leo seemed as unbothered by it as Alice was.

Jess wasn't on the cheerleading team. She didn't have the coordination but last year, she watched the tryouts in an effort to support Brittany and Cindy who were both desperate to be on the team. This year, they were doing it again, except this time Brittany was leading the routines.

Cindy grabbed Jess's hand and yanked her from the group. She stumbled forward and turned to the others. "Sorry! See you at lunch!"

They melted into the chaos. It was such a relief to hear Jess wanted to sit with Alice at lunch, and not the other Honeycombers. Alice couldn't handle it if Jess completely disappeared from her life.

Leo looked at her. He had a calming presence. "Hey, at lunch, can I have your pudding cup?"

***

Bobby

Bobby wore a red cocktail dress under one of Johnny's shirts, which had sleeves that hung over her wrists. Her unbrushed curls were smashed under a sparkly beanie. It had cat ears. Her face was covered by giant, tinted sunglasses because the sun was too bright today. Was it always this bright?

Johnny grabbed her arm, lifted her into his arms, and twirled around. The movement made her sick but she swallowed the nausea. He set her down and she stumbled. He wrapped his arms around her, his hands caressed her waist. He'd been very happy with her lately, ever since the first poker game.

She chuckled. "Hi."

"Hey," he kissed her. "Hungover?"

"Stop yelling," she groaned. "And yes. You were there. We drank half the club."

They went club-hopping last night. She wasn't sure whose idea it was, it could've been hers, but they competed in several drinking games and danced until Bobby's body surrendered to exhaustion.

Johnny pressed her against the lockers, body pushing against hers, warm and tough. He held her hips. She stood on her toes and they kissed. His lips were chapped. The kiss was rough, lazy, and he smelled like alcohol. Could it be from last night's partying or was it from his usual morning routine? His hand drifted down her thigh, fingers tickling her bare skin. He lifted her leg, so she could hook it to his hip but they were interrupted. Part of her was glad.

"No PDA in the hall!" Principal Penez shouted. He was an older guy. He dyed his hair black and wore power suits every day. His glasses were rectangular and his gaze was serious. He probably wasn't popular in high school. He made sure they knew they were being watched, then he walked away.

Bobby looked at Johnny. "Next time, more water, please."

"You wanna know a hangover cure that's foolproof?" he asked.

"It's not grass juice, is it?" she yawned. "'Cause I've had that and it's disgusting."

"No," he chuckled. He pulled a metal flask from his backpack and handed it to her.

She raised an eyebrow. "Rum?"

"I'm not a pirate," he said. "It's whiskey."

A billion bees relentlessly buzzed against her skull. She was nauseous and physically exhausted. She wanted to sleep. Maybe she could catch a nap in one of her classes. She held up the flask, put it to her lips, and threw her head back, sucking down as much as she could before her throat burned.

She gasped. "Okay."

"Feel better?" he smiled.

She shook her head. "Not even a little bit."

He kissed her forehead. He put the flask back and wrapped his arm around her. Heading down the hall, they were surrounded by chaotic voices and laughter, which made Bobby's headache worse. She held his shirt to try and keep herself steady. He squeezed her shoulder, not as a threat but even so, it made her tense. She didn't flinch. If she flinched, he'd get mad. She didn't want him to get mad.

"There's another game in a couple of weeks. Big winnings," Johnny said. "With you playing there's no way we can lose."

"Is it a good idea to go to all these games? We already won a bunch and those big, large, really large men were really really really angry, right?"

Bobby won every poker game Johnny found. He was proud of her. When he counted their winnings, he'd list the things he could do with the money like buy a fleet of yachts and a bejeweled camel, stuff like that. Bobby was proud too. Her dad taught her well. But the losers were mad. She played against criminals, not only Betty's people but also Markinson's people and lower gang members.

Markinson's men were the scariest. Every single one of them seemed to have large scars on their faces. Some of their scars looked self-inflicted. She didn't know much about Markinson but she definitely didn't want to piss off his henchmen. They'd do something terrible to her.

"Babe, if you're scared, we can split it a different way," Johnny shrugged. "I'll take seventy and you'll take thirty, instead of fifty/fifty. That way I take more of the risk."

"Thirty percent? That's not fair," Bobby said. "I'm the one who plays the games."

Every poker game she played was set in a dark room. She swore the shadows housed hungry, slimy demons who wanted to eat her. Each man at the table had a weapon, guns mostly, but she wasn't afraid. Johnny was liked by Markinson's men and everyone else in the city was afraid of Casey - Cece - so they wouldn't touch her.

Bobby was the only girl at the table.

A flickering orange light hung above them. The men smoked cigars and cigarettes. They tossed in their chips - plastic poker chips found at a dollar store - and readied their cards. Bobby watched for their tells and did the numbers in her head. She didn't need to see what they had to know who would win.

Sorry, boys, she laid down a royal flush. *Guess I'm lucky.*

She acted cool but on the inside, she was doing a happy dance. Johnny high-fived her, kissed her, and laughed. The first few games were fun. Winning felt great and she needed the money for bills and such, then her opponents started getting angry. They'd glare at her or swipe everything off the table in frustration. Morey, a Burrows businessman, threatened her life.

Bobby told him that Cece would feed him his toes if he tried anything.

"And I know when and where the games are," Johnny scoffed. "Without me, you wouldn't get to win, *we* wouldn't have anything," his voice softened, rubbing her shoulder, he said. "I'm just looking out for you."

She tried to believe him. She wanted to believe him. But for the last few weeks, it felt like all he cared about was the money. She liked the money too but Bobby didn't want to risk her life for it. Why did he?

He pressed her against the lockers, smiling. His wicked and beautiful smile. He kept her still, inching up to kiss her with his hot, whiskey-scented mouth. She took a deep breath. Why did she love him? Was there something wrong with her?

She groaned, stomach-churning and mouth-watering, she shoved Johnny out of the way and darted into the girls' bathroom. Her heels slipped on the tile and she stumbled into a stall. She yanked off her sunglasses. She ate a bag of M&Ms and two tiny bottles of 7up for breakfast, both of which splashed into the toilet water, the whiskey too. Fizzy mud in the toilet bowl. Her stomach squeezed its emptiness. She shifted off her knees and sat down, body aching. Why did she always overdo it? Why did she have to wake up like this?

"Babe?" Johnny shouted from the hall. "You okay?"

"Yeah," she groaned. "Yeah, I'm good."

She put on her sunglasses and yawned. She probably looked like the hipster version of the bird lady in *Mary Poppins*. But cuter. She lay on the floor, stretching her arms above her head and leaning her legs on the side of the toilet. She glanced around the stall at the walls covered in permanent marker. Different handwriting, words, names, pictures. Some were inappropriate, others were simple. On the stall door were the words BOBBY JONES IS A WHORE written in perfect cursive.

"So, what do you think about that poker game?" Johnny asked. "In a couple weeks."

Her head was a boulder. She didn't want to argue. He'd nag her until she agreed or worse. Her bruises hadn't healed from the last time she disagreed with him. It was easier if she did what he wanted.

"Whatever you want." Bobby closed her eyes.

***

Tommy

Dave's constant finger tapping echoed through the empty room. His nervous habit was enough to send Tommy running out the door but he didn't, he didn't complain either, because he knew what Dave was thinking. Dave didn't like to remember his childhood. For a while, he escaped his darkness, but now, the ghosts of his past were coming back to haunt him.

"I'm telling you, he's gonna kill me." His fearful tone shattered his usual calm, cool persona, which Tommy found less than comforting.

Casey shrugged. "It'll be quieter around here."

"You suck," Dave said, too distracted to think of a better retort. His dad was a psychotic jerk obsessed with fire who made Dave ashamed of his own name.

Tommy didn't know much about Ted Marson, other than a few infamous stories spread across the Burrows, and the vague details of his and Dave's last encounter.

"I get it but what are the chances he'll come after you?" Tommy needed to soothe his friend's worries before Dave spiraled into a panic. "He just got out, he's working for Betty. You're probably scared about nothing."

"I'm scared because my old man is free," Dave said. "You know what I did to him, man, he's gonna want revenge. I'm so screwed."

"Yeah," Casey ate a pretzel.

Tommy looked at her. "You're not helping."

"I wasn't trying to."

"You've made that obvious."

"That was the goal." She ate another pretzel.

Sally was in the back hall doing inventory. She let the kids hang out when the club was closed because she figured it was better than the streets which Tommy would've agreed with except Sally did business with every crazy, violent criminal in the city. Mostly, she traded information. She knew everything going on in the Burrows and had several grudges against her.

"She doesn't get it," Dave glanced at Casey. "She's an orphan."

Casey threw the small, wooden bowl filled with pretzels at his head and when it hit him, she smirked, satisfied with the wound she gave him. The salty snacks scattered everywhere.

"Hey!" Dave yelled, rubbing his forehead. "What!"

"You kind of asked for it," Tommy said.

"I was stating a fact."

Tommy sighed, shaking his head, while Casey tried to kill Dave with a glare. As Betty Beater's students, the three of them shared many horrible traumas not even the most twisted mind could imagine, but the reasons they each became trapped under Betty's thumb were worse. If Tommy could erase his childhood, he would, without question.

"Look, Betty wants Ted for something," Casey clicked her tongue. "She's got him held up somewhere, just find and avoid him."

"How do I do that?" Dave asked. "If Betty didn't tell her champion anything, then she only told her inner circle. Hobbs and those guys would rather die than betray her."

"I can use facial recognition software," Tommy said. "I'll hack into the street cameras and some satellites and we'll find him in no time."

"I love it when you talk tech," Casey chuckled. He smiled.

Dave rolled his eyes. He'd been Tommy's best friend for a long time. They met after Betty found Tommy in an alley, drenched in the rain, hungry, lonely, and ready to give up on himself, much like his mother already had. He was broken, which Dave related to, saying it meant he wasn't the only one who had barely survived a nightmare.

He had watched Tommy and Casey's relationship develop, he supported Tommy's feelings for her, but that didn't stop him from rolling his eyes and scoffing every time they acted like a couple. "You guys are gross."

El scooted in beside him. He wrapped his arm around her. Her long, light tan hair looked like a doll's, and her skin was perfect porcelain. She wore black leggings and a big, dark blue T-shirt as a dress. She had several scars on her body, three on her neck. Tommy didn't bother asking where she got them but he assumed the scars were from training with her father. The man known as Markinson.

"Why are there pretzels all over the floor?" she asked.

Tommy and Dave answered at the same time. "Cece."

Casey smiled.

"Oh, got it," El said. "Nobody working for my dad knows anything about Ted's release."

"Damn it," Dave sighed. He rubbed his eyes, exhausted and paranoid. He'd been searching for his father - without meaning to - in every corner of the Burrows, waiting to pay for what he convinced himself was a terrible mistake. "Thanks for asking around."

"Guess we'll have to wait till a building starts on fire," Casey said.

"That's a good backup plan," Tommy nodded. "But I'm still gonna try facial recognition."

"Fine. If you wanna do it the easy way."

"I can sleep over tonight if it'll make you feel better," El said. "I know Cole's there but I want to be there too, if you need me."

"Nah. Nobody needs to get killed because of me," Dave said, fingers galloping on the table. "I already asked Cole to stay with Tommy, and his answer was 'If you stay, I stay', so."

"Lifers," Casey said. She'd been making that joke since he and Cole became roommates.

Dave shook his head. "I can't believe I did this."

"You didn't do anything wrong," El said. "And it wasn't a mistake."

"Eh," Casey bobbed her head. "That's debatable."

Tommy put his hand over her mouth, so she couldn't make any more unhelpful comments. She leaned back and crossed her arms, annoyed.

El rubbed Dave's shoulder, trying to comfort him, but he barely noticed the gesture. She grabbed his hand and stood up, tugging his arm. "Alright, come on."

"What are you doing?" he asked.

"We're going for a walk," she said.

Dave smiled at her flirtatious look. As his oldest friend, El had met his father, she understood Dave's fears better than Tommy could. But unlike Tommy, El wasn't capable of sympathizing with the situation, because of her own father, she was taught to "suck it up," as she put it, which he guessed meant "be tough or die." Tommy never knew his dad, sometimes he wondered who the guy was or if they would've gotten along.

"A walk isn't gonna solve my problem," Dave stood up. El wrapped her arms around his torso and pressed herself against him. She leaned close to him, enough for their lips to graze but she didn't kiss him. He kissed her.

Casey rolled her eyes.

"It'll at least take your mind off it." El pulled Dave forward in the direction of the front door.

He chuckled. "Fine. If you insist."

Tommy removed his hand from Casey's mouth when Dave and El were gone. He had no doubt the casual couple were going to end up at Dave's apartment, either on his couch or in his bedroom.

Tommy leaned beside Casey and she looked at him. They could sit there, in the corner booth, for hours, playing cards, talking about anything, laughing, teasing each other. He could sit with his arm around her in silence and be completely content. He loved her scent of leather and sandalwood. He loved her fierce green eyes and blue hair. Everything about her was incredible.

"He's screwed," she said, yanking Tommy out of his daydream.

"Maybe." He didn't disagree but he wasn't ready to accept defeat yet. There had to be a solution, a way to save Dave's life. "But it's rude to remind him."

"Reminding him is half the fun."

He nudged her. She scrunched her eyebrows as if she didn't understand what he meant. She had to leave the booth, so he could get out. "I've got to start facial recognition. I can't do that from here," he said. "And you're blocking me."

"You should've thought of that before you sat down," she said. "You should've brought your laptop over here, instead of leaving it at the bar."

"I didn't need it then."

"Not my problem."

The corner booth was a wrap-around. He slid to the other side. She scoffed and he nodded for her to follow him. He unpacked his laptop and set it on the bar. His fingers flew over the keyboard. An expert pianist and his piano. The keys clacked and clucked with each press. He loved that sound. He nodded along to the code, mind racing with binary, algorithms, and encryptions. He could do this in his sleep.

Casey stood behind him, arms crossed. "If Betty doesn't want Ted found, then he can't be found."

"Probably but I can still give it a shot."

"I don't want him to die either." She paused. "Yeah, no, that's right." She'd never admit it but she cared about Dave too. "But what are the odds his dad doesn't come for him? The idiot called the cops that night. Once Ted's finished with Betty, she'll let him run wild."

"Which is exactly why we're gonna keep tabs on him," Tommy said. "When Ted's out of Betty's protection, it'll be easier to catch him on facial recognition and otherwise."

"Okay, so what are the odds Dave can fend him off?"

"There's a chance."

Betty trained all three of them. Dave had been under her thumb the longest but for some reason, she paid special attention to Tommy and Casey. None of them were sure why but Dave didn't care. He got more freedom. Not to mention, he grew up on the streets, more so than Tommy or Casey. He knew how to handle himself in a fight, especially against the man who ruined his life.

"Slim one at most," she said.

Tommy finished. He smiled at his work, nodded, and closed the laptop. He shoved it in his bag and hung the strap on his shoulder, turning to Casey. "You and I are Betty Beater's best, if anyone can do this, it's us. And Dave isn't helpless."

"I've yet to see otherwise."

"We'll cross that bridge when we come to it."

They walked side by side. Two parts of a well-oiled machine. Betty's machine.

As they left the club, Casey grabbed Tommy's wrist and wrapped his arm around her. He pulled her close, so they were walking together, footsteps synced. She held the back of his hoodie.

He'd do everything he could to protect Dave because Tommy understood having complicated parents.

"I've got an hour before my fight," Casey said.

He loved having her next to him. He hated remembering the time before she was in his life or before he met Dave, before he found Betty, before Tommy escaped his childhood. He squeezed Casey's shoulder to keep himself from drifting into his darkest memories.

Her leather jacket was cold and slick under his touch. He kissed her head. "Silent movies and popcorn?"

She smiled. "Read my mind."

Chapter 4

Jess

THE EGGSHELL-COLORED WALLS MATCHED the cotton candy pink carpet. The dresser stood next to the bathroom. The hall door was by the desk. A corkboard hung above it, framed by black tape, with pictures of Bennett and Layla, Brittany and Cindy, Jake and Tony but mostly, Alice and Jess. There was one of them by a tilt-a-whirl. Mason took them to the fair when they were nine. In the picture, they were laughing so hard, sick on hotdogs and rides. They had the best time.

The nightstand had pink polka dots painted on it. The lampshade was dark pink with white stripes. The round alarm clock was antique. The pillows and sheets were ruffled.

Textbooks, notebooks, flashcards, pens, pencils, highlighters, bookmarks, rulers, and novels were scattered on the bed. Jess was busy.

She had extra credit and homework to do. She needed to write a lesson plan for Alice's tutoring session and do some things for the student council. She was the sophomore class president.

Stress knotted in her belly. This was insane. It was too much for her to do in such a short time. She took a deep breath and piled her hair in a bun. She grabbed a pencil and started scribbling. She pushed through the hand cramps, headaches, and hunger until she finished a one-thousand-word essay, four math assignments, and the outline for Alice's next five lessons.

She sorted it by topic. They'd work on the subjects Alice had the weakest grade in and go from there. She put the plans in a folder and grabbed her vocabulary flashcards.

"Accede," she whispered. "To become a party to an agreement or treaty or give one's consent at the insistence of another... or... to arrive at or come into an office or dignity."

She checked the back. She was right. When she finished, she tied a rubber band around the neat pile and put it in her backpack. She packed the rest of her work and hung the bag on a hook next to her desk. Everything had a specific place.

She started on the student council work but her phone rang, so she answered it. "Hello?" Loud music blasted in her ear. Cindy yelled, "Jessica!"

"Cindy? Is that you? What-"

Loud rustling, then silence. Brittany spoke, "Hey. We're having a party at Cindy's place. You should come. Take a break from all the homework and stuff."

"That's a nice thought but I still have a ton of work to do," she said. "I can't bail on this."

"It's Saturday, Jess. That stuff is due on Monday," Brittany laughed. "Do it on Sunday and come over here. I need you. Tony came with a date."

She sounded half-drunk and all jealous. Why were they having a party? They threw a Halloween party a few weeks ago. Brittany dressed as Sandy from *Grease*, Cindy was a zombie bride and Jess went as a flapper. She loved the sparkly costume and feathered headband. She read a book in an empty bedroom, danced with Tony and he gave her a ride home. "I don't know."

"No! You have to. I can pick you up."

"No. I... I can walk. Cindy's is just a few blocks."

"Great! Come find me."

Jess hung up. She grabbed a jacket. Her bedroom was on the second floor along with her parents' room and the guest room. A full bath was in each. The stairs led to the living room where there was a white, L-shaped couch with solid-colored throw pillows and a cashmere blanket. Layla loved Cashmere.

A flat-screen TV stood on a dark wood console table with several drawers. The coffee table matched.

Bennett spent most of his time in the den behind the staircase. There was a leather recliner and every vinyl record from the sixties to the nineties. He loved music. He played guitar.

The kitchen connected to the living room through an archway. All their appliances were silver and the countertops were granite. The walls were seashell blue.

"Mom?" Jess went into the dining room. Layla used it as a home office. Their family never ate together. They only used the dining room as a family when they had company. Part of the "perfect" family picture her parents loved to show people.

Files from Layla's latest cases were spread across the long, rectangular table, which was also decorated with gold-painted candlesticks and a bowl of plastic fruit. Ted Marson's name was scribbled on one folder. He was released from Steel Prison three weeks before Halloween. People protested against it. They stood outside the courthouse and chanted a reprieve but it didn't work.

Jess glanced around to make sure Layla wasn't hiding somewhere, then she opened the file. Most of it was public information but at the bottom of the page was an address from six years ago. It could've been Ted Marson's old home. "Ames Street."

"Jessica!"

Jess dropped the file and turned to her mom. Layla wore silk pajamas and a furry bathrobe. Her hair was in braids. Jess folded her hands behind her back and picked her cuticles. "There's a party at Cindy's. I wanted to ask if I could go."

"Those files are confidential," Layla pointed at the table. "Why were you looking at them?"

"I... I was curious. I'm sorry. I just loved working with you and... um," Jess gulped. "I shouldn't have touched them. I won't do it again. I didn't see anything anyway."

Layla's stare was stern and withering, ready to slice you in half if you made one wrong move. "You can go to the party. Be home by eleven."

Jess nodded. She ran out of the dining room, through the kitchen, and into the living room. She slipped on her brand-new sneakers, which she didn't wear often but she felt the need to get away fast, so she decided against her favorite ballet flats. She ran out her front door, terrified that Layla would accuse her of lying and punish her without proof. She ran through backyard after backyard. A shortcut to Cindy's.

Cindy's family, the Cohens, owned a chain of successful, high-end restaurants.

The house was old, made of stone and brick with arched windows and a newly redone porch. The lawn was professionally landscaped. Multi-colored roses lined the path to the front door and there was a pool in the back. Cindy and her twin brother, Isaac, used to throw pool parties every year for their birthday because it was the only theme they could agree on. But now, Isaac went to a boarding school, so he was only home for holidays.

One girl was puking in the bushes. Another was passed out in the empty fountain, and from what Jess could tell, the girl was breathing. Her snores confirmed it. If the party just started, why were there people passed out already?

"I'm gonna do a flip!" one boy shouted to his friends. Six boys from the football team hung off the deck railing, whooping and shouting like idiots. One of them was going to break a limb.

Jess rolled her eyes.

Red, plastic cups were scattered everywhere on the lawn ruining the house's perfect, antique image.

The open front door led to a fancy entryway.

Missus Cohen recently refurbished the house as revenge against her husband. She always redecorated after one of their fights. The walls were dark tan and what once was white carpet, was now gray tile. A sharp chandelier hung from the ceiling. It glimmered and shined, beautiful and threatening right above Jess's head.

Photos of the Cohens family were on one wall, able to be seen by anyone who entered. Most of the photos featured Isaac winning academic rewards. The photos of Cindy featured her as a little girl, holding a stuffed lizard or her in the present wearing her cheer uniform. They weren't in many photos together.

Music blasted from every strategically placed speaker in the house. Jess's classmates danced on top of each other. She saw a lot of Honeycombers, which wasn't surprising. Some Nesters were huddled together in the corner, laughing to themselves. A couple of Burrowers were there too, the same ones who were at every Honeycomber party. One of which, wearing a gray trench coat, was selling drugs to one of Tony's friends. Marijuana, maybe? Everyone was drinking from a red, plastic cup. The stench of alcohol and sweat mixed, making Jess nauseous. Was it too late to leave?

"You made it!" Brittany slurred, smiling. She was drunk. She grabbed Jess's wrist and yanked her to the kitchen, where half the basketball team stood around the keg. A boy and girl were making out in the corner. There was puke on the fridge. Jess cringed. She should've brought wet wipes.

Brittany grabbed wine from the liquor cabinet -which was supposed to be locked - and held the bottle out. "Drink?"

"No," Jess shook her head. "Thanks."

Brittany yanked the cork. She put the bottle against her lips and tilted her head. Jess was amazed that she could drink so easily. Brittany would never drink cheap beer from a lousy keg but the Cohens' personal collection was perfect. She coughed. "Oh, geez."

"Too much?" Jess chuckled.

Brittany nodded. "Oh, yeah."

Tony walked in, eyes floating over Jess's body, he smiled. He was attractive and he'd made his interest in her obvious but she'd known him forever. They'd seen each other in diapers. Their parents were friends, co-workers, and Jess didn't see any reason to date him, especially since he was her friend's ex. It wouldn't be right.

"Wanna dance, Jessica?" he asked, looking at her like she was a prize he wanted to win.

"Uh, no. Thanks."

"Yeah, Tony, go away," Brittany said. "You're asking her to make me jealous and it isn't working."

"Seems like it is," he said.

She scoffed. "You're a cheater and a liar and a jerk."

"And you're a spoiled brat."

Jess left their angry, frustrated shouts and went into a semi-empty hall, where a few of her classmates were laughing about a recent football game. She should've brought a book. Parties were great but she didn't recognize anyone she liked. Brittany and Tony were the only people she really knew, and they'd argue all night if they could. Cindy was nowhere to be found.

"Jess?" The voice was familiar. His black hair, short and neatly combed, had grown out a bit. He wore a red vest, a white polo shirt, and tan khakis, the St. Hariot's uniform. His smile was shy and kind, a little timid. Other than slightly more mature facial features, he looked the same as he did when they were kids.

"Jake," she smiled. "What are you doing here?"

"Tony invited me," he leaned against the wall, trying to act cooler than he was. "I figured a few of us from St. Hariot's could crash a Morgan High party."

"It's not my party," she said. "I wouldn't know who's welcome."

St.Hariot's was a private school with a respected, unbeatable reputation. They were potentially the best school in the state. Layla wanted Jess to go there but she wanted to follow Alice to Morgan High. Bennett sided with her.

"So, listen," Jake chuckled. "My dad's been talking to your mom. Apparently, she thinks we're perfect for each other."

"Convenient," Jess said. They'd been toddlers together. They grew up together and their parents were best friends. Jess didn't see him the way Layla wanted her to. Their relationship was platonic and perfect the way it was.

"She says she still regrets not sending you to St.Hariot's," he said. "At least that's what my dad tells me."

Jess needed to change the subject. "How are you?" she asked. "We haven't talked in a while."

"Yeah. I think the last time we hung out we talked about Sigmund Freud," he laughed. "Good times." He shrugged. "I've been good, busy. I'm playing lacrosse this year."

"Wow. And that's fun?" She wasn't interested in sports.

"It definitely is. I love it. You should come to one of our games."

"I'd love that," she chuckled. "Text me a day and I'll be there."

He stared at her, loving and sweet. The same look he had when he gave her a Valentine's Day card in the seventh grade. Every class they shared, they'd sit and work together. They were both favored by their teachers. He smiled. It was a good smile, plain but handsome.

Her cheeks warmed.

"Do you wanna go out sometime?" he asked.

The words clanged against Jess's skull. She should've been flattered but all she felt was panic. Was he asking because he liked her or because he felt obligated? Because their parents wanted them to be together? Images flashed in her mind. She suddenly saw herself ten years from now, married to Jake with two kids living in a nice house. She was a successful lawyer and he was a surgeon like his mom. Was it a nightmare or a dream? It was the plan, exactly what Layla wanted.

"Jess?"

She gulped. "What?"

"Do you wanna go on a date?" he chuckled. He couldn't see how panicked she felt. She tried to find the right words. Jess kept hearing her mom's voice shouting *Say yes! You have to say yes.* Did she have to say yes? Her throat was dry. She didn't want to hurt Jake's feelings but she wasn't interested. Why did it feel like if she said no, she'd be doing something wrong? Layla would lecture her, make her believe it was the wrong decision. Her mom's voice drowned out her own.

She ran. She'd apologize to Jake later. Right now, she needed to escape. The walls were closing in and she couldn't breathe.

*****

Bobby

Johnny and a few of his friends decided to sell drugs to the Honeycombers at Cindy Cohen's party. He made good business. Bobby tagged along because she had nothing else to do. She still wasn't speaking to Casey. They hadn't spoken in months.

Bobby loved rich people's houses. They were like modern castles, elegant and fancy, beautiful and giant. Super huge. *Wow.* Not even in her wildest dreams, did Bobby imagine having a house like this.

The music made her body vibrate. Johnny pressed himself against her. The railing dug into her back. She was three steps above him, so they were equal in height. He held her close and caged her in with his arms. His kisses were hungry and rough. She couldn't keep up. His hands moved through her hair and down her torso, thuggish and careless. "Let's go upstairs."

"What?"

"Upstairs," he smiled. "There's gotta be an empty room."

Her blissful smile drooped. Panic crashed into her. Was he asking what she thought he was asking? Was he even asking? She didn't hear a question.

"Um.." she opened her eyes. "Uh…"

"Come on." He kissed her. Hard. He was warm and sweaty. He smelled of weed and Lysol. She knew for a while that he wanted to be with her like that but she wasn't sure. Here? Now? With people everywhere?

"I don't… Um, I don't wanna…" she hesitated. "No."

She shocked them both. His shock twisted into offense. "*What*?"

"I… I don't want to," Bobby said. "I said no."

He stepped away, staring at her as if she was crazy. She glanced around. Why did she feel embarrassed? There was nothing wrong with saying no. She had a right to that. Didn't she?

"What in the hell have you been doing?" he asked.

She whispered, "what?"

"Teasing me like that. Being like you are," he scoffed. "I mean, come on, you should want to, you look like you want to. You act like it."

Her breath overlapped and crashed against her ears, uneven and distorted like she was underwater. Why did she feel guilty? She shouldn't feel guilty. He had a few drinks and was probably pretty drunk. He didn't mean it. He couldn't, right? He said it before. He said and did worse things to her before.

"Johnny, I'm… I'm sorry. I just…" she paused. What was she apologizing for?

He shook his head and rolled his eyes. He pushed through the crowd until he vanished. She gripped the railing, trying to steady herself, trying to stay on her feet. Was she smaller? She felt smaller. She felt about two inches tall, not even. She wouldn't cry. Not here, not now.

Bobby was alone in a house full of drunk, blissful people. They didn't notice how sad or hurt she was. She wanted to scream. She wanted to tear apart the furniture and yell at everyone, scorn them for being happy.

She went to the kitchen. What was she looking for? Maybe Johnny, so they could talk, or maybe another familiar face, not that she had anyone. She pushed away her best friend. She'd done so many things wrong. Maybe she was born to make bad decisions.

She grabbed a red, plastic cup and filled it with cold, cheap beer.

She drank without mercy.

***

Alice

Alice stood in her kitchen and stared at her phone. Mason was back to his normal routine. He didn't come home, didn't call or text and she hated it. He got fired from another job. He'd been through seven in the last two years and it was ridiculous. She was sick of dealing with it.

The front door opened and shut. How? It was locked. Cece walked in and held up metal cups and takeout. "Chinese."

Alice gestured to the oven. "I already put in a pizza."

She put the takeout and cups on the counter, shrugging. "Guess China and Italy are joining forces to defeat our hunger."

"What happened to your eyes?" Alice asked.

Cece's arms were bandaged. There was a long scratch on her left eyelid and her right one was bruised. She clicked her tongue. "I had a fight last night."

"Looks bad," Alice said. It wasn't the first time Cece showed up with wounds and bruises. Half the time her arms and knuckles were bandaged, the other half she had bruises on her cheeks or chin. She didn't talk about her job. If the topic wasn't about Bobby, Cece's boyfriend, or his best friends, then she tried to avoid talking about it.

Wicker stools lined the counter. They were meant for a patio but Susan loved them. She bought them at a resale shop. When Mason first saw them, he tried to point out the fact they were outdoor furniture but Susan said there was no such thing. She rambled on for twenty minutes until Mason laughed, kissed her,

84

and agreed to keep them. It didn't matter anyway, the Johnsons mostly used to eat in the dining room together. Every night, they had family dinner and talked about their lives.

Cece fiddled with her necklace and unpacked the food. "I got kung pao chicken, dumplings, roasted duck-"

"You know," Alice said. "I'd really like to go to one of those soon."

"One of what?"

"Your fights. You said you get paid to fight, right? By this Betty Beater person. I wanna see it."

"That'll never happen," Cece said. She resumed unloading the food. "I got sweet and sour pork too-"

"Why not?" Alice asked. "You know all my secrets. You come over to my house, we meet at Linda's, you've met my dad. Eddie. I wanna see more of your world."

"My world is the Burrows, Al," she said, serious. "Gangs, fights, drugs. The worst part of Height City and you wanna go on a bonding trip? I'm the Crime Queen's enforcer. Trust me, you don't wanna see that."

"Cece?"

"Fortune cookie or fried rice?" She held up each option.

"There is nothing you do that can push me away." Alice kept her tone steady. She already figured out that Cece had trust issues and grew up in a harsher reality than she did. She accepted it.

"There's a difference between hearing stories about it," Cece dropped her shoulders. "And actually seeing it. You'd run at the first glimpse and I, shockingly, like hanging out with you, so no. I don't want to gi-" she broke off. What was she holding back?

The timer dinged. Alice grabbed an oven mitt and pulled out the cheese pizza. She put it on the burners and sprinkled on extra mozzarella.

Cece sat on one of the wicker stools and dug into the Kung Pow chicken.

"You stood by me when my dad disappeared," Alice said. "You sleep over when he isn't home, you listen to every story I have about my mom. You keep my powers a secret. You never ran."

"You're a superhero's only child," Cece said. "I'm a crime boss's prodigy."

"And?"

"We're not the same."

"You're really that scared you'll lose me?" Alice asked.

Cece dropped her gaze and fiddled with her necklace. She ate a dumpling and took a breath. It seemed difficult for her to find the right words or say them out loud.

"Yes," she admitted.

Maybe it was best not to push the issue. Alice didn't want to upset Cece or push her away; she decided to be patient. She'd learn more about who Cece was eventually, as soon as Cece trusted her. Maybe Alice didn't fully trust Cece either. She pointed at the metal cups. "What are those for?"

"Practice," Cece grabbed the cups and pulled them apart, setting them in a perfect row.

"Practice for what?" Alice asked.

"Your powers," she said. "I know you're not gonna be a superhero or join a circus but being a powered person is still pretty cool, so let's see what you've got."

"I don't know. It's-"

"I'm not taking no for an answer." Her determined gaze was more than enough to convince Alice.

She shrugged. Testing her powers could be fun. "Yeah, okay."

Cece came to Alice's side, then stepped behind her. Cece stood like Susan used to as if she was invincible, like nothing could tear her down.

Alice faced the counter. She took a deep breath and tried to relax her shoulders. She cracked her knuckles, psyching herself up, then straightened her arm and held her hand toward the first metal cup. White lightning flickered between her fingertips. A million little vibrations went through her body. Amazing. The faster the vibration, the brighter the light. There couldn't be a better feeling.

She zapped the cup. It flew across the kitchen, slammed against the wall, and fell on the floor. The girls laughed at the same time. Alice grabbed Cece's arm, too excited to stand still. She couldn't believe she did that. She zapped a cup off the counter. "That felt awesome!"

"Yeah," Cece smiled. "It looked awesome."

"Wow." Alice had never done anything like that with her powers.

Cece pointed to the next cup. "Hold on, Sparky. Let's see if you can hold it in the air."

"I don't know if I can do that," Alice said. She'd seen her mom levitate things but she'd never done it. She never learned how. "Maybe, uh."

"Try it," Cece stepped back and slid onto the counter, legs dangling over the drawers. She rubbed her bandaged knuckles. Her bruises must've been more painful than she wanted to show.

Alice held out her hand. She took a deep breath. Tiny lightning bolts sparked between her fingers. A million little vibrations - powerful, energetic, hypnotic - all through her body. She pictured what she wanted to do. She wanted to lift the cup. The image was crystal clear. Lift, not zap.

She zapped the cup but it didn't fly. The lightning danced around it, against the metal, connecting with Alice's fingertips. She held her breath and focused.

Slowly, the cup slid. Alice tried to control its movements. She pictured it sliding to the left and it did, then the right. The more lightning she gave, the faster the cup went. She tried to make it go in a circle, but when it started to, she got excited and it zigzagged to the right, then slid off the counter, flopping onto the floor.

Alice dropped her hand. Did she seriously do that? *Awesome. That was awesome!* She smiled. Her technique needed work but it was still super cool.

Cece chuckled. "Did you know you could do that?"

"Not at all."

***

Bobby

Bobby was certain she drank the rest of the keg. At least, it felt like it. Her vision looped, twirling and spinning. Everything wobbled or was she wobbly? People were starting to leave, ignoring her drunken stumbles around the house. She needed to find Johnny.

She faintly remembered a text to Tommy. Where did she leave her phone? It disappeared at some point. She should probably care. She couldn't afford a new one. She wanted her boyfriend. Was that insane?

She hadn't checked the pool.

She tripped on the sliding door. Pain made her knees shiver and beer splashed everywhere as her red, plastic cup rolled away. An imaginary hammer beat her skull. Twinkly lights reflected on the chlorine-filled water. Beautiful. What would it be like to be a mermaid? To swim in the water and never come up? It would blur the world, make everything quiet, maybe even easier.

Cindy, asleep on a lawn chair, clutched a stuffed dolphin.

Johnny was near a blow-up palm tree. His hands caressed Brittany's hips. Her arms were wrapped around his neck. They were pressed against each other, kissing like there was no tomorrow.

This couldn't be real. It had to be some sort of hallucination or mind trick. Maybe it was a nightmare. It had to be. The Eskimo kisses, the hand-holding, the inside jokes couldn't have meant nothing, then again, the poker games, the screaming, the fighting, and the hitting. It didn't leave much room for denial.

Bobby leaned on the doorframe and stretched out her legs. Hot, watery mascara drifted down her cheeks. The tears hurt. Her chest ached. Her heart had shattered, broken into a billion pieces, nothing more than a glass figure dropped on a hardwood floor. She didn't care. She didn't want to care. Why did she care? Why did this hurt so much?

"Bobby!" *Tommy?*

She stayed in the doorway and willed the world to disappear. Johnny and Brittany were tangled together, slobbering all over each other. Was there a brick to throw at them somewhere?

"I hate clowns," Cole said. He wasn't a very good whisperer. Bobby must've looked terrible. Mascara all over her face, smeared lipstick and dripping blush. She looked how she felt.

Tommy sighed. "Grab an arm."

The boys crouched at either side of her. They wrapped her arms around their shoulders and yanked her up, holding her waist with grips that were gentle, protective, and sturdy. They dragged her through the living room and entryway, ignoring the leftover partygoers, most of whom were passed out on the floor.

An old, black jeep was on the curb. Sally must've let Tommy borrow her car. Bobby leaned on him while Cole opened the door, and they lifted her into the backseat. She stretched out, extremely tired. Wait, since when was she barefoot? Where were her high heels?

Cole slid in on the other side and Tommy took the driver's seat. The doors shut. Her eyes were closed. She wanted to puke or did she need to puke?

She dry-heaved. This wouldn't be good for anyone involved. Her stomach twisted and knotted, gums watering, she sat up, ready to spew on Sally's ripped, leather seats but nothing happened. She sighed, head plopping on Cole's shoulder. He rubbed her back, gentle and comforting, making sure she was buckled in and safe. He brushed the beer-soaked, tangled strands of hair away from her face.

"Why doesn't he love me?" Bobby whispered.

Chapter 5

Casey

"She hasn't left in weeks." Casey stood on Bobby's rundown porch. A pink tricycle with rainbow streamers and peeled unicorn stickers leaned on the railing. The front lawn was overgrown and tangled. The kitchen window was boarded up and the siding was dirty.

"She's getting her homework done." Tommy was on the other end of the call. Casey got a new burner phone earlier that day.

She rolled her eyes. "Yeah, 'cause of me. A friend of mine gives me the work and I shove it through the broken window in the back."

"Are you ever going to tell me who this mystery Morgan High friend of yours is? 'Cause I thought everyone you knew either worked for Betty, Markinson, or went to Baltic here in the Burrows."

"Feeling insecure?" she asked.

He chuckled. "Just curious about your life."

She smiled. She loved the sound of his voice. She crouched down. The metal front door had an old Santa Claus plushie hanging from the triangle-shaped window. She kept the phone between her ear and shoulder as she picked the lock. "Time to smoke her out of her foxhole. How's the search for Dave's dad?"

"No facial matches. Whatever Betty's up to with him," Tommy sighed in frustration. "They're keeping it under lock and key. It's a good thing he hasn't come to find Dave."

"I asked around," she said. "The fire at Cruise Industries was Surge, not Ted."

"Isn't Surge the arsonist who took over for Ted?"

"That's the one." The lock clicked. Casey smirked and put the toolkit back in her jacket.

The kitchen was small. A thin layer of grease covered the black countertops and dirty dishes filled the sink. Crayon-colored stick figures and other messy drawings hung on the fridge. In the living room was a dusty green couch with a marinara stain on the middle cushion. The walls were plastered with pictures of Bobby as a little kid. Even as a toddler she wore crazy outfits. At nine, she had long hair dyed pastel colors.

Vincent was in some pictures. He looked kind and exhausted, especially in the ones where he was sick.

Casey used to be jealous of Bobby's relationship with her dad. They were best friends and he loved her so much, which showed in the way he looked at her. His baby girl. He welcomed Casey into their house and seemed to approve of the girls' friendship.

The day he died was awful.

Casey helped Bobby put the groceries away while Vincent napped on the couch. He'd been sick for about a year, maybe longer. At the time, Bobby did the housework, took care of him, and had two jobs. She paid the bills and the mortgage. The grocery store she worked at gave her free food and her neighbors across the street helped with chores and everything. The moment Vincent took his last breath, Bobby was clutching his hand, crying over her father's pale, lifeless body while Casey called an ambulance but it was too late. They couldn't save him.

"Hey, I have to go," Tommy said. "Dave just dared Cole to eat lemon-flavored soap."

"Text me later?"

"Definitely."

She hung up.

The stairs were old and creaky. Vincent tried to fix the railing many times but he never finished. He was a single father with three different jobs.

The hall to Bobby's bedroom was short and the door was orange, her favorite color. Big, bubble letters spelled her full name. Her bedroom was small with a window leading to the fire escape and a closet filled with colorful fabrics, animal prints, sparkly clothes, and high heels. Bobby owned one pair of sneakers, which were zebra-striped and made noise.

Each wall was a different color. Random blankets were piled on the bed, including the baby blanket Bobby's mom brought her home in. It was tie-dye with orange ribbons.

A diamond-shaped mirror - decorated with sparkly streamers and stylish hats - was on the yellow dresser.

Bobby sat on the floor, holding a joint between her fingers. Sparkly clips held her messy hair. She wore one of her dad's flannel T-shirts and pink underwear. She had one sock on, which had the word FABULOUS printed on it in pink bubble letters.

Smoke filled the air.

"You wanna talk about it?" Casey sat next to her and leaned against the bed, stretching her legs.

Bobby sniffled. "I'm sorry."

"For being a total bitch?"

"Basically."

"Apology accepted. T told me what happened."

"I should hate him, right? I want to hate him," Bobby cried. "But I... I don't know how to hate him. I hate myself for loving him."

Tears trickled down her cheeks. Without makeup, she was a simple beauty, nothing fancy or overdone, just Bobby, and she was beautiful. She put the joint in her mouth.

Casey sighed. "You have to go back to school."

"I can't see him. And her... No way," Bobby shook her head. "Besides, what's the point? I'm failing almost every class now and nobody's gonna be there to see me graduate in a couple years, and-"

"I'll be there," Casey said. "Plus, Vincent wanted you to graduate high school. Just 'cause he can't be there doesn't mean you can let him down."

"Even if I graduate, I don't know what I wanna... Want... wanna," she giggled. "What?"

She seemed weightless. Her laugh was vibrant and silly.

Casey smiled. She took the joint and put it in her mouth. She sucked and released the smoke. Bobby wouldn't stop laughing. She lay on the floor, curling her legs, bending her knees against her belly.

Casey laughed too. What was so funny?

***

Bobby

The next morning, they were in her bed. Bobby was lying on a furry body pillow that smelled like weed. She groaned and rolled over. Sunlight fluttered in through the window, making her face and body warm. Casey was tangled in the blankets. Her leather jacket and boots were on the floor. The joint sat in an ashtray between them.

Bobby yawned.

They stayed up too late catching up on each other's lives. They talked about everything; Casey's recent fights at The Arena, her new friend, her and Tommy's blooming relationship. When she told Bobby that they were together, she jumped on the bed and cheered, too excited to hold in her happiness. Casey tried to stay cool but she couldn't fool Bobby. They celebrated by spraying whipped cream into each other's mouths and finishing the joint together.

Bobby was so happy to have her best friend back.

The fuzzy, rainbow alarm clock beeped. She covered her ears. "No!"

Casey pulled a pillow over her head. "Shut it up!"

The beeps were horrid and loud. Bobby sat up. She grabbed the clock and slapped the 'off' button. It didn't work. The awful noise got louder.

"That's the last time I save a clock from the side of the road!" she whined. She liked it because it was pretty, but it never occurred to her that it was broken. Casey tossed the pillow off the bed and sat up. She snatched the clock and chucked it against the wall. It shattered. Gears, fur, and springs went everywhere. Quiet.

"Aw," Bobby frowned. "It was so pretty."

"Just get another one from Billy. He'll have them in his jacket." Casey lay down, blue hair spreading across the pillow. Her socks were white and decorated with angry emoji faces.

Bobby slid off the bed and went to her closet. She grabbed an adorable sequin top and a furry, faux leopard-print skirt. She loved the style but hated the idea of dead or skinned animals.

"I have to go to school," she said. "Are you gonna stay here?"

"Remember what we talked about, if he comes up to you," Casey said. "Punch him."

"Last time I tried to punch someone my hand hurt for a month." Bobby zipped her skirt. She bent forward and flipped her hair, brushing her curls with her fingers. She grabbed a pair of neon, peace sign earrings. She had tons of jewelry, most of which she got from resale stores and pawn shops.

"Yeah, you almost broke Cole's nose. That's why you need practice." Casey pulled a furry, turtle-shaped pillow over her legs. She was relaxed laying in Bobby's bed with one arm curled under her head. She closed her eyes, falling back to sleep.

Bobby put on mascara, red lip gloss, and eyeshadow. She created a gold rose color on her eyelid.

Makeup made her feel better, less naked. A protective shield nobody could see through. A mask to hide her pain. She admired her reflection. *Perfect.*

She grabbed her backpack, waved to Casey, and left the room. She loved her house. There were so many great, fun memories. She'd put on fashion shows for her dad on the stairs. They'd play poker at the kitchen table. She and Casey would fall asleep on the couch watching movies while Vincent worked late. He'd whistle when he did the dishes. The same tune every time.

Bobby walked to school. It wasn't close but the fresh air felt good. The houses in her neighborhood were cute. The road wasn't well-paved and the sidewalk was uneven.

A single mom and her four boys - the Hale brothers - lived across the street. Vincent used to help her sometimes and in return, she'd help him. The kids were mostly grown now. One worked for Markinson, another worked for Betty, one was in the Spades, and the youngest ran away. Bobby used to cheer for him when the boys played basketball in the driveway. Thinking about him made her blush.

One house still had its Christmas lights up. The one beside it was abandoned. Supposedly, it was haunted. Some little kids fabricated the story and gave the pretend ghost a name. Teenagers threw parties there.

Morgan High was in the Nests. Bobby wouldn't have been able to afford tuition if it weren't for her dad's life insurance. She never wanted to go to Baltic. Although she was proud to be a Burrower, it wasn't a good school, a bit dangerous.

She hurried up the steps. A meatloaf stench wafted from the cafeteria.

Bobby went to her locker, ignoring the stares. It wasn't a secret her boyfriend cheated on her. Johnny texted and called over the weeks, asking about poker games, but she didn't answer. She wasn't ready for it to be over but it needed to be. It was.

She shoved her backpack and its contents into her locker. Sparkly stickers were on the door and a disco ball hung in the corner.

Strong, muscular arms wrapped around her body and lifted her off the floor. The world spun, dizzying voices and nausea in an unsafe clutch. She knew his touch by heart. It made her entire body tense. Maybe she should've brought Casey as backup. He set her down and she wiggled out of his grip.

"Is everything okay?" Johnny asked. "You haven't been around."

She hesitated. "I saw you and Brittany Mikes after the party. I just saw you guys kissing but I'm pretty sure it was more." Anger twisted her insides. Maybe she should punch him, hurt him like he hurt her. She'd never be able to cause him enough pain but she'd rather be angry than afraid.

He frowned. "I can explain-"

"No. No, I don't... I don't wanna hear it," she pushed past him. "I'm done. I have to be done-"

"Hey, hold on," he followed her. "Listen-"

"NO!" She pictured their first kiss. He looked at her as if she was everything to him. Maybe she imagined it. His lips were soft and kind then rough, and his hand touched her cheek. An illusion for her benefit.

"Bobby," Johnny said. "This is ridiculous. You were probably drunk, seeing things-"

"No. No, I didn't imagine it," she shook her head. "No, I didn't want to have sex with you in a stranger's bedroom and you got mad! You cheated on me!"

People started to watch. She didn't care. She wasn't embarrassed. She didn't do anything wrong. He did. He did so many things wrong and she let him. No more.

"That's not what happened. You don't even know what happened," he chuckled. "You were drunk and right now, you're being dramatic-"

"I'm okay with that!"

"Alright. Look, let's talk about this somewhere private, okay? I-"

"You want money and you need me to get it," she said. "That's why all the poker games. You didn't even care that it made me nervous. You don't even care that they could come after us-"

It was a low blow but she needed to say it.

"Stop," he said, anger in his voice. The type of anger that scared her. She didn't move. She didn't back down. She wouldn't.

"I hate you," she sniffled. "I hate you for everything-"

"No, you don't," he said as if he knew, as if it were the truth. "You don't."

"I want to," she said. "I want to more than anything."

He took her hand. His fingers grazed her palm. She stood still and stared. She loved him. Why did she love him? Was she insane? She felt insane.

He pulled her close and brushed the hair from her cheek. She looked away. She was so sick of crying yet tears trickled down her cheeks. His eyes were deep, dark, and beautiful. He smiled. It made her heart skip but she couldn't tell if it was love or fear.

"I love you," he whispered.

She wanted to believe him. She wanted him to love her. Did either of them know what that word meant? She wasn't sure because she wanted to forgive him.

His lips pressed against hers. A familiar, broken piece of home. Was she crazy? She hated herself for wanting him back, for everything she let him do. She couldn't do it anymore. It hurt too much.

She yanked away from him. "No!"

He grabbed her wrist. She tried to run but his grip was too strong. It hurt. His fingers pressed into her skin, threatening to bruise her. This felt familiar. She whimpered. He grabbed her other arm and tightened his fists, swinging her into the lockers, her back slammed against the metal. CLANG. Pain shot up her spine.

He held her. She couldn't move. His eyes met hers. His face twisted into an eerie anger, making her heart race. She wanted to break free but she was trapped. Again. His breath burned her face and his gaze threatened to kill her. She knew that look.

"Wait-"

He clutched her chin with a bruising pressure.

Their classmates stared in silence. The large crowd formed a circle. Nobody did anything. What could they do? Did they know what to do? Bobby didn't know what to do.

"Let her go!" Mister Scotts yelled.

Miss Z shouted, "Johnathan!"

Johnny glanced in their direction but didn't let go. Bobby couldn't breathe. Hot, fearful tears smothered her hair and face, dripping onto his hand. He kept his focus on her. He wanted to do something. Something bad. Her heartbeat thundered and shook.

Johnny pressed his lips against her ear. He whispered a threat she couldn't understand, then his body released hers. She shuddered. He flashed his wicked smile.

Her energy drained. She slid down the lockers and plopped onto the floor, defeated.

Mister Scotts shoved Johnny toward the principal's office.

All eyes were on Bobby. She recognized most of them.

Alice Johnson's readily, protective glare showed how much she wanted to hurt Johnny. She looked ready to tear him apart. Were her eyes glowing? It had to be a trick of the light.

Brittany looked sympathetic, which was shocking. She was never sympathetic toward Bobby, in fact, she was the cause of most of her embarrassment and pain but no amusement showed on the Honeycomber's face.

Bobby felt the bruises on her cheeks. They matched the awful pain in her wrists.

Leo Scotts stepped toward her. He reached his hand out to help her up but Miss Z pulled Bobby to her feet before he could do anything. He melted back into the crowd, next to Alice.

Miss Z was a slender woman with blonde hair. She wore several bracelets on one wrist. The most notable was her gold charm bracelet. The charms were in the shapes of different landmarks around the world, which jingled as she wiped Bobby's tears.

"You're okay, everything's okay," she soothed. "Let's get you to the nurse."

Bobby nodded.

Miss Z led her away from prying eyes. She shouted for the other students to get to class.

Jess

Jess invited Alice to her house after school. They needed another tutoring session before the test. She unlocked the door and wiped her feet on the welcome mat. Black cursive letters on a fuzzy gray surface. The porch was small, cute with a white wooden banister.

"We're home," Jess stepped into the living room. Her parents were on the couch watching a *Cheers* rerun. They loved the show. It seemed to be the only thing they enjoyed doing together. Takeout boxes from Linda's Diner were on the coffee table. A tuna melt for Layla and a BLT for Bennett. Neither one knew how to cook. They probably ordered Jess a cucumber sandwich and put it in the fridge.

"We?" Layla stood up. When she saw Alice, she frowned. Her classic look of disapproval.

Bennett gave a friendly wave. "Do you want to come watch with us?" He gestured to his takeout box full of french fries. "They gave us too many fries. You're welcome to have them."

"Thanks, Mister Peace but we have to study," Alice held up her backpack. "We've got a history test and I am definitely not prepared."

"Ah, I used to hate history," he said.

Layla rolled her eyes at the conversation. "Jessica, I want to talk to you," she gestured to the kitchen. The edge in her tone made Jess nervous. She glanced at Alice, who gave a sympathetic, understanding shrug and went to get a french fry from Bennett.

Jess followed her mom into the kitchen. They faced each other, hidden behind the fridge, so the others couldn't see them.

"What is it? I have to study," Jess said.

"Sweetie, I'm worried. The Johnsons' reputation is... complicated," Layla paused. Her frown was a thin line, decisive, persuasive. She crossed her arms. "I'm afraid you may be falling into the wrong crowd. Alice's father is... tortured, and her mother left, and-"

Was she judging Alice for her parents' mistakes? How did that make any sense? Jess automatically felt defensive. She had to protect her best friend. "Her parents made those decisions. It doesn't reflect on what kind of person *she* is."

Layla thought for a moment. Jess snuck a glance into the living room. Her dad was still on the couch but Alice wasn't there. She must've gone upstairs.

"Brittany Mikes is the kind of girl you should be around," Layla said. "She does well in school, her parents are nice and involved in the community-"

"Her dad's the mayor," Jess hissed more venomously than she expected. Her mother loved climbing the social ladder. The Mikes family was Honeycomber royalty. They weren't as rich as the Cruises or the Vances but they were respected and very influential. Layla loved anyone who could help polish her precious reputation.

Anger twitched inside Jess. Her friendships weren't for Layla to choose. "You like having that connection in your back pocket," she said before she could reconsider. "You can use my friendship as a bargaining chip, can't you?" She calculated her next words carefully. "Is that how you released a known arsonist, a known murderer, onto the street?"

Shock crawled across Layla's face. Her reaction wasn't what Jess expected, no shame or defensive excuses or insults, instead, Layla's face twisted in anger. Her gaze hardened and her frown deepened. Her glare made Jess want to shrink into a ball and disappear. She picked her cuticles. Maybe that wasn't the best way to confront her mother.

"Don't you ever speak to me like that, young lady, it's disrespectful and rude," Layla said. "I taught you better than that."

"Alice isn't a bad influence and neither is Brittany," Jess said. She heard about what happened at Cindy's party. Brittany kissed Bobby Jones's boyfriend, rumor was they ended up in Cindy's parents' bedroom. Jess muttered under her breath, "Even though she made out with another girl's boyfriend-"

"Alice did what?" Layla asked, appalled.

"Brittany, not Alice. Brittany did it," Jess said. She wasn't sure why she mentioned it. She could've kept her mouth shut. Layla didn't need to know her friends' drama. Maybe she wanted to see Layla's reaction.

"Oh," Layla said. She shrugged. "Well, you teenagers can be dramatic with your hormones, so-"

When she thought Alice did it, it was wrong, shocking, but because Brittany did it, it was forgivable? How did that make sense? Jess didn't like it. She didn't like the thought of losing Alice either. She needed Alice. Alice was her breath of fresh air, the only person who understood how crazy Layla was and didn't judge Jess for not being able to stand up to her. Without Alice, Jess was weak. She didn't want to be weak.

"I have done everything you've asked of me since I was two years old." Jess couldn't stay calm. The words bubbled like lava ready to explode. When she was in the eighth grade, she had trouble in math. She was in honors English, it was her favorite subject, but math was tough.

Before the biggest test of the semester, she studied night and day, stress kept her from eating, she barely slept and she didn't shower for weeks. She made her fingers bleed because she picked her cuticles so much but after the test, when she saw her grade, the world ended. She got a 'B'.

Layla told her it wasn't good enough. She said Jess was slacking off, she wasn't fulfilling her potential, and how dare she be so lazy. Jess called Alice in tears, feeling like a failure. Alice talked Jess out of hating herself and offered to come over with comfort food from Linda's Diner. That was the moment Jess decided she wanted to go to Morgan High. If Alice was going to go there, she wanted to be there. She needed Alice if she was going to survive her mother's expectations.

"Alice has been my best friend for a long time," Jess said. "I'm not going to stop being around her because *you think* her parents are messed up," the anger swelled. She started getting angry about everything in her life. "And you, you want me to go to Zak City Law and marry Jake and-"

"Because it's your dream," Layla said matter-of-factly. "You'll be an excellent lawyer."

Jess lost her voice. She was always working toward that goal, toward Zak City Law. It made her parents happy. She was going to go to the same college they did, where they met, where every member of Bennett's family had gone. It was a piece of her. They'd be so proud. They'd been talking about it since before she was born. She never thought about another future. Should she? "I... I... yeah, um," she forgot what she was going to say.

Layla nodded. "That's what I thought. I'm trying to help your odds, you know that," she put a hand on Jess's shoulder, which was weird. Jess kept herself still. Layla rarely showed physical affection. "Now, it'd be rude to ask Alice to leave, so consider tonight your last tutoring session. I'd be happy to refer her to a professional."

Jess wanted to argue but they'd end up going in circles. "Okay."

Layla patted her head. It made Jess feel like a dog. "I'm doing what's best for you, to help you achieve our dream." She smiled. Her gaze softened into pride. Jess said nothing. Why argue? She'd be wrong no matter what she thought. She felt sick.

She hurried past her dad and ran upstairs.

She closed her bedroom door. "What chapter are we on?"

"The civil war," Alice said. "Are you allowed to have that closed now?"

"No," Jess dropped her books on the bed. Layla didn't want a lock on her daughter's door. She wasn't allowed to have it closed either. What was Layla worried about? It'd been like this Jess's entire life. Nothing ever seemed to be her decision, her privacy didn't exist and she was only right if she agreed with her mother.

"Is everything okay?" Alice asked.

Jess plopped onto the mattress but she couldn't sit still. She was too energized like she drank six shots of espresso. "I don't know. I... um, Jake asked me out at Brittany's party and-"

"He asked you out?" Alice smiled. "Wow! Wait, did you say yes?"

"No. I don't like him like that," she said. "My mom likes him for me. Only because he's from a respectable family, and he's going to follow the plan his family laid out for him like my mom did for me-"

"I thought you liked the plan," Alice said. "What happened?"

"I thought so too." She liked the security of the plan. It was clear, precise, achievable, but Jess wasn't sure it was what she really wanted. "I don't know. I've been questioning some things. I don't even know if I should. I just..."

"It's your life. Your mom should be happy if you're happy."

"That was your mom." Jess couldn't believe she said that. Every time Susan was mentioned Alice became sad and stiff. She'd fold into herself, into the memories of being abandoned, Jess assumed. Ever since Susan left and Mason started drinking again, Alice changed, she used to be eager and willful, but now she was an empty shell, not really anything except lonely.

But it didn't seem to affect her this time, which was weird.

"I'm sorry," Jess said. "I shouldn't have said that."

"It's okay. Just because she... She left me," Alice rolled her lips. "Doesn't mean you can't talk about her."

"I'm sorry," Jess said by instinct. "I should've been a better friend this year and last summer." She didn't mean to drift away from Alice. It just happened. "With the internship and Brittany and extra credit and student council," she looked down at her folded hands. "There's no excuse."

Alice shook her head. "No, just because I froze doesn't mean the world did." She gently took Jess's hand and intertwined their fingers. It kept Jess from picking her cuticles. "You were moving forward, having a life and I was dealing with my own stuff. I couldn't let go-"

"Past tense?"

"I don't know yet," she frowned. Alice looked like her dad when she was upset. "I still miss my mom every day but it's getting easier, little by little."

Jess missed Susan too. She missed being able to turn to Susan for comfort or advice. Susan liked to bake and cook. She knew the girls' favorite snacks, so when Jess came over, she'd make chocolate chip cookies, caramel popcorn, and her fantastic vegetable pizza. The way she and Alice interacted - warm and loving. No sense of obligation or pressure - made Jess wish Susan was her mother too.

She still couldn't believe Susan abandoned her family. It seemed so unlike her.

"How's your dad? Any change?" Jess asked. She wasn't as close with Alice's father. She'd sit with him at Alice's basketball games and swim meets. Once he made a sign with Alice's name and jersey number on it, he waved it above his head and cheered as loud as he could. He wasn't quiet like Bennett was. Mason had a lively presence, at least, he did before Susan left.

"No, no, he still doesn't come home." Alice brushed the hair away from her face and curled it behind her ear. She shrugged. "Eddie checks up on me and sometimes, I stay with Mister Scotts and Leo when I don't feel like going home to an empty house but," she wrapped the sleeve of her sweatshirt around her fist and tightened her grip. Tears sparkled in her eyes but she held them back. "I'm tired, Jess," she sniffled, voice breaking. "I'm really really tired of feeling this way."

Jess scooted closer to her and put her head on Alice's shoulder. "You can stay here."

Alice chuckled. She laid her cheek on Jess's hair and wiped her eyes. "Your mom won't allow that, it's okay. I'll figure something out."

"Do you have any options?" Jess lifted her head to see Alice's face.

"I'm not sure yet," Alice said. She put on a brave expression, which meant she didn't want to talk about it anymore. "What about your problem?"

"My problem? You mean my mom?"

She hesitated, then nodded. "What do you wanna do?"

Alice's purple hair, Jess remembered the day they bought the hair dye. She was so excited to finally help Alice with something. She felt useless after Susan left. She held the pink dye in her hand and she knew what Layla would say. Jess didn't care because she was helping her best friend. She wanted to feel that again but this time, it'd be for herself.

She launched off the bed and ran to her dresser. She opened the bottom drawer, pushed aside her clothes, and took out a jewelry box. Its greenish-blue paint was chipped, and the wood was old and scratched. She bought it at Layla's favorite antique store.

Jess opened it and revealed a Zak City Law coursebook. She pushed it aside and yanked the false back out of the box. She grabbed the flamingo-pink hair dye. She stood up and turned to Alice. "I loved my streaks and I want them back. It's my body, so it's my choice. My mom can't dictate what I do with my hair."

"Are you sure?" Alice asked, uncertain. She was afraid of Layla too.

Jess nodded. She wouldn't let her mind change. She needed to do this. She needed to be her own person. She wanted to be strong. "Yes."

Alice shrugged and stood up. "Okay. We're gonna need bleach, tinfoil, the brush thing-"

"It's all in the locked hat box on the top shelf," Jess gestured to the closet. "Hidden behind my winter coats."

She could never be too careful when it came to her mom. If Layla thought her daughter was doing anything she disapproved of, she'd search Jess's room. She'd done it before. The woman didn't have boundaries. Once, when Jess was seven and didn't listen to her mom's orders, Layla threw away Jess's favorite stuffed animal - a furry, toddler-sized monkey with a sparkly tiara - as a punishment for disobeying her. When Jess cried about losing it, Layla ordered her to be quiet.

Alice grabbed the supplies and the girls went into the bathroom. Jess sat down and Alice began the process. The bathtub was big, triangular, and doubled as a shower framed by glass. Gray hand towels matched the ones in her parents' bathroom. The counter was white and gray. An air freshener was plugged into the outlet behind the door, making the room smell like pine trees. A big, vanity mirror framed with lights hung above the sink.

Alice smiled. "So, Jake asked you out?"

"Yeah, he did." Jess couldn't keep herself from blushing. It was the first time a boy ever asked her out on a date. She didn't expect it to send her into a spiraling panic. "I ran away from him."

"What?" Alice chuckled. "Seriously?"

"I felt terrible but I texted him an apology and a polite refusal."

"Nice of you."

"And you and Leo? Are you guys...?" Jess noticed Alice and Leo Scotts had gotten closer. They came to school together, hid during pep rallies together, sat together during their shared classes. Leo started joining the girls for lunch too. He liked tapioca pudding.

"God, no. He's great and all but," Alice shook her head. "He isn't my type."

"Got it." Jess's scalp started tingling. Was it the bleach? It was cold. She couldn't wait to have her pink streaks back. She couldn't wait to see Layla's reaction when she saw them.

Alice glanced at their reflections, still focused on Jess's hair. "Are you interested in anyone?"

Jess wasn't sure she ever thought about romance or relationships as something good, something she wanted. Her parents' example didn't give her much confidence in love. "Not really. Are you?"

"I don't think I have the energy for romance." Alice finished putting the bleach on Jess's hair and wrapped the specific strands in tin foil. It smelled sterile. "We have to give it a few minutes." She leaned on the counter. "So, what happened that made you want to do this?"

Jess picked her cuticles. Her questions started over the summer during the internship. She didn't know exactly what event did it, maybe the Ted Marson case. It was the first time she thought of her parents as liars or worse, criminals. They helped a guilty man get released from prison, a man they helped put away. Why would they do that? Why would they abandon their morals, hide the truth, and break the law? It felt impossible to believe but at the same time, Jess knew there was more to the story.

"Nothing specific," she shrugged. She didn't know how to explain it.

"If you say so," Alice said, unconvinced. "I think we need some music. What do you wanna listen to?"

"Something that sounds like independence and freedom," Jess smiled. Her excitement escalated. She was feeling bold.

"So, the national anthem?" Alice grabbed her phone and pressed the screen.

"No," Jess said. "I don't know, play something fun and upbeat."

"I've got the perfect playlist," Alice said. An energetic pop song blasted from the speaker. They created this playlist at one of their sleepovers during middle school. They chose each song together.

Jess laughed. They spent the evening gossiping and singing their favorite songs. At one point, they used hairbrushes as microphones and jumped on the bed. Alice dropped to her knees and played air guitar. Jess hit her with a pillow. They used to spend every weekend at each other's houses. They'd watch movies, play board games, and do their homework. They were inseparable.

The girls fell asleep, side by side. Their textbooks and notebooks were scattered on the floor. They didn't study much but Jess didn't mind. It was a great night. Alice seemed lighter, less depressed, and hopeless. Jess was glad to see she was starting to heal.

A terrible beeping woke Jess up. Her alarm clock was screaming, louder and louder until she yanked the pillow away from her ears and sat up. She reached over Alice and slapped the 'off' button. Silence. She sighed.

Alice wrinkled her nose. "You have morning breath," she whispered, eyes still closed.

"Good morning to you too," Jess yawned. Her breath did smell awful. She'd brush her teeth later, she didn't want to get up yet. She laid back down.

Her perfect brown hair now had vivid pink streaks. She loved it. She felt reborn, bolder, better. She bent one arm above her head and stretched her legs, copying Alice's pose. They lay in comfortable silence, drifting back to sleep.

"Jessica!" Layla's voice made Jess's skin tighten. The door opened and Layla's jaw dropped. She looked stunned at first, then angry. Her face hardened and her grip tightened on the doorknob.

Jess sat up, so her mother could have a better view. Her pink streaks meant disobedience, they meant defiance. Jess pushed away a smile. She'd remember the look on Layla's face forever.

A few seconds went by without a word, which made Jess nervous. She folded her hands in her lap and picked her cuticles. Why wasn't Layla saying anything? Did Jess accidentally give her mother a heart attack? What would Jess's punishment be? Maybe she'd take Jess's bedroom door off its hinges - a threat she'd made once before - or ground her until college. She waited for Layla to burst into a lecture or use guilt as a weapon but all she did was look at Alice. "You've corrupted my daughter."

Alice blinked. "Wait, what?"

"Mom!" Jess shouted. "It's not her-"

"Jessica, be quiet." Layla's glare made Jess stop talking. No matter what she said or what was true, Layla wouldn't believe her.

Alice opened her mouth but she must've seen the fury radiating from Layla's eyes because she didn't dare say anything. The girls shared a nervous glance. What should they do? Run?

"I want you out of my house," Layla pointed down the hall. She paused. Bennett stood behind her, no emotion on his face, no love, no compassion, nothing but a thin, tired frown.

"Layla," he said in a cold tone. Jess hated when they did this. When they fought, it was worse than when they avoided each other. They made a great team at work but at home, depending on the day, they were either strangers or enemies.

Layla stared at him, superior and spiteful. She was challenging him to stand up to her. She wanted him to back down, to obey her. "What?"

"Enough." He barely ever won their arguments. Most of the time, he didn't try. He didn't speak up unless he had to. It was easier to go along with what

Layla wanted but when it came to his daughter, he tried his best to fight Layla's word. He gestured to the staircase. "Breakfast's ready."

"Fine," Layla said through gritted teeth. She shot Alice a dirty look, then stomped downstairs.

Bennett waited for her to leave, then he grabbed the doorknob. His expression softened. "Alice, you're welcome in our home any time," he smiled. "And Jessica, I love your hair."

A wave of relief washed over her. She mouthed a quiet *thank you* to her dad, then he shut the door. Her shoulders relaxed but she felt nauseous, a little dizzy. Standing up to Layla was a lot tougher than she expected. She rubbed her temples, folded her hands in her lap, and picked her cuticles. A few of her fingers were scabbed.

Alice brushed her fingers through Jess's hair. "Maybe she's jealous," she twirled one of the pink streaks around her index finger. "We both know Layla could never pull off this look."

Jess chuckled. She appreciated the humor but it didn't take away the disappointment. Her mother was never going to be the person Jess needed her to be. Jess was a puppet and Layla was happily pulling her strings. How could she escape? Maybe she couldn't.

She felt tired. She wanted to go back to sleep.

Chapter 6

Casey

CASEY WAS SHOCKED TO learn Alice knew Eddie because she lived under Eddie's Bar. He didn't know the basement existed. If he did, he never used it.

The entrance led to the alley behind the building. Stained walls with portable heaters and fans everywhere. Half-broken twinkly lights lit the large room. An old, torn mattress sat in the back corner covered by tangled black sheets and white, circular pillows. A suitcase held all of Casey's clothing - several T-shirts, a few pairs of jeans, and a couple of other items - and an antique army trunk with rusted padlocks and faded green leather held her knife collection.

A mini-fridge was at the end of the bed. The extension cord went to the only outlet in the basement next to a TV from the nineteen-eighties.

The acrylic coffee table was the single nice piece of furniture, no chips or dents or stains. It was the first thing she got for the basement. Hobbs helped her move it in, then Bobby and Casey sat around it, eating french fries, as they fantasized about what the basement could be and where she'd put everything.

"By golly," Tommy said in a terrible British accent. They were watching a silent movie. The man on screen carried a briefcase with an endless scarf inside, dragging it along the sidewalk, but the man didn't seem to notice. He kept walking. "My thermal underwear seems to be falling out from my bag," Tommy finished.

Casey put her chin on his chest. She smiled. "By golly? Thermal underwear?"

"It's funny."

He had his arm around her. She was comfortably tucked between his body and the couch's back, coffee-stained cushions. None of the bottom cushions matched.

He smelled faintly of gunpowder and peach shampoo, which she loved. Her arm rested on his chest. She could feel the rise and fall of his breath, steady and constant, as well as his heartbeat. Its steady rhythm made her smile.

A woman appeared on the black and white screen.

Casey cleared her throat and got into character. She spoke in a terrible Irish accent. "My God! Am I seeing things or is that thermal underwear coming from your bag?"

"Why yes, it is," Tommy answered. "I packed it for my business trip today."

"Your business trip?" she asked. "Why do you need thermal underwear on a business trip? Is it some sort of fetish you have?"

"Fetish?" he laughed, breaking character. "Seriously?"

"You're the one who brought in thermal underwear."

"How dare you turn thermal underwear into something dirty."

"It's just a way for me to be entertained," she said.

"You're impossible, you know that?"

"You love silent movies."

"Yeah. They're cool. So what?" he asked.

"So..." She shifted onto her hands and knees, body hovering above his. He lay still, staring at her with his usual reserved, unreadable gaze but the way he focused on her made everything else disappear. He adored her, it was obvious. She smiled. "You're a dork and a computer geek."

"Proud of it," Tommy said. "Besides, you're my girlfriend so you can't complain."

"That term hasn't been approved." She kissed him. His hands rested on her waist, then slowly moved up her back. His fingers sent electric shivers up her spine and his body heat made butterflies dance in her belly. His hands got tangled in her hair.

She could kiss him forever.

She loved being near him, held by him. She lifted herself enough to look into his perfect brown eyes. Their faces were inches apart. He didn't try to kiss her again, instead, he waited for her signal, unlike when they were on a job together, then he usually called the shots.

"Who's deciding our labels again?" he tucked a strand of blue hair behind her ear, fingers softly grazing her cheek. "Because they're taking forever."

Casey wanted labels. She wanted to say she was his girlfriend and he was her boyfriend. There was no doubting they were a couple. She had a difficult time getting close to people, even when she trusted them. Her instinct was to keep everyone an arm's length away. She trusted Tommy more than anyone else, more than she thought possible, but she couldn't admit it.

Trust was dangerous. It made you vulnerable.

A rushed knock interrupted them. *Good, a distraction.*

Casey yanked herself off the couch's back and adjusted her T-shirt. A five-step stairway led to the door where three deadbolts were locked at all times. Eddie's Bar wasn't technically in the Burrows but it was on the border. She couldn't be too careful.

She opened the door.

Alice stood on the crappy, straw-like welcome mat. Her hair was twisted in a soaked ponytail and her clothes were drenched. Leftover rain drizzled from the gutter and puddles littered the gray pavement. She held a small suitcase. Casey couldn't tell if Alice's cheeks were wet from the rain or from tears. The desperation on her face begged for safety.

Casey grabbed her wrist and yanked her inside. "What are you doing here?"

"I was at home. I had my homework finished and I was going to bed..." Her voice cracked as she held back fearful sobs. "And I heard the door slam. He... he had blood on his hands."

"Your dad?" Casey asked. She wondered if the angry shouts she heard earlier had been Mason's. Rumbles happened all the time in Eddie's Bar. The Rattlesnakes, a biker gang, liked to pick fights with the retired veterans who hung out there but the veterans, with their guns and whiskey, didn't take crap from anyone. "What the hell did he do?"

"I don't know." Alice's voice shook. "But I'm scared to find out." She loved her dad despite everything he put her through. Casey admired how much Alice cared about people. If she loved someone, she loved them with everything she had. "Can I... could I stay here for a bit?"

"Yeah," Casey said without a second thought. She hadn't expected the drop-by and was a little embarrassed. The basement was a place to sleep. She found it when she was eleven, when she left St.Marian's Orphanage for good.

Tommy must've heard them coming because he was already on his feet. He wore his gray hoodie and jeans. He had a slight bedhead, thanks to the couch cushions. "You must be the mysterious friend from Morgan High."

"Hi," Alice gave a weak smile. "I didn't know Cece had company. Sorry."

He glanced at Casey, silently questioning the use of her street name. She told him to *shut up* with her eyes. He hid an amused chuckle but didn't reveal anything.

He held his hand out to Alice. "Nice to meet you."

"Al," Casey gestured to him. "This is T. T, Al."

"Tommy," he corrected.

Alice shook his hand. "Alice."

"I meant to introduce you two earlier," Casey lied. She was a good liar but Tommy could see right through her. He grabbed his boots and his leather laptop bag. He was a hacker, computers were in his DNA and he liked to keep one on hand in case of emergency. "I'll see you in an hour."

"Yeah."

He kissed her cheek and whispered, "Cece."

"See ya!" she slapped his shoulder and shoved him out the door. He laughed as he left. Casey smiled to herself. She couldn't help it. His presence did something to her.

She wanted to tell Alice her real name but she wasn't ready. She needed the separation. If Alice knew everything about her, even the darkest parts, Casey didn't want to think about what would happen.

"Your boyfriend seems nice," Alice said. "You guys are sweet."

"Not exactly the word I'd use," Casey fiddled with her necklace. "You can crash on the couch."

Alice put her suitcase on the coffee table. She sat on the armrest and stared at the floor. What was she thinking? Was she thinking about her dad? Her mom? She pulled her sweatshirt sleeves over her hands and hugged herself, rubbing her arms. Her body shivered but she did her best to hide it. She looked like a stray cat, unloved and in search of a home, reminding Casey of the way she used to be before she met Betty.

"What's in an hour?" Alice asked.

Casey shrugged. "The Arena. I've got a fight."

"Could I come?"

"I think I already answered that question."

"Months ago," Alice stood up. Her stubborn tone distracted from her overall misery. "Come on. I have to see your world sometime. The Arena, the fights, the boyfriend, they're all part of it."

The night in Alice's kitchen, Casey was surprised by the question. She hated the idea of a friend leaving her. She didn't have many loved ones or people to trust. She wanted to trust Alice but their lives weren't the same. Alice was Glisin's daughter, the heir to hope, but Casey was destined to be a criminal, the next Crime Queen.

"If I say no and lock you in here. Are you gonna use your powers to break out?"

"Sure. I'll burn your coffee table too."

"Wow, serious threat," Casey chuckled. She couldn't keep Alice blindfolded forever. Sooner or later, Alice would learn about Height City's shadows, about Casey's demons. Why not rip off the bandaid now, and let things get back to normal? Disappointment broke through Casey's emotional shields. Did Alice really mean that much to her?

"Fine. You can come."

Alice smiled. She had no idea what she was about to walk into. She gestured around the basement. "I like your place, by the way. It looks like a survivor's den or something."

What the hell was a survivor's den? This place was crap but Casey loved it. The basement was home. Her first real home. The first place she felt safe.

She glanced over Alice's outfit; gray sweatpants, sneakers, her sweatshirt, and a baggy top. It wasn't threatening or dangerous. It was lazy and comfortable.

"You're gonna have to change," Casey said. "You don't look like a Burrower."

"What do Burrowers usually wear?"

Casey pictured Bobby's closet. She looked at her suitcase. "Good question."

***

Alice

A tattered, red curtain hung from the doorframe. Spray-painted letters spelled out THE ARENA. The building was at least thirty-five stories tall. It looked un-cared for, abandoned. Trash and popcorn littered the sidewalk. The crumbling brick walls were covered in graffiti and all the windows were boarded up.

Alice followed Cece into the rundown lobby.

People were everywhere, dressed in dark colors, thick coats, gloves, hoods, and hats. Each person looked ready to defend themselves from everyone else around them. They screamed and cheered, talking about who Cece's next opponent might be and how fast Cece would beat whoever it was.

The center cage looked like something a lion tamer would use to whip its beasts into submission. Why'd it smell like raw fish?

"Intense," Alice said.

Cece bobbed her head. "You have no idea."

They pushed through the crowd. A line of Burrowers pointed to a desk built into the floor. A boy with charcoal brown hair stood behind it wearing a brown, rugged leather jacket and simple jeans. The people in line handed him their money - bets, Alice assumed - and he sorted the different bills into a metal box.

A girl stepped up to the desk. She handed him her bet and greeted Tommy who was casually leaning on the desk. He didn't seem on edge like the others, he was relaxed yet ready for a fight if one were to start. The boy in the brown leather jacket flashed the girl a charming smile. He said something and she chuckled.

Tommy rolled his eyes.

The boy gave the girl a pen. She scribbled something on his arm, then walked away. The boy shoved his arm in Tommy's face, showing off whatever the girl wrote. "Three out of five numbers."

"Are you sure that last number is real? She might've given you a random number, you know, so you'd stop bothering her," Tommy said.

"Jealous?"

"Nope."

The boy smacked Tommy's head, telling him to *shut up* without words. Alice could tell they were great friends, best friends, connected like her and Jess.

"You look hot," the bookie said when he saw her.

Alice glanced at her outfit. She wore one of Cece's black tank tops under a loose flannel T-shirt, which lay open on her torso. Her jeans were slightly ripped. Her hair was in a loose bun, falling around her face, framing her cheeks, and her makeup mimicked Bobby's. She blushed at the compliment but he wasn't her type. She smiled. "Thanks."

"This is Dave," Tommy said. "The Arena's bookie."

"So," Dave focused on Cece. "What the hell is she doing with you?"

Cece frowned, unamused. "What does that mean?"

"Hot girls run in packs," he smiled. "Donkeys are loners like you."

"Says the horse's ass." She tucked her necklace under her fitted tank top. She made sure it wouldn't slip out or fall off. She glanced at Alice, unsure, then turned to Tommy. He nodded as if she had asked him a favor.

He kissed her. "I can hold your necklace for you."

"It's my lucky charm."

He smiled. "Good luck."

Cece patted Alice's shoulder and followed Dave to the cage.

Alice stood beside Tommy and crossed her arms protectively over her chest. This crowd was loud, sweaty and everyone had some sort of weapon. She tried not to be uncomfortable but this entire situation was new and scary.

"Cece! Cece! Cece! Cece!" People raged. They pumped their fists above their heads or clapped as loud as they could. If they weren't chanting her name, they were whooping and screaming things like "Fight! Fight!" or "Nobody betrays Betty Beater!"

Who knew Cece had a fanbase? Alice wasn't sure what she'd been expecting but she couldn't have imagined anything like this.

Dave locked Cece inside the cage and climbed the wall. He hung off the twine-like bars and turned to the crowd, holding a microphone against his lips. "Tonight's challenger! Is a Markinson man. And if that weren't crime enough, he wanted to come meet the champion! What's dumber than that!"

The Burrowers roared. Alice covered her ears.

Tommy handed her some earplugs. She chuckled and put them in. Every voice, scream, and noise became muffled. It was much easier to focus.

Tommy put another set in his ears.

***

Casey

Casey stretched her arms above her head. She was nervous. She never got nervous before a fight but with Alice in the crowd, it felt different. Tonight would decide whether she lost a friend or not. She'd let her mask crack and that was terrifying.

El came into the cage. She wore blue jeggings and a pastel green top. Her doll-like hair was braided in a bun. El was Markinson's daughter. She couldn't be here. It was dangerous enough that she and Dave had an on-and-off relationship. He was a Betty. It was practically forbidden.

"Cece!" he waved her over. Desperation lit his face like a neon sign. He cared about El more than he'd ever admit. He'd known her since before his dad went to prison. They'd all known her since they were kids. She was part of their crew.

Casey clenched her fist and went to the fence. "What's she doing here?"

Dave shook his head. "I don't know but you can't kill her."

"Rules say-"

"You have to knock her to the floor, not kill. Kill is Betty's preference. Don't follow it this time." He let the slightest bit of emotion creep into his voice. He wanted her to know how serious this was. He needed El to be okay.

"Just 'cause you guys sleep together doesn't mean I've gotta go easy," she said. "If Betty doesn't want her dead, she'd tell me."

"If you do it, there'll be war," he said. "Besides, it's El."

His eyes begged her to go easy, to let El live.

Dave was right. If Casey spilled the blood of Markinson's daughter in the cage, then he and Betty would go to war. Height City would be torn apart and destroyed. More than that, El was a friend. She spent most days with the group, laughing and joking. She teased the boys, she helped Casey perfect certain gymnastic moves. And Dave cared about her.

Casey hated that her loved ones had power over her.

"You need a new panty dropper," she said through clenched teeth. "Because El is the Markinson me."

"Ew," he shook his head. "Don't put it like that."

She rolled her eyes. She met El in the cage's center. They stood as if they'd both win this fight. The siren blared and everyone shut up.

El swung her fist. Casey blocked. She kicked El in the stomach, then the knee. She twisted El's arm, spun around, and flipped the girl over her back. El's feet slapped the floor and she yanked away from Casey.

Their fists flew, heavy breath echoing. Casey tasted blood on her lip and felt the bruises on her skin. Her body worked off muscle memory. It automatically dodged and blocked and when she found an opening, it obeyed.

El favored her left.

Casey kicked but El dodged, ducking under Casey's foot. She grabbed her fist. She swung Casey against the fence and held her arm in a hurtful stretch, one move and Casey's shoulder would dislocate.

"There's a rumor going around Markinson territory," El said. "One of Betty's stole from one of my dad's inner circle members after a poker game."

Casey stomped on El's foot. She twirled, blocking El's arm when she tried to punch. Casey put a knife to her neck. They froze. The blade hovered near El's skin. With one swift slice, Casey could kill her. Part of her wanted to do it, her insides ached to end El's life but she didn't. She couldn't.

El chuckled. "You can't kill me."

"Nobody stole anything," Casey said. "Why couldn't you tell Dave your gossip?"

"My dad said to lay low for a while. He doesn't exactly approve."

"Shocker. So what? Lost your mind without the boy toy?"

"The rumor is a ringer was thrown in." El wouldn't come to The Arena without a purpose. She wasn't stupid. She wasn't allowed to be here, she was heir to Markinson's kingdom, which meant she was Betty's enemy. She knew that.

Her arms dangled at her sides. She wasn't bothered by the blade against her throat.

"A ringer... Of Betty's?" Casey asked. "Is there any proof?"

"No, but the source is someone you know."

"Someone I know?" Casey crinkled her eyebrows. Who'd start a rumor that could spark a war between the crime lords? Who would want to threaten the existence of the lower gangs? This rumor could split the underworld in half. Whoever lost their money - during the poker game or after it - would go after the ringer. Who'd be that crazy or vengeful? *Johnny.*

She scoffed. "That little weasel."

"Your friend is in real trouble." El grabbed Casey's wrist, snatched the blade, and swung Casey to the side, when she let go, Casey slammed against the cement floor, and pain shot through her arm. She scrambled to her feet and stumbled, bones aching.

They had to put on a show.

El tossed the knife and lunged into a cartwheel. As she flipped, Casey jumped and grabbed the cage's ceiling, fingers fisting in the holes, her body dangled.

El slammed against her feet like a skinny boulder. She fell. Casey dropped and grabbed El's left ankle. She lifted her leg and stomped on her knee. SNAP.

El screamed.

"I'm really sorry about this." Casey knelt on El's torso. She grabbed El's hair and knocked her head against the cement, not too hard but hard enough. Her eyes closed and her body relaxed.

Casey sighed.

Dave yelled into the microphone, "Fifteen seconds!"

The crowd roared.

The boys opened the door. Tommy quickly kissed Casey's cheek and followed Dave to El. They dragged her unconscious body out of the cage and disappeared into the crowd.

Casey ignored the intense ache throughout her body. She shoved past the Burrowers as they screamed her name and congratulated her. What would Betty think? Would Betty have wanted her to kill El? The voices blurred and meshed as the questions tried to overwhelm her.

She found Alice by the entrance. This was it. This was where she lost a friend. This was the moment Alice would tell her that she was a horrible person, that she didn't have a soul. Casey wasn't ready to hear it, to lose her, but she wanted to get it over with. It was nice while it lasted.

Alice grabbed her hand and yanked her outside.

***

Alice

Alice never took her eyes off the fight. Cece's movements were panther-like. She was swift, strong, and knew exactly what she needed to do. Absolutely incredible.

The night air was cold, it chilled Alice's bones, or maybe it was the memory of Cece's fight. The city lights blurred the sky, distorted the moon, and kept the world a million miles away. The Burrows were darker than the Nests and the Honeycombs. Less lively, less vibrant.

A soda can crunched under Alice's foot.

Worry and uncertainty cracked Cece's blank expression, which made Alice want to say the right thing.

"You do that most every day for a crime lord," she said. "You... you beat people up, like the people who disobey her or to... To initiate them... or...?"

"Pretty much. I do other things for her too. Worse things," Cece couldn't look Alice in the eye. No wonder she didn't want to show Alice her world. "Tommy too, and Dave sells drugs for her. That wasn't a normal fight either. It's complicated but-"

"You kill." Alice figured as much but to see it opened her eyes. She knew Height City had violence and darkness. Her mom used to fight the monsters lurking in Height City's shadows. Alice watched the news and she heard the rumors but now it was real. It wasn't a story on a screen or a quiet whisper. She never realized how sheltered she'd been.

"Yeah, I kill," Cece said. "Kill the champion, you become the champion."

Alice should fear a teenage killer. The things Cece did were screwed up and terrible, more so because she was totally fine with it. Both their realities were extreme. Alice was raised by a superhero. Glisin embodied hope and justice for Height City. She brought light to people's lives and defended those who couldn't defend themselves.

What had Cece gone through to make her so okay with violence, horror, and the bruises on her skin? She looked death in the face and served it too.

This was the girl who helped find Mason when he went missing. She slept over when he was gone. She protected her best friend. Was she truly something to be feared or was she someone who needed to be saved? Either way, they were bound together by Susan's secret.

Alice stepped toward Cece but Cece stepped back. She held her hands in a defensive gesture. Alice grabbed her wrists and yanked her into a hug. Her arms folded loosely around Cece's neck and stayed there. She wanted to show Cece this didn't change anything.

Cece stiffened, her body tense. For a few seconds, she didn't move, then she wrapped her arms around Alice's torso and relaxed. Loud chants and cheers rang from inside.

"You don't hate me?" Cece sniffled. "Why the hell aren't you running for the hills?"

"No offense," Alice chuckled. "But with my powers, I could probably take you."

"Debatable."

They pulled apart. There were no words for this moment. It was a simple, quiet breakthrough that they'd remember forever.

Alice smiled, "Linda's?"

"Absolutely," Cece said.

They locked arms and started walking. Cece's arms and cheeks were black and blue. El had a mean left hook and got several good hits in. She moved almost as fast as Cece.

"Burrower Alice is kind of chic."

Alice didn't agree but she found the observation amusing. "I think she looks trashy."

"Well, Dave definitely approved," Cece smiled. "Bobby would too."

"Jess wouldn't."

***

Dave

Dave held El's legs. Her broken knee was bent the wrong way and it freaked him out. He couldn't look at it without feeling sick. Tommy held her shoulders. Her head injury wasn't horrible, no blood or bumps or cracks. Casey hit it hard enough to knock her out. Dave doubted Casey could get any scarier.

"Sally's gonna kill me." Tommy shoved El into the backseat.

"It's not my fault you keep borrowing her jeep."

"She'd never let you borrow it." He closed the door. He took the wheel and Dave got in the passenger seat. Multi-colored beads decorated a little liquor bottle hanging from the rearview mirror. Sally had several CDs on the dashboard, mostly classic rock and some country albums. She played most of the songs at her club.

"I'm getting a van anyway," Dave said.

Tommy started the engine. "A van?"

"Yeah. I can woo the ladies and drive around," he shrugged. "Plus a roof over my head would be nice."

"A roof without Cole, you mean." Tommy drove out of the alley and onto the uneven road. The yellow lines were faded.

El lay in the backseat. She looked as fragile as a crystal vase. Her fists must be made of iron. Dave was a little surprised she survived Casey's talents. He'd trained with Casey for as long as they'd been friends, he knew how well she could

124

fight. Why would El risk coming to The Arena? What possible reason could she have for risking her life?

Dave smiled at the scent of her bubblegum lipstick. "The dude makes sock puppets. I don't even know why."

"They're for the kids at St.Marian's Orphanage." Tommy was laser-focused on the road but his hands were lazy, fingers hanging off the steering wheel.

"The place he and Casey grew up?" Dave asked.

He nodded. "Yeah. He makes the sock puppets for the kids and takes them over there."

"I'm shocked the nuns let him."

"Yeah, Casey is too."

"She ever go with him?" Dave glanced at the backseat. For some reason, he felt like El might vanish into thin air but she was still asleep, chest rising and falling, which meant she was still alive.

"Casey would never go back there," Tommy said. "Not after everything they did to her."

Dave didn't know much about Casey and Cole's lives before he met them. Neither one of them liked to talk about it, so the subject was left alone but Dave knew it wasn't a good childhood, almost as bad as his or Tommy's.

The Burrows' public clinic was a small, rundown building. It was a dirty turquoise color with a flat, white roof. There was a truck bay behind it for medical supply shipments. Sometimes, the shipments were hijacked or sabotaged. Nobody did anything about it.

The inside was a mess. The tile floors hadn't been swept in years. The heat was broken and fluorescent lights flickered from the ceiling. The nurse at the front desk, looking bored and exhausted, handed out prescriptions.

Dave and Tommy carried El through the lobby and dropped her on an unattended gurney. Tommy grabbed a knee brace from an unorganized shelf and secured it on El's leg. She was still sound asleep. She didn't snore or move. Her dad was going to be pissed about the injuries. What lie would she tell Markinson to keep him from waging war on Betty?

"Is she your girlfriend today... Or?" Tommy asked.

Dave chuckled mockingly. "Very funny," he rolled his eyes. "You know, I could ask you the same thing about Casey."

"It's not the same thing." Tommy wasn't wrong. He and Casey were more together than Dave and El had ever been but Dave still liked to tease him about the fact they couldn't define their relationship out loud. The truth was Dave had never felt that way about anyone. He'd never been in love and he doubted he ever would be. With all his trauma and baggage, he wasn't worth being loved in that way, which was fine. He didn't need the heartache.

"I'm gonna get a doctor," Tommy said, then walked away.

Dave patted El's unbroken knee. His eyes drifted toward the people in the waiting area. One man gently bobbed a crying baby in his arms; another looked older and half asleep. He had a prosthetic leg; a seventeen-year-old girl held a pregnancy test. She wasn't with her parents.

Dave froze at the glimpse of a man. The man's hair was charcoal brown like Dave's except his hair was short, almost a buzz cut in the back and fuller on top while the man's hair was long, shoulder-length. He had a bushy goatee and a thin mustache. He wore a black, leather vest and ripped pants. The burn marks on his fingers sent Dave into a spiraling panic.

The man vanished out the back door.

Dave stumbled. He couldn't breathe. Was he breathing? His heart banged against his ears. Bang. Bang. Bang. Rageful fists on a helpless woman's body. Ted's knuckles were so bloody. The body was black and blue. Bruises covered her belly, arms, neck, and head. Her agonized screams echoed in Dave's mind like an Earth-shattering whistle.

He grabbed the phone and hid in the closet. The dial tone was clear as day and the operator's voice was unforgettable: *911, what's your emergency?*

The worst night of his life.

"Dave?" Tommy's voice was a million miles away. All Dave could focus on was the memory, the images, the noises. He couldn't feel his heart but he could hear it. Was he stumbling? He couldn't catch himself. Tommy caught him and lowered them both to the floor.

Dave took a deep breath, pulling himself from the panic. The floor was solid and stable under his hands. The wall was sturdy behind his back.

"You okay?" Tommy asked. "What happened?"

"Nothing." Dave's dizziness faded. He took deep breaths, calming his heartbeat. The memory drifted back into the darkest corners of his mind. He used Tommy as a crutch and stood up.

"Maybe you should sit again," Tommy said. "In a chair. Till-"

"I'm good, man," Dave pulled away. "I'm good."

"You sure?"

"Yeah, I'm gonna go."

"Uh... okay," Tommy said. "I'll stay with El."

Dave gave a shaky thumbs-up and left the clinic. He took deep breaths of the fresh air. He needed to clear his head. He couldn't have seen his father. It couldn't have been Ted Marson, right? Ted was hidden somewhere waiting for instructions.

Dave didn't pay attention to where he was headed. Muscle memory took him there. He'd lived in the same place since before his dad went to jail. He and Cole had been roommates for almost that long. The building was tall and old with dark blue, cement walls. Half the apartments were abandoned and the plumbing sucked.

A homeless man – with a dusty beard and a glass eye - lived in a cardboard tent outside the door. He often talked to the sign labeled AMES STREET.

Dave went through the tiny, mold-scented lobby and entered the stair-well. He lived on the second floor. The narrow hall had wallpapered tile for floors and gray walls. Apartment 8B.

He reached his keys into the lock and froze. Did he see what he thought saw? He really hoped not. Maybe it was a trick from exhaustion or trauma. He turned.

An old photo was taped to the wall. It featured an eight-year-old Dave standing beside his parents. He could barely remember being happy. He missed the clueless feeling, not knowing about his father's sins or his mother's fears. His mom's long, red hair was beautiful. Her smile was wide. People said he inherited her eyes and his father's everything else. He hoped the second part wasn't true.

He took the photo off the wall. It was the same one Ted took to Steel Prison. On the back, there was fresh ink. The messy handwriting read:

The Adler Building.

***

Jess

Jess took confidential files from Layla's briefcase and left the house. She was pretty sure she lost her mind or was body-snatched but she couldn't help it. She had to read them. She went to Linda's Diner for some privacy.

The diner was deserted except for herself, the owner, and Bobby Jones.

Jess knew her from school but they never spoke. They never made eye contact and weren't in any of the same classes. She knew the rumors and why Brittany started them but she didn't know if they were true.

Bobby sat in the booth by the left window and Jess sat in the booth by the right one. They faced each other but they were worlds apart.

So far, Jess knew Layla and Bennett helped put Ted Marson in Steel Prison.

He was sentenced to life behind bars for murdering his wife, Cynthia Marson. He committed several other crimes, including arson, but those were never brought to court. Jess's parents also helped get him released. They fabricated new evidence that somehow proved Cynthia committed suicide but according to the coroner photos Layla had hidden in her briefcase, suicide was impossible. Over ninety percent of Cynthia's body was covered in bruises. Half her skull was caved in. It seemed like even after she died, Ted kept beating her.

One street name popped up on almost every paper. Ames Street.
Why was it important?

***

Bobby

Bobby's head hurt. She couldn't believe she spent the entire year partying, drinking, and napping. She was behind in every class. Luckily, Mister Scotts and Miss Z convinced Principal Penez to give her an extension.

Bobby worked on extra credit stuff too. Math came easy but the other subjects weren't her favorite. She liked numbers. They made sense for some reason.

Jessica Peace was there when she walked in. All Bobby knew about Jess was that she was a top student, a teacher's pet, an overachiever, and a rich kid. She was also friends with Brittany and Cindy, who Bobby hated.

***

Alice

Cece and Alice stood in front of Linda's Diner. Their best friends were on separate sides of the building, each one framed by a different window. Neither paid attention to the other. They were both busy.

Jess picked her cuticles, staring at several papers spread across the table. Homework, probably, or something for the student council. Bobby had headphones on. She bobbed her head to whatever music was playing in her ears. She stared at the papers in front of her like they were written in a foreign language. She looked ready to jump up from the table and storm out of the diner.

"Now it feels weird to go in," Cece said.

"Agreed," Alice said. She wasn't sure it was a great idea to see Jess after the night she'd had. And she didn't know Bobby very well. She didn't want to let anything slip or reveal something Cece wanted to keep hidden. Their friendship included. "Neither of them know we're friends, right?"

"Uh-huh," Cece clicked her tongue. "Now what?"

"Back to your place?"

Their friends were isolated from each other. Lonely. Alice didn't like it. This night wasn't what she expected. When Mister Scotts dropped her off at home, she made a sandwich and started her homework. She couldn't have predicted Mason coming home the way he did. He didn't know she was there. He kept muttering things to himself as he washed the blood off his hands. What did he do? Did he hurt someone? Alice didn't want to know, so she went to Cece's. It was the first place she thought of.

"It's our place," Cece corrected. "At least until you find a permanent address."

"Deal. I'll find one soon, I swear."

"Okay, till then you're on the couch, and if you snore, I'll throw a pillow at you."

"I might whimper. I have nightmares and my powers act up too."

"You're not gonna accidentally toast me, are you?" Cece asked. "'Cause that'd put a real damper on the roommate thing."

"I promise that won't happen," Alice said. "I'll put it in writing if you want."

"Alright. Now let's talk about rent."

Alice laughed. "You're funny." She wrapped one arm around Cece's shoulders. She was looking forward to living someplace safe. She wouldn't have to worry about her dad or wonder where he was all the time. The distance would be good. "I think I'm gonna practice my powers when we get back."

"Those poor cups," Cece smiled, arm around Alice's torso.

***

130

Jess

Jess saw Linda wave to someone through the window but didn't see who it was. Her focus was on the files. She picked her cuticles as her thoughts swirled. She could figure this out. She just needed to think. Maybe cleaning something would help, she could offer to sweep up for Linda. The distraction might prove to be beneficial. Or coffee. Coffee always helped.

Linda slid two plates on the table. Blueberry pie and chocolate cake.

Jess moved her work. "Sorry, I didn't order anything."

"She did," Linda gestured to Bobby. "Darling."

She glanced up. It was the first time either of them acknowledged the other.

Linda's voice was kind. Her southern accent was thick. She wore a cute yellow dress with red buttons and a white collar. Her tan hair was clipped to the back of her head. The wrinkles around her eyes made her seem wise. "You two darlings used to pop in here all the time with your parents," she said. "Never noticed each other. Well, there are only two of ya sweet cheeks in here now, so y'all are gonna sit together, eat some cake and pie, and have an old-fashioned chat."

It was true. Bennett and Jess loved this place. They'd get to-go orders and bring them home. And Jess would come with Alice's family when Susan didn't cook. They'd play songs on the jukebox and talk about their days. Sometimes, Mason would bring them after Alice's games, he let both girls order any dessert they wanted.

"But... um... sorry, We..." Jess was uncomfortable. "We don't know each other."

Linda put her hands on her hips. "Do you want these free desserts or not?"

"I... I do," Bobby raised her pencil. "I want my pie."

"Then come sit with this perfect stranger." Linda wasn't taking no for an answer. She winked at Jess, then went to stand behind the counter and started refilling salt shakers.

Bobby piled her books and journals into her arms and came to the table. She sat across from Jess. They were silent, staring at each other. How was one supposed to start a conversation with someone they didn't know? Someone they had nothing in common with.

"I'm Jess or Jessica Peace, I guess."

"Bobby Jones, my friends call me B."

They shook hands and glanced around. Jess felt stiff. This was weird, wasn't it? She was sitting with a girl she only knew by reputation, a supposed slut, her friend's enemy.

"You like cake," Bobby chuckled.

Jess looked at the piece of double fudge, chocolate cake on her plate. "Oh, yeah. It's a regular of mine."

"That's cool. I like pie, so..."

"So does my best friend. She loves the custard pie here."

"My best friend prefers cake," Bobby bobbed her head. "Butterscotch cake. She really likes that flavor. And she could eat a can of frosting in one sitting," the words spilled out of her mouth. She didn't pause once. "I mean, it's insane, I can't believe it. She's so funny-"

"Bobby?" Jess asked.

"Yeah?"

"This is weird for me too. Can I ask you a question?"

"Sure. I mean, if I can ask you one."

"The rumors... Um... about you," Jess picked her cuticles. "They're not true, are they? Brittany made most of them up after you, uh-"

"Yeah," Bobby looked down at the table. "She did," she gulped. "My turn?"

"Yeah. Go ahead."

"I hear you're, like, really smart and everything, so could I.." Bobby paused. "Maybe you could help me with my schoolwork? In return, I'll buy you another piece of cake, I swear."

"It's a deal," Jess smiled.

Bobby chuckled. "Okay. Good."

Chapter 7

Jess

JESS READ LAYLA'S PAPERS backward and forward several times over the last few weeks. The only solid clue she found was an address. Ames street. She wanted to know what was there and she had no idea why. Another mystery for another time.

She weighed the pros and cons. The first con was she'd be disobeying her parents. Though she already stole from Layla - and dyed her hair again without permission - so maybe disobeying wasn't so bad.

Pro, she might finally learn why her parents helped a known criminal get out of prison. She needed to know why they lied. What did they gain from it?

Con, it could be dangerous.

Pro, she was already in the Burrows. She wanted answers more than anything. She wanted to prove her parents weren't criminals. They had to have legitimate reasons for their actions. The bottom line? This mission was insane and Jess didn't care.

She found the address. A dark blue, cement apartment building with a cardboard fort in front of it.

She parked, muttering positive words to help make herself feel brave, trying to psych herself up for what she was about to do.

An hour before this, she finished the last student council meeting of the year. She signed early bird yearbooks and made plans with Alice for later that night. They were going to meet at Linda's.

"You can do this." Jess got out of the car and locked the doors.

Bennett would kill her if anything happened to his Range Rover. He loved this car. It was his second baby.

Police sirens echoed in the distance. A car backfired and she flinched. Could it have been a gunshot? She read many articles about crimes in the Burrows. Murders, thievery, it was an endless pool of danger. The garbage smell was overwhelming. She'd need six showers after this. Maybe she should've brought a weapon or some sort of protection.

She hated being unprepared.

Buttons were in the cramped entryway, each one labeled with a different apartment number. Which should she choose? She'd have to try them all.

She pressed one and waited. No answer. She pressed another. No answer. Another and nothing. She kept trying until finally, one buzzed.

Apartment 8B.

"Who is it?" a voice glitched in the speaker.

Jess cleared her throat. She tried to sound confident. "Package for 8B."

The voice didn't answer, instead, there was a loud buzz. She pushed the door open and went inside. The empty first-floor hall led to a dusty stairwell. The railing was broken and the steps were carpeted with blue and green squares. If these weren't the people Jess was looking for, she'd go door to door and ask about Ted Marson. Someone had to know something about him.

Apartment 8B had a dark green door with brown edging. It wasn't special, it looked like every other door in the hall except for the wooden welcome sign hanging from a rusted nail in the center. She knocked, feeling more anxiety than she'd ever felt before. She picked her cuticles.

She hoped this wasn't a mistake.

A boy with short, blondish hair opened the door. He wore a loose, white T-shirt and colorful plaid shorts. He looked at her pink streaks, tilting his head, he crinkled his eyebrows, particularly interested in them.

"You have pink hair." His matter-of-fact voice was the same one from the speaker.

"Yes...?"

"I should get pink hair. I'd look good with pink hair," he said. He seemed to picture it, distracted by the image, then he pulled himself back to the current situation. "Anyway. Where's the package?"

Jess gulped. She folded her hands behind her back, so he wouldn't notice her cuticles. The habit was revealing and annoying. She couldn't stop. "It was a lie. I apologize," she said. "I'm a junior reporter for the Height City Gazette and I'm writing a piece on Ted Marson. A source led me to this address."

She couldn't believe how steady her tone was.

"What source?" another boy came out from behind the door. He had charcoal brown hair and his deep blue eyes looked like the night sky without the stars or moon. He wore a black T-shirt and pajama pants with little race cars on them.

"He was behind there the whole time," the first boy did jazz hands. "Magic!"

He went back inside.

The second boy stared at her, seemingly impatient.

"Uh, the eyewitness from the night he was arrested," she said.

He leaned against the doorframe, casual but guarded, and held the door still. His charming smile seemed to mock her like he knew something she didn't. He was attractive in a bad boy, breaking-the-rules sort of way, and obviously, he knew that. "Funny. I don't remember talking to any junior reporter."

Her heart dropped into her stomach. "You're the eyewitness?"

"Yeah."

"Huh... Well, that complicates things." She gulped. Now what? She was caught in a lie without an escape plan. She wasn't prepared for this.

"What are you really doing here, Honeycomber?" The judgment in his voice hinted at how much he already hated her. His eyes floated over her body. She scoffed. Was he serious?

"My parents put Ted Marson in prison and helped him get out," she said. "I'd like to know why."

"Your parents put my dad away?" He said with less hatred, raising his eyebrows.

Jess's jaw dropped. "Did you just say-"

"What do you think I was doing there that night?" he asked, slightly annoyed. He seemed tired of the conversation. She guessed he didn't like talking about it. She wouldn't either, if it were her story.

"I didn't know."

"I'm a minor, those files were sealed," he said. "Nobody knows I was the witness except for my dad, me, a couple of chosen friends, and apparently, your parents." He shifted his casual stance. Tension spread into his shoulders. "Look, you want answers?" he asked. "Here you go, your parents were either bought or threatened by Betty Beater. The queen of crime herself." He said the name like he was summoning a monster. "She needs my old man for something."

"I don't understand. My parents aren't criminals." Jess may not have been happy with her mother but that didn't mean she wanted to believe Layla was capable of breaking the law, of allowing a killer to roam the streets. Questions swirled through Jess's mind, making her dizzy. This answer wasn't good enough. "Who's Betty Beater?"

She didn't know a Betty Beater. Her parents never mentioned anyone by that name.

"She's a crime lord like Markinson," the boy said. "They've got territory all over the city. They'd be killing each other if there weren't for the truce."

"I don't know what you're talking about," she said. Jess wanted to understand but she didn't. She didn't know who Betty Beater was, she didn't know who Markinson was, she didn't know about whatever truce they had. She hated how clueless she felt.

He didn't seem surprised. Did he expect her to be clueless?

"Go back to your castle, princess," he chuckled. "You don't belong here."

The boy with the blondish hair reappeared. He nudged the second boy out of the way and held his hand out to shake hers. She didn't take it. They were strangers. She didn't trust them. She didn't know them.

"Okay," he dropped his hand, unoffended. "I'm Cole. This is Davey."

"Dave," the second boy said.

Cole waved away the correction. "Anyway, it's nicely to meet you...?"

"Jessica," she answered. "Or um, sorry, I'm Jess."

"Pretty name. Wanna come in?"

"Does she wanna *what*?" Dave disagreed.

Jess ignored him and smiled at Cole. She kept it polite but felt the uncertainty in her face. She didn't want to be rude. "I don't think, um-"

Cole lifted his finger, signaling for her to wait a minute. He disappeared into the apartment. Dave and Jess looked at each other. She didn't like him. He didn't make a good first impression and something told her, he didn't like her either. He looked at her like she was the enemy.

Cole came back. He held out a taser. "Safety first."

"Uh..." she took it. "Thanks?"

"Wanna come in now?" he asked.

She nodded. "Sure."

Cole pulled Dave out of the way.

Their apartment was a mess. Clothes were everywhere. In the living room, there were two couches with a little trampoline sitting between them like a coffee table. The shaggy carpet underneath had glue and ink stains, and random bits of crafting supplies like googly eyes and yarn. A fish tank stood against the back wall; sock puppets were piled inside it and a duffel bag filled with something illegal, probably.

The kitchen didn't have an oven. Several large bags of different flavored chips were on the counter. Paper plates, Pop-tart boxes, and takeout napkins peeked out from a cabinet. Food-shaped magnets were stuck to the fridge. The hardwood floors had scuffle marks and weapons such as guns, knives, ninja stars, and nunchucks were piled in the open dishwasher.

A short hall led to what, Jess guessed, was a bathroom and a second bedroom. The first bedroom was a few feet from the front door.

"Right," Dave gestured to the taser. "'Cause now you can fend off the evil Burrowers if they attack you."

Cole slapped his head in an effort to get Dave to be quiet. "So, this is our castle. Welcome."

"It's nice." Jess didn't want to hurt their feelings but the place was a tiny landfill. It smelled like sweat and old turkey or maybe it was ham.

"Nice," Dave chuckled. "Code for crap pile."

"Okay." Jess turned to him. She was sick of his judgemental tone. "Obviously, you have an issue with me," she frowned. "Is it only because I'm a Honeycomber?"

"Pretty much," he crossed his arms. "You're a pampered, spoiled, sheltered princess."

"And you're a pompous, prideful, rude, dirty criminal," Jess countered. "But I'm not complaining."

He scoffed but smiled. His eyes floated over her again. Was he checking her out or sizing her up? She tried to use her mom's iron stare. Was it working? Probably not. Part of her agreed with him but she still hated the unfair assumptions.

She tempered her anger. She was there for a reason. She wanted answers. She adjusted her firm grip on the taser and turned to Cole. His eyes were kind and inoffensive. He wasn't rude like his friend, maybe he'd be more helpful.

He frowned. He turned to Dave. The boys seemed to telepathically communicate.

"Hey, if the Honeycomber wants to know, tell her," Dave shrugged. "I've got bigger problems."

"Ted Marson," Jess guessed.

Their eyes met. He didn't seem to like that she knew his business. His expression, although stubborn and tense, was unreadable. He pushed past her without a word. He grabbed an old photo from the fish tank and stared at it.

She didn't bother asking about it, he wouldn't tell her what it was even if she did. She and Cole sat on the left couch. It had pillows shaped like french fries, an ice cream cone, and a cheeseburger. A fuzzy blanket with a 3D mustache was draped over the back.

Dave sat on the right couch. The pillows were solid colors, red, blue, green, and yellow. The quilt draped over the back was pretty, sewn with intricate beaded patterns and colorful lace. It didn't seem to belong in the apartment, it looked like it should be on the end of a king's bed. Jess noticed initials were sewn on the corner, C.M. *Cynthia Marson?*

Cole started the explanation.

***

Bobby

Bobby handed in all her extra credit and homework assignments. Her tutoring sessions with Jess helped her finish in time. Jess was a lifesaver and unlike her friends, not a jerk. Now all Bobby could do was wait to see if she'd be a junior. She didn't want to be a sophomore again.

She stepped onto her porch and pulled out her keys.

A black van had been following her for the last week. It showed up at Morgan High, at Jess's house, Sally's Place, everywhere Bobby went. She knew why. Casey told her about the rumor Johnny started. The van must've belonged to the men who wanted their money back.

The keys jingled in her shaking hands as she tried to unlock the door. She yanked it open, ran inside, and shut it. Should she barricade it with furniture? Would it stop them? This couldn't be happening. She dropped her backpack on the couch and took out her phone. She closed the curtains and hid away from the windows. She pressed one. It dialed.

Casey answered. "What's up, B?"

Bobby whispered, "I'm gonna die."

"Are you high again?"

Bobby ran her hand through her curls. She tried to still her overlapping breath but her panic made it difficult. She needed help. She couldn't protect herself. Tears dripped down her cheeks and made her quiver, everything inside her was shaking. "No. I'm totally serious. The van is parked outside my house. It has to be those guys who I think I'm the ringer-"

"I'll be right there." Casey hung up.

Bobby tossed her phone on the couch. She didn't want to die. There were so many things she still wanted to do. She wanted to achieve her dreams, whatever they were. She hadn't figured it out yet. She wanted to know what her dream was. She wanted to graduate high school with her friends and see where life would take her.

She couldn't believe it. She used her dad's teachings to win money for her stupid, abusive boyfriend. Johnny used her for the money. He was getting back at her for the breakup.

He stole that money from Markinson's men, then spread the rumor about the ringer, and skipped town. He took everything else from her, so why not take her life?

Bobby went to the window and pushed the curtain aside. The black van was parked on the curb, blocking her escape. Men-shaped shadows moved around inside it. Those men were going to kill her.

She was going to die.

***

Dave

Dave occasionally glanced up from the photo in his hand.

Cole was giving the Honeycomber girl a summary of Height City's under-world; Betty Beater, Markinson, The Arena, Cece the champion, Thomas the tech support, the illegal poker games, the illegal street races, the lower gangs, Mick the Menace, the drug deals, the pay-rolled cops and lawyers, etcerea.

She was shocked, which wasn't surprising. Honeycombers were usually in the dark. They dressed up their corruption with fancy houses and respectable titles.

Dave couldn't imagine the questions and realizations rolling around in her head. He didn't know the lawyers who sent his dad to prison but he heard their names once or twice. He didn't know they had a daughter. He didn't care to know.

She was beautiful in a delicate flower sort of way. Her long, brown hair neatly framed her face and the pink streaks made her entire person more noticeable but she didn't seem to know that. Her kind, caramel-colored eyes held a spark of dangerous curiosity.

"Wow. That's a lot to process," she said when Cole finished explaining. He didn't go into too much detail, which was probably a good thing. Dave wasn't sure the Honeycomber could handle anymore life-changing informa-tion.

"Now you know," Cole said. "Do you want peanuts?"

"Peanuts?" she said. "No, uh-"

"I'm gonna get peanuts." He left.

Jess scrunched her eyebrows. When the door shut, she turned to Dave. "I thought he was getting peanuts?"

"He is," he said. "Buddy, downstairs, sells them."

"The homeless man?"

"I didn't say he was a good salesman," Dave shrugged. "He and Cole are friends."

"Oh," she said. "That's... Um, okay then."

Her confusion was hilarious. It was fun to see someone who didn't know Cole witness his weirdness. Despite the weird habits and messy craft projects, he was a good guy. He had a great heart and Dave appreciated their friendship.

He looked at the photo. Ted's handwriting looked like Dave's and it made him sick. "Hey, princess. What do you know about the Adler Building?"

"Why?" Jess's curiosity would've been endearing in other situations but Dave didn't like talking about his personal life.

He hated his father. He hated most of his childhood but it seemed he didn't have a choice right now. He needed her help. "My old man wrote the name on this," he jiggled the photo. "There's gotta be a reason."

"Okay, well, my parents work there," she said. "There's a lot of businesses in the building, including an accounting office, real estate office. A smoothie place."

"My dad was never one for smoothies," he leaned forward, elbows on his knees. "What about anything out of the ordinary, like people, or something-"

"Um..." she thought for a moment. He could practically see the gears in her head turning. He had never seen someone think so intently. She nodded. "The floor above the law firm is under construction. People are always going in and out, even on days when there isn't any noise."

"Construction site, huh?" Dave asked. "About a year or two ago, some agency, something like the FBI but weirder, was investigating the mayor's office. Markinson has a bunch of people on the payroll over there so he got them to pack up."

"Yeah?" she asked.

His thoughts rumbled in his head as he put the pieces together. His fingers galloped against the armrest, he counted each tap. "What if this is the same thing?"

"You think... What? The construction site is a smokescreen? Why?"

"Fred Willin and some others are on Betty's payroll," he said. "They could be investigating your parents' law firm to find evidence against her. She has eyes and ears everywhere, so she probably found out-"

"You think that's why they released Ted Marson," Jess said, catching up. "You think Betty fabricated evidence to make his conviction hollow because she needs him to do her dirty work."

"Exactly," Dave smiled.

She caught on fast, he was impressed. He frowned at the photo. The faces in it seemed foreign, distant. It was weird to see his mother smiling. The last time he saw her, she was black and blue, still and lifeless. It was hard to think of her any other way. "Adler Building. He's sending me a clue."

His dad wanted revenge. This was it. Ted was setting a trap for his son. He wanted to kill the eyewitness and do the job for Betty.

"There's a party tonight," Jess said. "All the partners and most of the lawyers will be there to celebrate this big trial they won. It'd be a good staging area."

"I'll check it out." He dropped the photo next to his mother's quilt. It took her weeks to design the beaded patterns and sew the fabrics. She gifted it to Dave on his birthday. She wrapped it around his shoulders and hugged him close, tight enough to make the shadows disappear.

He opened the door, ready to rush out and face his father. He stopped when he realized Jess was behind him. He looked at her, blocking her path with an outstretched arm. Her eyes met his.

"What are you doing?" he asked.

"Coming with you."

"That's hilarious," he pointed at the couch. "Sit back down."

"No." Her determination shined through her stare. "My parents are there and I need to make sure they're safe." Her serious tone told him she had more to say. "Besides, I know those lawyers. They come to my parents' yearly Christmas party and give me birthday presents. They'll trust me."

"And what?" Dave asked. "They won't trust me?"

"No, they won't. No offense." She meant it.

He raised an eyebrow. "'Cause I'm a Burrower?"

She shoved past him and went into the hall. She turned, slowly walking backward. He debated an argument but figured it'd be useless. "And a jerk," she said.

He followed her. "Sorry. I didn't have time to be polite, what with my dad trying to kill people and everything."

"My car's downstairs." She took out her phone. She pressed a button and put it against her ear. Her cuticles were peeled. Faded white daisies were painted on her short nails, and her little pearl earrings seemed cliche. Did every rich woman wear pearls?

"Hey, Alice. Sorry, but I don't think I'll be able to make it to Linda's," Jess said into the phone. "I'm going to the Adler Building. It's a long story. I'll text you."

She hung up. She put her phone in her pocket and tightened her grip on Cole's taser. Dave couldn't believe he gave it to her. Cole wasn't one for weapons, guns or knives, or anything deadly, so he used other forms of protection. The taser was only one of his various tools. He must've really wanted her to trust them.

"Voicemail?" Dave asked.

"Yeah."

The silver Range Rover parked on the curb must've been expensive. He could tell it was hers by the way she froze. Its tires were replaced with cinder blocks and the passenger seat window was broken. The contents inside were more than likely stolen.

She gasped. Dave laughed.

Jess slapped his shoulder. "It's not funny! My dad loves this car!"

"It's pretty funny," he said. "I can't believe you didn't take the bus."

"I didn't know this... Would.." She huffed. "Shut up!"

"Come on. My motorcycle's this way."

"Motorcycle?"

They went to the alley beside the building. He ripped a bright blue tarp off his motorcycle. It was an old model, vintage, with black paint, a new engine -

he updated it a few weeks ago - and faded letters that said Ridley. Two helmets hung at either side of the back pouch, both locked on for safekeeping. Dave held one out to her.

"I am not getting on that deathtrap," she said. "The articles I've read are-"

"You wanna save your parents or not?" he jiggled the helmet. He didn't care if she came with him or not, he was going to face his father, no matter what. He waited, holding the helmet toward her, while she fought her goody-two-shoes instincts. She snatched it from him.

"If we crash," she warned. "I'm going to sue you."

He smiled. Making her angry was fun. He got on the bike and she sat behind him. She wrapped her arms around his torso, fingers clasped at his front. He started the engine. Their bodies pressed against each other. Her sweaty, delicate hands were shaking.

They sped out of the alley and her tense grip tightened.

Dave loved the freedom. The world was there for the taking, ready to be conquered. The wind whipped against his helmet and his heart jumped with each increase of speed. He wanted to do a wheelie but he didn't. It'd probably give the princess a heart attack.

Jess squeezed his stomach tighter, trying not to fall off.

Chapter 8

Bobby

DEAFENING SILENCE AND HORRIBLE waiting. The intense hammering of her heart made her ribs sore. Her hands were clenched between her knees. Hot tears dripped down her cheeks, making them pink. Her shallow, overlapping breath made calming down impossible. Bobby wanted to smoke to calm her nerves but her stash was gone.

What would her dad think about this? Vincent would've choked Johnny if he found out he'd hurt her so many times. He wouldn't have approved of the drinking or the drugs. She hated herself for being such a disappointment.

"B!" Casey banged on the back door. Bobby flinched. Could it be a trick? "B, open the damn door," she jiggled the knob. "It's me."

Bobby obeyed and Casey bull-dozed in. Tommy followed her inside and closed the door. Bobby jumped into his arms. It felt good to be hugged. She needed comfort. Maybe he could steady her, help diminish her fears. She stood on the tips of her toes despite her heels. He held her close, rubbing her back, one hand cradling her head. They let go of one another.

Casey stood in the archway between the living room and the kitchen. Her fierce green eyes were stuck on the van, which was still parked outside, taking away any chance of escape. Even if Bobby did leave, those men would find her eventually. She couldn't run.

"It followed me home," Bobby said. "They're gonna kill me."

"No," Tommy put a hand on her shoulder. "They just want their money back."

"I didn't steal anything," she said. "I won those poker games fair and square... Well, except for the fact that they were illegal. That's not the point!"

"You split the money with Johnny, right?" Tommy asked. "Where's your half?"

"I used it to pay the bills and the mortgage, I was like four payments behind," Bobby said. She tried her best to keep up with the expenses. She didn't do a great job. After her dad died, she quit both her jobs and started partying. She was too wrapped up in her grief to care about anything, even her own well-being.

She started playing poker at Sally's Place to make money but the men she played against were Betty's people or lower gang members, they feared Cece, so when Bobby won, they backed down, too afraid of what Cece might do to them if they harmed her. Bobby never should've agreed to play against Markinson's men.

She was exhausted. It was too much. She couldn't handle it. She felt the uncontrollable need to cry, so that's what she did. "I'm such an idiot. I can't believe I did this," Bobby's voice cracked, quivering with each sob. "I believed his lies and his beautiful, jerky eyes... And my life is ruined. I'm dead. I'm literally dead. I-"

"Zip it," Casey said. "We'll fix it."

"Yeah, and B, Johnny did this," Tommy said. "You didn't."

"I shouldn't have cared about him." Bobby wondered where Johnny was now. Was he in a different city or headed to an island somewhere? She couldn't believe how stupid she'd been. How could one person make so many huge mistakes?

Casey crossed her arms. "T, plan?"

He scoffed. "Really?"

"Well," she shrugged. They needed a plan and Tommy was the plan man.

He shook his head, rolled his eyes, and started slowly pacing back and forth. He rubbed his hands together as he whispered along to his thoughts. Bobby tilted her head. She couldn't understand what he was saying or what was going through his mind, a million scenarios all with a different outcome. She knew he had a process but this made her dizzy.

Casey smiled as she watched him. Her pride in his mind was only one reason Bobby loved that they were together.

He turned to the girls. "Bank accounts."

"Huh?" Bobby scrunched up her nose.

Tommy took his laptop from his bag and set it on the coffee table. He opened it. "I can hack bank accounts here in the city and have the cash wired to one of Markinson's. They'll get their money and you'll be safe."

"Yes! Yay! I like that, yes," Bobby clapped. Her relief and excitement lasted four and a half seconds.

"What's the catch?" Casey asked.

Tommy's fingers flew across the keyboard. "I need time."

"I'll buy you some." She pulled a knife from her boot and headed to the door.

Bobby had seen Casey's vast knife collection and the way she used a blade. She practiced and trained for hours every day, even when she wasn't training with Betty or the boys, she'd twirl the knives and throw them into a target board. Her skills were intimidating.

Tommy whistled and she turned. He tossed her a gun. She caught it. "What's this for?"

"Just in case." He went back to work.

Casey rolled her eyes and left the house. Bobby watched Tommy. She had absolutely no idea what he was doing but she hoped it would work.

***

Casey

Casey twirled the knife and cocked the gun. She preferred blades and Tommy liked firearms but she could be flexible. The black van shone in the sun. It must've been newly washed and waxed. She banged her fist on the door.

When it slid open, an older, scruffy man appeared. He must've been part of Markinson's lower command because she didn't recognize him. He was a henchman, a lapdog. She glanced past him. There were five other men in the van, the driver included. The youngest one had red hair and freckles. Austin Hale. He used to live across the street from Bobby.

They all held automatic weapons and had extra ammo.

She was flattered. They must've known she'd be here.

"Cece," the scruffy man said. "I knew the thief was one of Betty's."

"She ain't the thief," Casey said. "One of Markinson's boys stole the cash and started the rumor that she was the ringer. Your money's halfway to Crescent City by now."

"I don't believe you," he said. "Everyone knows you two hang out." Casey's friendship with Bobby wasn't a secret. Under normal circumstances, their connection would protect Bobby. Nobody messed with Cece's crew unless they wanted their eyes stabbed out. "You're lying to protect her, simple as that."

"Fine. Call El," she shrugged. "We'll hash it out. Make a deal."

"El's out of town," Austin said. He had known Casey and Bobby since they were kids. His younger brother, Justin, used to be their friend before he left town. "Markinson sent her to recover after her knee surgery."

"Yeah," the scruffy man chuckled, amused. "He's pretty upset with you. I'd be worried."

"He can't touch me," Casey said. "Betty wouldn't let it happen."

He twitched with excitement. His trigger finger itched, she could tell. The other men eyed her, ready to pounce if she made one move they didn't like. Markinson's men were known to be unstable, dangerous. They weren't afraid of Betty, or Cece, they weren't afraid of anything, not even their own demons, Markinson made sure of that.

"Look," she said. "We can get you the money. We just need time."

"You're out of time," the scruffy man said. "Markinson doesn't like to wait."

"Markinson is king," Austin said as if he were reciting poetry. The ridiculous catchphrase made Casey want to roll her eyes but she refrained. It'd only piss them off.

"Forty minutes." She kept her face neutral, unwavering. She stood firm, confident, and ready for a battle, the way she was taught. She casually adjusted her grip on the gun to make the men notice it.

They weren't worried.

"You've got twenty," the scruffy man said. "Make them count."

Casey nodded once. She went into the house and locked the door. Bobby turned to her with wide, hopeful eyes and a fearful tone. "So?"

"Twenty minutes," she said. "T?"

"It'll be close," he bobbed his head. "But I think I can do it."

"You think?" she asked.

His fingers clanked on the keyboard, fast and focused. He was the best hacker in Height City. He could do it, he had to, but she was still worried. She fought the urge to fiddle with her necklace. She wouldn't show her nerves, it'd be admitting defeat. She'd never admit defeat.

"I think," he repeated.

Bobby glanced between them. "And if you can't?"

"Then we're sitting ducks," Casey said.

Bobby whimpered. She hugged Casey, arms wrapped around her torso. She rested her head on Casey's shoulder, failing at her attempt not to cry. Her tears smothered Casey's favorite jacket. *Damn it.* She could always get a new one. She couldn't get a new best friend, another Bobby. She gently played with Bobby's fiery curls and held her while she cried. Casey glanced at the clock. *Twenty minutes.*

***

Dave

Dave parked in front of the Adler Building. The pressure on his stomach released and Jess stumbled off the motorcycle, yanking off her helmet. Her hair was fluffed, messy, and her breath was heavy. She seemed panicked, shaky, and bug-eyed. Was she terrified or exhilarated?

"Fun, eh?" he locked their helmets on the back pouch.

Jess scoffed. "No!"

He laughed and shoved his keys in his pocket.

They went into the building and hurried through the lobby. Crystal vases with fancy flower arrangements sat on every table. A few late-night workers sat on couches in the wall-less waiting areas, sorting papers, dusting antiques, or texting on their phones. A janitor mopped the white marble floors. He was doing a good job because Dave could see his reflection. Jess's too. She looked worried.

They ran into an open elevator and she slapped the button. The rumble could've lulled anybody to sleep but Dave was too anxious. He was wide awake. The rapid beating of his heart made him nauseous but he ignored it. He ignored the sweat sliding between his fingers and the constant image of his mother's dead body. He needed to focus.

Jess picked her cuticles. Now, he knew why they were peeled.

Dave took out a gun that Tommy built. He checked the magazine and quietly counted the bullets. He needed enough ammo to get this done. He couldn't hesitate. He took a deep breath.

"That's a gun," Jess's nervous tone shook. "Do you really think you'll need it?"

"If he's already up there," he put it back in the holster. "Yeah."

"Maybe we should've called the police. We still can-"

"Half those pigs are Betty's. If she wants my old man to do something, they're not gonna stop him," he chuckled. "Hell, they might help."

"What if... Maybe you could talk to him," she said. "You're his son, he'll listen to you."

"That's a fantasy, princess. He hates me. If we're gonna help your parents and those other people, I've got to deal with him." Dave never expected to see his father again. He assumed, or maybe he hoped, Ted would've been killed in prison. Dave had killed before, he tortured and hurt people, as a way to survive. He learned what he was capable of, and he didn't doubt he'd be able to take his dad's life.

"You're going to kill your own father?" Jess's caramel eyes were glossed in sympathy, sparkling in the crappy fluorescent light. She'd never done anything like this in her life. He could see it on her face.

"You shouldn't have gotten in the elevator." His frown deepened. His reflection was silver and distorted, twisted in a way he always knew. He felt it in his gut. The trauma of that night and the regular darkness of his everyday life kept him grounded.

Jess more harshly picked her cuticles.

It took three seconds for the elevator to open. Three seconds for Dave to feel the sweat on his fingers, the ache of his nerves, the echo of his breath. He contemplated death and murder. It was him or Ted tonight. They couldn't both survive.

He immediately left the elevator and felt Jess hesitate to follow. Nonetheless, she was right behind him. They stood side by side.

Lawyers sat at a long, oval table in the glass conference room. They were stiff, glancing at each other, as sweat dripped down their foreheads. They were shocked to see the two teenagers. They obviously recognized Jess. Their terrified gazes were glued to her presence as if they could somehow will her to disappear, get her away from the danger. Celebratory champagne had been poured. The bottle was next to a partially cut cake and a fruit plate. A cork lay in the corner.

Ted leaned on the doorframe. He looked the same as Dave remembered, older though with graying hair and pale, probably due to living in a prison cell. He was less angry and more amused with a gun in one hand and a match in the other. He must've heard the elevator. They should've taken the stairs.

"Oh my God," Jess whispered. "Is that-"

Dave looked down. Gasoline smothered the floor. Why didn't he see it when they came in? The soles of his boots were drenched. Jess's ankles were covered. It smelled like home. *Dad always did have a tendency for drama.*

"Glad you could come," Ted chuckled. "And you brought a guest!"

His father's laugh sent shivers up Dave's spine. Jess shifted on her feet but stayed beside him. She kept her eyes on Ted and her hand behind her back. Dave couldn't tell what she was doing. He stayed focused on his dad.

"Got the invite," He kept his voice blank, no emotion. "Thanks for that by the way."

"Well, I figured a family reunion was in order." Ted gestured to Jess with the gun. She stiffened and Dave put his arm in front of her. He felt oddly protective of her. This was his mess, not hers, he didn't want her to get hurt.

His dad laughed. "Her family's here too," his amusement became quiet anger, a threat he couldn't wait to act on. "Aren't they?"

"What?"

"Yeah. I saw a photo of her on one of the desks. Wait, let me guess! Peace, right? I'd never forget that name." Ted twirled into the conference room and walked around the table. He went to a woman in a black pantsuit. Her brown hair was short. Ted put the gun against her head and she whimpered. The man next to her stared at Jess, ready to jump through the glass and shield her.

"Mom," Jess whispered. "Dad."

"This is the bitch who helped lock me up!" Ted laughed. He tightened his fist on the woman's hair and smiled at her tears. "Of course, she couldn't have done that if you hadn't turned me in," he gestured to Dave with his gun. "Guess I've got a lot of people to be mad at." He waved the gun above his head. "It's hard to focus on just one!"

Dave kept his arm in front of Jess. He was frozen, waiting but ready. "What are you gonna do?"

He heard a beep. He glanced back. Jess was holding her phone behind his back. She had dialed a nine so far. Two more numbers to go. Her hands were shaking. He needed to buy her time. If she called the police, maybe they'd come and cause a distraction. They'd catch Ted's attention and Dave could take his shot.

Ted left the woman sobbing in her seat. He waved his gun at Jess's dad and came to the door. He bobbed his head in thought and wiggled the gun. His unstable act didn't fool Dave. Ted was as sharp as he ever was, lazy and careless but prepared. He had a plan. He always had a plan.

Dave lowered his arm, slowly reaching for his holster.

Ted shot his gun in the air. Jess gasped and dropped her phone. It splashed in the gasoline and automatically dialed. Did she get the two other numbers in?

"Hey, Jess," a voice glitched.

"Alice! Help! We're at the Adler Building and-"

Ted shot the phone. Jess screamed and jolted sideways. Gunshot. Dave turned his head. Wide-eyed, he looked at the girl next to him. She was frozen, her face as white as a snowflake. Red liquid seeped through her yellow top. Time slowed. Her eyes, blank and distant, drifted to Dave.

She stumbled and the gasoline splashed. Her parents' screams echoed. They were so far away.

Dave ended up behind Jess. He hooked his arms under hers and helped her fall. His knees splashed, jeans drenched in the gasoline. Her blood mixed with it, copper and car exhaust. Her gasps were shallow but her eyes were open. She was alive for now.

Ted laughed. "Poor girl. She won't get to feel the heat."

"Bastard!" Mister Peace stood up. "You sick son of a-"

Ted scraped the match in one swift motion. Tiny flames danced on its tip. Dave glanced at the lawyers and looked at the girl with the pink hair. She'd die in his arms. They were all about to die.

Ted dropped the match.

***

Bobby

Bobby nervously played with the sequins on her tutu. She shook her head and willed the tears to stay away. What was the worst part? Dying or what came after? Were heaven and hell real? If so, where would she go?

"One minute," Casey fiddled with her necklace. Her leg bounced along to the constant tapping of her foot. Bobby hated the fact that Casey was nervous, it meant things were bad, really bad. She should've told Casey and Tommy to leave when they had the chance but they'd never listen.

Tommy typed as fast as he could, sweat dripping from his brow. His hands were so fluid on the keyboard. The screen was filled with blinking letters and symbols Bobby didn't understand. She found comfort in the confusion.

"Guys..." she whispered.

Casey looked out the kitchen window. "They're aiming."

"When did Height City National get digital security!" Tommy yelled. "Seriously!"

Casey went over to him.

Bobby stood between the kitchen and the living room. Automatics were aimed all along her front lawn. The men were ready. The van was on the street. The same street where Vincent taught Bobby to ride a bike. She was so happy to finally get rid of the training wheels. The wind had been cold. The sun had been warm. Her dad's proud laughter mixed with the sadness of letting go. She hoped, wherever he was, Johnny would choke on that stolen money.

"I can't believe this," Tommy shouted. "This is ridiculous-"

"Duck now, complain later," Casey said.

Bobby turned to them. "Guys-"

The windows shattered. The glass shards were sharp and sparkly, raining alongside the bullets. Tommy spun on his knees, grabbed Casey, and yanked her to the floor. He held her with one arm and covered his head with the other. She folded her body close to his.

Drywall cracked. Picture frames fell. Dishes broke. A bullet plunged into Bobby's shoulder. Her blood splattered across a drawing she made in first grade. The faded memories of late-night popcorn, dressed-up dolls, jumping on the bed, pillow fights, dance parties, and falling asleep in her dad's arms were destroyed by a hurricane of gunshots.

The next bullet hit her thigh. The world spun, blurring in a sea of dreams and foolish hope. She plummeted to the floor. A rainbow glimmered against the glass shards next to her. *Gorgeous.*

***

Casey

Deafening silence.

The thunder ended, and Casey lifted her head. Tommy's arm protectively hugged her torso. Their bodies were stuck together like two sardines in a can. She felt his anxious heartbeat beside hers.

"You okay?" he whispered.

She nodded. She shifted onto her hands and knees. His arm fell away from her body. He brushed the pieces of drywall from his hair. His computer was in pieces. Everything was in pieces. The floor was covered in a sea of bullets and glass. The couch was shredded and the coffee table was broken in half.

Bobby lay a few feet from them, her body still and her eyes closed. Blood pooled underneath her, drenching her hair and staining her skin. There was too much blood, Casey couldn't tell where it was coming from. She couldn't tell if Bobby was breathing.

"She isn't." Casey glanced out the window's empty frame. The men were coming to make sure they finished the job. Tommy sat up. He yanked his hoodie off and revealed a solid-colored T-shirt. He crawled to Bobby and attended to her wounds.

"She's got a pulse," he said. "It's weak but it's there."

Casey grabbed the gun she lost in the hurricane. She stayed low. Her boots didn't make a sound as she hurried across the kitchen floor. She hid between the window and the front door.

Five pairs of footsteps.

Tommy worked expertly on Bobby's wounds. She looked dead. Bobby was a lot to handle but she was Casey's safety net made of sunshine. She couldn't lose her.

She adjusted her grip. What was left of the door crashed off its hinges and a man stepped inside. She aimed. Blood splattered on the wall and a piece of his skull shattered on the floor. He dropped.

She stepped over his body. *One down, four to go.*

They aimed their guns but it was too late. She shot one and used him as a shield. The bullets flew into his standing corpse. Blood showered the porch, droplets scattered in her hair, and decorated her clothes. *Three down, two to go.* Splinters flew against her face, chopped by gunshots.

She dropped the body and aimed, fast. Twin holes in their foreheads. Their bodies fell, sprawled out on the grass like slaughtered lawn gnomes. Five down. No Austin. He must've made a run for it, knowing he couldn't beat Cece. He'd tell Markinson everything.

This would take some explaining.

She ran back into the house. Tommy knelt beside Bobby. His hoodie was drenched in her blood. He held it against her wounds and pumped her heart, impressively calm.

"Call an ambulance," he said. "Now!"

***

Alice

Alice ran as fast as she could, legs aching. The night was somewhat cold but the adrenaline pumping through her veins and the fear in her heartbeat kept her warm. Jess's scream had been faint and glitchy but the gunshot was clear.

Orange light radiated the ink black sky. It would've been beautiful if it weren't so horrific. She heard the terrified screams before she saw the people. Hundreds of civilians stood on the sidewalk across from the Adler Building, recording every moment of the nightmare with their phones and cameras.

One sobbing woman screamed out for her husband, begging the police to let her through, so she could see if he was alright. Another man was crouched beside his two little kids, covering their eyes, as he watched the flames flicker and dance.

The police kept everyone away, so the EMTs and firemen had room to work. The EMTs used oxygen masks and smoke ventilation to help those the firemen had carried out of the danger. They shouted orders to each other, spraying the rageful flames with bursts of water but there was no way they could put it out.

At best, they were only buying a few seconds' worth of valuable time.

The Adler Building was engulfed in heat and screams. Every single floor was filled with flames waving in the windows and ripping apart the already crumbling walls.

Whoa, Alice gulped. She searched the crowds for her best friend but the only familiar face she saw was Savanna Ann.

Savanna Ann, the Channel Six reporter, stood in the middle of the street, facing a news van and camera crew. Curly wisps of black hair framed her tan skin. She wore a white pantsuit with a gray skirt. Her nails were perfectly manicured and her makeup was professionally done. "That's right, folks, what you see behind me is the largest fire Height City has seen in years. The last fire of this magnitude caused hundreds of casualties and it looks like this one will take even more lives."

Alice didn't see Jess.

She was still in the fire. The entire Peace family could be bacon and there was nothing Alice could do. Her heart thumped. She'd lose her best friend forever. Her best friend was going to die. Her heart hammered. Panic took control, energy surged in her eyes, and lightning flickered between her fingers. Her powers were ready, desperate to be used. *Maybe I can do something.*

She pushed away her doubts, her fear, and uncertainty. She didn't need that now. She had to act.

She rushed into an empty alley a few buildings from the crowds and fire. She glanced around to make sure no one could see her. The heat of the fire surged through the city's streets like a cancer, it made her palms sweat but she ignored it. Intense energy drifted through her body, speeding up as it coursed through her bones and muscles until she couldn't feel anything else. Her body burst like a glass bulb shattering because of too much power, a much needed deep breath.

She launched off the ground. Deadly orange light blurred the faces below, causing the chaos to melt, the screams silenced by disaster. What did the people see? Alice imagined herself as a fantastic lightning bolt shooting across the sky.

The flames, heat, and smoke got denser as she got closer. She knew what floor the law firm was on. She'd gone there once or twice to meet Jess. Bennett gave her a tour.

Alice punched through the windows, smashing them to pieces and a million glass shards skidded across the floor. Crouching on one knee, her body reformed. Dazzling flames caged her in, angry and chaotic, clawing at her skin. They looped and twirled, burning chairs, tables, and magazines, everything.

The lawyers were contained in the conference room. The glass acted as a shield against the fire. They were unconscious but alive. Layla and Bennett lay by the door, bodies pointing toward their daughter.

Jess's clothes - a long sleeve, yellow top, and a long, jean skirt - were soaked in blood and gasoline. She looked frail, still. Was she breathing? Dave lay beside her, unconscious. His hands were painted in her blood. He had tried to stop the bleeding.

Alice yanked her hood over her head in the hopes it would protect her. She covered her nose and mouth with her sleeve, coughing. Smoke shredded against her lungs, stealing her breath.

There were too many people to save. She couldn't get them all out in time. There had to be others on different floors. People she couldn't see who needed their lives saved. People with families, loved ones, children, homes, neighborhoods, jobs, hobbies. She couldn't leave them. She needed to think of something that'd save them all. And fast.

The sprinklers weren't on. It was an automatic system, they should've turned on the moment the fire started. Someone must've turned them off somehow. If she triggered one, maybe the others would start. *Maybe.* It was a lot of lives to risk on a maybe. Did she have a choice?

The spigots were connected to metal pipes wrapped in wire. She wiped the sweat from her forehead and tried to ignore the burning sensations threatening to peel off her skin. Smoke stung her lungs and protective tears shielded her eyes. She punched her hands into the air, electricity blasted from her fingertips and rageful power squeezed her insides. It tore at her organs and clenched her muscles.

It was the most power she ever used.

Broken lights exploded. Sharp glass shards rained above her, shimmering in the flames. Fire mixed with lightning. A war between allies. Her power overwhelmed the system. Wires sparked and spigots turned: thunderstorm.

Her knees buckled and her arms went numb. She felt as light as a paper bag, empty and sore. Her battery was drained, exhaustion seized her limbs. She needed to sleep for a thousand years.

The flames died, slowly diminishing in the water. Her sweatshirt clung to her skin while her hair twisted in clumsy, wet strands. Alice didn't care. Everyone was safe, including her friends. She saved them.

Jess and Dave still lay beside each other, drenched in blood and gasoline, but they were alive. Any second now, the EMTs and firemen would rush out of the stairwell and attend to Jess's wounds. She'd be okay. She had to be okay.

Alice turned toward the broken windows, too tired to stand. Her vision blurred at the edges, she was seconds away from passing out. Height City was a distant shadow, not a single artificial light was on for miles, more than six blocks had lost power. Did she do that?

Millions of beautiful stars surrounded a mysterious full moon hovering above the city. It'd been a while since Alice saw the sky so clearly.

She chuckled. *Wow.*

***

Jess

Thoughts swirled in Jess's mind. Surgical masks, blue gloves, and complicated-looking machines faded in and out of her blackening vision. Cold air tickled her skin. She couldn't think. It was all blurry and faint, miles away from wherever she was. She couldn't focus. She could barely stay awake. She couldn't stay awake.

When she finally regained consciousness, she realized she was in a hospital room. The bed was lumpy, uncomfortable, and the gown she wore was thin. Too thin, she felt naked. Her body hurt. She couldn't tell what part of her body was more sore. An IV peeked through the many bandages wrapped around her right arm. Her left arm was bandaged too.

She turned her head on the overly fluffed pillow. She expected to see someone else. Maybe her mom would be armed with an angry but caring lecture or her dad would be clutching her hand, desperate for her to wake up. Instead, Dave sat at her bedside, tapping his thigh.

"Where..." her thoughts were jumbled and slow. She couldn't remember how she got there. She couldn't remember anything after the gunshot. How did they survive?

He sat up. "You're awake."

"My parents," she groaned. "Where are they?"

"They're getting treated for burns and smoke intake."

His arms were bandaged like hers. The shadows under his eyes made him look exhausted. There was guilt in his eyes as if he had done something wrong. Did he think he was the reason for what happened? She remembered that he tried to protect her. He never wanted her to get hurt.

She felt the bullet wound in her skin, the sore edges, and the stitches. The giant bandage covered half her belly. It couldn't be worse. She thought it would've hurt more but the nurses probably gave her some sort of pain-relief drug. Which liquid in what IV bag? There were five.

"I'm sorry, princess," Dave said. "I should've taken the shot."

"It's not your fault," she whispered. "I don't blame you for hesitating. He's your dad. It couldn't have been easy for you."

His eyes widened. Was he surprised? Did he expect her to yell at him? She couldn't feel anger right now. She couldn't feel much of anything. There were too many medications floating through her veins, making her feel nothing but exhaustion, but her tired thoughts were crystal clear. She couldn't blame Dave for what happened. Ted was his father, that meant something. She would've been more worried if it had been easy for him to kill Ted. Dave was a good person despite his terrible first impression.

He took a deep, shaky breath and chuckled, relieved. He gestured to her belly. "You had about four surgeries, you know? It's been intense."

"You waited here?" She didn't expect him to take an interest in her recovery or her life, for that matter.

"Yeah. I had to get treated for the fire and um," Dave shrugged. "Another friend is here... and... I... I," he leaned forward, elbows on his knees. He reached out and gently touched her fingers, enough to show he was worried about her. "I wanted to know you were okay."

She took a deep breath. It hurt. "I'm okay."

"Do you mind if I stick around? Just till your parents kick me out."

"Sure," she smiled. "You can stay."

***

Alice

Alice sat in the hall outside Jess's room. Her skin was pale. There were bags under her eyes and she'd been napping on and off all night. The doctors checked her but there was nothing wrong with her. She just needed to sleep for a few days. She texted her dad but he never answered. She didn't know where he was.

"Al," Cece had pieces of Bobby's shattered porch and droplets of blood in her hair. She and Tommy were at the hospital when Alice and Dave arrived with Jess. They gave the highlights of what happened at Bobby's house, the shooting, and Markinson's men. It seemed like a crazy day for everyone.

"Is Bobby okay?"

"She's still in surgery. This isn't about her, you need to see something."

Cece helped Alice stand up. They went to an empty waiting room with dingy wallpaper and a bad diaper smell. An old, heavy TV from the nineties was bolted to the ceiling.

Savanna Ann was on the screen, standing next to a picture of the Adler Building Fire. The volume was off but the headline read: LIGHTNING BOLT SPOTTED. Of course, people saw Alice. How stupid could she be? She never considered the consequences of stopping the fire, of revealing herself to the entire city.

"Okay..." she sighed. It was hard to focus, she had a headache. "So.."

"I called Betty to cover up those Markinson men's deaths and..." Cece shoved her hands in her jeans pockets. "She mentioned this. Rumors are already spreading about the next Glisin."

"The next... Me?" Alice chuckled in disbelief. "I'm not... I'm not-"

"You used your powers in public, given for a good reason but people talk," Cece said. "Destroyer and her gang of misfit toys are the only openly powered people around here. People are scared of them and your mom could fight them. They think you're gonna take up her mantle."

"Me?" she asked. "But..."

Alice shook her head. She never seriously thought about being a superhero, being like her mother. It didn't seem possible. Height City was littered with corruption and crime, murder and chaos, hate and shadows. She couldn't be its sign of hope. She didn't even know the extent of her powers. How could she consider fighting for the city when she didn't know her limits?

"I'm not my mom. I can't be. I just wanted to save Jess."

"They don't know that," Cece pointed to the TV. "Height City wants a new hero."

Alice's head hurt too much, she couldn't think about this now. She could barely stay awake. Her eyelids were heavy, her muscles were numb, and her stomach had folded in on itself. She was starving, she needed food and a long nap. "I can't do this right now. I feel like crap."

"Yeah," Cece said. "You look it too."

Alice rolled her eyes. "Gee, thanks."

They headed to the hall outside Jess's room. The floors were white, textured tile and the walls were painted the same color. It'd make you dizzy if you stared too long. Did sick people have a smell? It wasn't clear but disinfectant definitely did. Nurses wore scrubs printed with different patterns and the doctors looked identical in their lab coats.

Tommy met the girls at a row of chairs across from the door to Jess's room. He'd gone off with his laptop. Alice wasn't sure where he went or what he'd been doing. He rubbed his eyes. He looked tired, so did Cece. He wrapped his arm around her, either using her to comfort himself or trying to comfort her. She leaned her head on his shoulder, and he kissed her forehead.

"Did you do it?" she asked.

"They got their money. They'll leave her alone," he said. "She'll be out of surgery soon. Did Betty punish you for killing those guys?"

"No, but Markinson is gonna be pissed," she clicked her tongue. "Betty will take care of it."

"She always does."

"No kidding."

"Food!" Cole dropped two big, brown paper bags on the chair next to Alice. She saw several foam boxes in each bag, all labeled with the same neat handwriting. The smell of french fries made Alice's stomach grumble. She didn't know it was possible to be so hungry.

She crinkled her eyebrows. "How'd you know we were here?"

"Tommy called," Cole said. "I thought you guys would be hungry."

Tommy plopped down in the chair on Alice's other side. Cece sat on his knee and leaned against his shoulder, arm around his neck. He kept her steady with one arm around her waist. Cece never looked more relaxed than when she was in his arms. It was nice to see her at ease.

Cole handed Tommy a Monte Cristo and gave Cece two BLTs. One of which had a note with Bobby's name on it.

"What are you doing here?" Dave came from Jess's room. He'd been there, covered in sweat and guilt, during Jess's surgeries. He gave Alice a vague explanation of what happened and didn't say another word. He stared into the distance, distracted by the memories replaying in his head. Alice didn't blame him for what happened. She knew it wasn't his fault. His many apologies proved how guilty he felt.

Hopefully, Jess didn't blame him either.

"Pancakes for you," Cole handed him a box. "I figured if we're gonna camp here then we need supplies."

"Good idea," Tommy said. "Thanks."

Cece ate a french fry. "So, your dad skipped town, huh?"

"Seems like it," Dave sat next to her and Tommy. "He always comes up with an escape route," he tapped two fingers on the box in his hands. "I figure Betty paid him and he ran."

"Johnny too," Tommy said. "Facial recognition isn't picking either of them up."

Cece lifted another fry in celebration. "Good riddance."

Alice slapped it with her own french fry. She dipped it in a puddle of ketchup and tossed it in her mouth. Cole got her a cheeseburger with everything on it. She wouldn't have chosen anything different. She bit into the burger. Her friends ate their food and talked about the events of the day, catching each other up on everything that had happened. Alice felt good. She felt happy.

"Where'd you get the food?" Dave asked. "It's not from Buddy, is it?"

"I got it from Linda," Cole said. "She sends her love."

Part 2

Chapter 9

Alice

"ALICE!" MASON YELLED. HE made his anger clear yet he wouldn't stop following her around the house. When she was four and didn't want to wear pajama bottoms, he'd chase her until he caught her. He'd blow a raspberry on her belly and call her a troublemaker. This time it couldn't be made into a game.

She spent the summer living with Cece in Eddie's basement. He didn't know they were there but she visited him when her dad wasn't around. She didn't tell Mason where she was. He didn't care until the Adler Building Fire. The story was on every news channel for weeks. The lightning bolt was a featured part. Of course, he knew it was her. He started calling her after that but she never answered. She did text him to tell him she was okay, which was more than he ever did.

"I don't want to talk to you!" Alice yelled. "Leave it alone!"

"I can't leave it alone. You know that. You used your powers in public!" he said. "That wasn't just stupid and reckless, it was dangerous! Someone could have found out-"

"I know!" she faced him. "But Jess was gonna die. Her entire family was gonna die along with a bunch of other people. I had to do something! I *could* do something."

"You could have died!" he said. The last part of that sentence dangled silently between them. *You could have died like your mother did.* Susan used to say Alice looked exactly like Mason when she was angry, they had the same crease between their eyebrows, the same scowl, and the same pout in their chin. Right now, they were probably twins.

"We need to talk about this idea you have about moving in with your teacher," he said. "And you need to tell me where you've been the last three months."

"Staying with a friend. I came home to get more clothes and-"

"And what?" Mason crossed his arms. "You're going to stay with a man you barely know? Isn't he your math teacher?"

"You don't even know why I left, do you?" She tried to hide the unevenness in her tone. Tears creeped up behind her eyes but she didn't let them flow. She needed to stay calm if she was going to win this argument.

He took a deep breath and sighed. "I assumed it was about your mom-"

"No. No, it was about you." Anger made her muscles tense. She wanted to scream at him, to make him feel her pain. "You never came home. I was left here all alone. You don't drive me to school. You're always drunk. You get mad when I try to talk to you about her! About anything!"

It was great to finally say the things she'd felt for so long. A weight lifted off her shoulders. But it felt like a betrayal. This was her dad. A man she loved and admired. He read her bedtime stories and taught her how to ice skate. He played basketball with her and taught her how to dunk. He helped name her stuffed animals. He was the only family she had left but he was too fractured to care about her.

"I needed time," he said. "It's been hard without her-"

"I know," she cried. "That's why I needed you."

His face fell into grief and guilt. He couldn't look her in the eye. She wanted him to say something, to give her an explanation for his actions and choices, maybe some promises about getting better, even if they were a lie. She needed to know he loved her. Or did that die with Susan too?

He was silent, unsure of what to say. Alice rolled her sweatshirt sleeve over her fist and pushed her hair behind her ear. She wiped her tears and nodded. She wasn't going to get what she wanted from him. She wasn't going to get the answers she needed or the empty promises she'd settle for.

"Mister Scotts drove me to school and home most of last year," she sniffled. "Now he's offered me a room at his loft. He said he'd love to talk to you about it but um, I'm taking it whether you like it or not because... I," she silenced her sobs, acting strong despite the fact her heart was breaking. "I'm not supposed to be alone in this, Dad."

She searched his eyes. What would he say? Would he make this harder than it had to be? Would he make her stay?

"Okay," he whispered, defeated.

She didn't hope for a different answer, so why did it hurt so much? If he didn't want to be her father again, that was fine. She couldn't watch him fall apart anymore. If he wanted to stay in this misery, he could do it alone.

They stared at each other, hollow love between them.

"I can just back out and close the door." Cece stood at the front door. Alice didn't hear her come in. Did she pick the lock again and come in without permission? She stood there, waiting for an answer.

Alice shook her head and wiped her nose. "No, we're done. Come on in."

"Who's this?" Mason asked.

"I'm Cece."

"She's the friend I've been staying with," Alice said. "You guys have actually met."

"Yeah, around this time last year," Cece chuckled. "I helped Al and Eddie shove you in his car and you threw up on my shoes."

He cleared his throat, embarrassed.

Alice almost felt bad. What did he think of her friend? Cece wore ripped jeans and a gray, cropped T-shirt under her leather jacket. Her blue hair was falling out of a black, spider-clip at the back of her head. Her silver, angel wing necklace hung placidly on her neck. She looked like a Burrower.

"She's here to help me pack," Alice said. "Mister Scotts's son will be here in a little bit, so if you're not at the bottom of a bottle by then, I'll introduce you."

His frown tightened. He didn't counter the bold statement, probably because he couldn't. Mason usually started drinking right at noon or sooner, depending on the day.

He went into the kitchen.

Alice led Cece to her bedroom and closed the door. She grabbed her camera and set it on the desk.

Cece hopped on the bed, body bouncing against the mattress. She looked at the Glisin poster, then at the family photo on the nightstand, chuckling. "Who would've thought an ordinary housewife was a superhero?"

"Apparently, nobody." Alice grabbed the photo. Her mom and her dad looked so happy in it. Mason might as well have been a different person then. She dropped it in her suitcase, which lay at the bottom of her bed filled with folded clothes, a toothbrush, a hairbrush, her original photos, a baseball cap, and her phone and computer chargers.

"You know, I think that night he puked on B's shoes," Cece said. "I took them 'cause we were fighting. It made her so mad."

Alice smiled. She appreciated Cece being there for her over the summer. They had a great time as roommates, watching movies, gossiping about the Burrows, and getting takeout. The couch was surprisingly comfortable. They also hung out at Cole and Dave's apartment, which was fun. The boys seemed to enjoy their company. She'd hang out with Jess in the day while Cece trained and did jobs for Betty, and she'd hang out in the Burrows at night. The perfect in-between.

"Thank you for everything."

"Of course," Cece shrugged. "It'll be nice to have my own place again though." She made it clear that Alice was welcome to crash at Eddie's basement for as long as she needed but staying with Betty Beater's champion proved to be troublesome. "When's Leo coming to pick you up?"

"I'm not sure but I have to be ready by then," Alice crouched down. She flipped the suitcase's lid and tried to zip it shut. It wouldn't budge. It was too full. She was bringing anything she thought she might need or want. She didn't want to have to come back home if she didn't need to. It'd be easier to stay away rather than come and go. She groaned.

Cece smiled. "I could sit on it."

"Or I could get a second suitcase." Alice left the room. She could see Mason downstairs in the dining room, sitting at the table with a beer in one hand and a bottle opener in the other. She didn't wait to see if he'd drink it. She pulled the cord to the attic and the ladder unfolded.

"Since when do you have an attic?" Cece asked.

"Since we moved here."

They climbed through the square hole in the ceiling.

Dusty chairs from an antique dining room set were piled in one corner but the table was missing. Black, metal file cabinets filled with important papers were next to an old ping-pong table leaning against the wall. Alice went through a big ping-pong player phase when she was ten, she and Mason played almost every day for two months. He'd use his left hand, so she'd win easier. His old laz-E-boy recliner was in another corner, it had torn leather and stained cushions. When Alice was two, she got the flu and puked all over it.

Boxes were everywhere, each labeled with a different sticky note; Wedding china from Susan and Mason's casual, backyard barbeque reception. Vases from Susan's first attempts at pottery. Yearbooks from Mason and Susan's youth and favorite toys from their childhoods, including the baby doll Susan gave Alice when she was five. Susan loved pretending to take care of it when she was a kid but Alice was never really interested in baby dolls. Other items were scattered around the attic like old cassette tapes, Susan's Walkman, a CD player, and the golf clubs Mason never used.

Mason and Susan were pack rats when it came to their pasts.

At six, Alice convinced herself a monster lived in their attic. She kept hearing noises at night, which turned out to be a bat. Mason chased it around the attic, swinging a broom at it until the bat flew out the window, screeching at him. It took three days to clean the mess Mason and the bat had created. Susan laughed so hard at his heroic act.

Alice missed hearing her mother's wild, noticeable laughter.

"There should be a suitcase here somewhere."

***

Casey

Alice started her search. She was so comfortable surrounded by her family's history. Casey liked the old mementos of a once happy family. She couldn't believe people kept everything from their lives. Other than her necklace, she barely had anything to treasure. She didn't know what it was to have a family, let alone possessions that resembled unconditional love. She wasn't sure it really existed. It was an act people put on for good measure.

An antique, Tiffany lamp with a colorfully tiled shade sat on one of the boxes. It looked like it should be in an old mansion, not a cramped townhouse in the Nests. Casey rubbed the lamp as if it were magic. It looked like it could be. *Damn, no genie.* She was disappointed.

There were a lot of antiques and random boxes in the attic, most of which seemed meaningless but not to Alice. For her, each item held a memory she never wanted to forget. Casey didn't know what it was like to lose a family, she never felt that safety or love. She wished for it almost every night when she was a kid but she learned the hard way that wishes didn't come true. Magic didn't exist.

Her bruised fingers glided over a dusty, pleated gown. It was a soft pastel green with spaghetti strap sleeves and a fitted waist, a cross between a sundress and a ballgown. Simple and sweet. She lifted it to her torso and pressed the back against her chest.

She turned to the large, antique mirror sitting against the wall. Its thin, gold-painted frame sparkled in the sunlight fluttering through the half-closed shutters in the window. The mirror was broken in several places, every piece was held together by pure willpower. Casey's shattered reflection mimicked her movements.

***

Alice

Alice turned to search another area. She swore there was a suitcase somewhere.

Cece stood in front of the antique, Adeline mirror Alice's grandmother gifted Mason and Susan for their ten-year wedding anniversary. Susan's mom owned an antique shop, she sent things she thought the family might enjoy. Susan didn't talk about her mother. The few details Alice knew about her grandmother weren't enough to imagine an entire person, let alone a family member.

Alice knew Cece hadn't shared everything about her life due to gaps in her stories. It was harder for her to keep certain things a secret since they became roommates but that didn't stop her from trying. Cece still had demons she didn't want to share. Alice didn't want to push too far. She trusted that Cece would come to her when she was ready.

"She wore it to her senior prom," Alice gestured to the gown Cece was holding.

Cece froze. She spread the gown against her body, acting as if it were made of porcelain. The fabric was bumpy against her leather jacket. It would've looked

177

beautiful on her. Cece's reflection was in pieces, broken beyond repair, she had never looked more honest.

She turned and dropped the gown on the floor. "What?"

Alice smiled. "My mom. That was her prom dress."

"A superhero and a prom queen," Cece said. "What couldn't she do?"

"She actually was prom queen," Alice chuckled. "The crown is here somewhere. It's plastic and bedazzled."

"That was supposed to be a joke. Didn't know it was true." Cece crouched down to pick up the gown. She paused, head turned toward a pile of boxes hidden under a fuzzy, plaid blanket from Mason's childhood bedroom. The boxes weren't labeled. Alice assumed they were filled with her dad's stuff.

"Al." Cece poked her finger through a hole in the corner of one of the boxes. She ripped and clawed at the cardboard until a bunch of brown leather journals spilled out onto the floor.

Alice had never seen them before. She knelt beside the pile and picked up one of the journals. She ran her fingers over the soft spine. The name Smith and the number three were sketched on it. Whoever had hidden the journals didn't want them to be found.

Cece held up the journal she had grabbed. It had the same name on it but a different number. "Smith as in John?"

Alice shook her head. "Susan Smith. My mom's maiden name."

"So, these are your mom's?" Cece said. "Must've skinned a lot of cows."

Alice flipped through the journal's worn, rough pages, which were blank except for the dates at the top. Black ink. She grabbed another, then another. Every single one was the same, blank with dates at the top. Different numbers were sketched on each spine. "Why would she have a bunch of blank journals? It doesn't make any sense."

Cece held up an open journal and tapped the date. "They're not blank."

"What? Invisible ink?"

"Hey, the woman was Glisin," Cece clicked her tongue. "Maybe her identity wasn't her only secret."

***

Dave

"If you have a membership here, does that mean you're a Honeycomber?" Tommy asked. He and El had been chatting since they got in the car.

Dave walked between them. He asked them to come for moral support in case he needed backup. They were at the Height City country club, exclusive to the rich, powerful, and snobby. Honeycomber territory.

Markinson had a membership.

"My dad's a crime lord. I'm pretty sure I'm a full-blown Burrower." El wore a black bikini and her hair was looped in a bun. She had a scar on the knee that Casey had broken. It took two surgeries for it to heal. Her dad sent her to a physical therapy center after the fight, it took months for her to finally walk again.

She wasn't angry about what happened. She went to The Arena, she knew the risks.

The smell of her bubblegum lipstick mixed with the chlorine-scented water. The pool was a giant, rectangular-shaped hole surrounded by white, wicker beach chairs. Some had umbrellas, others didn't.

Some middle school aged kids were playing water volleyball, splashing and laughing. A few Honeycomber boys about Dave's age were dunking each other underwater. He swore he recognized one of them as a customer he had last year. A group of girls lay on several big, donut-shaped floaties, tanning their smooth skin.

A brick path led to the outdoor bar. Several Honeycomber adults were chatting and laughing, sipping smoothies with fancy fruit and straws. They were probably talking about the vacations they had taken over the summer or when their next big party was going to be, whatever rich people talked about.

"I'm really not up to date on the rules," Tommy said.

El chuckled. "You can have my copy of the guidelines."

"Appreciate it," he said.

Sweat slid between Dave's fingers. He wanted to blame the hot day, the sun beaming down against his face and body, but when he saw the girl sitting in the lifeguard stand, the uneasiness in his nerves strengthened and he knew the sun wasn't to blame.

Jess wore a white one-piece bathing suit that hugged her delicate curves. Her hair was tied in a side ponytail, her pink streaks spiraled along her shoulder, and Wayfarer sunglasses were balanced above her forehead. A yellow umbrella shaded her from the sun. A book lay on her bare legs.

Dave couldn't help but smile when he saw her.

He visited her in the hospital almost every day. He'd sneak in when her parents weren't there. At first, it was to check on her, to make sure she was okay and Ted didn't ruin her life or her health, but then it became about her company. Dave learned things about her; the way her face lit up when she learned something new; the way she laughed at a joke; how focused she became while reading a book; how determined she was to succeed at everything; how easy it was to talk with her.

Dave never expected to like her but he did. He liked her in a way he had never liked a girl before. He didn't realize how far he had fallen for her until she was released from the hospital and they didn't speak for most of the summer. Not seeing her, not teasing her, or speaking to her drove him crazy.

"There's the entire reason you brought us there," El said, pointing at Jess. She wasn't offended when Dave asked to come with her to the country club. It wasn't weird for him, why would it be weird for her? They were friends first. When he told her why he wanted to go into Honeycomber territory, she laughed and teased him about liking a rich girl.

"There's a lot of Honeycombers here," he said. He was already really nervous and the presence of so many Honeycombers didn't help. It was good to know he wasn't alone.

"That's why we're here," Tommy patted Dave's shoulder. "For moral support... and a burger." He knew about Dave's crush before Dave did. When Dave recruited him to come to the country club, Tommy's exact words were *Finally, you figured it out*, which was annoying on multiple levels.

"Exactly," El said. "Besides, she's just a girl. I'm a girl and we dated. Hell, you were completely comfortable with me." She raised her eyebrows suggestively.

Dave rolled his eyes. "Thanks for that."

"I didn't need to hear that either," Tommy said.

El laughed at their discomfort, elbowing Dave's shoulder. "I'm sure you'll be fine."

"Excuse me?" Brittany Mikes asked. She wore a pink, frilly bikini and wedge sandals. Her long, reddish-blonde hair hung over her shoulders and waist, half clipped behind her head. Dave recognized her from not only the pictures on Jess's phone but also from the news. Her family was famous in Height City and her father, Mayor Mikes, was one of Betty's secret employees. He took office after Destroyer killed Mayor Porter, the night Glisin died.

"Hey," Brittany chuckled. "My friend and I are doing dares and this is stupid." Her flirty smile and seductive stare were focused on Tommy. "She dared me to come and ask for your number." She gestured to Cindy Cohen across the pool.

Cindy wore a plaid one-piece bathing suit and no shoes. She waved to the group, laughing.

Dave smiled. *This will be entertaining.*

"Uh... I have a girlfriend," Tommy said. "Sorry."

"I thought you were undecided," El teased. "But you have been together for a really long time."

"Practically forever," Dave said. "It's kind of weird."

"Yeah," El nodded.

Tommy glanced between them, annoyed. "Okay, shut up."

"I just need your number to win the game," Brittany said. "It doesn't even have to be your number, I mean, nothing has to happen. I could have anyone -"

"You're doing great so far," El gave a thumbs-up.

Dave laughed. "Maybe next she'll use the flexible line. It's very popular."

Brittany glanced at him and El. Her annoyed frown signaled how much she hated being made fun of. Dave couldn't blame her, they weren't being very kind, but he was enjoying himself. The nervousness he'd been feeling about talking to Jess had lessened and the knot in his stomach had untwisted. He felt a little more ready to brave asking her out on a date.

"Who are they?" Brittany asked with venomous disgust.

"Well," Tommy sighed, pointing to Dave. "One's the bane of my existence-"

Dave nudged El's arm. "Hear that? I got a promotion."

"Congratulations," she said. "I'll bake a cake."

"Listen, I'm flattered but I'm already with someone," Tommy said. "Sorry."

"Alright," Brittany shrugged. She looked at El like she wanted to rip out her hair but she looked at Dave like she was trying to figure out whether or not he was worth her time. It was hard to tell what she thought of either of them. Did she hate them? Was she threatened by them? Dave wondered if Jess had told Brittany about him, if so, what did she say?

The tension in Tommy's shoulders eased as soon as Brittany was gone. He would never betray Casey or their relationship, he loved her even though he hadn't told her. He slapped Dave's head, unamused by his and El's teasing.

Dave rubbed the wound but laughed at Tommy's annoyed expression.

They went to three unattended beach chairs. El dropped her purse on the one with an umbrella and rubbed the fresh bruises on her neck. Ever since she got back to the city, her dad had been assigning her jobs, dangerous missions she tried to avoid talking about. "You could've given her Cece's number."

"Brittany?" Tommy chuckled, shaking his head. "No, she'd be decapitated by lunch," he gestured to the outdoor bar. "You wanna get a smoothie?"

"Definitely," she said. "Dave?"

"No, thanks." He nodded to the lifeguard stand.

El and Tommy shared a smile, wished him luck, and went to get their smoothies.

Dave took a deep breath. Being nervous was new, he never had any problems with girls before. It was easy for him to charm them. But this girl was different. Jess was unlike any girl he'd ever met. She proved that when she followed him out of the Adler Building elevator.

***

Jess

As she read, Jess let herself get absorbed into the world of written words. She loved Shakespearean. There was something about the way the words were said, it romanticized the idea of love and life and made it medieval. She thought the story was outdated, of course, but it was still fun to imagine.

After she was released from the hospital, Jess started physical therapy. Layla hired the best in the state and insisted on three times a week. She also wanted Jess to take another internship but Jess wanted a simple, relaxed summer vacation. She argued with Layla for days until Bennett intervened. The compromise was that Jess would volunteer at their country club. It wasn't a law internship but it'd still look good on her college applications.

Most days, her friends, Brittany and Cindy, came to enjoy the sun and the smoothies. They practiced their cheer routines by the pool. Their mothers came to the country club too, as well as other bored housewives and socialites, who were eager to sneak a peek at the new pool boy.

Jess could've sworn the manager hired him for the women's enjoyment.

Sadly for those housewives, the pool's bar didn't serve alcohol. There'd been an incident and a lawsuit, and they had to stop.

"Hey, princess." Dave stood below her. He wore striped board shorts and nothing else. His stomach, flat and solid, matched his muscular arms. Most of his skin, including his abs, was covered in scars, wounds from what looked like blades, burns, and bullets. His unbrushed hair was in disarray but he didn't care. He probably thought it made him look better.

Jess wasn't sure why Dave visited her in the hospital every day. At first, she figured it was guilt because of his dad and her injury, but the theory unraveled when Dave kept coming back. He'd sneak in, so her parents never saw him. He'd bring limo jello he took from unattended cafeteria carts and one time, he brought Jess a bunch of balloons he stole from the gift shop.

She was in her hospital bed, staring at a book, but she hadn't had the energy to read. She had a headache and her stomach was sore. She couldn't sleep either, thanks to the relentless nightmares featuring the fire, the gunshot, and Ted's evil laughter.

Dave walked in carrying several colorful, sparkly balloons, each saying GET WELL SOON in various fonts. He looked extremely proud of himself for stealing them. *What do you think? I thought we could tie them to your bed*, he said.

No way! My mom will definitely notice those, she'll ask who brought them, Jess said.

So, lie. Say something like, I don't know, a handsome, dashing volunteer wanted you to have them. Dave didn't wait for her to answer, or comment on the fact he called himself "handsome," instead he tied the balloons to her bed and smiled - His charming, flirty smile - then casually laid next to her. *Or do you think "handsome" is too close to the truth? Might be the detail that reveals it's me.*

Jess rolled her eyes. *I seriously doubt that.*

She learned that Dave loved to work on cars and motorcycles; he loved pumpkin pancakes; he appreciated his friends and loved them more than he'd admit; he was smarter than he gave himself credit for; he was damaged and he knew it.

"Hi," Jess closed her book. "What are you doing here?"

"Come down here." He gestured to the ground.

She set her book on the armrest and climbed down the short, wooden ladder. The cement stung her toes, so she slipped on a pair of sandals. The sun's heat screamed against her skin, making her sweat. The light breeze blew through her hair and helped cool her off. "What are you doing here?"

He shrugged. "El has a membership."

"Your, uh, your ex-girlfriend?" Jess didn't want to be insecure but she definitely felt that way. Dave told her stories about Ella Markinson. He had known El since he was a kid, she was his first kiss. They weren't in a serious relationship but he had mentioned they were constantly on and off. "Are you guys together again?"

"No," he shook his head. "No, we're just friends."

"Oh," she smiled, relieved. "Okay."

He chuckled. If he noticed the fear that had crossed her mind, he didn't mention it. He gestured to the book she'd been reading. "What are you reading?"

"*Romeo and Juliet*," she said. "The first time I read it I was in seventh grade. I fell in love with it. I love the writing, the story is a little, uh.." Sometimes, she forgot some people didn't have the same interest in books that she did. She had to keep herself from bursting into a monologue. "Sorry, it's just, well, it's a book, so-"

"So, you could talk about it for hours, I know," Dave said. In the hospital, he listened to her talk about several books she had read. He sat there, on the end of her bed, eating jello, as she described her thoughts, the characters, the themes. At the time, she thought it was pity or guilt that made him stay but maybe it wasn't. He smiled.

"Yeah...well, um." She felt nauseous but in a really good way. It was hard to describe. Every part of her body tingled, like warm shivers, when he stared at her with those handsome blue eyes. She was at a loss for words. What should she say? She had never felt like this before.

"Do you wanna go out sometime?" The question poured out of his mouth as if he'd finally gotten the courage to ask it. He tapped his thigh, waiting for her answer.

She opened her mouth to say something, to say yes, but she didn't hear any sound. She tried again. "Out? Like out on a date?" she chuckled, shock mixed with her nerves. "With you?"

"That's the idea." He glanced at her bathing suit. His eyes lingered and she scoffed. Was he seriously checking her out again?

She shoved him. "Don't do that!"

Dave stumbled, probably to humor her. She wasn't strong enough to actually knock him over. He laughed and lifted his hands in the air. "Alright, I'm sorry, is that a no?"

"It's..." she picked her cuticles. "It's a yes."

He smiled, more excited than she'd ever seen him. He looked like he wanted to hug her but he didn't, instead, he stepped closer, two inches away from her. Her body stiffened, suddenly the sun wasn't the only thing making her sweat. Her cheeks warmed as butterflies danced in her belly, a million little electric shivers drifted through her veins. Her heart jumped out of her chest when he touched her arms.

His gaze floated over her lips as he slowly ran his fingers from her elbows to her wrists. He locked their hands together, fingers intertwined. She couldn't pick her cuticles. She gulped.

"I really like that bathing suit," he whispered.

She chuckled. "I noticed."

"You know what would make it even better?" He smiled. "If it was wet."

Her gaze narrowed. She frowned. "*What*?"

Dave yanked her against him and lifted her up, belly bent over his shoulder. She could feel the shape of his muscles, how strong his body was. He twirled and she closed her eyes. The world whipped and bounced, light and dizzying.

Laughter burst from her throat, she didn't mean to laugh but she couldn't help it. His grip on her legs was sturdy, solid. He wouldn't drop her, hurt her, or let her fall. He'd keep her safe without trying to control her, he proved that when she followed him into the Adler Building elevator.

When he let go, Jess crashed against the cold water and drifted down to the pool's floor. Pieces of the sun danced across the cement like beautiful ribbons blowing in the wind, calming and distant, magical and untouchable. She swam up and broke the surface, gasping. "Not funny!"

Dave laughed, standing at the pool's edge, his fists shot triumphantly into the air. "Pretty funny."

***

Bobby

Sitting beside Bobby's feet were two suitcases and a duffel bag filled with her favorite clothes and shoes, three hairbrushes, the stuffed animals and toys she couldn't part with, photos of her and her dad, her lucky sewing kit, a toothbrush, toothpaste and her dad's old collection of handcrafted poker chips. Her makeup had its own container complete with foldable shelves and hidden pockets.

The shooting destroyed her house. The broken windows were boarded up and the new door had a different lock. Bloodstains were smeared on the shattered porch and the front lawn. It wasn't her childhood home anymore. It was empty and alone.

She sold everything she didn't need or want and pocketed the cash. Now all her belongings fit in three bags. At least, she was alive. The doctors said she was lucky.

It hurt when she moved her leg the wrong way or when she stretched her shoulder too far. Her whole body was sore. She did her best to regain her strength but she hated exercise, so the boys helped her. They all knew how much she loved to dance, so Cole bought a Wii game, Just Dance, and they'd take turns playing it with her.

Sally drove her old, black jeep up to the curb and parked in front of the house. She waved, leaning over the steering wheel. She wore a gray tank top under a loose denim shirt with brass buttons. Her beautiful black hair was tied in a fluffy bun at the top of her head, allowing her gold hoop earrings to stand out at either side of her face.

Bobby shoved her stuff in the back seat and climbed into the passenger side. She slammed the door. She hated that she wasn't allowed to live in her house anymore, the home Vincent worked so hard to pay off, the place where all her favorite memories were. What jerks got to make these decisions anyhow?

"The bank owns it now," Bobby said. "I don't have a home anymore."

"You can stay with me," Sally rubbed her shoulder. "I've got the space."

Bobby closed her eyes. She couldn't believe how much of a screw-up she was. She ruined everything, her entire life, and lost it too. She lost her home, her dad, her dignity, and faith in her own judgment. She never should've trusted Johnny, she never should've loved him. She'd never wish pain on anyone but she wanted him to suffer in some way. She couldn't blame it all on him, she made her choices and she had to deal with the consequences. How could she have been so stupid?

"I won't stay long," she sniffled. She didn't want to cry. "I'll find somewhere permanent."

She asked Sally for help because, at the time, Alice was living with Casey. There wasn't room for all three of them in Eddie's basement. Sally didn't need to be convinced, she had always been there for the kids whenever any of them needed help.

"Whatever you need." Sally drove away from the curb.

The image of Bobby's childhood home glimmered in the rearview mirror. She could almost see the house as it used to be; the clean, blue siding with yellow edging and a white, metal door. The screen around the solidly built porch. Vincent's freshly washed car in the driveway and the sidewalk chalk scattered across the lawn. As a little girl, she'd play in the grass, dancing and attempting to cartwheel, while the boy who lived across the street played basketball with his older brothers.

It was a simpler time before death and pain ripped away her innocent bliss.

Chapter 10

Alice

Leo and Mister Scotts lived in a two-bedroom loft or it counted as a two-bedroom. Leo's room was a bridge-like upstairs surrounded by a metal railing. It was above the den they made into Alice's room. They put up a room divider to give her privacy. A floor-to-ceiling, colored window connected the two rooms. It had a great view of the Nests and the rest of Height City.

Alice made herself comfortable with the twin-sized bed from their neighbor and the hand-me-down nightstand from Mister Scotts. Her favorite sports and band posters were scattered on the walls while her original photos were clipped to twine hanging along the ceiling. Several floating shelves held books, her alarm clock, her photography supplies, and a few other random things. Her clothes were on a portable rack next to the bed. She didn't mind not having a closet.

"Have you seen my math book?" she shouted.

"Have you seen my history book?" Leo yelled back.

"No!" Alice came out of her room and Leo ran down the metal staircase that led to his. They glanced at each other and started searching the open-concept apartment.

The little office area included a leather swivel chair and a desk with two drawers, where Mister Scotts graded his students' papers. A bookcase filled with nerdy knickknacks and family photos stood behind the desk. Each photo featured Leo in a different stage of his childhood.

The living room was the loft's center with a simple area rug, a circular glass coffee table, and several lamps. Two big, cushioned reading chairs were on either side of the L-shaped couch, which faced a flat-screen TV that Mister Scotts had no idea how to use. He wasn't very tech savvy, he had to use four different remotes just to get the TV to turn on.

His bedroom, next to the front door, was hidden behind a potted plant with giant leaves. He watered it every morning. It used to be his wife's.

Alice moved in at the end of summer, now it was Fall and school had been in session for a little over two months. The three of them learned to co-exist. At first, things were rocky, she and Leo fought over the bathroom and the boys' snores kept her awake at night but eventually, they all got used to each other. Alice liked living with them so far. Mister Scotts cooked dinner almost every evening, and on the weekends, they did a game night, or sometimes, they all watched movies together.

One thing was for sure, the Scotts boys never made Alice feel alone.

"Eggs!" Mister Scotts lifted the pan and Alice ducked under it.

She sorted through the pile of junk mail on the kitchen counter, which separated the kitchen from the living room. The kitchen had a six-burner stove that Mister Scotts used to cook. He kept several cookbooks and recipe journals in the dishwasher, which didn't work and leaked whenever it was used. Alice learned that the hard way. On the fridge, magnets shaped like sushi and clown faces held grocery lists, to-do lists, photos of the boys, and messy drawings Leo did when he was in kindergarten.

Leo flipped the couch cushions. "Find my history book?"

"I'm looking for my math book!" she said.

Leo found the car keys and turned to his dad. "Is this the extra set or the main set?"

"I have no idea," Mister Scotts plated the eggs. "Put them over there."

Leo slapped the keys on the counter. He went back to searching the living room. He wore a gray T-shirt with white letters that said: I'M NOT PROCRASTI-NATING, I'M DOING SIDE QUESTS. His wardrobe was filled with nerdy T-shirts exactly like it. He checked under the coffee table.

Alice pulled an inappropriate magazine from the junk mail. A woman in lingerie was posed on the cover.

"Uh... who's is this?" she held it up.

"Dad," Leo narrowed his gaze, humorful. "Do you have something you wanna confess?"

"Hilarious," Mister Scotts frowned, unamused. "It must be the neighbor's."

"Where do I put it?" Alice glanced at the cover. The woman was beautiful, even if she weren't wearing less than a bikini, her body stretched in a way that made Alice's face warm. She couldn't imagine why anyone would ever choose to work as that type of model but she decided not to judge.

Leo backed up toward the front door and gestured for the magazine. Alice tossed it to him and he ran out into the hall. Who knew he could catch? "Find my history book!"

"I'm looking for my math book!" she searched the cabinets, most of which held every type of pot, pan and chef's tool. Alice didn't know what half of them were and the other half she knew very little about but depending on the recipe, Mister Scotts used them all. Cooking made him feel artsy.

"You've got two eyes so look for two books," Leo closed the door. "The magazine is on the welcome mat."

"Good. Time?" Mister Scotts asked.

Leo looked at his comic book-themed wristwatch. "Almost seven."

Mister Scotts grabbed three plastic baggies from a drawer and dumped some eggs into each one.

Leo raised his eyebrows in question.

Alice stood up and shook her head. She had no idea where her math book could've gone. "That's it, I can't find it anywhere."

"Did you leave it in your locker?" Mister Scotts asked.

"No, I had it last night when I was studying with Jess."

"Hey, what was she complaining about?" Leo grabbed a fork and a ceramic, gnome-shaped pepper shaker. He took one of the baggies and doused the eggs inside. He took a bite and nodded happily.

Alice looked under the couch. "She's stressed out with student council, party planning committee, her honor classes," she checked each chair, no math book. "Plus, her boyfriend likes these sci-fi movies and she's been watching them for him."

"She doesn't like sci-fi?" Leo asked. "Hey, I already checked there."

"She likes romantic comedies and documentaries," Alice wasn't sure where else to look. How did her math book vanish into thin air? "Did you find your history book?"

"Oh, now you care."

"Yeah, 'cause if you found it, you can help look for my math book."

"Nice," Leo chuckled. He took another bite of his eggs. "But no, I haven't."

Mister Scotts handed Alice her own egg baggie. He clapped his hands, grabbed his briefcase, and went to the door. He gestured for them to hurry. "We need to go. Come on."

Leo grabbed his backpack and swung it on his shoulder. He ate another egg. "What about our books?" he asked with a full mouth.

"You can look for them after school," Mister Scotts said. "Maybe now you'll remember where you put things. Take responsibility for them."

"It's the action figure incident all over again," Leo walked out the door. "I was nine!"

Alice laughed. She grabbed her bag and her camera.

The hall was wide with walls of exposed brick, pale blue carpet, and wooden doors. The few apartments on their floor were occupied; some college kids lived in one. They threw parties late at night and smoked pot; An old lady with six cats lived in another. One of her cats liked to escape and explore the building; a couple with a newborn lived next to her. The baby always started crying around four in the morning; and the super. He was a chubby man who kept to himself unless someone needed him to fix something, then he was happy to help.

"What's with you and the camera?" Leo pressed the elevator button.

Alice shrugged. "I don't know, I just take it everywhere."

"What do you take pictures of?"

"My friends, buildings, random people, I don't know. Anything and every-thing, I guess."

"Why?" he asked. That seemed to be his favorite word. His observations and fascination with the world made him unique but sometimes, it got to be a little overwhelming. "Why do you love it so much?"

"I guess..." she paused. Alice wasn't sure how to describe it. She started taking photos when she was a kid after Mason gave her his old camera but the hobby really absorbed her after Susan died. It was comforting to be behind the lens. "I like capturing a moment. It's probably why I take lots of candids, so the photos don't look stiff or fake. I like people how they already are."

When the elevator opened, the three of them piled into it. The full-length windows were locked from the inside and tinted to the outside. Alice enjoyed watching the shift of the buildings and the way the road and people got closer as the elevator rumbled gently, taking them down to the first floor. The building had a stairwell but it was only used for emergencies.

Mister Scotts had his gray Honda parked across the alley. He started mutter-ing complaints about being late as he started the engine and pulled out of the parking lot.

"Hey... uh," Leo cleared his throat. "You're friends with Bobby Jones, right?"

"Sort of." Alice had spent time with Bobby while she was living with Cece but they never spent any time alone together. Still, she considered Bobby a friend. She aimed the camera at Mister Scotts. Alice loved his suede elbow patches and his thick, fuzzy, gray hair. He wore a white bowtie with red cherries printed on it.

"Is it a good photo?" he asked.

She smiled. "I think so."

She turned to Leo and lifted the camera. He covered his face. "No! A camera to me is like sunlight to a vampire."

She shoved his arm down. He stuck his tongue out and she took the picture. She laughed. "See? That wasn't so bad."

"I'm pretty sure I'm turning to dust," he said. "Thanks a lot."

"Drama queen." Alice looked out the window.

The Nests were wide awake, buzzing with early morning risers. A golden retriever and its owner jogged past a woman sitting at the bus stop. She slowly pushed a stroller back and forth while a man wearing bright yellow rain boots read the newspaper. Everyone seemed alive, relaxed, no worries at all.

The morning was like any other. Alice went to her classes, did the work, and talked to the few people she had to. Miss Z partnered her with Tony for a presentation project and it was the most awkward hour ever.

Usually, she'd have lunch with Jess and Leo but Jess was busy with student council work, party planning committee, and newspaper; something new she decided to try. Alice didn't mind, she was busy with something of her own.

She went to the girls' bathroom.

Cece sat in the window, one leg bent against her chest and the other dangling outside. Her head and back were leaning on the frame. "You know I don't go here, right?"

Alice dropped her backpack on the floor. "I know but this is important."

"Well, I was shaking down a fence," she said. "So this better be good."

Alice knelt next to her bag and unzipped the front pocket. She pulled out one of the brown, leather journals from her attic and held it up. "My mom wrote something in this and the others. I need to know what and probably why."

"Dude, you're on repeat. Should I slap you, so you stop skipping?" Cece said. "I thought you were over this. You were busy with your new roommates and we tried-"

"I know, okay? I know," Alice said. "We tried blue light, a pencil, regular lamps, I can't think of anything else. What are your ideas?"

"Do you have a penny?" she smiled. "Maybe it's like a scratcher."

"I seriously doubt it but I'll give it a shot."

"I was kidding." Cece slid off the windowsill and crouched beside it, back leaning against the wall. She scanned the bathroom as if she were checking for monsters, then made a face that meant she thought this was crazy.

Alice couldn't blame her. She felt crazy. She sighed. "I have not lost my mind."

Cece made another face that meant she disagreed but she didn't say her judgments out loud. "Look, I get it. These are Glisin's words," Cece said. "Who wouldn't want to read them? But this is getting to be a wild goose chase."

"She wasn't just Glisin. She was my mom," Alice said. Her grief made her voice crack. She'd been doing so much better, she felt less hopeless, less alone, but these journals reminded her of everything she had lost, of the memories she'd never make, and the happy family she still mourned. "She could've written something for me. A letter or a note, I... I have to know."

Cece's shoulders slumped, love and annoyance crawled across her face. She snatched the journal and flipped through the pages. "I don't know what to do either."

Alice groaned and pulled her hood over her eyes. Maybe she wasn't supposed to see what secrets or last words were written in Susan's journals. Maybe it was a lost cause. Maybe Susan hid them for a reason. Maybe she never wanted her daughter to know about them.

The door opened, and both girls went still, rigid, like deer caught in a car's headlights. Were they about to get caught? Alice wasn't sure what rules she was breaking but at that moment, she didn't doubt she could be punished or get detention, except it wasn't a teacher, it was Jess.

Jess carried a binder stuffed with several pieces of loose-leaf paper, two yellow notepads, and what looked like a million Post-its as well as her student council papers, homework, extra credit, and her newspaper notebook, which was basically a bunch of rough drafts for articles she was working on. She had neon orange highlighter ink in her hair and droplets of black, pen ink on her fingers. She slapped her things on the counter and groaned, exhausted.

"You didn't lock the door?" Cece asked.

Alice shrugged. "Oops?"

Jess looked at their reflections then turned, eyes wide. "What's going on?"

"Cult," Cece said.

Alice shook her head. "Nothing. We're just talking."

"Isn't that how a cult starts?" she asked. "Talks, gatherings-"

"M'kay," Alice said before Cece could keep talking. "This is Cece. Cece, this is Jess."

"Dave's friend," Jess guessed. She and Dave officially started dating before school and from what Alice gathered, the couple was completely smitten with each other.

"Friend is a strong word," Cece said. "But yeah, more or less." She wouldn't admit it but she cared about Dave. If anything, she enjoyed bickering with him. "You're the Honeycomber girlfriend."

"He told you?" Jess blushed. She must've liked hearing that Dave called her his girlfriend. "Um, sorry," she frowned, serious, and the color in her cheeks drained. "It's just that we talked about keeping it a secret for now."

"She knew," Cece pointed to Alice, who raised her hand.

Alice knew Jess's relationship was supposed to be kept a secret from Layla and Bennett, not from their friends. "Yeah, Leo also knows now, so."

"So, does Cole and Tommy and El and Bobby," Cece counted the names on her fingers. She waved her hand for emphasis. "Guess the secret's out."

"Okay," Jess said, annoyed with Cece. "Well, keep it to yourselves for now, please," she smiled. It was nice to see her happy. "It's new and good and we... um, I don't want my mom or anything else ruining it. What are you guys talking about?"

"Invisible ink," Cece said. Where was she going with this?

Alice decided to jump in. She rolled her lips. "For a school project."

"I haven't heard about an assignment involving invisible ink," Jess said. "What teacher?"

"Um..." Alice turned to Cece for the answer but she shook her head. Alice gave up. She held up the journal. "We found this in the attic when I was moving out and it has invisible ink. I don't know how to get it to appear."

"It was your mom's, wasn't it?" Jess asked. "About her being Glisin."

Blank confusion seized Alice's mind. Did she hear that sentence correctly? She looked at Cece for the answer but Cece looked as shocked as Alice felt.

Cece scoffed. "You told her? You couldn't have mentioned that?"

"I didn't... I don't think..." Alice couldn't find the right words. She didn't think she told Jess, she didn't remember telling Jess anything. How did she know?

Jess sat with them, creating a messy triangle. She chuckled, a little proud and slightly embarrassed. "I kind of figured it out."

"How?" Cece asked.

"The Adler Building Fire," Jess said, turning her focus to Alice. "Alice, you weren't there when I was shot but I did call and tell you where we were," she shrugged. "Somehow you ended up on the victim list in the Height City Gazette and with that lightning bolt spotted at the scene... I already knew powers could be hereditary." Jess smiled. "So, I put two and two together."

"You... you didn't tell me you knew," Alice said. "All summer-"

"You didn't seem like you wanted anyone to know. The lie about Susan abandoning you guys and that you never wanted to talk about it," Jess paused. Her frown deepened. She figured it out on her own, Susan's identity, Susan's death, everything. "I'm really sorry. She was an even more fantastic woman than I thought she was. And powers or not, you're my best friend."

Alice chuckled. A giant elephant had been pulled off her shoulders. So many times, she wanted to tell Jess. She never wanted to lie to her best friend, the girl she grew up with, the girl who knew and loved her mom almost as much as she did. This was a dream come true. Jess wasn't mad or betrayed, and now she could mourn Susan's death, and Alice didn't have to keep secrets from her anymore.

"You made one of those detective boards, didn't you?" Alice asked. She could picture Jess sitting in her bedroom, staring at old newspaper articles about Glisin while she sorted through her memories of Susan and put all the pieces together.

Jess nodded. "Definitely."

They laughed and hugged. Alice remembered when they were seven, they fought over a popsicle. It was one of their worst fights ever. They didn't talk for an entire day and when they got home from school, they immediately made up.

"Not to interrupt this touching moment," Cece held up the journal. "But do you know anything about invisible ink, Jessie?"

"It's Jess," she corrected.

Cece shrugged. "Don't care."

"Wow, okay," Jess scoffed, offended. "Well, what have you tried so far?"

"Shading it with a pencil, using one of those invisible penlights, and holding it up to some lamps," Alice said. "Nothing's worked."

"I suggested scratching it like a lottery ticket," Cece said.

"I thought that was supposed to be a joke."

"May I?" Jess reached for the journal but didn't take it, Cece gave it to her. She examined the pages with an intense focus. Alice could almost see the twirling gears in Jess's head, working the problem as she tried to think of a plausible answer. She stood up and set the journal on the counter.

The others followed. Their reflections stood side by side in the foggy glass.

"Cruise Industries' Powered Person Study says that no two powers are the same unless genetically transferred, even then it's a coin flip. You can't really be sure," Jess said. "So, what if the invisible ink is somehow activated by Glisin's- Susan's abilities?"

"Meaning?" Alice asked.

"It'd be the perfect way to keep whatever she wrote a secret because only she could see it."

"One problem," Cece said. "She's six feet under."

"Okay, wait," Alice tried wrapping her mind around the explanation. "You think the ink would appear when she used her powers on it." Something didn't add up. "Why would she need to read her own secrets?"

"Memory loss?" Cece guessed. "She took a couple of famous beatings-"

"It's just a possible theory," Jess said. "We could try other techniques like heat or using some sort of liquid. Maybe a gel-"

Alice stared at the journal. Susan knew death was a risk. She knew all the risks of putting on her mask. If someone learned her identity and threatened the right person, she'd willingly use her powers on the journal. Why would she make it so easy for them? She would've somehow protected herself and her family. She wouldn't have written anything for herself. It wouldn't have made sense.

"Al? Al!" Cece snapped her fingers.

Alice shook herself from her thoughts. She glanced between her friends. They stared at her curiously.

"You zoned out," Jess said. "Are you okay?"

"She didn't need to know her secrets, it would've been stupid to write them down," Alice said. "Unless they were for me. She wanted me to find the journals."

"Technically, I found them," Cece said.

"Are you really searching for credit right now?" Jess asked.

"Fine. Unimportant," Cece gestured to the journal. "So, what? Susan wrote whatever she wrote for you, so you could find those... For what? Insurance policy?"

"Exactly," Alice said. "So, my powers should activate the ink."

"So, I was right," Jess smiled, proud and fascinated. She stood a little taller.

Cece clicked her tongue. "Now who's looking for credit?"

"No, I, I wasn't," she paused. "I was just pointing out that I, I," her shoulders slumped. "Oh, never mind."

"Yeah, and I found the journals," Cece slid onto the counter, legs crossed like a pretzel. "We'll get congratulatory cupcakes after this."

Alice took the journal and went to the first page. It was rough under her fingers. She could smell Susan's mango perfume, old and faded. The memory of a happy home and an undeniable legacy. What if she was wrong? What if it didn't work? What if Susan didn't leave anything for her and this was all a fantasy Alice created in her head? Even if disappointment was an option, she needed to know.

She took a deep breath. Her heart thumped in a hopeful rhythm. Lightning flickered between her fingers, rippling and glistening across the blank page. Black ink emerged. Small, cursive, all capital letters. The same writing on every grocery list, every sticky note, and every permission slip Susan ever wrote or signed. It was perfect.

Alice chuckled. "It worked."

They all shared an excited glance.

***

Leo

Leo tossed his pudding cup in the trash and left the cafeteria. He didn't sit with Alice and Jess, which was fine. They were busy. He liked being by himself. It gave him a chance to watch people again. He used to do it all the time during his freshman and sophomore years. He found that people were more real when they thought others weren't paying attention.

He turned the corner and headed to the library. He had homework to finish for his next class. He could've done it the night before but he decided to play video games instead.

Bobby Jones was outside the library doors, leaning against some lockers with a laptop sitting on her outstretched legs. She wore a baggy flannel top made tight by a glittery orange belt. The red skirt underneath was short and layered.

Upon seeing her, Leo gulped. He had never actually spoken to her but Bobby was one of his favorite people to analyze. She always walked confidently in her dazzling outfits. She definitely stood out amongst a crowd.

He first noticed her freshman year when Brittany Mikes tripped her in the cafeteria. Spaghetti splattered all over Bobby's chest, ruining her outfit and makeup. People laughed, Brittany and Cindy high-fived, and Bobby ran out of the cafeteria in tears. The next period, she acted like nothing happened and walked tall as she headed to her next class. There were conflicting rumors about what started Brittany and Bobby's rivalry, most of which could've been true, like the one theorizing Bobby stole the role Brittany wanted in the freshman play. Leo wasn't sure what to believe.

He took a deep breath. *Okay, she won't bite. She's just a girl, you can do this.* He gathered his courage and went up to her. "Hey, uh, whatcha ya doing?"

Bobby looked at him. Her dark hazel eyes, surrounded by light green eyeshadow, had enchanting gold speckles shimmering near her irises. Her long eyelashes were black and curled, probably due to mascara, and her lips were pink, pretty. Her makeup had a woodland fairy vibe to it. "Leo Scotts, right?"

For a second, Leo forgot how to speak. He nodded. "That's, that's me. How'd you know?"

"A friend of a friend moved in with you," she said. "And uh, well, you're the teacher's son. I like him, he's nice. Mister Scotts, I mean."

"Yeah. He's a great dad too," he chuckled. The mention of his dad helped loosen his nerves. "You're Bobby Jones, right?"

He felt it was polite to ask.

"The one and only," she scrunched up her nose. "Okay, this is gonna sound really weird but can I borrow your hat? It's just that Sally's shower is broken and I haven't been clean in two weeks, and my hair is oily and gross, and I hate it, and-" she broke off, sighing. The words spewed from her mouth in an elegantly hyper babble. It was cute but she didn't seem to think so. "I mean, it's your hat-"

Leo pulled off his gray beanie and held it out to her. His hair probably looked crazy but he didn't care. He didn't need to look good for anyone. It wasn't like people noticed him or even knew he existed.

Bobby's hair didn't look bad either, her fiery curls were gorgeous, wild, and soft. Her lips parted in surprise. She hesitated before she grabbed the beanie and put it on her head. She tucked it over her curls, each one poked out in adorable, little puffs. He wanted to touch one, play with it, but he didn't. It'd be weird.

"Who's Sally?" he asked. He sat next to her, inviting himself into whatever she was doing.

Motels were listed on her laptop's screen.

"Uh, she's.. I guess my roommate," Bobby said. "Um, my house got foreclosed and I needed somewhere to stay. She's kind of the Burrows' wolf mother, it's complicated."

"Basically, she let you stay with her 'cause you didn't have anywhere else to go." Leo realized his bluntness could've seemed mean and wished he would've been a little gentler with his response. He didn't want to be rude or hurt her feelings.

Bobby nodded once. "Basically."

"Um," he pointed to her laptop, desperate to change the mood of the conversation. "If you already have a place to stay, why are you..."

"The motels, right, yeah," she gestured to the screen. "I'm a bother, so I want to go and get my own place before, I, well, I," she paused, reconsidering her next words. "Before I overstay my welcome."

Her fists tightened on the sleeves of her flannel shirt. Her nails - short and slightly bitten, painted with black, sparkly polish - dug into the fabric as if she were using it to push away a bad memory.

"I doubt she'd let you stay if she thought you'd be a bother," Leo said. He wanted to comfort her but he didn't know how. He didn't know her well enough to say the right thing. He wasn't sure he ever said the right thing whether he knew the person or not.

Bobby scrunched her eyebrows. Was she confused or surprised by what he said? Her expression could've meant both. Maybe she was offended. "You obviously don't know me," she said in a soft whisper as if she were trying to warn him away from her. She looked at her shirt, squeezing its sleeves, like she was hugging the person who wore it before her.

"Can I help?" Leo asked. He doubted anyone would ever see Bobby as a bother but he didn't want to argue with her. He wanted to make her feel better.

"Why?" she narrowed her eyes.

He shrugged. "I have no life?"

"You seem pretty alive to me. You gotta have friends. Girlfriend? Boyfriend?"

"Loner," he pointed to himself. "On Saturdays, I play Scrabble with my dad. It's fun. I'm the champion by the way. Have been for a while."

She covered her mouth, muffling her laughter. She shook her head. "I'm sorry. I didn't mean to, it's, I'm a jerk. The jerkiest jerk."

"Nah, it's okay," he chuckled. He didn't mind being a dork. He loved being at home with his dad, playing games or watching movies, or by himself, reading comic books. "What do you do on Saturdays?"

She looked at the floor.

He knew the rumors as well as anyone else. Bobby Jones, the slut, the whore, the loser. Burrows' trash as Brittany called her. She'd come to school hungover or tipsy, exhausted from partying. Her and Johnny's public fight didn't help matters. Leo remembered the finger-shaped bruises Johnny left on Bobby's face, her tears and the terror, how small and broken she looked. That day, all Leo wanted to do was help her up and get her away from the crowds but he never had the chance.

He couldn't imagine what else happened between the ex-couple. He didn't want to imagine. The shooting at her house wasn't a secret either. Supposedly, it was a drive-by gone wrong.

"Um... you know, I, I used to..." she frowned. "I don't, uh, anymore. I don't know."

He didn't want to push her to talk about it. He shouldn't have asked. "Okay," he nodded.

She shifted her position.

Leo didn't mean to make her uncomfortable. He took the laptop and set it on his knees, scrolling through the list of motels. He didn't recognize any of their names but most of the addresses were in the Burrows.

Bobby watched him, unsure. She glanced between him and the screen, her expression reminded him of an abused puppy that had finally been adopted. He hoped she wouldn't send him away, he wanted to keep talking to her.

"It looks good on you." He pointed to his gray beanie on her head. He meant it. The beanie looked better on her than it ever did on him.

She adjusted it, tucking it tighter around her curls. She blushed. With pinkish cheeks and a sheepish smile, she looked beautiful but then again, she was always beautiful.

She scooted closer to him. Their shoulders bumped and Leo's heart stopped. His face warmed and he became highly aware of his nerves. He smiled. It was a weirdly satisfying feeling.

***

Tommy

"I have no idea what this thing says." Dave slapped the book shut. He'd been trying to read it for over twenty minutes and he'd gotten as far as the third page.

Tommy couldn't help but laugh. He shrugged. "It's Shakespearean."

It was nice to see Dave determined to succeed in a relationship, it proved how much he actually liked Jess, how much he wanted to be with her, understand her. He dropped the book on the bar. "No, it's confusing."

"Why are you reading *Romeo and Juliet*?" Sally asked. She faced the boys from behind the bar, wiping the wood with a damp rag. She already swept the dance floor and cleaned every booth.

"His girlfriend likes it and they have nothing in common," Tommy said. "So, they made a deal-"

"She watches my favorite movies and I read her favorite books," Dave said. "But I can't read what I don't understand." He had given Jess his collection of *Star Wars* DVDs, so she could watch them, and she gave him five of her favorite novels, including *Romeo & Juliet, Jane Eyre,* and *The Book Thief*, which was also a novel Tommy happened to enjoy.

"So, tell her that," Sally said. She was vaguely interested in the topic. Tommy couldn't understand why she let them hang out at her club when it was closed. Nobody else was welcome inside until the open sign flickered on, so why a bunch of random street kids?

"How do you do it?" Dave asked. "Be all relationship-y with Casey."

"She can't even admit we're in a relationship," Tommy said. He didn't have a problem with it, he and Casey both understood what they were. Boyfriend. Girlfriend. Together. Whatever you wanted to call it. He didn't need a label to know how he felt about her and he hoped she felt the same way.

"Okay, maybe you're not the best example," Dave turned to Sally. "Sally, you ever dated anybody?"

"I had a few romances in my day. Want to know what made them work?"

"Aren't you single?"

She frowned at the question, eyebrow raised. The same face she made when she reached for her shotgun, which was the exact reason no one ever messed with her, insulted her, or broke her club's rules. She had extra ammo and wicked aim, she wouldn't hesitate to blow you away.

Tommy laughed so hard that a little soda spit out of his nose. "Way to catch flies with vinegar."

"What?" Dave asked. "She is!"

"For that, you're washing the dishes," Sally whipped her rag and a little water splashed Dave in the face.

He saluted her. "Yes, ma'am."

"Now, here's my advice," she said. "Every relationship is different and if you're concerned about something that has to do with yours, talk to the other person in it."

Dave squinted as if he didn't understand, as if she were talking crazy. He turned to Tommy and held up the book. He didn't want to talk to Jess about it because he was afraid, he didn't want to disappoint her or for her to think he was stupid. Dave might put on a good show but his insecurities ran deep.

Tommy nodded. "There's a cliff notes version."

"Thank God," he sighed.

Sally rolled her eyes. "Hopeless."

She walked away, shaking her head. She did her best to help them. Mostly, they weren't interested in her help or thought they could handle things themselves. They were usually wrong. Sally gave them advice, free food, and drinks, she had their backs when other Burrowers came after them, she even gave Bobby a home. Tommy appreciated her, sometimes he wished she was his mother.

The front door swung open, jingling a little bell, and Cole ran into the club. He looked wide awake, bug-eyed, like when he first competed in a Burrows' street race. He didn't win but he got addicted to the thrill of the speed, the action, the open road, and he decided to start racing regularly for money.

He tripped on a chair, knocked it down, and bent forward, staggering toward Tommy and Dave. He grabbed the bar and gasped for air. He held up a finger, signaling that he needed a minute.

"Did you run here from our apartment?" Dave asked.

Cole wheezed, heavy panting made his chest rise and fall in quick, uneven spurts. He stood straighter and nodded furiously. His face was red. His and Dave's apartment wasn't too far from Sally's Place, a few blocks, maybe. Still, Cole was a racer, not a runner. "Guess... who's... Mick's..." he bent down. "Oh God."

Mick the Menace was an independent assassin who did jobs for Betty and Markinson. He had a tiny kingdom in the middle of two giant ones. He was also famous in the Burrows for his temper toward his girlfriends.

"You look like you're gonna pass out. Sit down." Dave climbed up onto the bar and hopped behind it. He poured water into an empty beer mug and dropped a couple of ice cubes in it. He handed it to Cole, then plopped back onto the barstool he'd been sitting on. Cole sat on the third barstool in the row, so Tommy was positioned between them.

"Mick's got a new girl," Cole huffed. "Paisley."

The second Tommy heard that name, his stomach flipped, dropped thirty stories, and smashed into his gut. Cold sweat drained the color from his knuckles. He held the bar to keep himself steady, to keep himself from fainting or punching a wall, he wasn't sure. He wanted to do both.

He couldn't breathe. Why couldn't he breathe? He needed to breathe. He needed to stay calm.

His friends stared at him, worried. They both knew who the name belonged to, what the person meant to him, and why she was important. If she got hurt or worse, Tommy wasn't sure how he'd handle it.

"Is the other one...?" Dave asked.

Cole shook his head. "They haven't found her body yet."

Chapter 11

Alice

"You've read every single one of those. It's not gonna suddenly change after four months. Put it down and eat a cake pop or something." Cece sat on the counter, legs dangling over the edge. Her boots were on the floor, so her polka dot socks were exposed. Under her leather jacket, she wore a black, full length T-shirt to hide whatever horrible injury she got while threatening a man's life for Betty Beater.

"What?" Alice glanced up from the journal. She sat on the girls' bathroom floor, legs crossed like a pretzel. Her sneakers and messenger bag were next to her in the corner as well as her backpack and camera. She read all the journals, most of which were completely blank. Susan never had the chance to write in them. Others were half full, some lines were in code.

Alice was back to the first journal because it made the most sense. She highlighted phrases, dog-eared pages, and used sticky notes to mark certain sentences. She read it so many times, she basically memorized it.

"Hello?" Cece waved her legs to get Alice's attention. "A cake pop-"

"What are you talking about? What does a cake pop have to do with any-thing?"

"You really should've signaled before you left the 'no humor' zone," Cece said. "Look, I get it, you're upset but your mom died suddenly, she just didn't have time-"

"No, I know. It's not... It's not that." Alice closed the journal. She used her finger as a bookmark. Reading the journals, seeing her mom's handwriting, it was a more emotional experience than she expected. It made her realize how little she knew about Susan.

Susan wrote entries about certain fights she had with Destroyer or Mama Smoke - Destroyer's second-in-command - and the other members of Destroyer's infamous powered-person gang. Nothing too detailed but enough to get a picture. Alice recognized some of the fights from the news.

She thought she knew her mom. She thought she was included in Susan's secrets but apparently, Susan wore more than one mask. Alice doubted anyone knew her true face.

"Then what is it?" Cece asked.

Alice leaned her head against the wall, legs bent by her chest, arms resting on her knees. "She knew how to use her powers, she taught me to control mine... sort of..." she paused. Susan taught Alice that her powers were part of her as much as her skin or her blood were part of her. They reacted to her reactions, so Susan taught Alice to keep herself calm and present in any situation but their lessons never went further than that. "But she could do amazing things with her powers, you know?"

"I might have seen a couple of news stories," Cece smiled. A couple was an understatement. "She couldn't transform into lightning like you, it was different. Less stable, less natural."

Susan's lightning seemed less pure than Alice's because of its blue tint. She couldn't transform for as long as Alice could either. Susan never said why. Either she didn't know or she lied. Alice wasn't sure what to believe now. "She was still powerful. She was amazing," Alice shrugged. "All I can do is blast and move a cup across a clear surface. And I've been practicing for... Well, you know."

Susan could use her powers to levitate things, move things. Sometimes, she used her lightning to light matches or warm her tea when it got cold. Once, when a car thief was racing through the streets of Height City and the police couldn't catch him - they chased him for twenty blocks - Glisin used her powers to stop the car. Navy blue lightning crackled from her fingertips, connected to the car's hood, danced against its metal, and lifted it into the air. She swung it above her head and dropped it on the other side of the street. The thief didn't know what to do.

A helicopter from Channel Six caught it all on camera. Alice remembered sitting on her couch, staring at the TV, amazed by her mother.

"I thought you didn't want to be a superhero," Cece said. "So, why does it matter?"

"No, I... I don't want to be, it's just that my powers are... they're a gift. This amazing gift that I don't know anything about." She set the journal down and looked at her hands. Her long, thin fingers and the plain lines on her palms. When she was little, she wanted nothing more than to be like her mom, then Susan died, and being a hero seemed less exciting.

She stopped using her abilities because it felt wrong without Susan there to be her teacher. Alice never thought one day she might want to see what she was capable of but the Adler Building Fire woke something up, a fascination she never realized she had.

"I barely knew I could do what I did for Jess," she leaned forward, running her fingers down the journal's soft, leather cover. "I don't know what my powers are capable of. I don't know what I'm capable of," she looked at Cece, wanting to show how serious and desperate she felt. "I'd like to find out."

Cece rolled her eyes and muttered a few mean, creative curse words.

Alice felt defeated. Was it possible she somehow disappointed her mom? Would Susan have wanted Alice to stop using her powers or would she have wanted Alice to keep using them despite her absence? Alice wasn't sure. She wanted to talk to her mom so bad, more than anything.

"I'm probably gonna regret this but," Cece slid off the counter. "You said that journal mentions someone named Karen Micheals?"

"Yeah. A few times. Why?"

Cece took out her latest burner phone and dialed. Alice stood up. She hugged the journal against her chest and came to Cece's side. The phone clicked and Tommy answered. He sounded distracted.

"Hello?"

"Hey, I need something," Cece smiled. Did she know he couldn't see her? She must've memorized his number because she didn't keep a contact list. She switched phones every two weeks.

"Not even a hello?" he asked. "Really?"

"Hi," she said. "Okay, can you find someone for me? The name's Karen Micheals."

"I could. Who is she?"

"For all I know she's a cross-dressing midget," Cece said. "But it's really important that I get an address or a phone number or something."

"And why do you need to find a cross-dressing midget?" he asked.

"'Cause I'm in a good mood?"

Alice crinkled her eyebrows. "What?"

"I don't know," Cece waved her away. "Shut up."

"Is that Alice?" Tommy asked. "Is this about her powers?"

The girls shared the same astonished expression. Alice slapped Cece's shoulder as a punishment for telling Tommy about her abilities. How could she? Alice understood they had a connection, they were in a relationship but Alice's powers weren't Cece's secret to tell. If anything, the fact she told Tommy was a betrayal of their friendship.

Cece shook her head. "I didn't!"

"Then how did..." Alice grabbed the phone. "How'd you know?"

"There was a camera across the street from the alley you hid in the night of the Adler Building Fire," he explained in a kind tone. He wasn't judging her for missing it. "Usually, the blackout would've wiped the feed but," he chuckled, proud. "I found it. I used facial recognition to ID you."

"I didn't even think of security cameras," Alice said, feeling stupid.

Cece clicked her tongue. "Wow, you're really bad at this, aren't you?"

"Not helpful."

"I erased it from the digital world so nobody will ever know," Tommy said. "I haven't and I won't tell anyone about your powers. I know it's dangerous and it's your business, and apparently, Cece's."

Cece bit her lip, shrugging and nodding.

Alice smiled. It was nice to know she had people she could trust. She never thought she'd be adding Cece's boyfriend to the list. "Why were you looking at the footage in the first place?"

"Betty wanted to know who the lightning bolt was," he said with a hint of warning. Alice glanced at Cece to see if the mention of her and Tommy's employer caused any worry or fear but her expression was blank, unreadable.

"I told her I looked but I couldn't find anything," Tommy said. "Not a single scrap of evidence that revealed your identity."

"You sure she believed that?" Cece asked.

"I made sure no other hacker in the world could find it," Tommy said. That didn't answer her question. Alice had been told stories about Height City's unofficial Crime Queen. Stories that involved torture, murder, and fear like teaching young kids - Alice's friends - to be killers, soldiers, all in the name of keeping her crown, her control over the unknowing inhabitants of Height City.

Like Destroyer, the Crime Queen was ruthless, cunning, and strategic. If Alice learned anything from the stories, it was that Betty Beater was a force to be reckoned with.

"I'll start the search for Karen Micheals but you guys need to be careful," Tommy said. "If Destroyer thinks there's a new superhero in town, she'll crawl out of the Trenches just for the entertainment of a potential challenge."

"Don't worry, there's not a new superhero here." Alice handed the phone to Cece. She looked at Alice as if questioning the sentence. Alice meant what she said, she wasn't a hero, and she wasn't sure she wanted to be. Her mom was the hero, not her.

Alice leaned against the counter. She flipped the journal over in her hands, feeling the softness of the leather, the roughness of the pages, the texture of the ink. She closed it and set it by the sink.

Cece spoke into the phone. "Don't be mad I lied, I," she sighed. "It wasn't my secret to tell."

"I already have a list of stuff you can do to make it up to me," Tommy said.

"Oh yeah?" Cece chuckled, relieved. "What's the first thing on the list?"

"A massage and I get to choose the takeout we get for the next month."

Alice could hear the love in their voices. It reminded her of the way Mason and Susan used to talk to each other, with love and adoration, like as long as they were together, then the world made sense and nothing else mattered. Part of her wondered if she'd ever have that, if she'd ever find the one person who made her feel safe and cared for, the other part believed she was like the rest of the world, maybe she'd never find the right person to fall in love with.

Cece hung up. She stuffed the phone in her pocket. "Alright, now we wait."

"This is great." Alice put the journal in her messenger bag and wrapped the torn strap around her torso. When she swung the backpack on her shoulder, the weight of her textbooks made her stumble. She hated having so much work but doing it at the counter with Leo while Mister Scotts made dinner, she didn't mind the work, it was actually pretty fun.

"You don't even know if this woman is alive," Cece said. "That journal is from when you were a kid, you know, things might've happened."

"It's still a chance, no matter how small," Alice said. She found a gateway into her mom's secrets, a path to learning about her powers, and she wasn't ready to give up hope yet. She wasn't sure how to imagine someone she had never met. Her mom never mentioned a Karen Micheals. The journal didn't say what she did or how close the two used to be. It only mentioned Karen's thoughts on certain subjects. Based on that, she sounded like some sort of scientist.

Alice went to open the door.

"Mind if I come?" Cece asked.

"Come where?"

"Out into the hall. It occurs to me that I've been to this school a lot in the past few months and I've yet to see what's outside the bathroom door."

"It's just a hall," Alice shrugged. "But sure."

***

Casey

Casey wasn't sure what she expected but it wasn't this. Wide halls with fake, tan tile, white walls, and gray or dark brown lockers. Colorful posters, covered in glitter glue and stickers, advertised the many clubs the school offered and wished good luck to all the sports teams. One banner hanging along the ceiling screamed GO FALCONS! While yellow and blue decorations showed the school spirit.

Chaotic teenagers - Honeycombers, Nesters, and Burrowers - roamed the halls, heading to class, trying to catch up with one another, talking to teachers, goofing around. The bits of chatter, the slamming lockers, and the squeaking footsteps made Casey a little jumpy. It was a vague reminder of St.Marian's but with several improvements.

"What do you think?" Alice asked.

"Did you ever see *Fast Times at Ridgemont High*?"

"I hated that movie."

"Exactly," Casey shrugged.

They stayed close together, side by side, except out of habit, Casey fell a step behind, so she could guard Alice's blind spot. From this position, it'd be much easier to catch or stop a threat from getting to her friend. It was how she protected Bobby and Cole too.

A boy appeared at Alice's other side but his focus was on Casey. "You don't go here."

His beige-colored hair was hidden under a black beanie. He wore jeans, recently ironed, and a graphic T-shirt. The image on the front was of an astronaut holding balloons. The balloons were the planets and Pluto was floating away. He favored his right arm but from the way his index finger was bent, it seemed he had broken it at some point, probably as a kid. His left shoelace was untied, one wrong move and he'd trip into the lockers.

"Perceptive," Casey said. "Who are you?"

"This is Leo," Alice gestured between them. "Leo, this is Cece."

"Cece," he repeated. "What, are you a runaway?"

"Something like that," she said. He didn't know how accurate his guess was. He stared at her, eyebrows crinkled, as if he was trying to remember where he recognized her from. Casey didn't like the idea of him asking any other questions, so she took control of the conversation. "Nice of you to let Al crash."

"Oh, yeah," Leo smiled. "She's practically part of the family now, gave me a run for my money on Scrabble night." He nudged Alice's shoulder, an affectionate, brotherly gesture. "And with her around, my dad stopped trying to teach me to cook."

"I heard she burned the casserole."

"Yeah. We ordered pizza that night," he chuckled. "She's gotten a lot better though, even knows what a whisk is."

"I've had trouble with that one myself. Always thought it was a magic wand," Casey said. She didn't cook. She could heat frozen fries or tater tots in an oven or make toast, and if she was feeling really bold she'd boil pasta and add cheese to it.

Alice opened her locker and shoved her books inside. It was decorated with pictures of the city, of Jess and Leo, and Mister Scotts. One photo featured Casey at Linda's Diner, sitting on the counter, with a plate of french fries on her lap. She was blocking the camera with her hand and rolling her eyes, which seemed about right, only the image was edited to be in pieces like a shattered mirror, and another image was faded into the picture, one where Casey was laughing. Alice must've taken it when she wasn't paying attention.

"I wasn't that bad," Alice said. "I made those blueberry pancakes and they were fantastic."

"They were shaped like blobs," Leo said. "But yeah, they tasted good."

"See?" she smiled. "I'm a rocking chef."

"Sous chef," Casey corrected, tearing her focus away from the picture.

It was good to see Alice happy. It was a nice change from when they first met but it also felt like the first step toward losing each other. Alice had Leo, and Jess, and Mister Scotts, she had a new family and a new honesty with her childhood best friend, why would she still need Casey? The second step toward losing their friendship was Alice learning about her powers. After all, how could a superhero and a future crime boss ever be friends?

"Oh, did I tell you about that motel Bobby and I found?" Leo asked, looking at Alice.

Casey did a double take. "You what?"

He glanced at her. "Yeah, I've been helping Bobby look for motels to live at. The first one we found smelled an awful lot like mold," he scrunched his nose in disgust. "And the second one had water damage and at the third, there was this sleazy landlord who tried to offer her a discount for, well," he paused. "Let's just say it wasn't a nice discount."

"Sounds like the Burrows," Casey said. Why didn't Bobby tell her about this? Bobby was safe and protected where she was. She had a roof over her head, solid walls, cooked meals, an air mattress to sleep on, and company. It was a good setup and Sally would never kick her out.

"I keep telling her we need to look in the Nests," Leo said. "Sure, they're a little pricier but they're nicer," he shrugged. "But she wants to keep checking places out in the Burrows."

"Where is she?" Casey asked. "I need to talk to her."

Leo pointed to a locker down and across the hall.

Bobby stood in front of it, holding three hardcover textbooks and a spiral-bound notebook. Under a purple, eighties-themed jacket complete with a fitted waist and shoulder pads, she wore a white, knee-length sundress with a furry zebra-striped collar. Her sparkly, black heels shimmered in the fluorescent lighting and her panda-shaped purse hung from her shoulder, swinging from side to side, as she got ready for her next class.

Casey shoved through a group of Honeycombers, threatening them with her glare. She squeezed past a couple of Nesters and headed straight to Bobby. Two Burrower boys with lower gang tattoos practically broke their necks when they jumped out of her way, arms held up in surrender.

They must've recognized her as Cece.

She stood behind Bobby, arms crossed. "You could stay with me if you don't want to stay at Sally's."

Bobby almost dropped her books. She turned, lips parted in surprise and eyes wide. Her lavender eyeshadow and gold-speckled mascara made her look like a rock star. "What are you doing here?"

"Why didn't you tell me you were looking for a place?" Casey asked. "Why isn't Sally's good enough?"

"I, I, I knew... I knew you'd try and talk me out of it," she closed her locker. "You need to go, you can't be here, you don't go here. I'm gonna get in trouble, I'll-"

"B." Casey held a solid tone, it meant her patience was wearing thin and Bobby better have a really good explanation. The same tone could also mean she'd handle something if it needed to be handled and no questions should be asked. She used it on Bobby several times.

"Can't we talk about this later?" she whined. "Please."

"No, we can't." Casey lowered her voice, careful in case others were listening. "Motels in the Burrows are dangerous, you know that. It's where business is conducted, I would know," she pointed to herself. She'd done several bloody jobs in Burrows' motel rooms, it wasn't pretty. "Now you wanna go live at one? Don't you trust Sally? She wouldn't kick you out-"

"Exactly! Sally wouldn't. I don't want to end up being hated by her." Tears filled her pretty hazel eyes, she shook her head. "I have a tendency to screw up-"

"That is not true," Casey scoffed. "You're-"

"I almost got you killed!" Bobby yelled. She shrunk back into herself and they both glanced around to check if anyone had heard her. The random teenagers went about their business, yelling, laughing. A few boys wrestled each other by the water fountain, some girls traded makeup tips by a French club poster. It was all very mundane and ordinary. Alice and Leo were the only ones staring at Casey and Bobby but luckily, they were out of earshot.

"B, that wasn't your fault," Casey said. "The shooting was-"

"I called you because I was scared and they basically blew up the house." As much as she tried, she couldn't keep her voice steady, it cracked with emotion, allowing the shame she felt to be heard from miles away.

Casey hadn't realized how hard it had been for her.

"We got lucky," Bobby said. "But... but if we hadn't..."

"Nice outfit," Brittany scoffed, her tone dripping with sarcasm. She wore a cashmere turtleneck top and black pants. Her hair was tied in one big, fishtail braid. Casey recognized the mayor's oldest daughter from the news and from Betty's personal archive, where she stored evidence and information on her employees. Brittany Mikes, Honeycombs' queen and Bobby's nemesis, not to mention, she'd made a move on Tommy before school started.

"What's with the blue hair?" Cindy Cohen chuckled. "Trying to be a mermaid?"

"No, but I'd love to drown you," Casey mocked her laugh. It took all her self-control not to slam their heads together. "Now, can you two leave by yourselves or do you need to be kicked to the curb?"

***

221

Bobby

"You look like you should be working the curb," Brittany said, acting superior. She was good at acting like she owned the world. Bobby glanced between her and Casey as the two glared at one another, each one challenging the other. She knew exactly where this was headed and it wouldn't be good for anyone. She needed to stop it, but how?

"Let me ask you something," Casey said in her nicest tone, which sent shivers down Bobby's spine. "Are those deflated balloons on your chest real or plastic? I just can't tell." She stepped toward Brittany, ready to slap her into next week, but Brittany didn't back down. If anything, she seemed more angry.

Casey reached for her boot. *Oh no.* She'd scare the hell out of both Brittany and Cindy, which would probably result in Bobby getting expelled. She couldn't have that. She needed to stay in school, she needed to graduate.

"Please don't," she whispered.

Casey ignored her, too focused on Brittany. She kept her arm stretched toward her boot, ready to grab a knife and twirl it or wave it, whatever she was going to do with it, anything was possible. Her fierce green eyes were glued to Brittany, staring her down, strong and menacing.

Cindy stood near the two girls, entertained. She didn't know that right now her friend didn't hold any power. Casey didn't care if they were Honeycombers or from influential families, she'd threaten their lives just to make a point.

"Burrower," Brittany hissed.

Casey's hand was on her boot. "Honeycomber."

"Criminal."

"Bitch."

"Hi!" Alice laughed. She put herself halfway between the two. She grabbed Casey's shoulders and gave her an intense look. Casey met it. She didn't protest when Alice yanked her away from the situation.

Leo came to Bobby's side, took her hand, and led her to safety, fingers loosely intertwined. His hand was warm, a little sweaty, but his touch was kind and gentle.

Bobby tried to convince him to stop helping her search for motels but he was insistent. He liked her company; he said she made him laugh and since he had never been to the Burrows, he figured she was a good tour guide. She wasn't sure if he meant the nice things he said or if he was only trying to flatter her but either way, after the last motel with the sleazy landlord, she didn't want to go to the places alone.

"You okay?" He took her books, one arm folded around them, and he rubbed her shoulder. She was too focused on Casey and Alice to really notice his affectionate touch or the fact that he hadn't stopped staring at her since he came to her rescue.

The two girls understood each other's movements and expressions. It was weird to see someone else read Casey so well, and Casey had lowered her emotional shields enough to let Alice take a peek into who she was, not enough for Alice to get a whole picture but still.

"What were you gonna do?" Alice asked. "Stab Brittany in public?"

"I figured I'd wing it," Casey turned to Bobby. "Now back to you-"

Bobby couldn't take it anymore. Her anger boiled over, she was ready to explode. "I've been dealing with Brittany and Cindy's crap for years, okay? I'm not helpless or, well, I don't want to be," she sighed, releasing the steam rising in her chest. "You have to stop protecting me, stop coming to help every time I screw up, you can't keep forgiving me either," her voice broke. "Why aren't you mad at me? Why haven't you realized-"

"B, you haven't left me yet so why should I leave you?" Casey's solid tone made Bobby furious.

Alice and Leo stood together, silently watching the argument with interested eyes.

"I mess up! I always mess up!" Bobby yelled. "You could've... you could have died." She loved Casey more than anyone else in the world. "I can't be the reason you die-"

"I'm not going anywhere!" she shouted. "And you need to deal with it!"

"Stop protecting me! Just stop it!"

"Fine!" Casey said, shoulders relaxed. Her stance was rigid and her expression stayed tense, angry. "I'll stop protecting you! Hell, I'll hold your heels while you take a long walk off a short pier!"

"Thank you!" Bobby took her books and stomped away.

***

Jess

Electric guitar riffs, wild drumbeats, and fantastic keyboard solos blasted around Jess's bedroom. The tempo was fast and the rhythm was aggressive. The lyrics had something to do with justice or possibly war or revolution. She couldn't tell but it was fascinating.

She sat on her freshly made bed surrounded by notebooks and textbooks for each of her honors classes, vocabulary flashcards, folders for every club she had joined, homework, extra credit, and her laptop, which needed to be charged. She joined the student council again as well as the party planning committee and the Morgan High newspaper. She convinced Layla it'd spice up her college applications.

Being busy kept her from thinking about the fire. She still couldn't remember what happened after the gunshot, other than blood and pain. At night, she'd wake up as if she were stuck inside the flames, unable to escape but instead of Ted holding the match, it was Layla.

Jess rubbed her neck, feeling sore. She still had a lot more to finish.

Her window slid open and she smiled when Dave climbed through it. He wore his brown, rugged leather jacket over a plain navy blue T-shirt and jeans. His hair was messy, probably from wearing his helmet. He took his boots and set them under the windowsill. He came to the bed. "What do you think of the band?"

"It's not particularly to my taste." Jess enjoyed a few of the bands he showed her like the Renegades, an independent punk and classic rock band made up of four teenagers about their age. And she liked some of the famous rock bands but the metal bands gave her a headache.

"They're telling their truth, it's a story, you like stories," Dave said. He sighed. "So, you don't like it?"

"Not really." She stood beside the bed and stretched her arms above her head. She'd been sitting in the same position for two hours, studying. She needed a break. "But I like those sci-fi movies, at least the science part of them was really cool."

"The violence is my favorite part," he said.

"It's still common ground."

"That it is." He gestured to the mess on her bedspread. "Planning the next big school dance?"

"Among other things." She went to the stereo on her dresser. She turned the knob, silencing the music, and put the CD in its case.

Dave was right behind her. His hands, gentle and strong, drifted from her shoulders to her wrists. His fingertips sent tiny jolts over her skin. "Do you ever not study?"

She faced him, bodies an inch apart. She wasn't sure how it was possible but his eyes seemed bluer tonight. The first time Dave was in her bedroom he went through her books and looked at the pictures on her corkboard. He flopped down on her bed, folded his arms behind his head, and smiled flirtatiously as he teased her about climbing through the window. They figured out that if he climbed the sycamore tree in her backyard, he could get to the low roof shingles and crawl right up to her room, easy, and Layla would never know.

"Yes, I'm on the party planning committee and I hang out with Alice and you," she pulled him a little closer, enough to feel his body against hers. She held the lapels of his leather jacket. "And I write articles for the newspaper. In fact, I just finished one about the sixtieth anniversary of the school and I'm planning a dance for it."

"I stand corrected," he said, half joking. "You really like working on the newspaper, huh?"

"I really do." Her excitement felt like a billion jumping beans exploding with energy in her chest. "It's so much fun. The research part, the fact-checking, the writing. Seeing it published." Her first published article was about one of the first football games of the school year. She wasn't a sports fan but taking time to understand the game, writing about the players, and feeling the fans' excitement fascinated her. She still didn't get the allure of football but the experience was fun. "I know it's only a school paper but it's amazing."

"You're adorable when you're being a dork," he smiled as if she were the most amazing person in the world. It made the butterflies dancing in her stomach multiply. He moved his hands down her arms and interlocked their fingers. He kissed the scabs on her cuticles.

Although her instinct was to pull away, to be embarrassed and hide her nervous habit, she didn't. She let him hold her hands, keeping her nerves at bay. "I've even researched some journalism schools." She didn't expect to love the newspaper and writing as much as she did. It was a great surprise. "I know it's probably stupid and pointless but I can't help it. I can't stop thinking about it."

"You've got a year to decide what you want to be, right?" Dave asked.

"My mom wants me to be a lawyer." It was simple. Jess could tell her parents she wanted to explore journalism or writing or any future outside Zak City Law but they wouldn't help her or accept it. It was law school or nothing. "I have to follow the plan."

"Zak City Law, marriage, kids," he said, almost bored. His grip tensed but his lazy, stone expression didn't change. He stared at their interlocked fingers. "Guess I don't fit into that, huh?"

They'd been dating since the beginning of the year. They hadn't discussed the future. Dave always changed the subject when Jess tried to bring it up. They never officially told anyone - other than their closest friends - about their relationship. In some ways, it was easier but in others, it hurt.

"Are you saying you want to fit in?" She tried to read his face but it didn't indicate what he felt. He was good at hiding his thoughts and emotions. A skill he probably learned from Betty Beater.

"One day at a time, right?" He leaned closer to her, erasing the last inch that kept them apart. The heat of his breath made her blush and his touch made her heart jump. She loved being able to feel his heartbeat, racing and excited, like hers. Hands on her waist, he kissed her, which made sparks explode throughout her body.

"I've been thinking," she pulled away from him. He tried to kiss her again but she dodged it. "Maybe we should tell them."

"Tell who what?"

"My parents about us."

"You wanna tell the Wicked Bitch about us?" He took his hands off her waist, breaking whatever romantic moment they had been. He didn't seem happy with the idea. "Won't she turn me into a toad?"

"Layla hates toads, if anything, she'd turn you into a hamster," Jess said. She thought joking about it would help lighten the subject but Dave wasn't amused. She cleared her throat. "Sneaking around isn't practical. If we told them, we could live outside my bedroom."

She wanted to take Dave to her favorite bookstore or to Moon Park. She wanted to go out with their friends as a couple. She loved their bubble but the longer they stayed in it, the harder it would be to pop. Like ripping off a bandaid, she wanted to tell her mother and stop worrying about getting caught.

"We could do that now. I could take you to the Burrows," he said. "We could play pool at Eddie's Bar or dance at Sally's Place, sit in the corner booth-" he broke off, smiling. He pulled her against him, as close as they could be. "For the record," he kissed her, gentle and slow. "I don't mind being in your bedroom."

She liked having his arms around her, strong and supportive, muscular. He was the first boy she knew who had actual muscles. Tony and Jake played sports and worked out but they weren't as finely tuned as Dave, maybe it was a Burrower thing.

"We can't go to the country club though or go to dances. You can't even park your motorcycle outside my house." She wasn't sure how to convince him it was a good idea, maybe she hadn't completely convinced herself.

He sighed, fingers tapping her waist. She tried to read his mind but couldn't. What was he thinking? She tried fixing his messy hair but only seemed to make it worse. She gave up. "Something wrong?"

"No," he paused. "Just... you're a Honeycomber. You're gonna go to college, and," he seemed to reconsider his next words. "And I'm gonna end up nowhere good." What wasn't he saying?

"You could be better, be more, if you wanted to be," she said.

He laughed.

She knew how he felt about his upbringing. He hated his childhood. He hated his father. Ted defined him in a way Jess couldn't understand yet. She didn't know how he felt about his mother. He didn't talk about Cynthia often, a few minor details and tidbits but nothing of substance. He talked about his friends more than anything else. He was more connected to them than his parents.

He shook his head, still chuckling, and he kissed her.

She stretched against him and wrapped her arms around his neck.

"So, what do you think?" she didn't mean to smile but she couldn't stop herself. "About telling people who aren't in the inner circle about us?"

"Well... " he dropped her into a dip, one hand grasped firmly on her back and the other held her waist. "I am a good dancer." He pulled her up and kissed her again. At first, it was light, playful, then it became deep and wanting, distracting. She didn't want it to end.

Dave had the ability to make her forget about the stress and pressure of her everyday life. She didn't have to be the perfect daughter or the perfect student. She didn't have to constantly impress him or succeed for him, she could be herself, imperfections included.

She pushed his jacket off. He took it from her, ready to toss it somewhere, but the door cracked open, so like a horse getting whipped in the ass, Dave ducked into the closet.

Jess closed the door and slapped her back against it. Heart pounding and breath heavy, she picked her cuticles. At this point, they knew the signs of invaded privacy and impending doom.

Layla walked in. "Jessica, I wanted to make sure you're studying." She wore a fuzzy bathrobe and big bunny slippers. "The SATs may be in the Spring but they're coming up fast. You need to ace them."

"Mm. Mm-hmm," Jess hid her hands behind her back. "I'm studying."

"Have you practiced your college essay?" Layla didn't notice Dave's shoes by the window or the open curtains. If she had, she'd be ransacking Jess's entire bedroom, throwing pillows, lecturing her about lying and keeping secrets, how wrong it was, how horrible and disrespectful. Funny, how Jess had to respect Layla's privacy when Layla didn't respect hers.

Jess didn't make eye contact. She went to her desk, grabbed a folder marked with her perfectly neat penmanship, and handed it to her mom. "I wrote six versions for you to approve."

"Good girl," Layla patted her head. "I'll look them over and give notes, so you can correct all your mistakes, then we'll work on combining and choosing," she smiled. Her condescending, I-own-you smile. "Okay?" She spoke to Jess like she was a six-year-old who needed supervision and hand-holding.

It made Jess feel incompetent. She wasn't incompetent. "Yes, Mom." Her tone stayed obedient.

Layla nodded. "Good. Now, get back to work."

She left the door wide open. When Jess closed it, she put her desk chair under the knob, so it couldn't be opened from the hall. She still wasn't allowed to have a lock, which was demeaning on many levels.

She turned and smiled, as Dave crept out of the closet and hurried over to her. He kissed her quick, then lifted her up, one arm secured her waist and the other held her thigh. She wrapped her legs around his hips and wrapped her arms around his neck, squeezing his shoulders.

"We're getting better at that," he chuckled. They had almost gotten caught a few times in the beginning but they learned how to avoid her parents. Neither Layla nor Bennett suspected a thing. It was kind of fun being rebellious.

"Maybe we should start with my dad," Jess said. "Let him tell my mom."

Dave kissed her, deep and needing, and carried her to the bed. He gently dropped her on the only empty space, his weight hovering against her body, warm and toned, his heart pounding almost as fast as hers. She swore she saw stars as his beautiful, dark blue eyes focused on her.

He traced her cheekbone, then his hand drifted down her side. He kissed her and the world became quiet. Her parents didn't exist, the expectations, the stress, the work, the pressure, it was all silenced by his lips and she loved it.

"Or we could keep sneaking around." He moved his lips across her skin and onto her neck, so she tilted her head back. His kisses were careful, strategic, as if she were made of some sort of delicate glass. She bit her lip, gripping tightly to his T-shirt, pulling him closer until the space between their bodies disappeared. Dave kept his hands on her waist but his fingers were anxious, shaky. He lifted himself off her, again breaking the moment. "I wouldn't want to be turned to stone by Layla's death stare."

Jess didn't want to talk about her mom anymore. She didn't want to study or think about studying or worry about the future. She wanted to stay in the moment. She needed to stay in the moment. The more she thought about her future, the more she realized she had no power over it.

She pulled off her shirt and tossed it on the floor. Her bra was simple, pink, she liked it.

Dave glanced at the scar on her belly, the one his father had given her. He didn't have to feel guilty, it wasn't his fault but he couldn't seem to believe it. He saw the scar and an apology immediately formed in his eyes.

"Dave," Jess said. She hated the look on his face.

Her voice brought him back to reality. He smiled at her - his charming, casual smile - and yanked off his T-shirt, revealing the faint but permanent scars on his torso. He didn't talk about his wounds. She knew a few of his scars were from his dad, another couple were from sparring with Cece or Tommy but the others were total mysteries.

Jess wondered what they were from. Dave might never tell her.

He kissed her.

Chapter 12

Jess

JESS KEPT QUIET AS she tiptoed down the stairs and peeked into the living room, hidden behind the wall so her mom wouldn't see her. Layla stood by the coffee table, packing case files into her black, five-hundred-dollar briefcase. Jess wondered what sort of cases they were for; were they for legal lawsuits or something for Betty Beater?

One night while Layla and Bennett were at a Honeycombs' event - Jess told them she was sick, so she wouldn't have to go - she snuck into the dining room and went through Layla's private files, including insurance documents, birth certificates, and bank records. She learned that after Ted Marson was released from Steel Prison, exactly ten thousand dollars was wired into Layla and Bennett's shared account, which meant there wasn't a threat to their lives but they voluntarily worked for the Crime Queen. They helped release a known murderer, a violent killer, for money.

Who else in the Honeycombs was secretly a criminal? Jess kept her questions to herself. Even if she wanted to confront her parents, it'd only make things worse. Besides, she had other things to worry about. "You can do this," she whispered, picking her cuticles.

The same night she found the payment, when her parents got home, she heard them talking about her. The conversation rang in Jess's head like an annoying little bell.

She's talking back, she's in her room all the time, she's disagreeing with me, it's like she's completely forgotten how to be civil, Layla said. *And now missing the party, you know, she was lying about being sick, I cannot believe you let her stay home.*

She's a teenager, it's a phase, she'll go back to being herself soon, Bennett said. *You have to be patient, it's not like her grades are slipping.*

Jess hoped he was wrong. She didn't want to go back to following orders. She didn't realize how different she'd become until cotillion. Key Hotel hosted the ball every year, it was one of the most attended events in the Honeycombs. Jess looked at her reflection, wearing a fancy, white ball gown, elbow-length gloves, and pearl jewelry, and felt foreign in her own skin. While all the other girls, including Brittany and Cindy, laughed, squealed, and complimented each other, Jess stood by herself, wondering what the hell she was doing there.

"Jessica, did you remember to get a ride with Brittany? I have court, so I can't drive you to school and your father left already for that meeting." Layla's shouts were stressed, tired. She must've stayed up late working on her case.

Jess hid her hands behind her back. She took a deep breath. If this didn't go well, at least she and Dave had a plausible escape route. "I remembered but uh, Brit couldn't do it. So," the dryness of her throat made it hard to speak. "I had to ask someone else."

Maybe Dave was right. She should've snuck out the window.

"Who-" Layla turned, eyes flitting over Jess's person. Her face twisted in hatred or maybe it was disgust. Either way, she wasn't happy with Jess's outfit. Jess expected this reaction but it still scared her. She wasn't sure she'd ever stop fearing her mother.

"What the, what are you wearing?" Layla managed to say through gritted teeth.

Jess gulped. She wore a black pencil skirt and a fitted white tank top under a pink, slightly see-through, floral blouse with poet-styled sleeves. She couldn't take all the credit for the ensemble, it was Bobby who suggested a new wardrobe and took Jess shopping at her favorite boutiques and thrift stores in the Nests.

Layla didn't wait for an answer. "I don't like it." When she slammed her briefcase shut, Jess flinched. "Go put on one of your polo shirts and the jean skirt I got you for Christmas."

"I, uh, I can't. I threw them away." Jess hated feeling guilty for something she did even if it wasn't wrong. Why couldn't she have clothes she liked? Why did she need her mom's permission for everything? She may fear Layla's wrath but she was tired of not feeling like her own person. She wasn't a puppet or a pet, she was a daughter. She liked this outfit. She liked her pink streaks. Why was that wrong?

"You what?" Layla asked, appalled. "Why would you do that?"

"Because I don't like them, I never really liked them." Jess tried to seem confident, shoulders back, chin held high, but it was difficult. She kept her hands behind her back, picking her cuticles until one of her fingers started to hurt. "I wanted to change my style, update a little. And it's not like what I'm wearing is inappropriate, it's just different, right?"

She didn't mean for it to sound like a question but she couldn't help it. She wanted to shrink under Layla's terrifying, iron stare. Her mom didn't say anything at first, possibly calculating the number of punishments she could give Jess before she went to college. Jess needed a paper towel to wipe the sweat seeping from her armpits. She hoped her deodorant wouldn't rub off.

"We don't have time for this," Layla said. She looked angry but her tone was cold, detached. "If you didn't get a ride with Brittany, then who? Cindy? Alice?"

"My boyfriend," Jess closed her eyes and braced herself for disapproval, a lecture, anything and everything her mom could dish out. If the outfit didn't piss her off, then this new information definitely would.

She and Dave were happy and stable. She loved being with him. She loved when he listened to her read her favorite books out loud, she loved when he teased her and tried to distract her while she was studying, she loved hearing his stories from the Burrows and curling up in his arms. She wanted to take the next step, and the next step was making their relationship public, specifically telling her mother.

"Boyfriend," Layla repeated as if she were wrapping her mind around it. "Okay, who is it? Tony O'Hare or, oh, Jake. I love Jake. He's such a good boy, well-groomed, and his parents, well," she chuckled. Jake's mother was a surgeon and his dad worked for Cruise Industries. "I should invite them to dinner-"

Before Jess could correct her, a familiar engine thundered up the driveway. Dave came like he said he would. Part of her thought he might make a run for it. She gulped. Her nerves tightened and she felt sick, she ignored the nausea and ran to the front door, beating Layla there by a few seconds.

Dave stood on the front porch, white as a sheet, each hand tapping one of his thighs. She had never seen him look so afraid, not even before he went to face his father but maybe that was because Ted was a devil Dave understood and Layla was an entirely new animal.

"Who's this?" Layla stood behind Jess. Her voice was eerily calm.

"Mom, this is Dave," Jess kept her arm stretched between them in case Layla tried to choke him or something. She kept herself still, trying not to show her panic. She didn't want to show fear. "He and I have been seeing each other since, well, technically the end of summer, you two have actually met, uh-"

"I know." Layla's glare could set fire to the ocean, she might've been trying to turn Dave to dust with only her eyes.

He squeezed Jess's hand, either for comfort or strength, she couldn't tell. His palms were smothered in sweat and his stance was tense like he was being stared down by a giant, rabid polar bear. Jess felt terrible but she loved that he liked her enough to do this.

Her mother's face was a lecture in itself, disapproval, anger, shock, disappointment. Jess could almost hear the speech about how she needed to focus on schoolwork, she didn't have time to date, she was busy, and this boy wasn't right for her, he was a Burrower, a criminal, and she should be with someone better, someone Layla wanted her to be with.

"We should go," Dave nudged her shoulder. His face screamed *Get me out of here*.

She nodded. "Yeah. I have to get to school."

Jess held tight to her backpack as they ran down the porch's steps and hurried to the motorcycle - which Dave had secretly named Ridley - parked next to Layla's SUV. It faced the road, anxiously waiting to help them escape. Dave handed her a helmet and took the front, hands firmly gripped on the handlebars. He loved his bike. He always looked excited when he was about to drive it, and he spent his free time updating and working on it.

Jess sat behind him, fingers clasped against his chest.

"No!" Layla stomped toward them, ready to grab Jess and smack Dave. "That thing is a danger-"

The loud, thunderous roars of the engine drowned out her disapproving shouts.

Dave's belly rippled under Jess's hands when he laughed. She smiled. They raced down the driveway and away from her house, escaping Layla's anger. Jess would have to go home and face her parents eventually but right now, she could enjoy the ride.

The first time she rode this motorcycle was with a stranger, an annoying boy who hated her, to stop his crazy, violent father from killing her parents. She was terrified they'd be hurt, that she'd never see them again, and it was awkward holding onto someone she didn't know. She could've sworn she stopped breathing. But now, the world glided by in beautiful blends of color and architecture. The city's buildings were tall, intimidating, filled with secrets and sins. Some were built before and during the ninety-twenties, with vintage windows and exposed bricks.

People blurred into the scenery, faint and far away. Jess didn't focus on the crowds, instead, she looked up at the sky. Strips of fluffy clouds decorated the deep blue background while the sun shone over everything, chasing away the shadows.

The cold wind froze Jess's fingertips but she held on, feeling free.

When the motorcycle turned, it tipped so far, Jess wondered if the road would ripple like the ocean if she ran her hand across it but, of course, she knew that was logically impossible. Under her fingers, Dave's heart hammered with excitement, and hers matched it. She put the tip of her nose against his back, the smell of his leather jacket mixed with the many scents of Height City.

They pulled up to the school and parked beside the curb. The regular early birds glanced at them, most of whom were Honeycombers and Nesters, a few Burrowers. After they saw the couple, they went about their business, forgetting Jess and Dave existed, which was a relief.

Jess used Dave's shoulder to steady herself as she got off the bike. She un-buckled her helmet and smoothed out her hair. Her racing heartbeat started to calm but she still felt exhilarated. She loved being the girl on the back of the motorcycle.

"Well," Dave took off his helmet. "She didn't kill me, so it went better than I expected."

"Are you sure you're okay with this? Her," Jess glanced at her classmates. A group of Honeycomber girls were standing by the front steps, staring at them and whispering, amongst them were Brittany and Cindy. They didn't look happy. "And everybody else knowing about us? I know you agreed before but-"

"I think I'm good," Dave spotted the girls too. "How do you feel?"

Jess thought she'd be more nervous or freaked out but she wasn't. She wasn't having second thoughts or doubts, she wanted people to know they were to-gether. She didn't want to care about other people's opinions, it was exhausting. "Good, really good," she chuckled. "Text me later, we'll go on a real date, one that doesn't start in my bedroom."

"I'm in." He hooked his arm around her waist and pulled her closer, holding the motorcycle steady. "As long as it can still end in your bedroom."

She rolled her eyes but couldn't hide her smile. She kissed him, quick and teasing, trying to show him how excited she was. She wasn't going to answer his question though, at least until she decided what she wanted to do.

"And I get to plan it," he said.

"Hmm..." She pretended to think. Jess usually preferred to be the planner but it wouldn't kill her to let him do it. She raised an eyebrow. "Any hints?"

"Armed robbery?" he joked. She hoped it was a joke.

He kissed her, one hand traced her cheek and the other tightened on her waist. Her arms lazily laid on his shoulders, fingers clasped behind his head. She suddenly didn't care about her friends watching them or any other Honeycomber who might judge her for being with a Burrower. If they disapproved, fine.

"I don't think I can fit that into my schedule."

"How about pool at Eddie's Bar?"

"That sounds perfect." She gently put their foreheads together. "You'll have to teach me how to play."

"I can do that," His hand drifted up her arm. He glanced down at her outfit. "You look really good."

"You're not so bad yourself." She pulled away, holding his jacket's lapels. She kissed him.

He smiled, eyes half closed, entranced by her touch as if she was a dream come true. No one had ever looked at her like that before, not even the boys who claimed to like her. Dave kept her close, hesitating to let her go. "You sure you don't wanna skip school? I could buy you breakfast, we could hang out at my place."

She was tempted but she couldn't. "I'll see you this evening for our date."

She took his hand from her waist and played with his fingers. He watched her back away from him, nothing could've ripped his gaze away from hers.

She smiled. "Bye."

"Have a good day," Dave said. "And don't forget to learn something."

Jess ran into the school. The other students ran up and down the halls, laughing and chatting, slamming their lockers and preparing for class. A few Nesters were sitting in a circle on the floor, finishing their homework, while Tony and his friends tossed a foam football back and forth. Principal Penez started yelling at them about how unsafe it was.

Jess couldn't stop smiling or thinking about Dave. She couldn't wait for their date. She wondered if she should tell him she already knew how to play pool but decided that it'd be best to let him teach her. She had to choose an outfit too and come up with a way to get out of the house without Layla knowing.

"I have so many questions!" Cindy hooked her arm with Jess's. "First off, a Burrower, have you no shame?"

Brittany locked arms on Jess's other side. She was trapped between them with no way out. They both wore their cheer uniforms except Brittany also had a sweatshirt tied around her waist, and Cindy carried a new designer purse. Jess wished she would've seen them coming, she could've gotten away.

"He's a good guy. He's nice to me," she said.

"He's hot. Well done," Brittany nudged her shoulder.

"Okay," Cindy scoffed, disagreeing. "Weren't you just at Jake's lacrosse game? Nose in a book. Did you two have a fight?"

"Jake and I are friends, we have been for almost our entire lives," Jess said. Why couldn't people understand that? "We both understand that, besides, he has a girlfriend now who isn't me."

He told her about his new girlfriend at his lacrosse game. He offered to introduce them. Jess was happy for him and she was so sick of people, of Layla, pushing her toward him.

"Fine, okay," Cindy said. "But a Burrower? You're a Honeycomber, we co-exist because we have to but it's the law of the jungle out here, baby, and what you're doing is unnatural."

"There's nothing wrong with a little taste," Brittany said, mostly to Cindy. "But Cindy's right, you guys have different futures. Let me paint you a picture," she made a frame with her fingers. "Ten years from now, you're going to be a gorgeous, fashionable, successful lawyer, probably married," she raised her eyebrows as if it were a prediction, not a guess. "Kids or no kids, that's your choice." But it wasn't, not if Layla got her way. "But at that same time, he's gonna be in an orange jumpsuit, if he lives that long."

Jess remembered Dave's similar argument. She wished it wasn't right but if things continued they were going, if she went to Zak City Law, she would lose him but Jess didn't want to think about that. She didn't want to think about the future.

"We're better than them," Cindy said. "Take the slut, Bobby Jones, for example, she's a Burrower and dresses like a freak, she's gonna end up being something shameful-"

Jess yanked her arms out of theirs. *Enough is enough!* "You do realize that you two started all the rumors about her, right?" Her tone was determined and angrier than she anticipated. She couldn't believe they were being so horrible, so mean and heartless. Were they actually starting to believe their own lies? "You guys told everyone she slept with half the football team freshman year, you ruined her reputation."

"She made out with Tony in front of everyone while he was still with me, and she was with that loser Johnny something," Brittany said, offended. It was a sore subject.

Jess remembered leaving the gym that day after cheerleader tryouts, Brittany and Cindy were trying to guess whether or not either of them made the team while Jess finished sorting through her extra credit work. They found Tony and Bobby standing in front of his locker, arms wrapped around each other. Their tongues stuck down each other's throats. Neither one seemed bothered by the little audience that had formed. Almost everyone had seen or heard about it by the end of the period.

Brittany cried in the girls' bathroom for an hour before she faked a stomachache and went home. Her first crush, her first love, had betrayed her.

"That was wrong," Jess said. "It was also wrong of you to make out with her boyfriend at Cindy's house sophomore year. You were doing it to make Tony mad, right?"

Brittany looked at the floor, shifting on her feet. She knew it was wrong. She was heartbroken after Tony cheated on her, both times. She wondered for months how many other people he had been with while they were together. Why would she do the same thing to someone else?

Cindy crossed her arms and glared at Jess with vivid anger. Jess didn't say anything or move, she waited, she wanted to see what their reactions would be.

"I have to go." Brittany walked away.

"See what you did?" Cindy said accusingly. She shook her head. "You know, Jessica, I can't believe you're making such insane decisions." She twirled her finger near her ear, then put her hands on her hips. "You're supposed to be the sensible one."

"Wow, okay," Jess scoffed. She hated being judged. "Why don't you go complain to Brittany's ex, or I'm sorry, your current boyfriend, right?" Jess learned about Cindy and Tony's fling a little after school started, at first it was little things she noticed like Tony's letterman jacket at Cindy's house or the scent of her perfume on his shirt. Jess's suspicions were confirmed when she walked in on them making out in the janitor's closet. "You still haven't told her, have you?"

The anger on Cindy's face was replaced with sheer embarrassment. She made her hands into fists, wanting to punch Jess but she didn't, instead, she stomped her foot like a toddler and walked away.

Jess sighed, allowing the tension in her shoulders to cease. She leaned against the lockers and let her backpack drop onto her wrist. She was tired of secrets, of judgments, and of being controlled.

Everyone in her life seemed to have some sort of sin to hide or judgment to make about her except Dave and Alice, of course. When Jess first figured out who Susan was, she couldn't believe it. She couldn't believe the woman she admired so much was actually Glisin, and that her best friend had lied for years about it but Jess understood why Alice did it.

She could only imagine the kind of threats Alice had to hide from.

Jess turned her head, watching the crowds of loud, energized teenagers, and spotted Alice going into the girls' bathroom.

***

Alice

Alice received a text from an unknown number. BATHROOM, NOW. It could only be one person. Alice took her stuff and hurried to the girls' bathroom. She found Cece sitting on the windowsill, one foot against the frame with her knee against her chest. Her hands were stained in fresh blood. Alice didn't want to guess where or who it came from. Cece twirled an elegant, silver knife with a textured, leather handle between her fingers.

"Just get off work?" Alice dropped her backpack on the floor but kept her messenger bag wrapped around her torso. She unzipped the front pocket and took out her mom's journal.

"Finished early," Cece said. "Thought I'd give you the good news."

"Good news?"

The journal's leather cover had become familiar to Alice. She read it before bed every night, not for the information but to see her mom's handwriting. She could almost hear Susan's voice behind the words, soothing and caring. Sometimes, she fell asleep with the journal lying open on her chest or next to her pillow. She'd wake up and put it in her bag, unable to part with it.

"My guy found Karen Micheals," Cece held up a sticky note.

The address was written in blue ink. Alice didn't recognize it but then again, she could barely believe it was there, it was real. Part of her doubted Tommy would be able to find anything that had to do with Karen Micheals. His handwriting was oddly neat, precise, medium lettering.

"He did it?" Alice smiled. "That's where she lives?"

Cece clicked her tongue. "Not quite. It's her last known address and it's from four years ago." She made it sound like a credible lead, not a loss. "What do you think? Wanna jump down the rabbit hole?"

"I can't right now, I'm in school," Alice gestured to the door. "The classes are right out there and the bell is gonna ring soon."

"So, skip," Cece shrugged. When she pointed out the window to emphasize her point, her jacket shifted and revealed a giant, fresh bloodstain on her cropped, gray T-shirt. What the hell did she do? She wasn't harmed like on other days. She had bags under her eyes as if she had stayed up all night but she was wide awake, no other sign of exhaustion.

Alice ignored her dark suspicions. "I can't skip, I live with the teacher. He'd notice if I was gone." She held her hand up before Cece could say anything. "And before you suggest a cover story, I can't get one, I won't put Leo in that position."

It took all her self-control not to take the sticky note and run toward the address written on it. She had an agonizing need to learn about her mother's life, the life Susan had while behind her mask.

"We could kidnap the principal to hide your absence but uh," Cece clicked her tongue. "That might bring up a whole new set of problems."

Before Alice could reply, Jess walked in. *Seriously? Again?* Alice had to start remembering to lock the bathroom door when she was meeting with Cece.

"What are you guys doing?" Jess asked.

"Hi," Alice sighed. "Nothing. Cece's boyfriend found Karen Micheals but-"

"He did? That's amazing!" She smiled. "Let's go meet her."

"We can't... We have school."

"Al's a little nervous about meeting her mom's journal topic." Cece shifted off the windowsill, stood up, and reached her hands above her head, stretching her back. "Don't you wanna meet this chick?"

Alice imagined what Karen Micheals looked like, spoke like, and acted like so many times. Would she know things about Susan that Alice didn't? Would she be able to answer the chaotic questions tumbling around Alice's mind? Would she be able to help Alice learn about her powers? Or was all this a waste of time?

"We should go," Jess said.

"Wait, what?"

"What 'we'?" Cece asked.

Jess glanced between them. She ignored Cece completely. "I have a meeting with the party-planning committee but I can skip it," she shrugged. "I want to go. I figured out the invisible ink, so I should come, I want to see this through."

"You haven't missed a day of school since you had chicken pox in second grade," Alice said. Maybe this was a filmed joke, it had to be some sort of prank or hallucination. Jess was extremely proud of the fact that she had the best attendance record at Morgan High. Why would she offer to ruin it?

"You solve one problem and start thinking you're Veronica Mars, is that it?" Cece asked.

Jess rolled her eyes. "At least I don't dress like a cheap knockoff of Buffy the Vampire Slayer."

Cece raised an eyebrow at the insult. She wasn't amused and Jess wasn't backing down.

Alice glanced between them. She wasn't sure what was happening but she needed to stop it. She did want to meet Karen Micheals, more than anything, maybe it was now or never. She needed to do it before she started doubting it, before she talked herself out of doing it.

She grabbed her backpack, shoved the journal in her messenger bag, and tied her hair into a ponytail. She texted Leo to cover for her. He'd have to figure something out, and she'd need to create a really good lie to tell him about why she needed him to cover for her.

Her friends stood inches apart, stubborn and unwavering, which were two things they had in common. Neither one seemed to like the other although they didn't really know each other.

Cece crossed her arms. "I've met doormats with better comebacks than you."

"What's it like to have the intellect of a monkey?" Jess asked. "No, really, I'm curious."

Alice zipped her sweatshirt, checked her bags and pockets to make sure she had everything she needed, then tossed her backpack out the window. She took a deep breath, readying herself for whatever she was about to find. She hoped this little mission wasn't a dead end.

She climbed through the window.

Four different bus lanes were in the Morgan High parking lot along with hundreds of parking spaces, all meant for guests, students, and faculty. A few of them were reserved for certain teachers, the principal, and other employees. A tall, chain-link fence surrounded the entire cement square, separating the school from the highway.

"Guys, are you coming or what?" Alice's question broke her friends' argument, as she hoped.

They looked at her. Neither had realized she moved away from them.

Cece chuckled. She flipped the knife and stuck it in her boot, crawling through the window with ease.

Jess grabbed her phone and followed. "How do we get there?"

"Sally's jeep is around the corner," Cece said.

"She let you borrow it?" Alice asked.

"Not exactly." She put her foot in the fence and climbed to the top, swinging her leg over the horizontal pole, she dropped to the other side, a perfect landing.

"You stole a car?" Jess asked.

"Don't judge, princess. You're dating a drug dealer."

Jess scoffed at the comeback. Cece smiled at her annoyed expression.

Alice tucked her ponytail under her hood and grabbed the fence. She carefully climbed to the top and swung one leg over the horizontal pole. She sat there for a few seconds until she gathered the courage to jump. She landed on her feet, stumbling, but she caught herself. It was a clumsy landing but she did it. She couldn't hide her pride. "Okay."

Jess took a deep breath. She not-so-gracefully got to the top and swung her legs over. She fell on her butt.

THUD. Cece took a picture.

***

Tommy

Tommy hated this street because it brought back memories that he didn't want anymore. It took a long time to push them down, to lock them in a box deep inside his mind, but now they bubbled up beside the worry he had for Paisley. Thank God, his friends were with him. He couldn't do this alone.

"It's not that I'm not happy about it, it's just.." Dave shrugged. "I'm not a Honeycomber. It's like a dolphin and a bear mating, you know? It looks weird."

"Jess doesn't seem to mind. You guys are going out tonight, right? To Eddie's?" Tommy tried to focus on the conversation more than the chaos going on in his head. He needed to stay present, not seep back into old nightmares. He glanced at Sid's Beauty Parlor, a square building with emerald-green awnings and a dark yellow door. The chalkboard on the sidewalk said something witty about cutting hair.

The owner was a friend of Bobby's. She liked going there for styling tips. Sid was also a lower gang member, he helped launder money for the Hearts.

"Yeah, but Eddie's is adjacent to the Burrows," Dave said. "So, it's no problem being there, but take me to a sushi joint in the Honeycombs, forget it."

"I like tuna," Cole said.

"Not the same thing."

"You guys already got past the Wicked Bitch," Tommy said. "The rest of your coming out should be a cakewalk."

"Layla's one scary broad. Her stare was like daggers, dude," Dave pointed to his eyes. He hadn't stopped talking about his relationship worries since he got back from dropping Jess at school. The entire night before Dave tapped his fingers over everything in sight, constantly worrying about what would happen when he and Layla finally met.

Tommy gave up trying to calm him down. It was a pointless effort.

Cole laughed. "Like Rose's mom. You're the bug!"

"Who's Rose?"

Cole's shoulders slumped. "Rose and Jack, Jack and Rose. *Titanic*?" he rolled his eyes at Dave and Tommy's clueless expressions. "It's time for a movie night."

"I'm not watching another chick flick with you," Dave put his hands up in frustration. "No matter how much popcorn, Twizzlers, and junk food you put out on the trampoline."

"It's a classic," Cole said. "Idiom."

"Idiot."

"Idiom, Davey." Cole started calling people "idioms" to annoy Dave. Once when Cole forced Dave to wake up before sunrise - he wasn't a morning person - he got tongue-tied and accidentally called Cole an "idiom" instead of an "idiot." Cole teased him about it, Dave threw a pillow at him and eventually, the joke caught on. Even Casey joined in on the joke and started calling people "idioms" to make Dave mad.

"I'll have a movie night with you, Cole," Tommy said.

"We'll watch *Casablanca*," Cole smiled. It was one of Tommy's favorite movies.

"Can we get back on topic, please?" Dave asked.

Tommy nodded. "Sure. What's that?"

"Layla hates me and Jess listens to her. I'm screwed."

"So, if Layla hates you, Jess hates you," Cole's eyebrows scrunched. "But they're different people with different minds and feelings. Jess likes you. I'm confused."

"You're always confused," Dave said.

Tommy chuckled. He understood that Dave's girlfriend had some issues with her parents but that didn't mean she couldn't think for herself. "Okay, Cole's right," he said. "Jess will make up her own mind. She'll probably learn how disgusting you are in her own time and you won't have to worry about the Peaces anymore."

Dave rolled his eyes. "Why do I talk to you people?"

Tommy's focus faded away from the conversation as he glanced at his surroundings; rundown buildings in desperate need of fresh paint, boarded windows, and locked doors even though the streets and sidewalks were mostly empty. This was why Tommy didn't like the Burrows.

He liked it in the sense that it was his home. He grew up there. He lived there. Certain parts were nice; Casey's favorite ice cream parlor, the pawn shop Tommy stole her necklace from, the garage Dave worked at. He also liked the skatepark he used to go to when he was a kid, it was the best escape from his reality that he could find. He hadn't been there in a long time.

But his favorite part of the city was the Nests because it was more lively, active but peaceful.

"Can you tinker with my car this weekend?" Cole said. "It needs a tune-up."

"Sure. What did you do to it this time?" Dave asked.

"Hmm. I was driving it in a race, and it went BRRRR... And CLANK CLANK... and YOW-"

"Stop making sounds! Jesus."

"You asked! Why did you ask if you didn't want to know?"

"I didn't know you were gonna open your mouth to answer," Dave said.

Cole rolled his eyes and shook his head.

They turned the corner. The dirty, windowless building was as familiar to Tommy as the memories he hated. A red, neon sign in the shape of a curvy woman lying in a seductive position hung above the door, moving her leg up and down. He hated that sign.

The inside was a large room filled with smoke from cigarettes, cigars, and joints. Muscular men with scars and bruises sat on couches along the walls and near the stage or at tables scattered everywhere.

Most of them worked for Mick the Menace but the others were either loyal to Betty, Markinson or they were part of the lower gangs. It wasn't hard to tell who was who. The lower gang members had tattoos. Depending on which gang they belonged to, they either had a red diamond, a red heart, or a black spade. And Betty's men, most of whom Tommy knew personally, sat far away from Markinson's men.

They all carried some sort of weapon. Tommy could see the holsters hidden on various parts of their bodies.

Many beautiful women wearing a variety of lingerie flirted with the men, doing lap dances and laughing at their jokes, they also carried drinks and lit cigars and cigarettes.

One woman with long, natural red hair danced on stage in front of a five-paneled mirror. She stretched for all to see, then twirled around a pole and dropped into a sexy pose.

Tommy hated this place. He hated the image of Paisley dancing in lingerie. He cringed at the several memories he had of her in front of the five-panel mirror or doing lap dances for her regular customers. It made him nauseous and itchy. He was definitely scarred for life.

"This place isn't all bad," Dave said, watching the woman dance on stage.

Cole slapped his head. "You have a girlfriend."

"Hey! I was making an observation," he rubbed the wound. "I wouldn't do anything. You'd probably feel differently if it were guys in underwear."

"Not the point." Cole wiggled a sassy finger.

Tommy went to the bar.

The bartender was a broad-shouldered man in a black, long-sleeved shirt. His hands were calloused, probably from holding different weapons, and burns marked half his face. He had a reputation, an impressive kill rate. He was one of Mick's many assassins.

"You're Betty's tech support." He wasn't pleased. "Tell your champion one of our guys is missing some fingers," he raised his eyebrows. "I bet she'll know where they are."

Casey tortured people for Betty all the time. It wasn't shocking news.

"What Cece does for Betty isn't my problem," Tommy crossed his arms on the bar, acting casual. He didn't show any sign of fear or worry. "But I'm sure your guy did something to piss them off, look," he lowered his voice. "I need to talk to one of Mick's girls."

"Alright. Close your eyes and point." The bartender gestured to every woman in the room.

Of course, Mick had been with them all. Or was the bartender purposely making this difficult?

Tommy clenched his fist, digging his nails into his palm. He was highly aware of the holster strapped to his belt and the one under his pant leg. If he had to, he'd use force, he'd fight his way through and they'd all be sorry they ever tempted his patience, but it had to be a last resort.

"Hey," Dave showed the bartender his fake ID. "Can I get a beer?"

"You think if we drink here, Sally will sense it and put us in timeouts?" Cole asked.

"She's not a bloodhound."

"She's already got eyes in the back of her head. Who knows what else!"

Tommy knocked on the bar to regain their attention. Dave and Cole understood the warning and shut their mouths. They had his back if this went south.

"Alright, what about his favorite girl?" Tommy asked. "He's always got one of those, right? I hear the newest one is named Paisley."

"She's here," the bartender handed Dave a beer. "She's not taking visitors right now, so I'll let her know you stopped by."

"No, I think I'll talk to her now." He didn't wait for the bartender's answer.

His friends each nodded, wishing him luck.

Layered, lavender curtains hung in an archway separating a short hall from the main area. The hall led to a private bathroom, a locker room for the strippers, and a small office.

Tommy almost saw his seven-year-old self sitting on the floor where he'd play with his toy trucks or read books or snack on whatever the other strippers brought for him like crackers and celery while Paisley finished her shift. She didn't always remember to bring food for him. Sometimes, she was too drunk or high to remember him.

He knocked on the door.

The overwhelming smell of hairspray and cigar smoke slapped him in the face. The woman was younger than middle-aged. Her long, reddish-brown hair was tied in curly knots decorated with pieces of thin, silver string. She wore a cheap fur robe over her white, lacey lingerie, which had a plunging neckline and fancy, striped tights. The birthmark on her left cheek was shaped like a tiny strawberry but the scar on her right one was a giant gash, a gift from one of her old boyfriends.

Tommy forgot how much he looked like her, especially their eyes. "Hey, Mom."

Paisley didn't look happy to see him. She gestured into the office, allowing him inside. The office was a little, square room with four tan walls and stained carpet. There wasn't a desk but there was a coffee table covered in piles of loose cash and pills.

She plopped onto the dusty leather couch and lit a cigarette. She took a big puff and leaned back on the cushions, sighing. "Thought you were working for that bitch Betty. Tech support, right?" she squinted, suspicious of his presence. "So, what are you doing here in Markinson territory?"

Her voice was hoarse and her words were slightly slurred. She had bruises on her thighs, probably from her newest boyfriend.

"Mick's an independent. I can be here if I wanna be here," Tommy said.

"True is true. But Mick ain't here."

"He's at Sally's. I know."

He asked Bobby to text him when Mick came and left the club. She was happy to help him safely check on his mother. She even told Sally to help her keep Mick distracted long enough for Tommy to get in and out of the strip club without any trouble. Sally agreed.

"Then you're not here on Betty's behalf." Paisley raised an eyebrow, waiting.

He took a deep breath and tucked his hands in his pockets. He'd have to wash his hoodie more than once to get rid of the hairspray stench. "I wanted to talk to you about, uh," he wasn't sure how to say it. "You're with him, right? With Mick. You're his favorite girl?"

"Sure am," she smiled, pride in her voice.

"Yeah. Well, you know how dangerous that is, right? He doesn't have the best track record with women. They just found his last girl's body in an alley."

Paisley took a long drag from her cigarette and set it in the ashtray. The look in her eye told him she couldn't be bothered with whatever he had to say. It was the same hateful look she got every time he needed something like socks or a new toothbrush and they couldn't afford it.

"You know why all those girls got on his bad side? 'Cause they didn't know how to treat him, they didn't appreciate what they had. I do." She pulled a thick, silver ring from her pocket. It had the initials M.M. engraved on the side. Mick the Menace. Tommy couldn't tell if Paisley was staring at the letters or at her reflection in the silver. "He treats me right and I treat him right."

"What happens when you do something he doesn't like?" Tommy asked. He wanted her to care about herself enough to leave, to care enough about him to stay alive, but past experience taught him it was an impossible hope.

She hesitated. "I won't."

He wanted to argue, he wanted to convince her to care, to leave, but his phone buzzed. The text was from an unknown number: LEONARD ALBINO. MAKE IT CLEAN.

Betty changed her burner phone every so often to keep herself hidden. The single identification she used was the red dress emoji. If she sent him these instructions, she either couldn't find Cece or didn't want her champion on the job. But why wouldn't she want her champion on the job?

Tommy hated the dirty work. He liked computers better. "I'll see you around, Mom."

His friends were still sitting at the bar, watching a new woman pole dance. She was blonde, wearing a bikini-like piece of lingerie with her hair styled in waves. Dave had drunk half his beer and Cole had ordered a Sprite. The bartender wasn't there, he must've gone to call Mick.

"How'd it go?" Dave grabbed his beer and slid off the stool.

Tommy shook his head. "Exactly how I thought it would but it doesn't matter, it's her life," he pushed the door open and his friends followed him outside. "We have another problem."

"A good problem or a bad problem?" Cole asked.

"What the hell is a good problem?" Dave sipped his beer.

"One that doesn't get us or our friends killed?"

Tommy showed them Betty's text. He'd get additional information such as an address or possible places his target could be or people his target knew, then after the job was done, he was supposed to text her back and erase the message. Rules were rules, and this wasn't his first time following them.

"That's a target text," Dave said, staring at the screen. "Why didn't she send it to Casey?"

"I don't know," Tommy turned his phone off and put it in his back pocket. "I mean, I can do it. She trained us both but it's not my usual department. I-"

"Guess it's a good thing you never miss," Dave patted his shoulder. "Sorry, man."

***

Alice

The abandoned, brick apartment building with tinted, bulletproof windows was surrounded by a tall, wrought-iron fence covered in thick, twisting ivy which had pretty purple flowers blooming from every vine. Sharp spikes kept intruders from climbing over the fence and a wicked metal gate blocked the gravel driveway, the only entrance to the property, while a sign stood next to it, screaming **No Trespassing!**

"Looks friendly." Cece sat in the driver's seat, arms folded on the steering wheel.

Alice was on the passenger side, staring at the spikes on the fence, and wondering who the hell this Karen Micheals person was. When she imagined Karen, this picture never made the list. *Why spikes?*

"Are you sure she still lives here?" Jess bent forward, leaning over the console between the two front seats. She picked her cuticles the entire ride there but looked more excited and curious than Alice had ever seen her. Her fears of disobeying and her natural curiosity were warring inside her.

Cece shrugged. "This address is from a couple years ago but the chick still owns it, so she's alive."

"Did Tommy find any more information about her?" Jess asked. "Like a job, other addresses, family members? Maybe a criminal record?"

"Nothing," Cece said.

Alice's stomach was in knots, her questions swirling in her head like a hurricane. She needed to know. She needed answers. She needed this to work. *Here we go.*

She shoved the door open and hopped out. Her new sneakers squeaked on the pavement. Mister Scotts bought them for her when he saw her old ones were falling apart. These had cushioned soles and didn't hurt to walk in but they felt foreign on her feet. She loved them but she missed her old ones.

Two slams followed. The other girls stood beside her on the curb.

Jess gestured to Cece's bloody shirt. "You should probably change."

"I think Sally keeps a change of clothes in the trunk, hold on." She rounded the jeep. Cece didn't tell them what she did or whose blood it was. Alice wasn't sure she wanted to know. It was easier to ignore her friend's job when it didn't stare her in the face. She loved Cece but Alice didn't agree with what she did.

"You have that face," Jess chuckled.

"What face?"

"The one you used to get before a race or a game like you were getting ready for the biggest moment of your life. Your mom had a name for it, um," she thought for a moment. "Your determined face," she nodded. "Yeah, that was it. That's the face."

Alice remembered feeling determined before one of her races or swim meets or basketball games. She wanted to do a good job, she wanted to make her parents proud and help her team to victory but she also loved the adrenaline and the exercise. She liked it when her muscles ached, it made her feel like she achieved something and she liked knowing she tried her best even if she didn't win. She never knew she made a face to reflect all that. Another thing Susan never told her.

"So, do we have a plan or are we going to be stupid and wing it?" Jess asked.

"The second one," Alice said.

Jess sighed. "Of course."

When Cece came back, she was wearing a clean, slightly baggy tank top under her leather jacket. Her hands were still red. That'd take some explanation. Maybe they could tell Karen, or whoever they were about to find, that Cece liked to paint.

They walked down the gravel path. Behind the metal gate, the driveway was cement. There wasn't a keypad or a speaker, just an old-fashioned lock. Cece knelt in front of it and took out her toolkit; a small leather pouch she kept in her jacket, which held an assortment of lock-picking equipment. When Alice first asked her about it, her exact words were *I never know when I might need to break in somewhere.*

Jess watched her, fascinated.

Alice glanced around at their surroundings. Most of the buildings along the street were empty, unkempt with overgrown lawns and boarded windows. She'd never been to this part of the Nests but she knew that Destroyer's past raids had caused people to lose their homes and their jobs, forcing them to move to cheaper neighborhoods or leave the city altogether. It was one thing to hear about it but it was another to see it. It would've been such a beautiful street, if not for its loneliness. It would still be a great place to take pictures.

The lock clicked. Cece smirked. "Tumblers, baby."

She slipped her toolkit back into her jacket and pushed the gate open. It squealed, making a nearby squirrel curiously perk up.

Jess raised her eyebrows. "Impressive. Illegal... But."

"Technicality."

They headed inside, the gravel path turning to smooth cement. The grass was cut at Alice's knees, dandelions and other weeds were everywhere, creating an overgrown, chaotic jungle. The tinted windows hid any sign of life that might be inside the building, and the only visible door had five high-tech, password-protected keypads, which didn't fit the vibe at all.

Cece stayed behind the others, head at swivel, watching their backs. Alice appreciated it.

Jess inspected the keypads. "Seems like a six-digit pin is needed for all five, which means we need to figure out five different sequences."

"Couldn't they all have the same code?" Alice was probably wrong but she still felt the need to ask.

"Doubtful," Jess said, matter-of-fact and focused. "We could, theoretically, use some sort of powder on the screens to reveal the fingerprints-"

"Three cameras in the grass, maybe more." Cece tapped the knife in her hand and a shine reflected against its cool, steel blade. The sun was behind the building, so something else was causing it, something low to the ground and hidden.

"So, someone is in there," Jess said.

The statement gave Alice hope. She examined the twelve-story building. Someone was in there and she wanted to know who. She had come too far to give up now. She needed answers. She needed to get inside but how? Five passwords all with six-digit sequences meant it'd be impossible to break in. By the time they found powder or something to help, the passwords could be changed.

An idea popped into her head.

She gestured for her friends to block the camera's view - they did - then Alice put her hands on the first keypad. All those practice sessions with the cups better have paid off.

Stay calm. She thought. *Control it.*

The steady thumping of her heartbeat wasn't affected by the billions of little vibrations flowing through her body, incredible, hypnotic energy, seizing her bones and stroking her muscles. *Perfect.* She focused it, picturing what she wanted to do, and lightning flickered between her fingertips, crawling onto the keypad. Her power surged against the system creating a slight jolt. She smiled. *It's working, yes!*

Wild sparks shot from all five keypads. She jumped back and stumbled into her friends. She didn't mean to do that. Each keypad blacked out at the same time. An alarm went off and a deep, automated voice started screaming *Intruder Alert. Intruder Alert. Intruder Alert.*

"That's a bit on the nose," Cece said.

Jess shouted, "What did you do!"

"I didn't mean to!" Alice yelled. "I got excited and surprised, I-"

"The keypads are dark now, does that mean you took out the system?" Cece asked.

She shrugged and shook her head. "I don't-"

Intruder Alert! Intruder Alert!

"The door," Jess said. "It'll be unlocked if you-"

Alice grabbed the knob and shouldered open the heavy, steel door. She tripped into a medium-sized lobby with simple, smooth carpeting and tropical-print wallpaper. When the alarm shut off, button-sized pieces of technology scattered on the walls lit up, and lasers appeared, creating a deadly obstacle course.

The door slammed shut, leaving the girls without an escape.

Alice stood completely still, muscles tense. A laser barely grazed the tip of her nose while others surrounded her, trapping her in the center of the lobby. She was starting to regret coming to this place. What sane person had lasers in their entryway?

Her friends were fine, unharmed.

Jess stood behind and to Alice's left, panicked breath overlapping. Eyes wide, she stood between four lasers, one of which was right above her head, so she had to bend a little to avoid it. She probably wished she had stayed at school now.

Cece stood a few feet from Alice's right. The lasers' reflections shined off her leather jacket, one came close to her belly and another was between her legs. She stood still, casual, with no panic or fear. If anything, she seemed annoyed, muttering about how she could've possibly gotten herself into this situation.

The wall in front of them split open. *A secret elevator?*

A woman wearing a white lab coat and fuzzy, puppy-pattern pajamas stepped into the room. She glanced at each of the girls, cautious when it came to Cece and Jess, but when she saw Alice, her face shifted from anger and suspicion to sympathy and pride. She tapped the high-tech tablet in her hands and the lasers vanished.

Alice rubbed her nose. She could breathe again.

Cece readied her knife, prepared for a fight.

"You're Christina Martin," Jess said, staring at the woman.

Alice wasn't sure why she recognized the name. She didn't recognize the woman. Her golden brown hair was styled in a pixie cut, flattering her round face. She looked tired and kind like an adorable old woman but she was probably a few years younger than the age Susan would've been now.

"This might be the obvious question," Cece said. "But who the hell is Christina Martin?"

"A few years ago, a Cruise Industries employee stole a piece of experimental technology from the company. Brad never said what exactly it was but he and his board wanted to sue," Jess explained, eyes locked on the woman. "They hired Mister O'Hare, Tony's dad, to represent them, which is how my parents found out but at the last minute, Brad changed his mind. The employee disappeared and the crime never made the news or the papers. It became a rumored scandal in the Honeycombs."

"So, this chick's a thief?" Cece said. "Respect."

"I'm not a thief," the woman said, offended. Her voice was sweet, almost timid but also serious and focused. "I didn't steal it for myself. The technology was supposed to help counteract Destroyer's abilities," she turned to Alice, ignoring the other girls. "I was working on something, a defensive weapon, to help your mother finally defeat her rival but she died before I could finish it."

Alice barely registered the words. Memories of that night flooded back into her mind's eye; sneaking out her bedroom window, climbing down the trellis, crawling through the crowd, the sparks, the fight, Glisin's death, were all jumbled in a sequence of haunting images and echoing screams.

Her mom could've been saved? Susan didn't have to die? Destroyer could've been defeated?

This was her, the woman from the journals, the woman Susan trusted with her identity and secrets. Why didn't Susan ever mention her? What did Karen know about Susan that Alice didn't? Who else knew who Glisin was behind her mask?

Alice couldn't speak. She couldn't think. The tropical wallpaper - pink and green palm trees and gold coconuts - started spinning. The ground seemed to shift under her feet. Was she about to faint?

She managed to say. "Karen Micheals."

The woman smiled. "Hi, Alice."

"Wait a minute," Jess said, giving Alice a chance to catch her breath. "How are you both women? Karen Micheals and Christina Martin?"

"Martin is my maiden name, I changed it after the lawsuit," she spoke politely. "Brad is a very powerful, rich man. I learned something about his past and used it to save myself. He dropped the lawsuit and he paid me to leave town, he didn't want me telling his secrets, but I couldn't..." she paused, trying to keep her voice from breaking. Tears made her eyes sparkle. "I couldn't leave knowing Susan's daughter was here without her, so I changed my identity, making my middle name, Karen, my first name."

"That's why T couldn't find anything on you except this address, it's the only thing connected to your current identity." Cece gestured to the walls where the lasers had come from. "What's with the crazy security?"

"Hobby?" Karen chuckled awkwardly.

"Hobby," Jess repeated in disbelief.

"Who are you? I know Alice, obviously, but you two aren't-"

"These are my friends, Cece and Jess," Alice gestured to each of them. "They helped me find you. They know everything." Her friends stood behind her, one on either side. She had so many questions, she didn't know where to start. "If you didn't... Why didn't you come to find me when she died? If you knew I was here. If you stayed for me-"

"I couldn't disrupt your life," Karen said. "You were in so much pain and Mason-"

"My dad knew about you?"

"Vaguely. Susan told him she had a partner but we never met, not until," she paused, hesitating. She was grieving Alice's mother too. Her plain, careful hands shifted on her tablet. "We met at Liberty Cemetery."

Alice could fill in the rest of the story. Mason and Karen met at Glisin's mausoleum after she died, after Karen went into hiding and Mason became a drunk. He probably told her to stay away from his daughter. Alice could only imagine the slurred screams and untrue accusations about how it was Karen's fault that Susan was gone. Mason needed a monster, someone to blame, and found her there waiting to be clawed apart. He wouldn't remember meeting her or what he said either, thanks to the alcohol.

Alice bent forward, holding her knees. Her heavy, uneven breath matched the quick pace of her heartbeat. This was too much information, too many questions to answer, where should she start? How was it possible to be so connected to a stranger?

Cece raised her hand. "If you got a bunch of hush money from Brad Cruise, why the hell did you buy this crap shack?"

"Couldn't you have said that in a more polite way?" Jess asked.

She shrugged. "Eh."

Karen smiled, not a sweet, sympathetic smile but a kind-hearted, mischievous, I-have-a-surprise smile. She backed into the secret elevator, gesturing for the girls to follow.

None of them moved at first, sharing the same uneasy glance. Jess and Cece both looked at Alice to see what she wanted to do. Did she trust this woman? Her two friends would follow her, no matter what she decided, whether she chose to leave or as Cece said earlier, go down the rabbit hole.

She led them into the futuristic box with white marble walls and silver doors. Once the big, high-tech screen scanned Karen's hand and confirmed it was her, the elevator started rumbling.

Alice shared another glance with her friends. Cece tucked her knife in her boot. Her weapon may have been hidden but she was still on guard, ready to pounce. Jess was more fascinated than afraid, asking Karen how she built the elevator, how the lasers worked, and about the hand scanner.

Alice wasn't sure what to feel; Excitement because they found Karen? Confusion because finding Karen brought up more questions? Relief because Karen seemed willing to help her?

When they reached the tenth floor, the doors opened, revealing a large scientific haven. Metal desks were lined in rows along the white, tile walls, each one with an assortment of beakers, vials, and test tubes filled with colorful liquids. Fancy computer screens bolted to various parts of the room showed different confusing symbols, theories, and other information only a genius could explain. A few locked, steel cabinets were in the corner, clipboards hung from the doors, listing every piece of technology, experimental device, or invention hidden inside. The entire place smelled like disinfectant and chemistry, if chemistry even had a scent.

"Whoa," Jess chuckled, amazed. "This is incredible."

"I may be in hiding but I still experiment and invent," Karen said, beaming with pride. "I used the," she glanced at Cece. "*Hush money* to update this place. I liked its old bones." She patted the wall. "My own little hidden scientific oasis."

"Not bad," Cece leaned against the wall. "So, you were Glisin's sidekick, huh?"

"Partner," she corrected. "But yes."

"You must've kept notes on her powers, right?" Jess asked. "How they worked."

"I did. You can read the binder if you'd like."

"I'd love to!" Jess smiled. She was practically hopping with excitement. She curiously read the clipboards and stared at the colorful liquids.

Alice laughed. It was amazing, she'd never seen anything like it, of course, she'd never actually been inside a laboratory before. She took specific notice of the few personal touches Karen added; the wooden, hand-carved coat rack decorated with different types of tropical birds holding several lab coats. One shelf, filled with research, held a clay vase decorated with little lightning bolts, which Alice recognized as her mom's artwork. To-go coffee cups from a place called Java Joe's were piled in the trash, and several pictures of Karen and an adorable pug in a turquoise collar were set close to the cabinets.

Alice wondered what things were on the other eleven floors.

Karen didn't know anything about the journals or the code Susan wrote in. She did create the ink that Alice's powers activated. She showed Alice the research it took and the many failed attempts she recorded while creating it. She showed the girls the devices and the tools she invented, most of which Glisin used to use in battle, like smoke bombs and thermal scanners. Alice realized Susan never was specific about where she got these items. Alice never really thought about it.

Alice had a new connection to her mom, which was better than she could've hoped for but she couldn't believe how much she never knew about Susan. Glisin kept so many secrets that it was hard for Alice not to wonder what else she didn't know. She ignored her growing uncertainty and focused on the reason she wanted to find Karen in the first place. Alice wanted to understand her abilities and their limits.

"Would you help us research my powers?" Alice asked.

Karen didn't hesitate to smile. She clapped her hands and sighed, dreamful. "I'd be honored."

Chapter 13

Casey

ALICE HELD HER HAND toward a glass vase filled with daisies, lightning flickering between her fingertips like a crackling white sparkler.

Casey loved how it looked, she could only imagine how it felt. She sat on one of Karen's metal tables, legs crossed like a pretzel. "What's supposed to happen?"

Karen was bent over the table, tapping a pen against a thick, spiral-bound binder filled with the detailed results from training sessions, blood tests, urine tests, and X-rays she had run on Alice. The scientist was thorough in her examinations. She ran complete physicals on Alice every week and kept track of how Alice's powers reacted to her emotions. She also created a tight, silver bracelet that tracked the wearer's pulse, which Alice had secured around her wrist.

"Given recent results, I know that her powers work on an instinctive level, which is not only different from Susan's abilities but it also seems that when Alice transforms, she isn't aware that she's transforming her clothes too," Karen spoke like a scientist, proper and overly invested. "I think it means she can temporarily transform something's cells into pure energy like she does her own body but she needs to practice and learn to be aware of what she's doing."

"Could she transform anything?" Casey asked. "Like anything *anything*?"

"Did you have something in mind?"

"No... just... Anything means people too, right?"

"Theoretically," Karen squinted, suspicious. "Why?"

The scientist didn't trust Casey, which made sense. Karen used to work with Glisin, a hero, and Casey was a criminal, a killer. She had to show Karen she wasn't going to hurt Alice or Jess or anyone else unless they deserved it. She wasn't sure she could prove that though, given who she worked for. She did care about Alice and Jess, even if Jess was really annoying.

"I think I've seen her do it, is all," Casey said. "It was like the lightning ate this kid she saved and a second later, he was fine standing on the sidewalk."

"That's amazing!" Karen laughed and scribbled the new information in the binder. She was ambidextrous, Casey noticed. And by the way, Karen moved her right hand, it seemed she broke it at some point, possibly while helping Glisin. Casey would've asked but she didn't want to give another reason for distrust. She kept her observations to herself.

Alice's lightning hit the vase, making it flicker in and out of physical existence. While it sparked and faded, the daisies started to fall but at the last second, the pulse tracker beeped and the vase exploded. Charred daisy petals and shimmering glass shards went everywhere.

"It was a good try," Karen said. She looked more disappointed than she sounded.

Alice sighed, shoulders slumped. "I got excited that it was working, and I messed it up," she tucked a loose strand of purple hair - most of which was tied in a ponytail - behind her ear. "Why is this so hard?"

"Least you're doing better with the other stuff. You can control the speed of a moving cup now, and those hot dogs I cooked on your palms tasted," Casey kissed her fingers like a chef saying *voila*. "Delicious." She wanted to bring marshmallows this time to see how well Alice could cook them, maybe make a couple of s'mores, but she didn't have time to get any on her way over.

"You weren't here the other day," Alice yanked off her sweatshirt and tied it around her waist. "I tried levitating a chair and almost burned off Jess's eyebrows-"

"I can't believe you didn't call me!" Casey laughed. "That's hilarious."

"Are you running every day?" Karen asked, interrupting Casey's amusement.

Alice nodded, "Every morning before school." Sometimes, she invited Casey to come with her on her morning runs. They'd race, and Alice would try her best but Casey would usually win. "And I've been using those breath exercises you suggested. And Jess read somewhere that yoga helps calm your body or your spirit or something, so I've started doing that too at sunrise."

"Every little bit helps," Karen scribbled in the binder. She smiled. "I like that Jess."

Casey rolled her eyes.

Jess acted like a fangirl when they first saw the lab, she also understood Karen's science speak, so they immediately bonded. They were both like Tommy, eager to learn and determined to understand whatever new information they came across.

"Where is Jessie anyway?" Casey rubbed her bandaged ankle. An opponent, a Diamond who disrespected Betty's rules, broke it during a fight, an attack Casey didn't see coming but she quickly regained the upper hand. She threw him against the cage's bars and stabbed him three times, plunging the knife in and out of his stomach, until he was choking on his own blood. She made sure the last thing he saw were her green eyes and blue hair. Luckily, she healed fast.

"SATs are tomorrow," Alice fixed her ponytail. "She's getting in one last cram session. I'm gonna study again tonight."

"Good luck with that." Casey slid off the table and kept her weight off her broken ankle.

Her body felt sluggish, tired, she hadn't slept. She spent the night with a man from Crescent City. He had information Betty needed and Casey got it. He screamed in pain and horror every time she used the rusty tweezers to rip off his fingernails. She would've jammed a corkscrew in his skin or dunked his head underwater, pulling him up just before he lost his breath, but Betty taught her to shake up her methods of torture once in a while. Either way, it worked. He cracked like an egg.

She took a shower before she came to the lab because her hair and clothes were soaked in his blood. It didn't bother her, if anything it made her feel more like Cece, more like Betty's champion, but it bothered Alice. Casey tried to keep that part of her life as hidden from Alice as possible. She knew it made her uncomfortable.

"Are you leaving?" Alice asked.

Casey wanted to hate it but she didn't. She loved the violence and the power it gave her. She never felt weak in the darkness. She understood how screwed up and disgusting it was. She lost her soul a long time ago. She wasn't sure she remembered having a soul, a conscience, a guiding light inside her.

Alice would hate Cece if she knew everything about her.

Casey lied about her name and a lot more. "Text me later."

***

Alice

Alice watched as Cece stepped into the elevator and used the hand scanner - which somehow read individual fingerprints and could identify their owner. Karen added Alice and Jess's prints to the system but Alice had to convince her to add Cece's - to scan her hand and the doors shut.

Alice wished Cece would talk to her. No jokes, the shadows under her eyes, the constant yawning, meant something was wrong. There were certain realities neither one wanted to face. Alice wanted to ignore them for as long as she could in hopes it'd go away.

"Let's do some blasts," Karen pointed to the wood panel hanging on the wall. "And remember, don't explode, keep your lightning contained within yourself, and don't stop. I can tell these exercises have helped build your body's tolerance to your power. Hopefully, you won't end up so tired this time."

"Okay," Alice untied her sweatshirt from around her waist and put it on the table. She held her hands toward the wood panel. She could tell how training with Karen had helped the control she had over her powers. She didn't feel clueless about herself anymore.

The vibrations started small, then got bigger, harder, pulsing in her fingers. She took deep breaths to keep herself in control, she focused on the rise and fall of her chest as well as what she wanted to do.

Lightning blasted the panel.

It wasn't the same feeling she had during the Adler Building Fire. No ripping organs or aching bones, just a tightening choke on her muscles. Cold sweat dripped down her forehead but she ignored it. The energy was cold on her skin but she could feel the heat around her.

The wood sparked.

The first time she did this, Alice almost set the lab on fire, so Karen covered the panel with some sort of lightning-absorbent tarp, which worked wonders for everyone's safety.

Her lightning brightened as the vibrations strengthened, tightening her skin, ready to overtake her. She kept herself from bursting, she kept her body in its physical form but it was difficult. Her body ached to explode, to shatter, but she wouldn't let it. She imagined the lightning in a glass bulb. If the glass broke, she'd transform. It was more tiring than she let herself realize. She gave as much power as she could but it didn't last long. Her body gave up.

She stumbled forward and the lightning stopped. She took deep, heavy breaths and closed her eyes, holding the table's edge to steady herself.

She needed to get better. She needed to hold on longer and not get tired. She needed to learn to manipulate and transform things. She wanted to challenge her limits and learn how powerful she truly was. So far, it seemed she could be the most powerful person in Height City, more powerful than Destroyer, not that she needed to be, right? She couldn't become a hero.

***

Tommy

The Castaway - Cole and Dave's car - was a cross between a race car and a white Mustang. Blue and orange flames were painted on its hood and dry dirt was splattered on the bumper.

Dave made sure it was the best car in the Burrows; working on it whenever he had time, updating it, always checking the engine, and buying spare parts from different chop shops around the city.

He and Cole found the poor car in a junkyard and decided to fix it together. They bickered over what parts were best, how to decorate it, who it actually belonged to, and what to name it. When Cole suggested the name "Gregorio," Dave wanted to drop the subject but then Tommy offered the name The Castaway. Both his friends agreed that it was a great name.

Tommy sat in a plastic lawn chair leaning against the wall with his laptop propped on his knees. To make sure she was safe, he hacked Paisley's phone. He found a message that said a large amount of money had been deposited into her account. His curiosity peaked and he hacked her bank records.

"Didn't Dave tell you not to touch anything?"

Cole shrugged. "Yeah but he left to get a part, so I'm doing it anyway."

The Castaway's hood was held up by a makeshift kickstand, so the engine was exposed. Tommy thought it looked like a giant hunk of dirty metal but then again, he didn't know anything about cars. He didn't understand the appeal. He'd much rather read binary and create code than risk getting smothered in oil. "He's gonna be pissed when you break something."

"Then I won't break anything," Cole reached under the hood. He muttered random, mechanic-like-sounding words to try and show he knew what he was doing. CLUNK. Something sparked, and he backed away.

Tommy raised an eyebrow. "Sure about that?"

"Shut up."

Casey walked into the garage. She wore a black T-shirt with a knotted hem which showed the scars covering her belly. Her jeans had black patches on the knees and thighs, and her leather jacket lay over a gray sweatshirt that almost matched Tommy's hoodie. Seeing her necklace hanging comfortably on her throat, as always, made Tommy smile.

She fist-bumped Cole. "Ready for the race?"

"I was," Cole said. "Then I found out Mick the Menace won his. We're gonna have to go up against each other in the final round," he paused, unsure. "If I win this one. Maybe I should bail."

"You can't do that. These races are the Burrows' favorite entertainment," Casey said. It was true. Burrowers loved a good, violent, chaotic race. "Just chill, and remember how much you'll win when you beat him over the finish line," she gently punched his shoulder, trying to be supportive.

Cole smiled at the gesture. He shook his head. "I don't know if I can beat Mick, you know? He's too-"

"Psychotic?" Casey asked.

"Exactly."

"Focus on beating the guy in this race first, then worry about Mick." Tommy didn't look up from the screen. He was on the cusp of a breakthrough, a pattern was starting to emerge, and he felt the need to follow it.

Casey tapped his shoulder. He moved the laptop and she sat on his lap. Arm around her waist, he set the laptop on her legs and continued scrolling. She leaned on his shoulder, gently combing his hair with her fingers, as she watched the screen.

"What's this?" she asked.

"My mom's bank records," he said. "I tapped her phone and computer to keep tabs on her. I saw a huge payment get deposited. It's too big to be a tip, something's up."

"I get that you feel responsible for her but she's a grown woman," Casey said. "She doesn't seem to want your help, T, maybe you should let her be."

He used to daydream about what his life would be like without Paisley's constant existence and in a sense, it'd be better. It'd be the same but without all the weight and worry. He could imagine her dead body in an alley too, beaten and bloody. He couldn't handle the guilt or the grief. She was his mother and her life mattered.

"I can't," he said.

Casey sighed. She wouldn't make him talk about it or explain his reasons which he appreciated. He wasn't sure he'd be able to explain.

He felt her heartbeat next to his, strong and constant. Her scars reminded him of his own, different but permanent, all over his body. Most he earned in training with Betty, sparring with Casey and Dave, or while he was trying to figure out how to survive on the street. Others Paisley gave him one way or another. Why did he feel indebted to a woman who considered him a burden?

"It's moments like these that make me glad I don't have any parents," Casey said. "What do you think, Cole? You too?"

"Orphan club number one!" Cole pumped his fist, leaning over The Castaway's engine.

Tommy shook his head, amused. He rubbed Casey's back, fingers drifting up her shirt, so he could trace the scars near her lower spine. She didn't tense at his touch or pull away, instead, she leaned closer to him, giving him permission to hold her, to use her for support.

She hooked her arm around his shoulders and kissed his forehead. He appreciated the comfort. He tilted his head back and looked up into her eyes. Her intense, beautiful, green eyes. She smiled, the quiet, loving smile reserved only for him.

"Hi," she whispered.

He kissed her, fervent and sincere, holding the laptop steady. He needed her to know how important she was to him, how much he needed her by his side. Casey was the one bright spot in his own personal darkness. He traced the tip of her chin, memorizing her features for the thousandth time, then cradled the back of her head, bringing her closer.

She cupped his cheek with a calloused hand, tough but kind, then she grabbed his hoodie, balling the fabric between her fingers, telling him how much she wanted him near her too. They smiled at the same time.

"Mind if I come over tonight?" Tommy asked.

She chuckled. "Why? Think you'll get lucky?"

"Betty has me doing something... Uh... bloody." He couldn't believe he wasn't just tech support anymore. He hated the dry blood on his hands, the screams of a victim, the shape of a threat on his lips. These jobs, kill orders, and torture sessions, were a nightmare he couldn't wake from. He never wanted to be built for the darkness but he was too good at being part of it. He hated how well he could scare someone, how he could find anyone's breaking points and exploit them. He knew what buttons to press, what bones to break, who to threaten. He loathed the twisted demons in the darkest corners of his mind.

"You're still having nightmares?" Casey asked.

He nodded.

Everything Tommy had done since he shot Leonard Albino - point-blank in the forehead from three rooftops away, the bullet broke his skull right in front of his wife - was on repeat every time Tommy closed his eyes; Shredding a coward's skin until he gave up information, shooting a man in the neck then the chest when he fought back, threatening a Spade member's girlfriend because he made Betty angry. Every horrifying action kept Tommy from sleeping through the night but it was easier with Casey next to him, she kept the darkness at bay.

"Hey, uh..." she whispered, so Cole couldn't hear her. "Do you think, um, because I don't have nightmares that I..." she paused. She knew what she wanted to say but she didn't want to say it. She nervously played with the drawstring of Tommy's hoodie, avoiding his gaze. "Am I numb?"

Her face was neutral, blank, but he saw through her mask; guilt and shame. He knew why she was asking. The same reason she went to Morgan High every day and lied to him for a year. Alice.

He didn't blame Alice for Casey's choices or for making her lie. It fascinated him how the girl with the purple hair turned Casey's world upside down. He wasn't sure if that was a good thing yet.

"You wouldn't be asking if you were." Tommy brushed away the tears trickling down her cheeks. She closed her eyes and let him hold her, comfort her. Seeing her cry was a privilege. He was honored to witness her vulnerability.

Doubts passed through her green eyes and vanished into thin air. He couldn't tell what she was thinking but he knew how she felt about herself. Tommy knew the kinds of nightmares Casey kept bottled up, careful not to let anyone else see her childhood demons.

"I hope you're right," she said.

"Aren't I always?"

"You don't want me to answer that."

"Wow," he said, acting offended. He moved the laptop. "Get off my lap. Go."

She laughed and did not obey. She clutched his hoodie and yanked him closer, erasing the gap between them. She cupped his cheeks, one hand on either side of his face, and kissed him, fierce and loving. Her fingers were calloused from the way she held her knives. He felt each one, rough on his skin. Her lips drew him in, incredible and mesmerizing. It felt natural to kiss her, hold her. He never wanted to let her go.

Her weight shifted off his legs and she stood up, winking. "See you tonight."

He smiled. "I'll bring Italian for dinner."

"Get the garlic bread." She patted Cole's shoulder. He mockingly swooned, making fun of their romantic moment, so she flicked him on the forehead.

He stuck his tongue out at her.

She left, chuckling.

Tommy scrolled through more of Paisley's bank records. An identical payment had been deposited into her account on the same date for several years. Why? Who was it from?

***

Bobby

The SATs were officially Bobby's least favorite school tradition. She couldn't afford college but she wanted to see if she could get in. Leo's studying inspired her. He was so nice, nicer than anyone she'd ever met. While helping her search for motels to live at, they had bonded. Leo never pushed Bobby or made her doubt what she thought. It was good, weirdly good.

They sat on opposite sides of Sally's cold, leather couch. The walls were covered in square, wooden panels, and the entire apartment was open-concept.

An air mattress, decorated with Bobby's ribboned baby blanket, several pillows, and ruffled sheets, sat at the end of the queen-size bed, which had simple, tan sheets and two fluffy pillows. A shaggy, black, and red checkered area rug sectioned off the bedroom, separating it from the kitchen and living room.

Besides the leather couch, Sally's living room had a flat-screen TV, an antique coffee table, and lamps decorated with colorful pieces of glass, each from a different broken liquor bottle.

The kitchen was simple. All along one wall, there was a crappy fridge, an oven, a dishwasher, and cheap, white countertops with black speckles.

Dragons were featured strategically around the room; a glass figurine on the bookshelf, a colorful tapestry above the bed's headboard, a bracelet in Sally's jewelry box, and a poster on the bathroom door that read:

Two dragons walk into a bar.

The first one says, "It sure is hot in here"

The second one snaps back "Shut your mouth!"

275

Every pair of high heels Bobby owned was piled next to the stairwell. Her clothes took up most of the closet space and the dresser drawers. Anything extra was scattered on the shelves, the floor, and the windowsill, wherever they had space. Sally wasn't bothered by the mess. She didn't complain or anything, which was confusing. Why wasn't she sick of Bobby yet?

Bobby didn't get it and she didn't want to tempt fate. Sally would get sick of her eventually, so Bobby decided to keep searching for a permanent place after the SATs.

"How do you keep getting every math question right?" Leo asked.

Bobby liked how amazed he sounded. He also seemed a little irritated, which made her smile. Nobody had ever been impressed by her before. Nobody had ever been annoyed by her skills either. Her face felt warm. She tried to hide her pink cheeks but he noticed before she could. He smiled.

"Uh, I guess," she chuckled. "Math has always come easy to me."

"I can barely do long division." He looked at the SAT prep packet on his lap, jiggling a pencil between his fingers. He wore gray sweatpants, a black beanie, and a black T-shirt that said BATMAN across the chest in block letters. Simple and dorky and unexpectedly handsome.

"I don't get why you wanna go to college," she said. "I'm not going."

"It's just an option. What I really want is to travel, leave this city, and see what else is out there," he said as if he had given it a lot of thought. "I've saved my allowance for years and from summer jobs and I don't know," he shrugged. "Maybe it's ridiculous."

She didn't think it was ridiculous. She'd known other people who wanted to leave Height City too, and if they could do it, so could Leo.

"I design clothes," she covered her face. She never said it out loud before, only Casey knew. Bobby's designs weren't great. She couldn't draw that well but she loved to sew and imagine the impossible dream come true; her designs, clothes she created, on the runway, in magazines. It'd be amazing.

"So... that means you design and sing," Leo said.

She peaked at him through her fingers. "How do you know that? Nobody knows that, I mean, except for the shampoo bottles and the showerhead, forget I said that. How do you-"

"My dad took me to see the freshmen play," he smiled. "I remember when you sang, you were really good. You got lost in the performance or the music or whatever... It was, uh," he blushed. "It was good."

Bobby remembered being so excited for the freshman play. She loved preparing for her auditions, choosing a song, and getting the part, she loved rehearsals too, the costumes, the spotlight, everything, then Johnny didn't show and when Brittany tripped her during the bows, a bunch of Honeycombers laughed at her. Bobby felt terrible, embarrassed, and frustrated. She was tempted to ask Casey for help getting back at Brittany but she didn't, part of her felt she deserved what she got. After all, she made out with Brittany's boyfriend in front of the entire school.

Bobby crawled off the couch.

In the middle dresser drawer, under her pants and shorts, was her most prized possession, a big binder drenched in glitter and lace. It held her ideas, designs, fabrics, and inspiration. She brought it over to Leo and dropped it in his lap. She wanted to share her impossible dream with him to thank him for sharing his dream with her.

He glanced at the binder, then looked at her. "What-"

"It's, um, my designs. They're top secret, so you can't tell anyone that I ever, ever, ever showed you but they're really special to me, part of my imagination, I guess, anyway, it's probably stupid but uh, yeah, you can," she gestured to the binder. "I mean if you want," she rolled her eyes at herself. Why was it so hard to show him? She was pretty sure she trusted him. She sighed. "Go ahead."

She sat next to him, their shoulders touching. She felt his body heat under the blanket they shared. She could curl into his arms and stay there, safe and comfortable forever, but that'd be weird, right?

He stared at each page with irritating patience. After a few seconds of silence, Bobby started worrying and wondering. Why wouldn't he speak? What did he think? Did he hate the designs? Were her designs horrible? She loved her work but nobody else would. Her designs weren't professional, they weren't good enough. She wasn't good enough.

She tied her hair up. She needed something to do besides wait for him to speak.

Leo chuckled. "I'm not a fashion-forward person-"

"I've noticed."

"-but I think these are pretty good. Magazine material, probably. Height City will love this stuff."

Casey said the same thing but Bobby doubted it.

"It's just a hobby," she closed the binder. "Nothing serious." She didn't understand how her friends kept supporting her, telling her she was good and all she seemed to believe were the doubts screaming inside her head. She didn't know how to believe the compliments even if they were the truth. "And, uh, whatever you decide to do, it's gonna be great," she smiled. She wanted him to believe in himself, believe in his dream, but Bobby wasn't sure she liked the idea of Leo leaving, which was odd because they barely knew each other. She shrugged. "I think... I mean," she didn't want to say anything wrong. "I hear that the world has a lot to offer."

"Yeah," he smiled. "It does."

His caring gaze lingered on her eyes, then her lips. Did he want to kiss her? Terror and infatuation mixed and rose in her chest. Old memories and new feelings. She wanted to barf and blush at the same time.

She turned her back to him. She didn't want him to read her nervous expression. She wasn't good at hiding her emotions like her friends were.

"What is that?" Leo's hand hovered near her neck, fingers gently tickling her skin, sending sparks down her spine. She liked his kind, gentle touch.

She didn't need to see what he was asking about to know what it was. She could have traced the faded line that went from the base of her neck to the bottom of her head. It was easy to forget it existed, out of sight, out of mind. Her dad told her it was a birthmark. No one ever noticed it because her hair hid it.

Once, when Johnny saw it, he traced it, making her freeze under his touch, then he squeezed it. He was mad. The way his fingers tightened around her throat...

She flinched at the memory. She hated remembering that relationship.

She loosened her short ponytail and her curls fell over the birthmark. She shifted off the couch and wrapped the blanket around her shoulders, pulling it tight in an effort to protect herself.

Leo stared, completely still and probably confused.

***

Dave

People who had favorite trees always seemed like lunatics. No offense to them but the concept of loving a birch tree over an oak was insane. But Dave couldn't judge those tree huggers anymore because he loved the sycamore tree in Jess's backyard. The branches were thick, sturdy, and led right to her window. The climb was great exercise and it had the best prize at the finish line.

It was late but Jess wouldn't be asleep.

The curtains were open and the lights were on.

Dave noticed the Peaces needed their gutters cleaned. Leaves, mud, and an abandoned bird's nest clogged the metal tubes. He reached one leg over and made sure his foot was planted, then he climbed onto the roof and crawled to her window. He slid it open easily. Jess didn't lock it.

He heard the water running and guessed she was in the shower.

Textbooks from each of her classes, thick notebooks stuffed with neon sticky notes, vocabulary flashcards, scribbled-on notecards, SAT prep packets, blank college applications, and a bunch of other school things were scattered on the floor.

No wonder Jess canceled their plans all week. She was busy losing her mind.

Dave secured the desk chair under the doorknob and grabbed her laptop. He lay on the bed. It was the most comfortable bed he ever lay in. What was the thread count? Seven thousand?

Rich people. He rolled his eyes.

He loved how the pillows smelled like Jess's rose-y perfume. Her scent made him smile.

He opened the laptop, intending to play an online video game while he waited but noticed her browser tabs all showed research into different journalism schools, internships at newspapers, blogs about getting careers in writing, debates about whether or not writing was a good career path, and colleges with specific English programs. Did Jess want to become a journalist? She loved writing and she loved the Morgan High newspaper. Her face lit up whenever she talked about it, which was often.

"What are you doing here?" Jess stood in the bathroom doorway. "It's almost two in the morning."

She wore gray, silk shorts - her legs were smooth, a little pale, - and a white tank top under a long, cotton robe. Her wet hair was braided and her pink streaks were vibrant.

She was innocent and annoying when they first met, another stupid, reckless Honeycomber but it was different now, she was different but also the same. Dave couldn't help but wonder why the hell a girl like her was dating a guy like him.

"I had an errand after Cole's race, thought I'd stop by," he slid off the bed and stood up. "Sorry, I probably should've texted." He gestured to the scattered books. "I see you've been busy."

"Yeah. I've been studying, quizzing myself on every topic to make sure I know the material," she picked her cuticles. "What errand did you have to run? Something for Betty?" She didn't ask about his work often, probably because he didn't like talking about it. He didn't want to freak her out but Jess's curiosity was undeniable, she wanted to know everything.

"Something like that," he winked. She made an annoyed face.

Dave rounded the bed and came close to her, pulling her against him, arms around her waist. He liked teasing her, it was fun. He also liked holding her. She was a beautiful creature with an intriguing wildness he couldn't totally figure out.

She smiled. "I have to study."

"I'm not stopping you." He kissed her. She didn't move away or tell him to stop, so he kissed her again, this time deeper, harder. Her lips were soft, sweet. He wanted to pull out her braid. He liked it when her hair was down, messy, not tangled or unbrushed but not perfect either.

She chuckled. "I'm serious," she tried to sound serious but she was holding his shoulders, keeping him close to her. "I need a perfect score, so I can get into Zak City Law or my backups, okay? You're distracting me."

"I am really distracting, aren't I?" He smiled.

Jess rolled her eyes.

If she wanted him to leave, she'd go back to focusing on her work. Dave would be more than happy laying in her bed, listening to her read or watching her gears turn. He loved how determined she could get, how hard she worked. Then when she got too stressed or overwhelmed, he could distract her with a shoulder rub or a joke, making her forget the weight her parents dumped on her shoulders.

"What are the backups?" he asked. He didn't know anything about the college process.

"Well, the law program at Miller... You know, in Crescent City. Billings Law in Beakins and some others too." A realization crawled across her face. "We never, um, we never talked about it, did we? What happens when I leave?"

The different cities were, at least, a few hours away. Dave didn't let himself think about what would happen when Jess left. He didn't think they'd last this long. He didn't want to hold her back, interrupt her future, or keep her from what she wanted. He didn't want to talk about it.

If they talked about it, they'd end.

"I saw your laptop. What's with all the journalism stuff?"

"Oh," she frowned. "Uh... just an idea I had," she shrugged. "It's stupid."

"You don't want to be a lawyer." He said because she couldn't.

The guilt lit her face like a bright, neon sign. It was a dead giveaway. Her face became stern, serious, ready for a lengthy debate. "What happens when I leave next year for *law* school?" She was trying to change the subject but he wasn't going to let her.

"You're a good writer, Jess. Your articles are awesome." Dave read her articles from the Morgan High newspaper. If she didn't show them to him, then Bobby did. "Do you want to be a lawyer?"

"How do you know? You don't know anything about writing or journalism. I've been researching it and the best journalists have something to say. They do things... They go into danger... I don't know if I could handle that," she said. "Besides, my mom would never approve."

He scoffed. Why did she always do this to herself? Why did she need Layla's approval? He didn't get it. "Who the hell cares what she says?" He threw his arms up, then slapped them against his sides. "Huh? It's your life, Jess, it's your choice."

"You know what." Her voice was strained, getting angrier by the second. "You work for a crime lord who tells you what to do." She threw her arms up. "You're a criminal. Do you want to be that forever? You could be a whole lot more but no, you-"

"Don't," he warned. He told her things. He trusted her with his secrets, his trauma. He didn't regret it but if she used it against him now, she didn't listen at all. He shook his head. "If you finally stand up to your mother, you won't die. If I disobey, I have to fight Betty's champion who is Cece and she's freaking unbeatable-"

"There has to be a way," Jess said. "You should be able to choose-"

"Look, who's talking," he gestured to her.

She scoffed. "This is different."

"Yeah! Yeah, it is, 'cause you won't die." He watched every fight Cece - Casey - had. She killed grown men at eleven years old. She knew how to break your spirit and rip out your will to live. Dave trained with her and with Tommy. She was as terrifying as she was annoying. She learned everything from Betty Beater. Dave learned things from Betty too like how to survive in the darkness.

He liked his life. It wasn't perfect, it was dangerous and he had to watch his back but he didn't know anything different. He wasn't sure he wanted anything different. He wanted to move up. He wanted a better rank, a more respectable title. Other than that, he was fine. He made good money. He had friends. Why did he have to risk everything for a change that could be worse?

"Let's drop it," Jess said, deflating. "Okay?"

Dave grabbed the laptop, opened it, and went to a specific tab showing an application to a journalism internship for this summer. He clicked APPLY and held it out to her. "Your information required."

"What are you doing?"

"Give it a shot," Dave didn't want his life to change but Jess did. She'd go along with her parents' plan, her parents' dreams for her, and be unhappy for the rest of her life. Dave didn't want her to have a life she didn't want. "See if you can handle being a journalist. I mean, you've dealt with Layla Peace your whole life, so I think you can handle anything."

"She'll hate me. I-"

"So, don't tell her."

They stood still, silent. A thousand doubts and uncertainties flickered through her eyes. He couldn't exactly read her mind but he knew she wanted this. She wouldn't have done the research if she didn't but she didn't want to disappoint her parents. He couldn't relate.

She snatched the laptop from him. "Fine."

They sat on the bed. He didn't say a word as she completed the application. Her fingers paused at every question. Eventually, she finished it. She picked her cuticles, staring at the screen.

Dave glanced between her nervous expression and the screen. Was she shaking? She was holding her breath. Was that sweat dripping down her forehead?

Dave pressed SEND. "There."

"I did it," she chuckled.

"You're gonna be one hell of a journalist."

"Maybe." She looked at him. Her stare made fireworks collide in his chest. She glanced at the books and SAT prep on the floor, then shifted onto her knees, full attention set on him. He traced her cheekbone, his fingers moving into her hair, he loosened her braid. And she kissed him.

Her hair fell over her shoulders, long and beautiful. He smiled.

She quickly sucked him back into the kiss, teasinging him with her tongue. He loved kissing her. Her robe fell over her elbows. She squeezed his shoulders, gripping his T-shirt as she pulled him on top of her. They lay down, his body above hers. Her legs bent on either side of him.

"Hm," she winced. "I think I'm on a pencil."

He laughed against her lips. She shifted. He grabbed the pencil, showed it to her, and tossed it on the floor. She chuckled, pulling him back down, leaving no space between them. He kissed her again, deeper, harder. She tasted sweet like candy. He slowly moved his hands under her tank top, only going as far as her scar.

Dave knew exactly where it was. He could almost feel it. The first time he saw it, he felt guilty. He thought about how he hesitated. He couldn't stop his father or the fire. He hated that Ted was still out there, alive, doing who knows what. Then Jess told him to think about it in a different way.

The scar meant Dave saved her life. He was able to keep her alive. She told him he was nothing like his father. He really wanted to believe her.

He shifted, lips slowly moving across her body. He lifted her shirt just enough to kiss the scar. For a few seconds, he paused, listening to her breathe, listening for her heartbeat, telling himself he didn't fail like he originally thought but he still felt guilty. Marsons were always guilty.

Jess sat up, changing their position. She yanked Dave's T-shirt over his head, fingers trailing his chest, hovering over his own scars. She wasn't horrified or disgusted by them or what they represented, his darkness, his trauma. One day, he'd tell her about each one but for now, he kissed her.

"Jessica!" Bennett shouted. He was in the hall.

They both froze.

Dave cursed under his breath. "You've gotta be kidding me," he sighed. He kept his voice low. "Don't answer it. Hopefully, he'll go away."

"He knows I'm in here," Jess whispered.

Bennett knocked. "Can I come in?"

Dave couldn't believe this was happening. He quietly ducked under the bed. Jess's feet dangled off the edge. He tickled her toes and she kicked his hand. He laughed.

"Come in, Dad," she said.

The door opened. Bennett's feet were kind of small wearing furry, colorful monster slippers, which Dave never would've predicted.

"It's late," Bennett said. "You should get some sleep."

"I want to remember the material for tomorrow," Jess said. "I should keep studying."

A pause. Bennett came closer to the bed. Dave tensed, every muscle in his body froze. He'd dealt with criminals and killers his whole life and never broke a sweat, so why did his girlfriend's dad scare him? The carpet made his bare back itch. *Crap.* Where the hell did Jess throw his shirt?

"What's this?" Bennett asked.

Jess stood. "Um, that's.. Dad, wait-"

The sheet lifted. Suddenly, Dave felt naked and not in a good way. Should he jump out the window? Being a human pancake would be better than this situation. He tried to cover his chest but it was no use. *Shoot me now.*

"Hello," Bennett said, frowning.

"Hey, Mister Peace... how's life?"

He raised an eyebrow. He didn't seem angry, just protective, but Dave could be really bad at reading people. Was it too late to find another hiding spot?

"You do know this house has a front door," he said. "And my daughter has a curfew."

"Technically, we're inside..." Dave gulped. "Uh, sir."

Did Bennett own a shotgun? Would he use it? He didn't seem like the type to go that far. Then again, he'd just found a shirtless boy in his daughter's bedroom. It didn't look good.

"Since we're all wide awake," Bennett said. "Why don't we go downstairs and have some leftovers? I'd like to get to know you better, Mister Marson."

"Dave," he corrected. "And uh, can I ask... What if I don't?"

Bennett smiled as if he held the winning hand in a high-stakes poker game. "I'll board up her window."

"We'll be right down, sir."

When Bennett was gone and the door shut, Dave felt himself relax. He could breathe again. He couldn't believe this was happening. He crawled out from under the bed and stood up.

Jess tossed him his T-shirt. He quickly yanked it over his head. "This is my worst nightmare."

She knelt on the bed and sighed. "At least my mom's out of town and my dad isn't that bad. You guys might get along."

"Might." Dave hadn't faced the Peaces together. He saw Layla briefly when he and Jess told her about their relationship. He wanted to stay away from both of them at all costs. No matter what. Zero interaction.

Jess agreed.

She kissed him, arms loosely folded around his neck. He could get lost in her rose-y scent if he let himself or her curious caramel eyes. She pulled away, hands resting on his shoulders. "Don't mention that you sell, you know, for a crime lord," she paused. "And everything will be fine."

"Someone's confident." He pulled the robe over her shoulders and tied it closed. He didn't need to be distracted while he talked to Bennett. "What if I say something that'll get us both in trouble... like what really happens when I come up here-"

"I'll deny everything and it'll be your word against mine," she smiled. She may not want to be a lawyer but there was no doubting she was trained to be one.

Dave held her waist and lifted her up. She was light, easy to carry. He swung her around, twirling, until she gripped him tighter. She laughed, which made him smile.

Maybe talking to her father wouldn't be so horrible.

He set her down and kissed her, gathering his courage. He reminded himself that he'd been through worse. "You think it's too late to jump out the window and make a break for my motorcycle?"

Jess shoved him out the door. "Very mature."

Chapter 14

Jess

THE LAST DAY OF school was fast approaching. Everyone was excited, talking about their summer plans and vacations they were going to take but Jess was freaking out. She had a million things to finish; the last student council meeting, articles for the newspaper, extra credit work, planning junior prom, and studying for finals. She didn't know how she was supposed to finish it all in time, especially when all she could think about was the journalism internship.

She wanted it so much. She'd be working with real journalists in a real newspaper office. It'd be a great learning experience. The possible rejection terrified her.

Band-Aids protected her cuticles.

"Guess what!" Brittany slipped and crashed into Jess. They stumbled against the lockers. The metal hurt Jess's bones. Brittany laughed, panting. Her face was red and sweaty. She didn't have cheer practice today, so it must've been something else causing the excitement.

"Hi," Jess chuckled. "What's up?"

"My mom and I are going to Europe!" she squealed. "Just me and her over the summer. It'll be perfect. We never spend any time together. I can't wait. This is amazing!" She grabbed Jess's shoulders and started jumping up and down.

Missus Mikes, the mayor's wife and a socialite, was chairman of several charities and planned popular social functions with the Honeycombs' Board of Pearls, an exclusive club whose members included Height City's richest society women. Both she and her husband were famous and beloved, as were their daughters, but behind closed doors, Jess saw a less appealing side to the happy family.

"I'm sure you'll have a great time."

"It'll be perfect, you know? We'll shop, we'll eat out, we'll explore. It's gonna be the best summer ever."

It was nice to see Brittany so excited. She and her mom didn't have the best relationship. Hopefully, this trip would fix it like Brittany wanted. Jess used to wish she and Layla could have a better connection but she abandoned that hope years ago.

Jess and Brittany headed down the hall. The other students were busy, excited. The Honeycombers were chatting about their summer plans in Europe or at their out-of-state vacation homes. The football team was discussing their last big home game and a bunch of Burrowers were sitting in a group, lighting cigarettes. Principal Penez stomped over to them, took their lighters, and started lecturing them about proper safety and school policy. He paused his anger to wave at Jess.

She smiled. He was a good guy and he liked her. He wrote a gushing, personal recommendation for her college applications.

"What's up with you?" Brittany asked. "It's like you're sleepwalking."

"I'm preoccupied. I applied for an internship and I'm waiting to hear back." Jess adjusted her backpack. She wanted to pick her cuticles but couldn't. *Stupid Band-Aids.*

"Another law internship? Wow," Brittany said, impressed.

Jess didn't want any information to reach Layla, so she didn't correct the assumption. It was better this way. The less Layla knew, the better. "When do you leave for Europe?"

"The last day of school, on the dot. I can't wait. It's gonna be great," Brittany clapped her hands, too excited to stand still. "I already told Cindy," she frowned. "Have you guys talked at all?"

"No," Jess hadn't spoken to Cindy since their argument about Dave. "She's being... I don't know. She doesn't approve of my relationship."

"So you and the Burrower are still together?"

Jess smiled. She didn't know how it happened but she might've started falling in love. Dave got under her skin like nobody else ever had. She loved when he kissed her or touched her. His careful fingers on her bare skin. The way he traced her cheeks and held her hands. The way he stared at her with his incredible blue eyes like she was the only thing he wanted to focus on.

She loved sneaking out to see him, staying at his apartment when her parents were out of town. She loved riding on his motorcycle. It was a freedom she never could've imagined. She loved how he pushed her to apply for the journalism internship. He wouldn't let her cower.

"Yeah, we're still together." She couldn't stop smiling.

"I have to get a boyfriend," Brittany groaned. "You're making my love life look pathetic."

Dave and Bennett were on good terms too. At their impromptu dinner of leftover takeout, they talked about music. Jess specifically brought up Bennett's interest in old records because she knew it was something they'd have in common. She wanted to control the conversation as much as possible. Dave recommended a band called the Renegades and Bennett played a song on his guitar. It was nice.

Jess liked her life. Everything was good. She hoped it'd stay that way.

***

Alice

Alice could feel the better control she had over her powers. It was incredible. All the work with Karen continued to pay off. The scientist was a great addition to her life. The Scotts boys were too. She loved them and their home.

"I wanna reclaim my title. I challenge you to another Scrabble match." Leo wore a gray T-shirt with a picture of two stick figures. One held the other's stick body and it said I'VE GOT YOUR BACK in block letters.

Where in the world did he get these clothes?

"Why would I agree to that?" she asked. "I'm already the Scrabble queen. Why would I give you a chance to steal the crown from me?"

"You stole it from me first and for that, you're doing the dishes tonight."

"You can't pawn off your chores 'cause you're a sore loser."

Mister Scotts gave them weekly chores. He kept it fair with a chart on the fridge. They each took turns doing dishes or vacuuming or dusting or taking out the trash. He helped them with their homework too and he cooked breakfast and dinner every day. He offered to make their lunches but they both refused.

He seemed to enjoy having Alice around, probably because she let him teach her to cook. Leo wasn't interested in food unless he was eating it.

"Nuh-uh," Leo shook his head. "I'm not pawning. I'm giving you what you deserve, alright? You stole my crown."

"And it fits me perfectly," she said.

He rolled his eyes. "Come on. I don't wanna do them. I hate dishes." He pointed at her. "I have other ways of getting you to do them like blackmail. Cece stole that thirty bucks from Dad's wallet," he raised his eyebrows. "You're the one who brought her into the house, so ha."

"Least I'm not scared of her," Alice said.

He threw his hands up. "She carries knives! Super cool for a video game but in real life, eh."

Cece came to the loft once or twice for dinner. Most of the time, she was on her best behavior. She kept her knives and scars hidden, so Mister Scotts wouldn't ask any questions. Leo didn't know much about her either. He knew she was a Burrower but that was it.

"What are you guys talking about?" Jess wore a white button-down top with short sleeves, a black pleated skirt, and stylish, lace tights. Her long brown hair and pink streaks were in thick curls draped over her shoulders and back.

"Alice is a Scrabble crown thief," Leo said.

"What?"

"Nothing," Alice smiled. "Have you heard about the internship?"

The three of them walked side by side down the hall, careful as they avoided knocking into the other students. Some Burrower girls stood by the drinking fountain doing each other's makeup, talking about boys, and from what Alice overheard, Cece the Champion's next fight, while a group of Honeycomber boys tossed a basketball back and forth, discussing Honeycomber gossip.

Everyone seemed rowdy and loud today, which was normal for the end of the year.

"Not yet. I'm anxious," Jess showed them the Band-Aids on her fingers. "I know I'll just be getting coffee, organizing, and doing whatever but," she smiled, a bright, excited smile she hadn't had in a long time. "I'll be learning from actual journalists. I'll get a feel for the field and see if it's the right thing for me."

It was good to see Jess was looking forward to the future.

"You're a dork," Leo said. "But I'm a nerd, so I have no right to judge."

"As long as you recognize it," Jess said.

He chuckled. "Nice."

"Okay, so what about after school? Any plans?" Alice checked her pulse tracker - Karen's invention - the number was steady. Her emotions affected her powers, so in training, to control her lightning, she had to control her reaction. It was hard not to get too excited or impressed with herself and her progress. Exercising her powers turned out to be uplifting.

"My dad is taking me to Moon Park. He was all excited this morning about this surprise he has for me." Jess shrugged. Her and Bennett's relationship wasn't perfect but they stuck together, maybe because they had a common enemy in Layla.

Alice felt a little jealous. She wasn't sure she'd ever talk to her father again. He hadn't called or texted since she moved in with the Scotts boys.

"Layla isn't going with you?" Alice asked.

"No. She has a meeting or something. What about you guys? Any plans?"

"Ah, yes, okay," Leo smiled. "So, my dad and I have a tradition. Ever since I graduated kindergarten-"

"*Graduated* kindergarten?" Jess asked.

He silenced her with his hand. "Yes, I graduated kindergarten, it was an accomplishment." His tone was stiff but light-hearted. "Okay? Anyway," he sighed. "We always go to Linda's Diner on the last day of school but he's busy, so we're doing it today."

"I get to come," Alice said with excitement that made her squeal. She wasn't sure she ever squealed before. She loved how included she was in the Scotts boys' lives. She felt like part of their family. Mister Scotts never made her feel like a burden and Leo treated her like a sister.

"Alice Scotts has a nice ring to it," Jess said.

Leo nodded. "I think so too."

"You guys are crazy." Alice liked it too. She liked to think she was a Scotts but it was a betrayal to her dad. Her powers connected Alice to her mom but her last name connected her to Mason. She wanted that connection, even if they never spoke again. Mason was as much a part of her as Susan was.

"Hey, hey, hey!" Bobby skated across the floor, her orange and red curls bouncing in several sparkly clips. She wore hot pink, fishnet, fingerless gloves, a black tutu, a black T-shirt with white letters that said RENEGADES on the chest, and a denim jacket covered in glitter. She looked ready for a party or a concert, not history class. She crashed into Leo, grabbing his shoulders, as he held her elbows and kept her from face-planting into the lockers.

"How does she run in heels?" Jess asked.

"I have no idea," Alice said. She was baffled by Bobby's ability to run in high heels. Alice hated heels. They gave her blisters.

"I found..." Bobby wheezed. "A place..."

"You found a what?" he asked. His eyes were glued to hers. He held onto her every breath.

She hopped. "A motel!" she said when she stopped panting. "I don't know why I didn't think of it before, duh," she bumped her hand against her forehead. "But it popped up. It's cheap, it's perfect and will you come to look at it with me?"

She looked at Leo with a bright, sweet smile. Black, sparkly eyeshadow decorated her eyelids and simple, pink lip gloss made her mouth shine.

"I thought you weren't looking for a place anymore," Leo said.

"I wasn't but summer is coming up and," she shrugged. "Please?"

Leo's face changed from an amused smile to a serious line. "Okay, yeah," he nodded. "Of course, um, I have to be somewhere right now but later? Text me the address."

She jumped and hugged him. He held her, hands steady on her back. Did he sniff her hair? He talked about her all the time. He smiled when her name came up and he loved to repeat his favorite stories about her. He used words like "adorable", "fun" , and "bright" to describe her.

Alice thought it was cute, Leo had a crush. She and Jess exchanged knowing glances.

Bobby released him, shattering whatever daydream he had slipped into. He cleared his throat and glanced at Alice, who smiled at him.

Bobby waved and walked away.

Leo watched her leave, shifting on his feet. His smile didn't fade. "What?"

"Nothing," Jess chuckled. "Nothing at all."

"Okay..." he paused, pointing down the hall. "Race you to the car?"

"Winner gets the front seat." Alice took off.

Leo yelled something about cheating and "no fair" but she didn't stop. She loved to run. It made her legs ache in a fantastic, addicting way. Lightning sparked in her eyes. She felt the energy but she kept it contained. Vibrations crept over and into her muscles. Her powers bubbled but didn't ignite.

Leo was right behind her. She smiled.

***

Dave

Dave parked by the curb. His motorcycle was ready for an escape.

The house was white with a red door, no chipped paint, no grass stains or dirt, and the sycamore tree in the backyard cast a shadow on the pointed roof. It had a two-car garage, so all it needed was a white picket fence and it'd be the picture of a perfect family home.

He got a text from an unknown number. It didn't have the red dress emoji but it did have Layla's name. She wanted to talk. Bennett probably told her about the somewhat pleasant chat they had the night he caught Dave and Jess together in her room. Jess thought it went well. Her window wasn't boarded up, which was a good sign.

Dave knocked on the door, fingers tapping his thigh. He thought he was nervous while talking to Bennett but even the thought of facing Layla alone made him want to puke. He faced criminals every day. Hell, he was one. Why did Jess's parents have this unnerving effect on him?

When Layla appeared, he gulped. She wore an expensive suit which probably cost more than it did to repair The Castaway or maybe it cost more than a sack of diamonds, Dave wasn't sure. Her stare could set fire to Antarctica. She gestured for him to come inside.

The couch was comfortable and firm, nap-worthy. He didn't dare move too much. He wasn't sure what he was supposed to do. He wasn't sure what exactly was happening.

Layla sat in the chair across from him. She faced him and crossed her legs. What was this? A business deal? Whatever it was, he was losing.

He gulped. "What am I, uh, doing here, Missus Peace?"

"I want to discuss the future of your and Jessica's relationship."

"Shouldn't that be up to her and me? It's... it's our-"

"No," she said, almost like someone would say *duh*. "Despite my daughter's brilliance, she's clueless when it comes to you." She narrowed her glare. "My husband is as well but I'm not fooled. I know what you are and what you've done." He stayed quiet. He didn't need to add gasoline to the fire, so to speak. Where was this headed? Layla continued, "Your father was an arsonist for years. When he was finally apprehended it was for murdering his wife, your mother. He beat her to death, yes?"

Ouch. Did she really need to bring that up? It wasn't something he wanted to be reminded of or think about. He looked at the floor. "Mm-hmm." His hands were clutched between his knees, fingers tapping. The movement kept him grounded.

"Then he was released," Layla went on, cold as ice. "And proceeded to set fire to the Adler Building. He almost killed my entire family, my co-workers. My daughter wouldn't have been there if it weren't for you. She wouldn't have been shot."

Dave knew Alice's secret. She wouldn't have saved everyone if Jess hadn't been there. Jess would've lost her parents. Besides, it was Layla's fault that Ted was released. Why wasn't she giving herself this lecture?

"Your daughter found me," he said. "She followed me, I couldn't stop her. I tried. I was there too. I was gonna-"

"Kill him," Layla said simply as if it weren't a big deal or a haunting decision. She nodded. "That's how I know you followed in his footsteps. You're a criminal, aren't you?"

He didn't need to answer. It was a rhetorical question. She knew what he was. Everyone knew what he was: a Marson.

Crime was in his blood. He was a Burrower, no matter what.

She kept talking. Her tone signaled that if he interrupted, he'd get hanged or something. "Your association with Jessica could cost her her life and if that weren't enough, she's smart, capable, and could rule the world one day but not if you drag her down to your level. One way or another, you're going to end up in jail. It's just a matter of time," Layla paused, letting her words sink in.

He couldn't look her in the eye. There was only one other woman Dave never could make eye contact with and her name was Betty Beater.

Layla uncrossed her legs and leaned forward. "I expect it'd take more than the truth to make you do what's best for her, so I'm going to offer you something." She reached into her purse. Her checkbook was black. She wrote in it and ripped out a check, handing it to him.

He took it. His eyes widened. "Five thousand dollars?"

"You can cash it as soon as you leave Jess's life for good."

Dave never imagined having this much cash. It was enough to pay off some of his debts. He owed people in the lower gangs. The money might save him from a beating. How could he refuse this intriguing offer? "You're paying me to break up with her?" he asked. He wanted it to be clear.

"She won't remember your name within a year, let alone the rest of her life. You should gain something for the inconvenience," Layla said. Her gaze softened, almost compassionate. It was creepy, scarier than her iron glare. "You're her rebellion against me, Dave. You're nothing but a phase."

The words rang familiar bells. He told himself the same thing once or twice. He figured it was his insecurities. He didn't want it to be true. He wanted to believe he and Jess were more than a fling, more than a phase. He never expected to fall for a Honeycomber.

Was Layla right? Was Jess going to break his heart?

He stared at the check.

***

Jess

Jess couldn't believe Bennett bought her a car. Her very first car. She loved how it smelled, she loved how Bennett was more excited than her. He plopped the keys in her hand and gave her an entire speech about how a car was a responsibility, she had to take care of it and be smart. It was fitting that he bought her the car since he taught her to drive and took her to get her license.

She couldn't wait to take a drive with Alice. They could get ice cream and ride along the river. It'd be a beautiful view, the sunset over the water. Jess wanted to take Dave out too but they probably wouldn't do much driving. She'd call them both later but now, she had homework to do.

She parked in the driveway and followed her dad into the house.

Layla sat in the living room. Her briefcase was open on the coffee table filled with case files. Why wasn't she working in the dining room? Was she waiting for them?

"She loves the car," Bennett smiled. "We should go out and celebrate."

"I'll drive," Jess held up the keys.

He laughed.

Layla's sad, disappointed expression made Jess's stomach tighten. Her first thought was: *Did I do something wrong?* But she couldn't have. She had gotten pretty good at keeping her life a secret from her mother. Layla couldn't know about the sneaking out or the skipping school, she would've said something earlier.

Bennett's excitement fell. His shoulders slumped. "What is it?"

Layla took a deep breath. "I invited Dave over-"

"What?" Jess asked before she could stop herself.

"Don't interrupt me," Layla snapped, standing up. "I wanted to get to know him better but I didn't know," she paused as if the words were hard to say. "I didn't know what he'd do."

"What are you talking about?" Jess asked.

"I invited Dave over," she repeated. "We were having a pleasant conversation, so I went to make us some tea, and when I came back, I found him rummaging through my purse." She spoke with sincerity but Jess didn't believe it. First, a pleasant conversation with her mother was impossible. And second, Dave would've told Jess about the invitation.

"I think he stole one of my checks," Layla said.

"He stole from you?" Bennett didn't sound convinced. He liked Dave. He didn't approve of their bedroom hangouts but he thought Dave was nice. Bennett didn't judge him for Ted's choices.

Jess shook her head. "He wouldn't."

"He did," Layla said. Her I'm-right-and-you-need-to-accept-it tone. "I'm so sorry."

Jess wished she could believe her mom but Layla made it clear, she didn't approve of Jess's relationship. She didn't approve of anything Jess wanted or cared about. Of course, she'd try to ruin it. What did she do? Why did she want Jess to believe Dave was a bad guy? *What really happened?*

Jess wanted the truth.

"Excuse me," she yanked open the front door and slammed it shut, keys jingling in her hand.

Bennett bought her a silver Prius.

***

Cole

Burrowers crowded the parking lot, most of them brought popcorn and hot dogs to snack on while they watched the race, others were making bets on which racer would win. Mick the Menace was the favorite choice, not Cole and The Castaway. The finish line was white, whoever drew it must've been drunk because it wasn't straight.

Cole walked it like a tightrope a couple of times, trying to distract himself but his nerves were making him shake. He raced a million times before but this time, he was scared. Mick hadn't arrived yet. The prize money was too good to pass up, so he'd be here. They'd race. It was inevitable.

"What's this do?" Cole pointed to the piece of the engine he didn't know the name of. The entire engine looked like a meshed jigsaw puzzle but it didn't stop his curiosity.

Dave slapped his hand away. "Don't touch that."

He was crankier than usual. Cole had experienced all of Dave's moods. Sad Dave, dramatic Dave, flirty Dave but cranky Dave was the least fun to be around. The only explanation was something must've happened with Jess.

"It's my car," Cole said.

"No, it's your car when you're driving it but it's mine the rest of the time." Dave grabbed a wrench. Patches of sticky, black oil were on his T-shirt. He used the wrench to tighten the same piece Cole had pointed at. "Now get the hell away before you break something," he paused. "Again."

"Idiom." Cole leaned against the passenger side.

Dave rolled his eyes. "Back at you."

Casey leaned beside Cole. She wore her leather jacket over a white T-shirt and long, jean shorts. Knives were hidden in her boots and her necklace was in the same place as always. Cole loved the story behind it. He wanted a love, a strong unbreakable bond, like Casey had with Tommy. He thought love like that only existed in fiction.

"We should videotape them bickering," Casey chuckled. "And send it to one of those TV contests."

"It'd be a hit," Tommy smiled, arm around her. He wore his gray hoodie and jeans. He was a few inches taller than her but when she wore her boots, they were about the same height.

Cole appreciated them coming to see him race. He needed the support.

Casey hooked her hand on Tommy's shoulder. "Have you found who owns that shell company yet?"

"No," he frowned. "Whoever's paying Paisley doesn't want anyone to know their identity. Every lead I find is a dead end." He shrugged. "I just don't get why they'd be paying her."

"It has to be something huge, I mean, for three million a year," she clicked her tongue. "It makes you wonder why she's still living in the Burrows."

"She's probably using it to pay her debts and buy drugs," Tommy said. The hurt in his voice was veiled by his matter-of-fact tone. "Doesn't matter. Everything leaves a digital trail, which means I can find it. I'll figure it out."

"If you need help knocking heads, I'm your girl," she smirked.

He kissed her cheek. They made a good couple.

Cole remembered how strange it was after their first kiss. He watched, alongside Bobby and Dave, as Casey and Tommy tried to figure out what they wanted to be. Cole knew they'd end up together, even before they kissed. When Casey came back to St.Marian's Orphanage, after she met Tommy for the first time, she was different. Meeting Bobby made Casey less angry at the world but meeting Tommy made her crave danger.

Cole's stomach grumbled. He wanted a taco.

"Oh, geez!" Dave bickered with the engine. "Damn it!"

"What's wrong with you?" Tommy asked.

"Nothing, I'm fine," Dave said. He seemed annoyed. At who? Cole couldn't tell.

He looked around the parking lot. Where the hell was Mick? The race was supposed to start soon. He tried to spot the large, scarred man known as Mick the Menace but all he saw were regular Burrowers. Most of them were from the lower gangs; the Spades, the Diamonds, and the Hearts. The Clubs didn't exist anymore and nobody liked to talk about why.

Cole couldn't believe his eyes. Was that Jess? She stood out like a sore thumb, the only Honeycomber in a crowd full of Burrowers. She didn't seem to care. Was she mad? She didn't look happy. *Oh boy.*

"Davey-" Cole said.

"Stop calling me that."

Cole pointed past his face. "Davey, look."

His eyes grew three sizes. He gulped. Usually, he'd be happy to see her. He'd get excited when Jess sent him a text. The first time she spent the night at their apartment, Dave cleaned his room, made his bed, bought candles, and took two showers. He loved going over to her house. He loved taking her out. He'd probably never admit it but he didn't have to, Cole saw it every time Dave looked at Jess; he was in love.

Her angry glare accused him of something terrible.

Cole glanced between them.

"She told you?" Dave asked.

"She told me you stole from her," Jess folded her hands behind her back. "What's your version of that?"

Tommy and Casey were as clueless as Cole was, staring at Dave and Jess. Seeing his friends in pain hurt him. Cole loved them. He loved when they were happy. Dave was his best friend. They drove each other crazy, as only roommates could, but moving into the apartment was the best decision of Cole's life. It was the first place he ever felt safe. St.Marian's Orphanage would always be part of him but it was never his home.

He awkwardly waved to Jess and backed away. He stood with Tommy and Casey. They watched with much interest. If only they had popcorn.

Dave couldn't find his voice. He stuttered and turned to them for help. This was painful.

Jess raised her eyebrows, arms crossed. "Well? Say something."

"Hey," Billy said. He didn't care that he was interrupting. He wore his signature gray trench coat, which had over a hundred hidden pockets and flapped around his body like a cape. His head was shaved and bruises - new ones - painted his right knuckle. He must've gotten into a fight with a client. Billy was the Burrows' salesman. He could get anything and he knew almost everyone. "Hear the news?"

"What news?" Tommy asked.

"Mick ain't coming. Nobody can find him, even better," Billy smiled. "His favorite girl's been missing for a couple days."

Tommy's color drained. His blank expression filled with worst-case scenarios. He stumbled but Casey caught him. She was his rock in the middle of a violent, crazy river. He clutched her wrist and tried not to panic.

"Who's Mick?" Jess asked.

Dave answered. "A racer like Cole... and uh, an assassin."

Her eyes widened and her jaw dropped. "What-"

"It's a Burrows tradition that he dates a girl for a while, then a few days after they fight... Her body ends up in an alleyway," he said. "Mick's protected on all sides though-"

"Oh my God!" It was so obvious that Jess wasn't from the Burrows. She spent time there, mostly at Sally's Place and the boys' apartment. Cole loved her as a person and for his roommate but the Burrows had a lot of traditions she wasn't aware of, most of which would make her sick.

Tommy's gaze darted to each of his friends. He closed his eyes. His chest rose and fell with rapid breaths as he tried to talk himself out of a panic attack. Cole hadn't known Tommy for as long as Dave had but he knew Paisley was a complicated part of Tommy's life like Ted was to Dave. Cole didn't understand the responsibility of being someone's child but it seemed like a lot of pressure to carry.

"I, I, I have to find her, him, or them, I have to find them," Tommy said.

"Go with Jessie," Casey said, steady as she held his wrist. She was the only thing keeping him from falling to his knees and drowning in his fears.

"That's not my name," Jess said. "And I didn't say-"

"You got here somehow." Casey used her don't-mess-with-me tone.

It was a scary voice. It gave Cole chills.

Tommy had a stuck-in-a-nightmare expression. Was he blaming himself for not being able to protect Paisley? For not convincing her to leave Mick? Was he imagining her body in a ditch or an alley? Bruised and bloody like the rest of Mick's favorite girls?

"Fine, yeah," Jess sighed. "Whatever you need."

"I'll go with Cole," Dave blurted out. When Jess looked at him, he didn't meet her gaze.

"Yeah, if Mick isn't here, then there's no race," Cole said. He tried to lighten the mood by adding, "I'm at your depository."

"Disposal," Dave corrected.

"Idiom," Cole countered. It was awesome when Dave's head looked like it was going to explode, an angry, annoyed face reserved only for Cole. Hilarious and so much. It made him laugh.

"Yeah... okay, okay," Tommy gulped. His voice shook and his hands trembled. Sweat dripped down his forehead. "We'll, We'll cover more ground if we split up." He started to focus on the situation, the plan, which helped calm him down. "But what are you gonna do?" he looked at Casey. "You don't own a car, and no, you can't steal one-"

"I'll take Davey's motorcycle," Casey said.

Dave held up a finger in disagreement. "Wait a minute-"

"Don't care, give me the keys," she squeezed Tommy's wrist. She brought his hand up to her lips and kissed his fingers, then his cheek. She whispered something in his ear. He nodded in response.

Dave muttered complaints and rude insults under his breath, tossed her his keys and she left.

"Bitch," he said loud enough for the rest of the group to hear.

Cole patted his shoulder.

They went to The Castaway.

Cole loved the driver's seat. He had full control over everything except the open road. Surprise mixed with solid ground. He loved racing. The speed, the cheers, the adrenaline. The first time he drove a car, he crashed it into a video store. It was an accident. He would've gotten arrested if it weren't for Casey. Her reputation as champion saved him.

He dramatically revved the engine. Dave rolled his eyes. He watched Jess leave with Tommy. When they were gone, he sighed and leaned back in his seat. It wasn't relief, it was guilt. He bent his elbow on the window and drummed his fingers against his temple. Cole wanted to ask if everything was okay but he already knew the answer.

They needed to focus. Paisley could be dead.

He slammed his foot on the pedal.

Chapter 15

Tommy

THE CITY LIGHTS GLIDED by, making the dull colors of every building blur. The Burrows were the most alive at night. Burrowers found comfort in the darkness. Tommy couldn't understand why. He'd been running from his trauma, from his darkness, since he learned how to run.

He clutched his phone, desperately waiting for any piece of news but he hadn't received a single text or call yet. His friends were still searching. He hated that he cared so much. Why couldn't he let go? Why was she still important to him? It didn't make sense.

All the pain, all the bad, it was all connected to Paisley.

Awkward silence filled the car. Tommy didn't know what to say to Jess, a girl he barely knew, his best friend's girlfriend. Her hands, steady on the steering wheel, never moved from the ten and two positions. She was laser-focused on the road. Was this a new car? It smelled new.

"Thanks…" he paused. "For helping me."

Was she uncomfortable too? Her posture, with her back straight and her shoulders back, seemed tense. He wasn't sure if it was because of him or the situation or maybe it was just her.

"You're welcome, of course," she said. She bit at her lip. Maybe she did feel awkward. "Can I ask, um, this woman with this dangerous man, Mick, who is she exactly?"

"My mom."

"Oh."

For some reason, he wanted to talk about it. He never wanted to talk about his childhood. He hated to revisit the memories he tried so hard to forget. Maybe it'd be best to talk to an almost stranger, someone who didn't already know him or anything about his past.

"Yeah." He took a deep breath. "She wasn't a good one. Some good times but mostly she ignored me, drank or got high." Tommy could picture the drugs and needles on his kitchen table and the loud arguments from behind his mom's bedroom door. "She dated guys who hurt her, who hurt me." He choked on the memories of random men lifting their giant hands to slap him in the face. "As crazy as I feel, as much as I want to hate her, she's my mom."

"I can't imagine..." Jess said. "I'm sorry. It must've been terrible."

"I just..." He searched for the right words. "I can't let her die."

She looked at him. The first time she took her eyes off the road. "We'll find her."

He wanted to believe her. He hoped they'd find Paisley in time and if they didn't, he'd have to deal with it. He turned to the window. He let his vision blur. The city lights faded in and out, unfocused and dizzying. He closed his eyes, feeling the car's gentle rumble, as he drifted into a memory.

He could almost smell the burnt biscuits and french fries. It was what Paisley stunk like when she came home from the diner she used to work at before she was fired. She'd complain about how badly her feet hurt and she'd bring home leftovers. Two foam boxes, each held a Monte Cristo sandwich, his favorite food. They'd sit together on their crappy couch, eat and watch Paisley's favorite soap opera.

He remembered the ridiculous drama and the warmth of the sandwich in his mouth. It was in between the bad times when she didn't have a boyfriend.

The night Paisley had her sixth fight with her fourth boyfriend was the same night Tommy got tired of seeing his blood on the floor. He ran. He needed to escape the angry, slurred screams. He didn't want to cry but he was in tears. He went as far as his legs could take him. He ended up in an alley. He was panting so hard he couldn't breathe and his whole body ached. He was hungry and tired. He didn't want to go home. He couldn't go home. Rain crashed against him, drenched his clothes, and made him shiver. He slid down the brick wall and plopped onto the cement ground.

He hugged himself, unloved, alone, and bruised.

It was the same night Betty found him. He could still picture her long, slender, red dress and diamond earrings. She smelled like expensive cigars. She held out her hand and offered him a chance. A chance to escape, a chance to learn how to protect himself. She changed his life.

His phone beeped. Was it Casey or Dave? Someone with good news? Any news? Knowing had to be better than not knowing. The text was from Bobby. Her contact photo was her in a black tutu and a sparkly beaded top, with her bright, confident smile, dancing to an ABBA song.

Danvers Motel. X.

X meant emergency.

***

Bobby

The angry screams were muffled behind the black door. Room sixteen. Two voices. Bobby recognized the woman's and the man's sent shivers down her spine. Was she about to listen to a murder?

The outside hall, on the second floor, was lined with doors to different rooms. It had a depressing view of the parking lot, which was pretty much empty. Not many Burrowers generally hung out at Danvers Motel, only if they needed to conduct business or hide from their enemies. The cold night matched the distant fog crawling across the cement.

The moon, cut in half, was terrifying surrounded by faded stars.

Footsteps clanked on the green, metal staircase. Leo appeared. What the hell was he doing here?

Bobby's heart dropped into her stomach. She shook her head. "No, no, no, no, no, no, no, no, no, no! You can't be here-"

"What?" he asked, confused. "But you asked me to come-"

"No, please- Ah!" THUD. *Paisley?*

Bobby whirled around and faced the door, stumbling backward. She tripped on her high heels but Leo caught her. He steadied her. That sound was too familiar. She could almost feel it. Johnny's strong, rough hands against her face. The tears, the screaming, the bruises, echoing in her memories like a scab that never healed.

"That sounded like someone got hit-" Leo said.

"It was."

"Maybe we should call the police. Do you know who's in there?"

"Someone important to my friend." Without thinking or a moment's hesitation, she threw herself at the door, body slapping against it. *Ow!* Pain. *Boy, was that a bad idea.* She didn't care. She raddled the doorknob and banged her fist on the door. "Paisley! Paisley, open the door, please. I can-"

What could she do? She couldn't fight like Casey or shoot like Tommy. She couldn't do anything. What the hell was she doing? She needed a weapon. Something hard. A fire extinguisher? She didn't see one. Her palms were hot, smothered in sweat, and her lips were quivering. Panic rose in her throat, ready to scream, she felt sick like she needed to puke.

Leo put a hand on her shoulder. He was still there?

"Who's Paisley?!" he asked. Panic and confusion were scribbled on his face. "What's going on!"

"Burrows tradition." She didn't know how else to explain it. Her voice shook. She needed to do something but she didn't know what to do. "Paisley!"

"What does-"

The door swung open. Bobby met the harsh glare of a very dangerous man. He was tall, muscular, and had a wide scar across his face. A murderer for hire and for fun. Someone the police wouldn't capture because he was protected by Betty and Markinson. Mick's skills, his kills, were famous. His assassins were terrifying, they worked under the radar, undetectable, and they were loyal only to him.

"Go away."

Bobby couldn't move. Her body was numb. Terror and fear held her limbs hostage.

Leo stood behind her, holding her arm. His touch was reassuring. Every part of him made her feel safe, even when he was shaking. She realized he was using her to keep himself steady.

She had to be brave. She wasn't alone and she sure as hell wasn't afraid. "No."

Paisley sobbed behind Mick, blood gushing from her nose. A fresh bruise was on her cheek and an old one was on her shoulder. Finger marks squeezed her neck. She seemed shocked to see two teenagers. She probably thought nobody would miss her. Nobody cared about her. Why not take her chances with someone who might?

"Walk away," Mick warned. Bobby was less than half his size. She was an ant compared to him. Small, insignificant but she wouldn't back down. She wouldn't let this happen. It was wrong. It was awful.

She needed to stop it. "Don't kill her. Please, don't kill her. Please."

Rage flickered in his eyes. He grabbed her hair, fingers clutching her curls, and swung her inside. When he let go, her body slammed against the carpet, pain punching her bones.

Mick yanked Leo into the room and shut the door. He locked it. They were trapped.

"Please, Mick," Paisley cried. "I love-"

He stepped toward her. She flinched.

He wrapped his thick fingers around her already bruised neck. He shoved her backward, slamming her head against the wall. She whimpered, completely still. His glare was pure evil and his grip was harsh, unforgiving, the same look Johnny used to have.

Bobby reached for her panda purse. Leo was crouched beside her, shaking.

"Where is it!" Mick screamed in Paisley's face.

She couldn't shake her head. All she could do was sob and beg. Nothing she did mattered. He'd do what he pleased. Bobby knew that. She experienced it; the helplessness, the fear, the pain.

She pulled a sequin-covered bottle of pepper spray from her purse, hiding it behind her back. She didn't have a plan but she had to do something. If she could get close enough, hopefully, luck was on her side.

Leo was trapped by his fear, sweat dripping down his face, lips quivering. Was he about to cry?

He glanced at her, then at the bottle. He looked unsure, shocked, then shook his head. He didn't want her to take the chance but Bobby had to, if she didn't, they'd all die for sure. She started to stand but Leo stopped her. He tried to put on a brave face but his fears cracked the mask. He took the bottle before she could stop him. What was he thinking? *What are you doing?*

Leo stood up. At first, he took slow steps, then he lunged at Mick the Menace, shooting the large, terrifying man's face with pepper spray.

Mick screamed and staggered back. Leo froze.

Paisley gasped when he released her throat. She fell, coughing.

Bobby jumped to her feet. She grabbed Leo's arm. He stumbled, stunned by what he did. She yanked him to the door and grabbed the knob. A gun cocked. She closed her eyes. That sound was familiar too. She pictured the many guns she'd seen before; the ones the men at the poker games had, the ones Tommy built, Sally's shotgun, the gun Vincent used to keep under his bed but not once had a gun ever been pointed at her.

She turned.

Leo's eyes grew six sizes. *Poor guy.*

They both stared point-blank into the barrel of a gun. Bobby didn't know what kind of gun it was, one of her friends would but she didn't. Mick's eyes were swollen but he could still see. He was angry, more angry than before and that was saying something.

Bobby squeezed Leo's hand. His sweaty fingers choked her palm.

Mick gestured to the other side of the room. "Against the wall," he focused the gun on Bobby. "Now."

She took Leo with her. They slid onto the floor, backs against the wall, shoulder to shoulder and hand in hand like warriors waiting to be executed.

Leo's hands trembled in Bobby's grasp. He couldn't let her go. His pulse was quick, panicked, and he was starting to cry.

Mick grabbed Paisley's hair and yanked her up. She screamed. He pointed the gun at her forehead, keeping her off balance, his grip tight around her body.

She begged for her life, for mercy, through desperate sobs.

"Where is it!" Mick yelled. "I know you took it!"

Bobby was solid. She should've been more afraid, maybe in tears or screaming but she felt distant, disconnected from reality, and numb.

Leo squeezed her hand like a balloon he needed to pop. He gulped. "He's gonna kill her in front of us, isn't he?"

"He'll kill us after."

"How are you so calm?"

She pictured herself in the dark corner of Johnny's bedroom, knees against her chest with tears and mascara trickling down her cheeks. The bruises made her body ache and tremble. His angry screams echoed in her mind, punishing her for nothing. "This isn't the first scary situation I've been in."

Bobby put her head on Leo's shoulder. His cheek brushed her curls. She looped her arm with his, locking them together, fingers intertwined. She kept his hands, smooth and sweaty, from shaking.

It was odd being the support system, the brave one. Usually, she was the victim or the coward. Not this time. She wasn't sure what she was. Leo's heart hammered against his chest. His breath trembled but Bobby's was calm, serene.

She didn't know why because she was scared too. She could hear Johnny's voice, telling her she deserved this.

Mick threw Paisley to the floor. She tried to sit up but she was shaking all over. He shoved her down, flat, and pointed the gun at her nose, legs straddling her hips and one hand holding her arm above her head.

All she could do was wait to die.

A thunderous crackle boomed from outside. Everyone froze. Bobby heard rumors about that sound on all the Glisin-devoted chat rooms and fan websites. Could it really be? She waited to hear another crackle but nothing happened. Silence. That was it? No fireworks or heroes? This was bad.

Mick readied his finger on the trigger.

The door burst off its hinges and flew through the air, pieces of black, shattered wood flickering with tiny, white lightning bolts. They went everywhere.

All eyes went to the doorframe.

Two girls stepped into the room. One had long, purple hair and white sparks in her eyes. The other one had shoulder-length, sky-blue hair and held a knife. They stood side by side.

"Alice?" Leo asked in shock.

Bobby laughed. *Casey! Yes!*

Alice's hands and eyes and lightning were amazing. It clicked. The Adler Building Fire and the lightning bolt. The next Glisin stood in this room beside the future Betty Beater.

Whoa, what a conflict of interest.

Gunshot.

Alice and Casey dodged and rolled. The bullet cracked the doorframe, wood chips splattered and Mick shot again. Alice ducked halfway out of the room.

Casey somersaulted onto her feet, facing Mick, she threw the knife with unmatched accuracy. The blade twirled twice in the air, then sliced Mick's fingers, fast and he dropped the gun. She smirked.

Bobby yanked Leo up. He was frozen in fear, staring at Alice and Casey, as he tried to wrap his mind around what was happening, but he let Bobby guide him toward escape.

Alice grabbed a terrified Paisley, helped her up and they all ran out of the room.

Paisley leaned over the railing, gasping through her tears. Her face was red, puffy, and her wounds were bad, black, blue, and bleeding.

Bobby felt oddly excited, high on adrenaline.

"What the hell is going on!" Leo yelled, finally finding his voice. He was more freaked out than anyone.

Bobby clutched his shoulder. She couldn't believe it. She personally knew the next Glisin. Glisin's daughter was standing in front of her. She squealed. "Alice is a powered person, isn't that incredible? I'm kind of, really jealous! I mean, wow-"

"I'll explain later." Alice ran back into room sixteen.

***

Alice

Alice didn't know how she could help but she had to try. She stood in the doorway, hands flat on the frame. She was ready to jump into the fight but Cece seemed to have it handled.

She ducked under Mick's fist, whirling around, she slammed her foot into his stomach. He stumbled. She punched. He grabbed her fist and yanked her close to him, back against his chest. Mick wrapped one arm tight around her neck. Was he going to snap it or choke her? She smashed her elbow against his belly, loosening his grip. She turned, grabbed his shoulder, and kneed him in the gut. He bent forward and she knocked his head against her knee, shoving him onto the floor.

She took a knife from her jacket, twirling it between her fingers. Breath heavy, Cece smirked, ready to stab him and happy she got to do it. The psychotic look in her green eyes proved her excitement.

Mick sat up, quick, as he knocked the knife from her hand, grabbed her wrist, and yanked her down. They rolled, wrestling, but he won. He crawled on top of her. He held her arms down, flat on the carpet.

She lay still, chuckling. Was she satisfied or amused?

He dug his knee into her neck and snatched the knife.

Adrenaline made the vibrations in Alice's body more intense, electrifying her bones and muscles in ways she never experienced. She punched her hand out in front of her and white lightning blasted against Mick, shoving him straight into the wall, slightly singed.

Wow. Who knew she could be such a badass?

Cece pushed herself to her feet without wasting a second, she snatched the knife off the floor and wiped the blood dripping from her nose. The red liquid seeped down her chin and her left eye was horribly bruised. Could she even see?

"Are you okay?" Alice asked. "You're bleeding-"

"Little ointment, I'll be fine." She touched her black eye, shrugging. "Thanks for the save."

"Any time."

They high-fived and folded their hands together, fingers intertwined.

Alice laughed. She never imagined herself in a fight, let alone being the victor of one. She was on top of the world. Who else could she blast? Who else could she save? Now, she understood why Susan always stood like she was invincible. Nothing could ruin this moment, nothing could touch her.

Pain. So much pain. Horrid, overwhelming pain. She glanced down and saw blood, it drenched her jeans and made her thoughts spiral. Her surroundings, the entire motel room, started to blur. The world tipped and she was on the floor. How'd she end up there? Her mind swelled with static. Her clarity drowned.

Mick laughed hysterically. He swung the blood-covered blade at Cece. She blocked his arm and went to grab the handle. He stomped on her ankle, grabbed her hair, and threw her to the ground.

The echo of her body slamming against the carpet was all Alice could hear.

***

Casey

He stepped on Casey's shoulder. His weight held her down. He twisted her arm until SNAP. She could almost hear the individual joints shatter, anger and pain flooding her body, she bit her lip to silence a scream. She wouldn't give him the satisfaction of hearing her cry.

Alice lay beside her in a puddle of sweat and blood. Her thigh was stabbed through.

Mick readied the knife to plunge into Casey's chest.

She wanted to fight. She wanted to kill him but she was paralyzed. It wasn't fair. She needed to save her friends. She needed to live. She wanted to live. Why couldn't she live? This was the first moment, the first fight, she ever contemplated defeat. She didn't want to accept it. She never lost, so why now?

Gunshot.

A piece of Mick's skull broke from his head and flopped onto the fuzzy, tan carpet. His blood splattered all over the cream-colored wall. He dropped, body beside her, she looked into his eyes. His stare was blank, emotionless, soulless, nothing inside, like every other body she'd seen but this time, it wasn't her victim.

She rolled over.

Tommy stood in the doorway, holding one of his guns.

He did it. He saved her.

Breath heavy, Tommy knelt beside her. He didn't look at Mick. He focused on her. It wasn't his first murder. He knew the darkness as well as she did but unlike her, he had a soul. This chipped it a little more. How long would it be before he lost it for good?

She sat up, using her good arm to support herself. Her broken arm hurt. She couldn't move her fingers but she welcomed the pain. It meant she was alive.

Tommy's hands, trembling and cold, hovered over her skin as he checked her wounds. The wild look in his eye told her how panicked he was.

"T," she whispered. He didn't seem to hear her. She touched his cheek. "Tommy."

He looked at her, stuck in the murder, leaning into her touch. "Are you okay?"

"I'm okay," she said. "Are you?"

He glanced at Mick's lifeless body but his usual reserved, focused expression masked his emotions. He clenched his fists to keep his nerves steady. He didn't answer her question. He yanked off his hoodie and made it into a sling. His medical training came from Moira, a member of Betty's inner circle. He secured the sling on Casey's arm and kissed her forehead, cradling her head.

She gripped his T-shirt. She wanted him close to her, either for her comfort or for his, she wasn't sure.

Jess knelt next to Alice. Bobby was nowhere in sight. Cole, Leo, and Dave were huddled together in the doorway, wide-eyed and panicked.

Chapter 16

Alice

ALICE HEARD UNCLEAR ECHOES and saw a bandage being wrapped around her thigh. The images faded in and out. Something pricked her arm. A needle? The pain subsided. She tried to whimper. Could they hear her? Wait, who was they?

"Do you guys not realize what we did!" Dave gestured to the dead body. "We killed Mick the Menace! We're so totally gonna die! His men are gonna kill us!"

"I don't... I.. we.. we.. he... Someone just died!" Leo was more freaked out than the others. Unlike the others, he'd never been in a situation like this before. How did he get dragged into this anyway?

Alice came because Cece asked her. It was that simple. She was insane, right? A friend asked her to come, so she did and put her life in danger. Then again, three people would've died if she hadn't.

"Mick's men are gonna kill us," Dave said. "They'll string us up and skin us alive."

"He was gonna... That guy, the... The dead... The, the guy," Leo pointed at Mick and gestured out the door. "He was gonna kill that woman... Wasn't he? Who is she!"

"Tommy's mom, Paisley Gleason." Bobby stood by the door, hugging herself. She looked like she might melt into the wall.

Cole and Jess helped Alice sit up. Her head felt clearer but she couldn't feel much of anything, her body or her muscles, everything felt sluggish, numb. Whatever they gave her did its job. She was wide awake. Her thigh was bandaged and the bleeding had stopped.

A glittery first-aid kit lay next to her.

"Your mom was dating him.. but.. Who... why are his men gonna kill us?" Leo asked.

Cece rolled her eyes. "You really couldn't be any more behind."

Tommy's hoodie held her arm like a sling. Her eyes were bruised and blood drenched her clothes. Was it her blood, Mick's, or Alice's? She leaned against the wall, legs stretched in front of her. Tommy crouched beside her, hand on her knee. They were closest to the body.

"Mick was an assassin. He worked for Betty and Markinson," Dave said, annoyed. "His men are assassins too. They won't like that we killed their leader."

"*We* didn't do anything," Tommy said. "I did."

"Wait a minute," Leo waved his hands, trying to put the pieces together. "So," he paused. He pointed at the dead body. "His assassin friends are gonna kill us," he looked at Tommy. "'Cause your mom was dating him and you killed him."

"More or less," Dave said. "We don't have time for this, what-"

"We get rid of the evidence," Cece answered his question before he could ask it. "Dumbass."

"Insults, seriously?" he scoffed. "At a time like this?"

"I'm multitasking," she shrugged her good shoulder, wincing.

"And you have superpowers?" Leo's tone was sharp. He focused on Alice. She couldn't tell if his gaze was more confused or hurt. She hated that she kept her secret from him for so long. She wanted to tell him so many times, ideally under better circumstances. She barely nodded before he shouted, "since when!"

"Birth." She braced herself for his reaction.

Dave waved his arms like a panicked goose. "Can we focus on the actual problem here! We're all gonna die!"

"Relax!" Jess yelled. She stood next to Alice. "We need to keep our heads, so we can come up with a plan."

"Agreed," Tommy said. He thought for a moment. "We have to wipe our fingerprints from this place and the weapons too, remove any trace that we were-"

"What about the shattered door?" Dave gestured to the splinters everywhere.

Alice had to admit that might've been overkill. She had better control over her powers but they were strong and sometimes their strength got away from her.

"Cops too," Bobby said. Alice almost forgot she was there. Her arms were tight around her torso. She was holding it together pretty well. How? Was she having flashbacks? "The gunshot was loud, people probably heard it."

"Most of the cops are on Betty's payroll," Cece said. "One word from me and they'll walk."

"How do we get rid of the body? We can't start a giant campfire and it'd be so absolutely stupid to load him in one of our cars and bury him somewhere." Bobby stared at the body. She wasn't terrified or disgusted. She was solemn. Mournful?

"Sulfuric acid," Jess said. "It will dissolve the flesh, the teeth, fingernails, everything within hours like he never existed. We'd need a container made of steel, or uh, polyethylene or-"

"I can get it. Billy owes me a favor," Dave said. "It'll take some time."

"How long?" Cece asked.

"An hour, probably two."

"That'll give me time to deal with my mom," Tommy said. Where was Paisley? Was she still outside? He kissed Cece's forehead and stood up. "B, you go with Dave. You've got some pull with Billy, right?"

It took a second for Bobby to realize he was talking to her. "Billy does have a thing for me," she stared at the fresh corpse. She nodded. "Yeah, besides, I have to get out of here. I'm gonna puke."

"Then we're taking your car," Dave said.

They left and Tommy followed.

Alice used Cole as a crutch and plopped herself next to Cece. She'd need to trash these jeans when she got home. If she still had a home. Would Leo tell his dad about this? About her powers? Would Mister Scotts kick her out? Would he hate her for lying? Did Leo hate her lying?

"Did we just, we just planned a cover-up for a murder!" Leo yelled.

"Well, *we* did," Cece answered. "You weren't much help."

He grabbed his head and shook it, muttering "this is insane" under his breath over and over again. He paced back and forth across the room.

Alice wasn't sure how to help him. She looked at the bandage wrapped around her thigh. When she tried to move her leg, pain seized her muscles.

She groaned.

Cole pulled out a granola bar. The wrapper crinkled and he licked his lips. It was covered in chocolate. Everyone looked at him.

Alice's stomach churned. Was he nuts?

"Really?" Jess asked.

He shrugged. "I'm hungry."

She made a face and shook her head.

Mick lay peacefully next to Alice's feet, quiet and lonely. An empty shell of a very psychotic, terrifying man. What made him choose that life? Why did he choose to kill? Was it about the money? The fear? Maybe he wanted respect. What made him think abuse was okay?

Alice refocused on her friends. Cole ate his granola bar. She wondered how many dead bodies he'd seen to make him so okay with this. Cece was silent, deep in thought, as she fiddled with her necklace and stared at the corpse. What was she thinking? Jess was trying to calm Leo down. She rubbed his back, squeezed his shoulders, and tried to explain everything the best she could.

Leo pulled away from her and closed his eyes, taking deep breaths.

"I'm sorry I lied," Alice said, not knowing what else to say.

He looked at her. The betrayal, the pain, the fear, and confusion were on his face. Tears shimmered in his eyes. "We've been living together for like a year," he turned to the others. "How did, how long have you guys known?"

"The end of your guys' freshman year," Cece was barely paying attention. "She saved some kid from getting hit by a car."

"Dave, Tommy, and I learned about her powers after the Adler Building Fire," Jess said. She hugged herself and looked down at her ballet flats. No guilt, no discomfort. She glanced at the corpse. She was handling the situation better than Alice expected. Jess kept surprising her.

Alice kept surprising herself too. She thought she'd be more freaked out, more scared, or worried but she wasn't. Maybe the adrenaline still pumping through her veins was keeping her from absorbing the situation or the excitement of the night hadn't worn off yet.

Maybe she'd be more panicked tomorrow.

"So, it's just me, Bobby, and that guy," Leo pointed at Cole. "Who had no idea."

Cole bit his granola bar. "I think it's awesome," he smiled. "You're like human lightning."

He wasn't mad? That meant a lot. Bobby didn't seem mad either. Alice was pretty sure she could trust them. If Cece trusted them, Alice had no reason to doubt them.

Leo took a deep breath. He wouldn't look at the dead body. "Who else knows?" he asked.

"Her dad and some chick named Karen Micheals," Cece said. "A friend of Glisin's."

"Nobody else can know. The number is too high now," Alice said. "My mom had a lot of enemies, and thanks to Cruise Industries everyone knows powers are somewhat genetic. If people found out, my dad, you guys, everyone I care about could be hunted down and killed."

Her parents used to warn her about the dangers of people learning Glisin's identity. Glisin was needed in Height City, they said, but many people - criminals, psychopaths, murderers - wanted her gone. They'd use her weaknesses, her family, against her, so Alice had to keep the secret, no matter what. She wasn't doing a great job so far.

"You want me to lie to my dad?" Leo shook her head. "I can't do that." He was close with his dad, more than other fathers and sons. In a way, Mister Scotts was Leo's best friend. "You shouldn't either. He's my dad but he's your, well... You know."

"I hate it. I hate lying to him but I can't risk it." She didn't know what else to say. What could she say? She loved Mister Scotts. He took her in when she had nowhere else to go. He supported her, he believed in her, he encouraged her, he taught her to cook, he bought her clothes and supplies and in return, she kept a huge secret from him. It wasn't fair. It wasn't right. He didn't deserve it but it had to be this way. He was safer if he didn't know.

"Please," she whispered.

Leo's eyes drifted from the others in the room - they stared at him, waiting - to the splinters on the floor, to the dead body. What was he thinking? What would he say? Did he hate her? Did Alice ruin their friendship? A friendship she counted on, a friendship she needed.

"I'll have to think about it," he said.

She nodded. "Okay."

***

Tommy

Tommy stared at his childhood home. A rundown, crappy house with dead rose bushes under the front windows, one on either side of the front door. He didn't want to go in. He hated this place. At the same time, he felt sorry for it. If those walls could talk, they'd be screaming.

He tried to focus on something besides the memories like the funny smell The Castaway had.

Paisley came out. She locked the door, probably from habit, and came to the car. Two duffel bags hung from her shoulders. She dropped the bags in the back, buckled herself in, and nodded.

Tommy hit the pedal.

"Thanks for letting me grab some things," she said. Dave had handcuffed her to the railing outside room sixteen. Tommy laughed so hard. He wanted to take a photo but didn't want to waste time. He needed to get his mother out of Height City.

"What'd you grab?" His tone must've made the question seem like an accusation.

She frowned. She turned and opened one of her bags. The contents seemed to be badly folded clothes, makeup, and a pack of cigarettes. "Not drugs, I needed money and clothes." She sounded tired. Her face was still red from crying. "I've been going to meetings, you know? I'm working on it."

"I've heard that before," he muttered. "If you're sober, why'd you jump in bed with an assassin?"

He wanted to scream at her. His anger was suffocating. If he let himself, he could lecture her on everything she did wrong. It'd take weeks. "It doesn't matter. I just want you gone. Once the news spreads about Mick..." he sighed. "They'll come after you if they can't find anyone else."

Paisley nodded.

Did she regret it? Her choices, his childhood. How stupid was he? Why did he still want her to care? It was pointless. She never cared before, why would she start now? Tommy needed her to leave, not only for her safety but for his own sanity.

"So, you're still friends with that Cece girl, huh?" Paisley asked.

"Since we were nine but, I guess," He wasn't sure he wanted to tell her about his current relationship status. She never liked Casey. "A little more than a year ago," he paused. "We're dating now."

"Betty's champion? You're with her?" she chuckled in disbelief. "You two always seemed close, by each other's sides since you met but," her face wrinkled with concern. "She's champion of The Arena."

"And I'm Betty's tech support... and other things." An image of Mick's corpse surfaced in his mind, fresh and clear; the bullet hole in the center of his forehead, his blood splattered on the walls, his void, lifeless stare. It wasn't unlike Tommy's other victims. It didn't matter how he chose to kill them; a bullet in the head, a bullet to the heart, a blade to the throat, a brick to the skull; they all ended up with the same plain, glossy-eyed expression.

He forced the memories to fade. He'd deal with it later. He had to stay focused on the task in front of him.

Paisley shrugged. "That girl, though, she always had a few screws loose-"

"You don't get an opinion on my life," Tommy said. "Not after everything you put me through."

"They weren't all that bad-" she said.

He tightened his grip on the steering wheel. One of his earliest, clearest memories was of Mark, one of Paisley's boyfriends. He bought her expensive wine glasses. They were nice glasses. She broke one by accident, a tiny little chip in the rim. She apologized profusely but Mark was drunk again. Usually, he would've hit her, slapped her across the face, but he didn't. Instead, he hit her son. Tommy still had the scar. "Yes, they were."

He parked near the bus stop. They were at the edge of the Nests, a few blocks from Eddie's Bar.

A deodorant ad was pasted to the bench. The sidewalk was empty except for a few cars and street lamps illuminated the road. The city lights drowned the stars but the moon was bright, peeking out from behind a cloud.

Tommy wished he were on his and Casey's favorite rooftop, so he could watch the sky. He liked searching for the constellations he knew. He only knew a few, most of which Cole taught him but his favorites were the ones he and Casey named themselves. He loved their rooftop. They found it when they were kids, one of the tallest buildings in the Nests. It had a perfect view of Height City, including the Honeycombs, the Burrows, and the river.

They could see everything but no one could see them. It was their escape from the chaos in the world.

"For what it's worth, I'm sorry." Paisley sat on the bench. Her bags were by her feet.

Tommy wished he believed her but he couldn't. It wasn't sincere. He wanted to turn around and never look back. He'd leave her behind. He'd never think about her again. He'd move on, healthy and happy, but something held him back. He searched for the owner of the shell company that paid her every year but he couldn't find any answers. He wanted to know. "Why is there a shell company paying you in monthly installments? I can't tell how far it goes back but it's been, at least, a few years."

She looked like she'd been caught committing a murder. "How do you know-"

"I hacked your bank records."

She scoffed. "You always were a smart kid, never immoral but then again with the company you keep-"

"Don't," he warned. "I've never asked you for anything. I want an answer, okay? You owe me."

She disagreed. He didn't care. Paisley took a deep breath. "I had an affair."

"And?" It was hardly shocking news.

She rolled her eyes. "We used protection. I was on the pill but somehow *you* happened." Her displeased frown hurt him. "I knew I couldn't be a mom. I proved that but I tried my best, okay?" She paused. What was she waiting for? Comfort? Reassurance that it was fine? She wouldn't get it. "Anyway, I wanted an abortion but I couldn't pay for it... For anything-"

"Drugs." Tommy knew his mom never wanted him or loved him but the confirmation felt like he'd been stabbed in the heart. He stayed neutral. He hid any hurt feelings he had with a simple frown and vague eyes. A look that took him years to perfect.

Paisley didn't need to know how much her words could affect him.

"I took a DNA test and sent it to your father, proof and a demand," she said. "He paid the amount I asked for and has been paying for almost eighteen years."

"You used me as blackmail for drug money?" he asked. He couldn't believe it. She didn't want him but she kept him for money. He didn't know how to respond, what to think. Who was rich enough to pay her so much? Who'd go to such lengths to protect their reputation? Who was that important?

Paisley was a worse person than Tommy thought.

"We had nothing." Her voice started breaking. "I had nothing!"

"You couldn't get your weekly fix so you had me to get the money!" Tommy wanted to grab her and shake her. He wanted to blame her for everything horrible that had ever happened in the world but he could only blame her for his childhood. She was the villain who acted like a victim. It made him sick. His clenched fists tightened, his nails were tiny blades against his palms. "Tell me I'm wrong."

"You don't understand."

No, he didn't. "Who is it? Who's my father, Mom?"

"Brad Cruise."

***

Casey

"How in the world did I get myself into this situation?" Leo held one end of the blue tarp, carrying a charred body that used to be Mick the Menace.

Alice used her powers to burn room sixteen and everything in it beyond recognition but to be on the safe side, Casey still wanted to melt Mick too.

The Danvers Motel basement was as crappy as a place could get. The fluorescent lights were dim, rats scurried in the corners, and the floors were stained in dry blood, which wasn't shocking. Danvers Motel was used for dirty work.

She'd done one or two jobs there herself, mostly torture.

She was an expert at cutting off fingers. Betty wanted her to learn every trade. She learned how long an average person could hold their breath, so she could waterboard and drown people without killing them. She learned how to shatter bones with a single move, how to scoop out someone's eyes.

The Exodontist, a professional torturer, ripped out teeth to get information. He could get any answers he wanted if he used his tweezers. Casey studied with him for a week, she learned a lot, including how gross someone's bleeding gums were.

"I've been asking myself that same question for the last hour," Jess said.

She and Leo carried the body down the stairs since Alice and Casey had broken limbs.

Nobody threw up or fainted, so it went well.

"Are you guys seriously complaining that your lives are interesting now?" Casey stood by the window. Her arm and face were sore, blood was in her hair, and she needed a nap. Unlike the others, she'd sleep like a baby after this.

Alice sat on the stairs. She hadn't said anything. Who would've thought? Glisin's daughter helped cover up Mick the Menace's murder. What would Height City's superhero think? Casey could only guess.

She never felt the need to make anyone proud. She owed Betty her life but their relationship was nothing compared to a parent and a child. Or was it?

"Why are we so afraid of these guys anyway?" Leo asked. "We've got my superpowered roommate and the ninja over there."

"Not a ninja," Casey said. "I'm just awesome."

Bobby's nineteen-eighties sports car pulled into the parking lot. It used to be her mom's. Vincent kept it. He would've fixed it for her but he never got the chance, so Dave fixed it. Bobby loved that car. It was one of her most prized possessions. She kept an old picture of her parents in the glove box. It was taken before she was born, back when they first met.

Dave opened the trunk. Cole went to help.

"Where are we going to dump it?" Jess asked. "After he.. It.. um-"

"Sewers. You wouldn't believe how many bodies are down there," Casey said. Betty and Markinson were careful. They knew how to make someone disappear and people knew it. If you asked questions, you'd disappear too or your loved ones would.

"Acid at the ready!" Cole yanked a barrel into the room. Dave followed with the second one.

Rotten eggs, burned flesh, and mold blended together. The stench made everyone turn green. Casey found it comforting. She joined the group by the tarp. The body was black, burned. The flaking skin started to peel off the bones. The rest of room sixteen looked the same way. Alice's powers were strong. Casey was impressed. She hoped Tommy was okay.

"How'd it go on your end?" Dave grabbed an apron, goggles, and gloves.

Bobby handed the other boys the same outfit. "A present from Billy."

"Who?" Leo asked.

"Everything in that room is destroyed," Alice said. "I made sure of it. There's no evidence."

Tommy walked in. His eyes were rimmed with red. He'd been crying. What did Paisley do? *That slutty bitch.* Casey should've punched her when she was handcuffed to the railing.

Tommy took an apron, gloves, and goggles and quickly put them on. "Security footage is wiped."

"How'd it go with *Mommy Dearest*?" Casey rubbed his arm. She wanted to hug him, hold him in her arms, and whisper insults about his mother until he cracked a smile but he was too focused, too determined to keep moving.

"It was awful," he said. He tied the apron closed. "But she's gone and she won't talk. She doesn't approve of us."

"That makes me feel good." Casey squeezed his shoulder. She'd comfort him later.

She sat beside Alice. They leaned their heads together, silently supporting each other.

Alice's jeans were drenched in blood and she whimpered quietly every time she moved her leg. Mick stabbed her good. The bandage around her thigh kept her injury from getting any worse.

Jess and Bobby stood on either side of the staircase. Bobby had bags under her eyes. Her arms were wrapped around her torso. She looked plain, stiff, nothing like herself. Casey was proud of her best friend's bravery. Between the two of them, Bobby was definitely the toughest.

Jess picked and bit her cuticles. Her fingers were torn and scabbed. Her left index finger was bleeding. She shifted on her feet. She couldn't stand still. The princess was handling this situation better than Casey expected. She had to admit Jess had guts.

The boys cut Mick's charred limbs with rusty tools they found in the basement. The ax had dried blood on its sharp edge. Dave and Tommy did the slicing and dicing while Leo and Cole dunked the pieces into the barrels of acid. Black flakes floated in the air.

Leo puked twice.

No fingernail, toe, eyeball, or strand of hair; nothing was left. The girls rolled up the tarp. Casey helped as much as she could but she was down to one hand. She couldn't do much except help Alice stand.

Bobby volunteered to trash the tarp.

The group stood in a not-so-perfect circle. They were bound together now whether they liked it or not.

"I'm never gonna sleep again." Leo ripped off his gloves. He pulled off the goggles and yanked the apron over his head. He'd probably be scarred for life.

Cole nodded. "That makes eight of us."

"I'll stay with the body, wait for it to dissolve then get it out of here. You guys should go home, get your minds off this. I'll let you know when it's done."

Tommy rubbed his face and ran his fingers through his hair. He sighed as if he hadn't taken a breath all night. His hands weren't shaking, they were steady and his gaze - kind, reserved, a little shy - was hardened. A new willingness to kill. It wasn't there before, Casey would've noticed. With Paisley gone, there was a certain amount of weight lifted off his shoulders but murdering Mick had taken its toll.

Tonight changed him. It'd change everyone.

He leaned on the wall and slid to the floor, exhausted.

"This secret doesn't leave this room," Casey said. She wasn't saying it for Dave or for Cole, even Bobby knew how to keep a terrible secret. Alice would take her guilt and Mick's death to her grave. It was the others Casey wanted to tell.

Leo was too new, too innocent, he'd crack if his dad looked at him wrong.

Jess was the wild card. Casey wasn't sure what would make her crack.

She laced her fingers with Tommy's and squeezed his hand. He didn't need to say anything. They didn't need to talk about it, not if he wasn't ready.

He kissed her forehead.

Casey didn't feel any different. Everything that happened tonight was normal for her, a regular work day except for the people. Her friends.

Usually, she'd be alone.

***

Jess

Jess headed to her car. She needed a billion showers and to sleep forever. What was she going to tell her parents? What lie would explain being out all night and smelling like heat and blood? Her stomach was upside down. Her fingers were bruised and scabbed. She couldn't believe she helped melt a body and burn the evidence. Why wasn't she more panicked? Leo's reaction was correct. He was terrified. Jess was too but she was also exhilarated, fascinated, which confused her.

Her trembling hand reached for the door but Dave grabbed it first. "You hate me."

Was he so concerned about their relationship, he'd bring this up now? This was the first real glimpse she had into his everyday life. A drug dealer, a criminal, a guy who was owed favors and knew people who could get sulfuric acid within an hour. How could she have been so clueless? The realization didn't scare her, not completely, but it surprised her.

"It's been a long night," she said. "Can we talk later?"

"No, 'cause if we're good, then," he shrugged. "I'll come with you and we can hang out in your room and forget tonight ever happened, at least until morning."

She pictured herself saying yes. They'd sneak into her room and shut the door. They'd lay together in her bed. She could read him a few of her favorite poems or they could watch a movie. He'd probably choose one of the *Star Wars* movies. He had a crush on Princess Leia. It didn't matter what they did as long as Dave held her. She could fall asleep in his arms and forget about the dead body, and the melting, the burning, and the terror. She wouldn't have to worry about her parents or the fact she was a criminal now, like them.

"Sounds perfect," she said. She frowned. She was probably going to regret this but she couldn't help it, Jess needed to know what happened earlier with him and Layla. "But first, I need to know what happened between you and my mother because I know she isn't telling me everything."

He nodded, hesitant. "She paid me to break up with you. I guess, it's her twisted way of protecting you from me, so she wrote me a check, and I-" he broke off.

She didn't need him to finish his sentence to know what he was going to say. She didn't mean to cry but the betrayal overwhelmed her. "You took it?" she scoffed. "Let me get this straight, my mother gave you an ultimatum, me or the money," her voice shook. "And you chose the money?"

She didn't want to believe it. How could he do that to her?

"It wasn't like that. I need it. I've got debts in the Burrows that could cost me my head but I was never gonna break up with you, Jess," he stared at her. His beautiful blue eyes made her heart jump. "I figured we could lay low for a bit." Dave held up a finger and reached into his pocket. He pulled a crumpled piece of paper out of his brown, leather jacket. He handed it to her.

She smoothed it out. She was shocked. "Five thousand dollars?"

"I would've told you I talked to her but we've been a little busy." Dave gestured to the Danvers Motel basement. If Jess never saw that place again, it'd be too soon.

"What did she say to you?" It didn't matter, the check was enough to prove Layla was a selfish, controlling psycho. Jess couldn't believe she had come from her. But she wanted to know. What would Layla say to get rid of Dave? How far would she go to craft Jess's life?

Dave hesitated. He tripped over his words. "Lots of things... You know? Made a few good points, I guess-"

"Good points?" she asked. "Like what? That you're not good enough for me? That your dad shot me, because first of all, I get to decide who's good enough for me, and secondly-"

"Am I your rebellious phase?" he asked. What did he mean by that? Was he her rebellious phase? "It's our timetable... It doesn't make sense." He had never looked more concerned or vulnerable. "You were mad at your parents about releasing my dad and you started dating me, you wanted to come out to your mom first. You knew she'd hate it-"

"I wasn't planning that. I needed a ride that day and I figured she'd be upset, so it gave us an excuse to get away." It sounded suspicious now. Those weren't her intentions. She cared about Dave. She fell for him in the hospital. He made her laugh. He listened to her rant about her favorite books. He gave her shoulder rubs when she was stressed. He braved meeting both her parents. He made her feel adventurous. Yes, her mom didn't approve and maybe she liked that. Would Jess use him without knowing it?

"Am I your payback for her controlling you? This journalism thing, me, is it all just a way to piss her off?" he asked. "How do I know I'm not a phase?"

His beautiful blue eyes begged her to say something. For once, he didn't seem sure of himself, he looked desperate and doubtful. He was doubting them, their relationship, everything. What if it was true and she didn't realize it? Layla's plan vs her own. Was it all rebellion? Did that make sense? Did she not know what she was doing? Was Jess ready to leave a secured future for one she could create?

"You should keep the money," she whispered. "You're right. Um, you need it, and I... I need to figure some things out, so-"

"Wait a minute." His grip tightened on the doorknob. "I didn't-"

"You're right, okay? I was angry with my parents and I wanted to get back at them. I wanted to get back at my mom... I don't know if you were part of that, or if, if journalism is..." she sniffled, tears threatening to rush down her face. "Give me some time. Let me figure it out on my own."

Dave stared in disbelief. He wasn't happy. He stepped back and gestured to the door. She opened it, got into the car, and he slammed it shut, cursing under his breath.

Jess held the steering wheel. *Damn it! Damn it!* She started to cry. She could've cried forever. She wanted to scream into her pillow and slam her fists into a wall. She wanted to yell at her mom.

Her heart cracked.

What else could go wrong tonight?

***

Alice

Alice held Leo's shoulder as he helped her to the car. She needed to hug her mom. She wanted to hear Susan's voice and smell her mango perfume. She wanted to go back in time and let her parents hold her. They'd whisper that everything would be okay and she'd believe them.

She had enough nightmare material to last a lifetime.

"How are we gonna explain that to my dad?" Leo was referring to her wounded leg wrapped in a bloodstained bandage. It hurt to put weight on it.

She shrugged. "I tripped?"

"That's a horrible excuse," he said. "We have to come up with something better. Hey, um," he glanced around as if people were watching them. The parking lot was empty except for the others in their group. It wasn't a busy night for Danvers Motel. "I won't say anything... About the zapping and the whooshing, and the flashing-"

Sweat covered his face, bags were under his eyes and he'd been shaking, trembling since they found each other in room sixteen. Some people weren't cut out for violence. Alice felt bad about Leo being involved. He wasn't like the others, he didn't grow up like they did. She wished he would've run before Mick trapped him but he'd never abandon Bobby. He was too good, which was why Alice trusted him when he said he'd keep her secret.

She sighed in relief. "Thank you."

"On one condition. Don't lie to me again?"

"Promise." She hugged him. She never wanted to let go. In his arms, she was safe. He was her best friend, one of her best friends. Alice couldn't wait to hear Mister Scotts's snores or maybe he'd be waiting for them. Maybe they'd get grounded. That'd be perfect.

"Hey!" Cole waved. He looked tired but he was wide awake. "We should hang out sometime." He focused on Leo. "Maybe we could go to Linda's Diner or Sally's Place or something. You're the newbie in the group, right?"

"I don't even know your name." Leo pulled away from Alice but he kept his arm around her torso. He kept her supported, so she wouldn't fall.

She smiled at Cole. His tone was matter-of-fact and his gaze was kind, a little mysterious. Alice wasn't worried about him blabbing her secret. He was trustworthy based on the things Cece said about him.

"Cole, I'm Cole." He held out his hand.

Leo shook it. "Nice to meet you."

Bobby hurried up. She already put the tarp, gloves, aprons, and goggles in her car. She pushed past the boys - focused on Alice - and chuckled. "Wow."

"Hi?" Alice asked. What was happening?

Bobby stared at Alice like she was the president or God.

Leo smiled at Bobby. He looked at her with love and light like she was the toughest person in the world.

"I know we're, like, friends but we're not friends-friends," Bobby paused. She shook her head. "Anyway, duh, um," she laughed at herself. She was cute like a puppy or a kitten. "I just wanted to say I really looked up to Glisin- your mom. I had her action figure and I would play with it all the time," she smiled. "She had her own talk show and," she waved away the memory. "I still have a graphic T-shirt with a picture of her, and it's... It's so amazing," she gushed. "To meet you, Glisin's daughter." She gestured to Alice like she was a Greek goddess.

"Wow." Alice didn't know what to say. She knew people adored Glisin but she never talked to a fan face-to-face before. It was pretty cool to have a fangirl. She wasn't sure she deserved the admiration. Glisin was the hero, not her.

"And hey," Bobby said. Her back straightened and she got all professional. "I design clothes, so... If you ever decide to become a hero or something," she shrugged. "I could design your uniform."

She smiled at Leo, blushing. The pink in her cheeks didn't match well with her red and orange curls.

Leo hadn't taken his eyes off her. He chuckled.

Alice and Cole glanced between them, then looked at each other. He nudged Bobby and she snapped out of whatever flirtatious, giddy trance she was stuck in. She played with the tulle on her tutu and walked away. Cole followed her.

Alice elbowed Leo, so he'd stop staring at Bobby. He opened the car door and Alice slid inside. She leaned against the seat and took a deep breath. Her pulse tracker was silent. It felt good to be somewhere safe. She needed to feel safe after everything that happened. She couldn't wait to get home. Home being Mister Scotts's loft.

Leo took the driver's seat. "Have you ever thought about it?" he turned the key and started the engine. The Honda needed a minute to warm up. "Taking up Glisin's mantle, I mean, trying to save the city and everything."

The idea crossed Alice's mind more than once. It was a decision that would define her life forever. She'd be giving herself to Height City. She'd be swearing to protect it no matter what. She'd have to sacrifice herself for it, if it needed her to, like Susan did. She wasn't sure if she could promise that. She didn't know if she was capable of that. "I'm not my mom. I'm not a hero."

"Cece said you saved a kid. You saved Jess, her family, and all those people in the Adler Building Fire. So, I beg to differ," Leo said. "And hey, your mom didn't have friends to have her back, you know, a team-"

"She had Karen. She had my dad," Alice shook her head. "There's a reason she kept the circle small, okay? If I did this, I'd be putting you, your dad, everyone I love in danger, and-"

"Height City has been drowning in corruption and crime for years, even while your mom was alive and fighting," Leo said. "It needs someone new."

Alice couldn't picture herself as a hero, as the next Glisin. One of her best friends was Betty Beater's sidekick. She helped burn evidence and a body. She hadn't graduated high school yet. She couldn't fight. She was still learning about her powers. There were so many reasons not to do this. Why would she choose it? "Why do you want me to do this so badly?"

He shrugged. "I mean, assassins, drugs, murder, dirty cops and God knows what else." He frowned. The seriousness in his face made her sit straighter. "I'm terrified. People need some hope, they need someone to take the lead, and it seems like you can be that person."

Can. That word meant something. She could be a hero if she tried. She could follow in her mom's footsteps if she wanted to. What would Susan say? What would she think? What would her advice be? She wasn't here. Alice needed to decide this for herself.

"I don't even know where to start."

"I guess we'll figure it out together."

Part 3

Chapter 17

Tommy

SUMMER WAS COMING TO an end and so was the paranoia about Mick's death. Rumors spread through the underworld like wildfire. Nobody knew Mick the Menace was dead. As far as anyone knew, Mick left the city to go on another bender and he never came back. People assumed he found another girl to favor, one who didn't live in Height City. Paisley was gone. She hadn't called or texted, which was fine. It was safer that way. The only evidence of Mick's demise was a charred motel room.

Tommy had new problems.

"You haven't told her yet?" Dave asked.

They were headed to Sally's Place. Garbage and cigarette butts littered the sidewalk. A few men with black Spade tattoos stood in a huddle, smoking joints, outside a liquor store. It had bright green awnings and a big, shamrock-shaped sign above the front door. An alley cat chased a couple of rats across the road.

Tommy flipped through the magazine in his hands.

He collected every scrap of news about the Cruises since he discovered who his father was. How was he related to Honeycomber royalty? He found the DNA test results in Paisley's closet, exactly where she said it'd be. He never thought he'd go back inside that house but he couldn't believe her without proof. It was true. Tommy was Brad Cruise's son. But Tommy wasn't interested in Brad. He was fascinated with his half-brother, Timothy.

"We've been busy. Betty's got us working different jobs. I haven't found the right time."

He thought he'd tell Casey about his new family tree when he went back to Danvers Motel that night but things happened too fast. They had to melt Mick's body before they got caught.

After he and Casey dumped the liquefied assassin into the sewers - Betty's special place for everyone she or her champion killed - Tommy was exhausted. He lay with Casey in his bed at his apartment and listened to her breathe. She fell asleep in his arms, head on his belly. He gently combed her blue hair with his fingers and watched the sunrise through his bedroom windows. The glass was hidden behind white, slightly see-through curtains.

What would happen to Mick's organization once his assassins realized he wasn't coming back? Where would Paisley go? Would Tommy ever see her again? Probably not. He wondered about his father and about Timothy. How in the world was it possible that Tommy had a little brother?

"I don't even know how I feel about this yet," he said.

"Well, you're gonna have to tell her sometime," Dave said. "Can I be there when you do? I'd love to watch her kick your ass, wait, scratch that, she might kick my ass too."

"Remind me why I told you again."

"'Cause I found the shrine under your bed." Dave walked in on Tommy looking through his collection of Timothy Cruise information; Gossip magazines with dog-eared pages, newspaper articles, and photos from the internet. It wasn't a ton. Timothy didn't have a busy social life. "You obviously wanna meet him."

"Maybe." Tommy closed the magazine.

They went into the club and sat at the bar.

Sally carried a box out from the back hall and dropped it in front of them. She ripped it open and started unpacking tall bottles of vodka. Gold hoops dangled from her ears. She wore a black tank top and jean shorts. Her nails, newly manicured, had little panda faces painted on them. Bobby's work, Tommy assumed.

"You excited for B to go back to school?" Dave asked.

"It's been nice having her around," Sally said. "She's happy for senior year though."

"I don't get it. Isn't school supposed to be hell? Something I never understood about Jess. She loves it. It's crazy." Dave ate a cheese puff from one of the snack bowls.

He and Jess hadn't spoken all summer. He was grumpy for weeks after the breakup. He missed her but God forbid he do anything about it, then one day, Tommy found him in bed with a redhead and Dave's heartbreak seemed fixed, but Tommy didn't buy it.

Sally dropped the Lost & Found box on the bar. She pulled out a white, lace bra and tossed it at Dave. It smacked him in the face and he blinked. "Your date from last night left this here this morning," Sally said, annoyed. "Says she found it under your bed and it isn't hers."

"Oh, right..." Dave stuffed the bra in his jacket pocket. "It's from Tuesday night."

"You must've slept with half the Burrows this summer," Tommy said. "Casey and I tried to keep count but we lost track a while ago."

"Keeping count is disrespectful," Dave said.

Sally's disapproval was written on her face but she said nothing. "I don't care what you do with your dates," she shook her head. "As long as you get consent, use protection and hide any item from any previous dates. I'm tired of dealing with angry teenage girls."

"I'll cleanse my apartment before I come back later," Dave said. "I promise."

"Good. And the other two things?"

"Taken care of." He pointed to the Lost & Found box. "Can I go through this?"

"Bobby called first dibs," Sally put it away.

"Damn it."

"What about you and Cece?" she asked.

Tommy glanced around the club in hopes she was talking to someone else but no one else was there. *Damn it.* He scratched his head. "What about us?"

"Protection, consent. You're not gonna be teenage parents, are you?" Sally wasn't going to drop the conversation. She had that look, the one that meant *Don't screw with me.* She wasn't uncomfortable either. How was she not uncomfortable? Tommy wanted to hide under a rock and never speak of this again.

He appreciated the concern and the questions weren't out of nowhere but he and Casey made sure they were safe in every way they needed to be.

"No," he muttered. Was his face turning red? It felt hot. "Can we stop talking about this now?"

"Casey as a mom," Dave laughed. "There's a scary thought."

Lorenzo, a somewhat chubby man with two scars on his right cheek, walked in. His right pinkie was missing. According to rumors in Height City's underworld, Betty cut it off and kept the finger as a trophy. The second part wasn't true, Betty would never keep a measly finger as a trophy. A severed head, maybe.

Lorenzo didn't pay attention to the boys. Why was he so pissed off?

"What do you need?" Sally asked. Her eyes were half closed but she watched his every move. Her tone changed from serious and motherly to professional and threatening.

"Some little bitch with red hair stole some cash from me. I need to know where she hangs out." Lorenzo was part of Betty's inner circle. Nobody stole from him or messed with him because it'd be disrespectful to her. Whoever stole from him was crazy to risk getting on Betty's bad side.

"No wonder he's in such a great mood," Dave whispered, leaning close to Tommy.

Tommy smiled. "Is he ever in a good mood?"

"She's a new player. People call her Red." Sally said. Was that pride in her eyes? Was she impressed? This must be one special thief. The last person to impress Sally was Casey.

"The same Red who stole from the Spades?" Dave asked.

"That's the rumor."

The Spades specialized in firepower and were led by Laurie Hale, the oldest Hale brother; he was a respected figure in the Burrows. People liked him. Who would steal from him? Who was this thief with the guts and skills to steal from the Spades and Lorenzo Wilson?

"This is one person?" Tommy asked.

"One tiny person, tech support," Lorenzo grumbled. He looked like a tomato when he was angry.

Sally popped the cork in one of the vodka bottles and poured herself a drink. Dave held out his glass and tapped the rim. *Nice try,* her face seemed to say. She put the bottle on the shelf instead of pouring him some. He frowned.

"Yeah, she's a good thief," Sally sipped her vodka. "I don't know where she's crashing but she comes in here sometimes and steals wallets."

"You let her?" Dave asked, shocked.

"You wouldn't even let Cece do that," Tommy said.

Before Casey was the champion, when she first started coming to Sally's Place, she wanted to learn how to pick pockets, so Dave showed her a few basics. She quickly topped him by stealing from seven different people in one night. She kept their IDs as prizes.

"Cece went from customers' wallets to my closet in four days," Sally said. "She still has my leather jacket."

Lorenzo wasn't happy with the change in topic. He never liked Casey. Tommy wasn't sure why, maybe because his nephew used to have a thing for her, then he left Height City with the youngest Hale brother. Tommy doubted their leaving had anything to do with Casey but Lorenzo always seemed to blame her for things she had nothing to do with or maybe he didn't like the fact Betty favored her.

Dave slid off his stool, went behind the bar, and poured himself a soda. He raised his eyebrows to ask if Tommy wanted some.

He shook his head. He wasn't thirsty.

Lorenzo watched the boys with an annoyed glare. He grumbled something too rude to repeat and looked at Sally. "When does Red usually show up? I need a time, so I can get my money back."

"Varies," she shrugged. She set the glass down and leaned against the bar, casual, lazy but the sharpness in her eye meant she was ready for anything. "You're welcome to come in, buy drinks, pay your tab," she smiled. She wasn't afraid of anyone.

"Why would he pay now?" Dave asked absently. "He's got the longest tab in the bet."

Tommy slapped his head. "You're not supposed to tell her that."

"Yeah, like she didn't know already." He rubbed his wound.

Several Burrowers had a bet going to see who could go the longest without paying their tab. At what point would Sally cut them off? That was the question.

"Ballpark it for me," Lorenzo said.

"What's the information worth to you?" she asked.

Lorenzo sighed. He grunted his annoyance, then told Sally about a large shipment of drugs down at the docks. The Diamonds - led by a woman named Sylvia - ran the Burrows' docks. The shipment would be at their stronghold, a warehouse overlooking the river, at midnight.

Sally nodded. She approved of the information. "The nights vary," she said. "But Red usually comes in around ten and stays for an hour or two."

"I'll see you tonight." Lorenzo headed to the door, grumbling to himself.

Sally lifted her glass and slapped it against the bar. CLANK. The vodka splashed, and Lorenzo turned. She had his and the boys' attention. A warning was written across her face. "You get your money but if I see you grab her or try to hurt her," her glare narrowed. "I've got my shotgun in the back and Betty owes me a favor."

Betty didn't owe favors. If she did, it was a big deal. Sally wouldn't waste it on a lowlife like Lorenzo to protect a simple thief. Nonetheless, it was a threat worth fearing.

Lorenzo's jaw tightened as he tried to hide how pissed he was. He shoved open the door and stomped out of the club.

"Is that true?" Dave asked. "Does the Crime Queen really owe you a favor?"

"Damn straight," Sally put the last bottle of vodka on the shelf. "Markinson too."

"Remind me never to get on your bad side."

"How do you think I've survived so long in this city?" she smiled. "I play the game right."

Tommy looked at his magazine. Honeycomber Central was a written media source dedicated to gossip and news about Height City's richest families. It had a website too. On the cover, was a picture of Jenna and Jeremy Vance - sister and brother - They wore black clothes and sad expressions. In the circle below them was a picture of Timothy Cruise smiling with his parents, Brad and Martha, who paid to build the new hospital wing. At least, that's what the article said.

They weren't strangers anymore. They weren't annoying Honeycombers anymore and Timothy wasn't just a clueless, privileged rich kid. He was Tommy's blood. Tommy had a family besides his mom. He had a brother.

He used to wish he had a sibling. He wanted a teammate, someone to stand with him when his mom's boyfriends got mad, drunk, or high.

Sally handed Dave the club's extra set of keys and grabbed her purse. "I'm gonna run to the store."

"What for?" he asked.

"Bobby ate all the sugary cereal."

***

Bobby

The lab was cold, sterile, and smelled like chemistry. Bobby wasn't sure if chemistry had a scent but she decided that was what the lab smelled like. She was excited to be part of the team. Well, she thought they were a team, the eight of them.

Pin cushions, needles, thread, buttons, Kevlar, leather, and different textured and colored fabrics were piled on the metal table. She'd been brainstorming for weeks. Her binder was filled with sketches and doodles of possible super-suit styles. She had a picture of Glisin on her phone - from the time Glisin was interviewed by Savanna Ann in front of City Hall - for inspiration.

It was time to start sewing.

Bobby couldn't believe her first public outfit would be worn by Glisin's daughter. No one would know it was a Bobby original but it still had to be perfect.

"Let me know when you're ready for my input." Karen wore a white lab coat over a collared shirt, corduroy pants, and a belt with a giant bow. She wasn't thrilled to share her workspace but she'd made it clear, she'd do anything for Alice. The plans for Alice's uniform needed to be top secret. Karen's lab was the only place to fit that description.

"So... it's true? You teched out Glisin's suit?" Bobby asked.

"I did. I helped design it too. Susan wanted something inspiring."

"It definitely was, I mean, I dressed as her for Halloween when I was nine," she chuckled. "I saw a bunch of little girls last year dressed as her. It's so amazing. She was..." Bobby remembered watching the news with her dad, cuddled in his arms as he snored, exhausted because of his illness.

The headlines about Glisin's heroics were always incredible. She was such a badass. She stopped bank robberies, killers, thieves, and saved lives.

Bobby watched her final battle from a TV screen. Savanna Ann listed the most famous fights between Glisin and Destroyer as the two women fought.

When her ashes fell, the world stopped spinning and Height City's hope dissolved. The underworld celebrated Glisin's death. Liam Hale threw a party at Sally's Place. It was the biggest party of the year and Sally made fantastic tips. Bobby was Johnny's date but she didn't feel like celebrating. She couldn't believe her hero was gone.

"Um," Bobby pushed away the memory. "Are you gonna use the same type of tech to help with Alice's uniform?"

"That's the idea," Karen said. She pointed to a locked, steel cabinet. "Everything I need is in there," she gestured to the rest of the lab. The organized shelves, the binders, the books, the research, the prototypes, and futuristic devices. "Make sure to keep everything organized, okay? I like a clean workplace. Everything is labeled, so it shouldn't be difficult to put things back."

"Oooh, uh.. I'll try." Bobby couldn't make any promises. Every time she started a project, it ended up a complete mess. It was her process. Genius was messy after all.

Bobby decided not to leave Sally's Place. She stopped looking for another place to live after Mick died. She needed to start believing she wasn't a burden to her friends or else, she might start searching for the wrong kind of love again. Bobby didn't want to make the same mistakes as Paisley.

She liked living with Sally. She slept on an air mattress and they had to share a bathroom but it wasn't that bad. Bobby felt safer, steadier than she had in years. She felt stronger.

The high-tech, futuristic elevator, which looked like it should be part of an alien spaceship, slid open. Casey stepped into the lab. She handed Karen a foam box and gave Bobby another, then sat in one of the swivel chairs, unzipped her boots, and put her feet up on the table. Her socks were green with little, dancing leprechauns on them. The rest of her outfit was as usual jeans, a T-shirt, and her leather jacket.

She stretched her legs and ate a couple of french fries from her takeout box.

Bobby opened her box and bit into one of Linda's awesome grilled cheese sandwiches. "I can't wait to start on this outfit. It'll be my best one yet and it isn't even for me."

"Al will love it," Casey said.

Karen gathered her work. "Wash your hands before you touch anything. I don't want my priceless inventions to smell like-"

"The best food in the world?" Casey ate another fry.

"Don't touch anything, period," Karen said. She took her tablet and went into the elevator. The doors slid shut, and the girls were alone. Finally, they could have a real talk.

Bobby swallowed her food. "Have you talked to Alice yet?"

"Nope," Casey ate a fry. "I think I'll wait."

"You've been waiting since she made this decision," Bobby said. "She deserves a conversation about whatever choice..." she paused. She tried to read Casey's stone-cold expression but it was impossible to know what she was thinking. "Unless you don't want to tell her because you-"

"B, you are the worst choice for a therapist." Casey took half of Bobby's grilled sandwich and pulled it apart. She ate half of the half and licked the cheese off her fingers.

"You need to tell her," Bobby said. "She deserves to be broken up with in a respectful manner."

"If I don't tell her, then it doesn't exist." Casey was more stubborn than a bull. A blue-haired bull.

Bobby hated to see her best friend torn between two loyalties. Betty or Alice, Betty or Alice, Betty or Alice. It was a choice that would define Casey's life forever.

"Do you not want to be Cece anymore?" It was a question Bobby couldn't answer. She'd known Casey for longer than she'd been the champion. She knew Casey when she was still an orphan, an angry, quiet girl searching for something she couldn't describe. The championship title, The Arena, it suited her.

"I can't remember when I wasn't Cece."

Bobby smiled. "I do!"

"If you say the day we met, I'm gonna throw a microscope at you." She ate three more fries.

"But," Bobby scoffed. "It's the perfect example."

She remembered going to the kitchen for some chips while Vincent was at work. Her long hair, dyed pastel colors, was braided over her shoulder. She grabbed a family-sized bag of Doritos and went back to her bedroom where she found a blonde girl sitting on the fire escape outside her window.

The girl was admiring the dreamcatcher Bobby made in first grade. It was blue with purple beads and yellow and brown feathers casting a giant shadow on her bedroom floor.

"It was the first time I snuck out of St.Marian's," Casey said, lost in the same memory. "You opened the window with your sparkly nails and your goofy grin and you offered me a Dorito."

Bobby smiled. She wouldn't give their friendship up for anything. Casey was the strongest person Bobby knew. Her fierce loyalty and her confidence were unmatched but sometimes, she'd forget she was a good person. Bobby was glad to be the one to remind her.

"Whatever you decide, superhero or Cece, I'm with you," she said. "I can be a superhero's sidekick and a crime boss's bestie," she shrugged. "Why not?"

"I can think of a few reasons."

"Don't care," Bobby said. She knew it was unrealistic but she didn't care. Things would work out the way they were supposed to, she had faith. "I like the plan and you're not gonna change my mind. I can do it all."

Casey's appreciative smile faded. Her face became serious, thoughtful.

Bobby waited for her to say something. She was ready to listen.

***

Casey

Casey could still see the body of her first victim on The Arena's cement floor. The coppery smell was the first thing that came to mind and without mercy, it sucked her into the memory. Blood drenched her skin and her blonde hair. He was the first among many. It was the day she became something. The first time she mattered. She took her chance. His life was the price of her success. She was shocked. She survived. She won. She killed someone.

"I've been Cece for a long time," she said. The name was heavy but she always wore it as a badge of honor. Now, she questioned whether she still wanted it or not. "I don't know who I am without being the champion." She shrugged. "What if I can't be a good person? What if I tell Al the truth, that I've been lying about my name, and she hates me forever?"

She lied to Alice about plenty of things. Casey hadn't told Alice anything about St.Marian's Orphanage or the scars it left on her skin. When Alice pointed out a murder in a newspaper or on the news, Casey didn't mention it was her who committed the crime. She tried to keep her work vague, limited, because if Alice knew the gory details, she'd leave. It was bad enough that Alice had been to The Arena.

"I don't know how she'll react," Bobby said. A pin cushion was tied around her wrist, a yellow tape measure hung around her neck like a scarf, and a pencil was tucked behind her ear. Her red and orange curls were secured in a spider-clip on top of her head. She looked like an actual fashion designer. "But I know you can be a good person. You are one," she meant it. She believed it, which made Casey love her even more, if that was possible.

"And my best friend," Bobby smiled. "She can be a hero."

"How are you so sure?" Casey loved the thrill of a kill or a steal. She loved the power she had during torture. Standing over someone, holding their life in her hands, she decided whether they lived or died. Maybe she was broken, so filled with dark choices and urges that she couldn't be fixed. What if fate wanted her to be the next Crime Queen? The next Betty Beater?

"I believe in you, always have, always will," Bobby said, dead serious and she wanted Casey to see it. She looked her in the eye. "It's totally okay to be scared. You've been the champion since you were eleven. It's gonna be hard not being part of the underworld anymore."

"I don't know who I am without it." Casey hated to admit it but her trauma, her darkest memories, her worst urges, kept her grounded. She needed the darkness. Without it, she'd float away or she'd fall apart. Neither option was appealing.

"I'd help you figure it out," Bobby said. "We all would, together, right?"

There was one more problem: Betty. The woman who gave Casey everything. She made her what she was. She saved her life. She gifted her with the name Cece. She trained her, taught her, fed her, and cared for her.

How could Casey betray her?

***

Alice

Locksley Gym was Alice's new favorite hangout. She found it by mistake when she left Liberty Cemetery after visiting Glisin's mausoleum. She wanted to tell her mom that she decided to continue the family business. She wasn't sure why she said it out loud. Susan couldn't hear her but maybe the cherubs were listening. Alice left a bouquet of daisies on the front steps.

The gym was one large, open-concept room. Dented, metal lockers painted different shades of blue lined one wall while gymnastics mats lay scattered on the cement floor and punching bags wrapped in duct tape hung from the ceiling. A balance beam was in the corner alongside several barbells, dumbbells, and a bench press. The treadmills squeaked and squealed whenever they were used.

Many sweaty, well-built men and women lifted the weights, sparred on the mats, and got fresh drinks from the water cooler. They were intimidatingly focused on their exercise.

Alice dangled from a steel pull-up bar. Her knees were bent, so her feet wouldn't touch the ground.

One hundred and ninety-seven, one hundred and ninety-eight, one hundred and ninety-nine, two hundred.

Fifty more pull-ups to go. She started doing a hundred sit-ups every night, fifty push-ups every morning, and she ran in Moon Park after school. Her muscles were more toned. She almost had abs like Cece.

She wondered what she'd look like with abs.

Alice started exercising months ago, since before she decided to become a superhero.

"Are you sure you've thought this through?" Jess sat on a metal bench. The book in her lap had large block letters on the cover and a picture of a bald man with a nice smile. The striped duffel bag sitting next to her held Alice's ragged, green sweatshirt, a half-filled water bottle, padded gloves, a change of clothes, deodorant, a couple of hair ties, and a mouthguard.

Alice wore a black sports bra and gray sweatpants with white, cursive letters down one leg. The letters were partly peeled and falling off, making it difficult to see they spelled the word BELIEVE. Her purple hair was in a ponytail and sparkly, little soccer balls were painted on her toenails.

Bobby did them for her.

"You asked me that already." She yanked herself up, straining to hold her weight. Her fingers were sore from holding the bar for so long. She did her best to keep herself up, breathing hard, but she couldn't.

She let go and her bare feet slapped onto the mat.

"Yes, but I made a pro/con list last night and there are more cons than there are pros," Jess said. She didn't disagree with Alice's decision to become a superhero but the idea didn't bring a smile to her face either.

Alice checked her pulse tracker. The number was steady. She sighed, wiping the beads of sweat from her forehead, she reached her arms above her head and stretched her back.

She split her free time between Locksley Gym, Karen's lab, and the loft.

Leo was excited about her decision to become a superhero, more excited than her. He took out all his old comic books and searched for inspiration for her code name. He had a lot of Batman and Spiderman comic books, which he insisted were called graphic novels.

"This crusade you're starting is dangerous," Jess said. Her tone was the same one she used to explain trigonometry to Leo, steady and clear. They spent hours on the couch, staring at their math books. He still didn't get it. "You could die or worse," she paused. "You could be captured and tortured and if we joined you, we would be too-"

"Joining me is your decision." Alice grabbed her water bottle, unscrewed the cap, and put it to her lips. *Refreshing.*

She wasn't going to force her friends to help her. Height City wasn't their responsibility, they didn't have Glisin's legacy to live up to but Alice did. Mick's death made her realize there was a lot of darkness in the world and somebody had to fight it.

"You haven't told me why you're willing to risk your life for this city," Jess said. "It's a noble thing to do and it definitely needs help but," she shook her head. "There are variables we aren't ready for, that you're not ready for."

Alice knew this already. She'd gone over it a thousand times. She knew the risks, she knew how dangerous it was. She knew it was a life sentence, a commitment she couldn't break. It scared the hell out of her. She was giving up things, normalcy for one, but she'd also be gaining. To her, the pros outweighed the cons.

"What's that?" she gestured to the book in Jess's lap.

"You're purposely changing the subject."

"Yep." Alice grabbed the padded gloves. Along with exercise, yoga, and training her powers, she was learning self-defense. She figured it'd be helpful while fighting crime. She didn't ask Cece to teach her because she was nowhere near Cece's skill level yet. Instead, she found a teacher at Locksley Gym and he gave Alice half off his usual rate on lessons.

"Teddy Jenson's autobiography." Jess drummed her fingers on the book's cover.

"The guy you've been interning for all summer?"

"He's the editor and chief of the Height City Gazette. He's an amazing journalist and I barely got any face time with him, but this morning, he called me into his office for a performance review. I was really nervous," Jess chuckled at the memory. "He said I was hard-working and skilled. He said I have potential and I shouldn't be afraid of it, which is also a quote from his book."

She loved the newspaper. Every day, she'd call Alice after work and tell her the best parts of the day. She helped proofread articles, she created a new filing system, and she got coffee for all the journalists. She wrote practice articles for herself on various events around the city and researched writing styles and famous writers.

"That's incredible, way to go, Jess," Alice smiled. "Does this mean you're finally gonna tell your parents you don't want to be a lawyer?"

Jess's expression tensed. She frowned and looked at the floor, apologizing without words. "My mom would be disappointed." Of course, Layla was her first thought. "And besides, I don't even know where to start. If I'm going to be a journalist after graduation, where do I begin?"

"What's Teddy Jenson say?" Alice asked.

Jess traced the pages. She read the book, at least, twice. With the way her mind worked, she could probably recite the timeline of Teddy Jenson's entire journalistic career with perfect accuracy. "He started with a blog called the Jenson News."

"Hey, you ready?" Rodrick asked, standing behind them. His toned muscles made his black T-shirt tight on his torso. He had broad shoulders, black, messy hair, and a couple of tattoos, one of which was the Chinese symbol for glory. His uncle owned Locksley Gym but Rodrick managed it. He was a black belt in several martial arts techniques and only a few years older than the girls. A Baltic graduate, in fact.

"Rodrick, this is my best friend, Jess," Alice gestured between them. "Jess, this is Rodrick, he's been teaching me self-defense four times a week."

Jess reached out for a polite handshake. Her eyes floated over his arms, pausing on his tattoos with a certain fascination. "Your tattoos are interesting."

"I hope that's a good thing," Rodrick smiled at her curiosity, still holding her hand. It took a few seconds for either of them to let go.

"It is," she said, blushing a little. Her face almost matched her streaks.

Alice bit her lip to keep herself from chuckling.

"Nice to meet you," Jess folded her hands in her lap. "Alice really enjoys your lessons."

"I'll have her wearing a black belt in no time," Rodrick said.

"Sounds perfect."

"I'll be right back." He went to get his mouthguard and gloves.

Once he was out of earshot, Alice laughed. "That was subtle," she said.

"What?" Jess chuckled. "I was admiring his tattoos, and sure, he's cute, I guess, muscular," she paused, trying not to smile. "Shut up."

Her expression fell. She was thinking about Dave. Their breakup broke her heart. Jess cried on Alice's shoulder for a week, talking about how confused she was, how horrible of a person she was for hurting him, for wondering if she somehow was using him, and how she needed to figure out who she wanted to be by herself before she could really be with someone else. She went through two boxes of tissues.

Alice put in her mouthguard. She hopped from one foot to the other, letting the mat cushion her feet.

Rodrick had pinned her a hundred times on this mat but it never hurt. She loved her lessons. A fake fight was almost as good as a real one. She didn't use her powers when she sparred with Rodrick because she couldn't tell him they existed. She also wanted to learn to fight without them. She figured she'd be even stronger, more prepared, if she didn't rely on her powers completely.

She took her stance.

Rodrick faced her. He gestured to her feet. "Don't favor your left. Stay to the right."

Alice put weight on her injured leg. It took two surgeries and weeks of wearing a cast but it was almost fully healed. She was proud of the giant scar

Mick left on her skin, it was a sign she survived something traumatic and violent, a sign she was strong. She'd always be proud of it.

"Ready?" Rodrick asked.

She nodded.

Alice ducked under his fist, knuckles barely missing her face. She punched him in the throat. He staggered back, quickly regaining his balance. She tried to kick him but he caught her ankle. He yanked her forward and she slipped. THUD. Her body hit the edge of the mat.

Sometimes she was better, sometimes she was worse. She needed to be the best if she was going to be worthy of taking her mother's mantle. Alice needed to be unbeatable if she was going to take on Height City's underworld. She wouldn't stop until she could win any and every fight.

Rodrick helped her up. "You good?"

"Yeah," she stretched her fingers and took a breath. "Let's go again."

***

Leo

"Sparky!" Leo smiled. It was a great name and he figured it made sense. Alice had a tendency to spark. Now that he heard it out loud though, it sounded lame.

Cole shook his head, unimpressed.

They sat across from each other in a booth by the window. They'd been at Linda's Diner for an hour but their brainstorming wasn't going as well as Leo expected. He and Cole had tasked themselves with creating a name for Alice's superhero identity. It had to be epic.

"Zapper," Cole smiled.

Leo shook his head. "No. What about Lightning Fingers?"

"Bright Light?"

They weren't getting anywhere.

Cole kept a list of all the names they thought of. How did comic book writers do it? It was harder than it seemed. Why did the name Superman or Batman seem so cool?

Leo grew up reading comic books. Mister Scotts gave him his first comic book when he was seven years old. In a way, finding out about Alice's powers was a dream come true, he could experience an actual hero's rise, but in another way, knowing her secret was a heavy burden. Leo hated lying to his dad.

"We're terrible at this." Leo dropped his head onto his arms, which were folded on the table. He needed inspiration. He needed a muse, ideas, maybe a giant, blinking arrow pointing to the right name.

Cole waved to Linda. "I need ice cream."

She finished taking an old woman's order and came over to the boys. The old woman wore a large, fancy wig and a pink mumu dress. The solid gold ring around her finger looked ancient. Something was engraved on it, probably a name, but nobody was with her.

Linda flipped the pages in her notepad and smiled. "What can I get for you, darlings?"

"Cookie dough ice cream," Cole said.

"Alright, any chili cheese fries today?" Linda scribbled in her notepad.

"Maybe later."

She turned to Leo. "And what do you want to fill that empty belly of yours?"

"Pistachio ice cream."

According to his dad, Leo shared the same favorite foods as his mom, a woman he didn't remember but somehow felt the absence of. He didn't have a void or anything but it would've been nice to know what his mother was like and what she would've thought of him.

His very full but ordinary life shifted recently. Leo was suddenly living in an action movie. The night of Mick the Menace's death still haunted him. The corpse, the blood, the gunshot, it was all too fresh. He'd probably never have a good night's sleep again.

"Linda, do you have any ideas for superhero names?" Cole asked. What was he doing? Was he crazy? What if she figured it out? Wait, how would she figure it out?

"What for?" she asked.

Leo cleared his throat. "A comic book." He glanced at Cole. "Yeah, we're writing a comic book and we can't figure out a name for the main character."

"What's she or he like, darling? It's personality that matters and manners. Everybody should have manners, don't you forget that." Her smile was as sweet as sugar but her gaze was ice cold, protected.

He was probably imagining it, he desperately needed some sleep.

"Purple hair, white lightning," Cole said.

Leo wasn't sure they should give specific details. Shouldn't they keep it vague? Maybe Linda would think their fake character was based on Alice. She wouldn't guess that it was actually Alice, though, right?

"Kind, traumatized, outcast, powerful," Leo said. It was easy to describe Alice. He lived with her, which was why he felt a little stupid when he learned she had powers. How did he not notice before?

"What's her real name, then?" Linda asked. Why did she have to ask questions? Why did she have to be so interested in their fake comic book? It was making Leo's palms sweat. His fingers were slipping off the table, so he gripped it tighter.

"Ally," he said. It was the first name he thought of.

Cole smiled. "Ally Scotts."

"Well, I don't know much about superheroes or anything like that new zippy lightning thing out and about in the city." She was talking about Alice flying over the city in her lightning form. Leo wished he could transform like that. It'd be cool. "I always thought it was creepy," Linda said. "Something those paranormal chasers would look for."

"Paranormal," Cole repeated. "Not bad."

"Doesn't fit," Leo said.

Linda chuckled. She patted Leo's shoulder. "I'll be back with y'all's ice cream."

He liked her. She was what he imagined his mom would've been like. Sweet, wise, and calm.

Leo only knew his mother from his dad's stories. Mister Scotts missed his wife, he still had their wedding photo hanging above his bed, but he wasn't consumed by grief like Alice's dad. He didn't fill his void with cheap beer and self-loathing.

Leo didn't realize how lucky he was until Alice told him about Mason.

"So, what fits? What name is good enough?" Cole asked.

Leo shook his head. He didn't know. He wanted the name to mean something. He wanted it to be memorable. It had to be deserving of not only Glisin, an incredible hero, but also of her daughter, Height City's next savior.

Alice would be a great hero, maybe better than Susan.

Chapter 18

Jess

Jess read Teddy Jenson's autobiography five times and six other books about journalism. She wanted to memorize every word. The internship opened her eyes. The articles, the research, the proofreading, the potential for adventure, the quest for truth, it was everything she hoped for and more.

I want to be a journalist. She had to whisper it out loud to make sure it sounded right. But she didn't know how to start. She researched college programs, other internships, blogs, everything until she realized she didn't want to wait. She decided a blog was the best option.

She asked Tommy to help her build a website.

They sat together in a booth at Linda's Diner. Linda was refilling salt and pepper shakers. An elderly couple sitting in another booth had ordered meatloaf and two iced teas.

Jess got Tommy's number from Cole. She wasn't sure what she was expecting when she asked for his help. That night, in the car, when they were searching for Paisley, it was intense and weird.

Dave told her about Tommy; how he designed and built his computer out of pieces he bought on the dark web; how he shoplifted Casey's angel wing necklace from a pawnshop in the Burrows; and how since they met, he constantly kept Dave out of trouble. Tommy was more light-hearted than Jess thought he'd be. Mick's murder didn't seem to weigh him down.

He chuckled with pride and gestured to her laptop screen. "It looks great."

Her website, officially named Height City Anonymous, was ready to go. Jess wrote over forty articles to add to it. She smiled. "Thanks."

"Have you picked your articles?" Tommy asked.

She nodded. "I have. One is titled *Honeycombers vs Burrowers*, another is *Inside the Adler Building Fire* and another is *The Truth about Ted Marson*. I have others too, of course."

She was proud of how well they were written. She loved writing. She loved researching and learning. Mick's death, that entire night, showed Jess she was tougher than she gave herself credit for. She proved she could handle a stressful, violent, vomit-inducing nightmare. She wanted to expose the truth. She wanted to show people what they couldn't see. She didn't see her parents' crimes. The world was a dark place, Height City had a lot of shadows, and she was curious to see what else was hiding in them.

She liked having a different purpose, a new future. It was exciting. She wouldn't let it scare her, not after what she and her friends had been through.

"Wait, what's that last article about?" Tommy asked. "The one about Ted."

"It's an article explaining how he was released from Steel Prison," Jess said. It took her a while to write it. She had to wait for her parents to leave the house, so she could go through their case files. She found the paper she used to find Ames Street along with several other informative papers and copied them with her dad's printer. Layla would never know Jess had them. "That it wasn't new evidence but that the Crime Queen ordered it."

"You can't post that on your blog." Tommy lowered his voice. "Betty would seek you out. She'll hurt you and your family just for pissing her off."

"That's why I'm hiding my identity," Jess said. She checked to make sure every detail in every one of her articles was vague enough to keep people from guessing who she was. "People deserve to know who really runs our city, don't you think?"

"People like being ignorant because the truth is darker than the lie." His set jaw and intense frown showed how serious he was but his eyes were filled with fear. He wanted her to be afraid too. "If you post it, you're putting a target on your back and your mom's back, your dad's, Alice's, and everyone else you're close to."

Jess didn't need a lecture. She wasn't stupid. She'd be careful. She wouldn't let herself slip up or make a mistake. She told herself she wasn't allowed to falter. She needed this. She needed a purpose, a future Layla couldn't dictate or control, and she needed Alice. With Alice's big decision to follow in Susan's footsteps, Jess felt her slipping away. She didn't want Alice to leave her behind.

"I won't post it yet," Jess closed her laptop. "Can I ask you another favor?"

Tommy shrugged. "Sure."

"Alice is moving forward with this whole superhero thing and I want to be part of it somehow. I've been reading books on computer science, cyber security, and coding," she said. Tommy smiled. Was he trying not to laugh? She squinted, a little offended. "What?"

"Nothing," he chuckled. "Sorry, I just never heard of someone reading a book to learn about cyberspace."

"That's actually what I wanted to talk to you about." Jess bought every book she could find about coding, cyber security, and computer science. She had two journals filled with notes. She quizzed herself on the information - she knew the material - but she wanted a teacher with actual, hands-on experience. "I think it'd help if you taught me some of what you know."

It was a big favor. It meant teaching the potential enemy. If he continued working for Betty and she worked with Alice, they'd end up on different sides. They'd be fighting each other. Tommy had to know that.

He didn't answer right away. He was lost in consideration, weighing his options. "Yeah," he paused. "Sure, why not? Let's meet back here later and have our first lesson."

She smiled. "Sounds great."

She didn't expect him to say yes. She put her laptop in her backpack, swung it over her shoulder, and waved to Linda.

***

Tommy

Tommy watched Jess leave the diner. She didn't stand straight, her shoulders were sort of hunched, like she was trying to hide but she had a determined stride.

She wanted him to teach her about computers. She had the same thirst for knowledge he did. It'd be fun to teach someone who'd appreciate his expertise. Even if they'd be on opposing sides one day, Tommy wanted to help her. He didn't know Jess or Alice that well but because they were important to Dave and Casey, Tommy would do his best to look out for them.

He grabbed his leather laptop bag, waved to Linda, and left the diner.

His day was free. He'd usually have to torture someone or hack something or assassinate an enemy but there was nothing on the schedule and Betty hadn't texted him. He was better at the bloody work than he liked to admit. Maybe part of him enjoyed it, which terrified him. He'd grown an iron stomach and unshakeable nerves.

Tommy thought about the gossip magazines under his bed, the ones with articles about Timothy Cruise. Maybe he should toss them.

He and Timothy looked alike, which was eerie. Tommy never looked like anyone except his mom. He wondered what else they had in common. Did they enjoy the same books? Did they like the same music? Did they share any interests at all? He wanted to meet his little brother but what if he wasn't good enough? What if he disappointed Timothy? What if he couldn't be a big brother? What if he did something wrong? His insecurities swirled, creating a hurricane of doubts and questions that clouded his mind and gave him a headache. He couldn't focus on anything else.

Somehow, he ended up in the Nectors, the neighborhood in the Honeycombs devoted to mansions and winter homes of Height City's elite.

He stopped at the Cruise Estate.

The whole property was protected by brick fences and metal gates. A smooth, black driveway led to a four-car garage and a gorgeous brick and stone building. Five stories, at least. Brick pillars supported a wrap-around stone deck and tall, arched windows were on every floor. Thick, white curtains kept the inside hidden.

Tommy shoved down his jealousy. He grew up in a crappy, two-bedroom house with a small kitchen, limited counter space, stained carpet and a broken toilet. Timothy had a mansion, a courtyard, and what looked like six acres of land. But it was good, he was lucky.

Nobody deserved to grow up the way Tommy did.

Why was he there? This was pointless. What did he have to offer a boy who had everything? A good family, a respected name, money, a bright future, and nothing to worry about. As Tommy turned to leave, a black Jaguar, newly washed and super expensive, turned into the driveway.

The passenger side window opened, revealing a woman with long, light brown hair twisted in a bun. She wore a three-strand pearl necklace, pearl earrings, and a long, black jacket with a white fur collar. Her gold wedding band had a diamond the size of a newborn's fist. *Martha Cruise.*

"Who are you?" she asked.

Tommy stared at her, mouth dry. Seeing her made him realize how much his existence harmed her marriage. Tommy was the product of Brad's infidelity. A crack in their commitment that she couldn't see. She'd hate Tommy. She'd have every right to hate him and he wouldn't blame her if she did. He deserved it.

"Nobody important. Sorry to bother you." He turned to leave.

"Why are you standing outside my house?" she asked.

He stopped. What could he say? He couldn't tell her the truth. He faced her.

He wanted to apologize to her but he wasn't sure what he'd be apologizing for. His birth, maybe? He didn't show his emotions. He kept a straight face, vague eyes, and a simple frown. He shrugged. "I was admiring the structure," he gestured to the mansion. "It's a beautiful house. Places where I'm from don't look like it."

"Where are you from?" Martha asked.

"The Burrows."

Her face became sympathetic, or was it pity? He could only imagine the stories she heard. The crime, the murder, some of it was true, some of it was dramatized. He was part of the problem. Betty Beater's tech support, her enforcer, a hacker, a criminal. "I'm not a bad person. I swear."

He needed her to believe that. He was starting to doubt it.

Her smile was kind. Whatever she thought, it wasn't rude or judgmental. "What's your name?"

"Tommy."

She gestured to the back seat but the windows were tinted, so he couldn't see what she was pointing at. "I just went to the grocery store and I bought enough food to feed an army," she chuckled. "Why don't you come inside and have lunch with us?"

"Us?" Was he ready to meet his father? No.

Martha nodded. "My son, me, and our maid, Fernanda. Brad, my husband, is on a business trip."

That made him feel better. He wondered if his father would recognize him if they ever came face to face, probably not. He didn't want to find out. But he was a stranger, why would Martha invite him to the dinner table?

"You don't even know me," Tommy said. "Why would you let me into your house?"

"You seem like a good kid. I'm giving you a chance to prove me right." She unlocked the car. It idled.

This was his chance to meet Timothy. Was he ready to take it?

***

Bobby

Bobby twirled around the corner, heels slipping on the tile, but she didn't stumble. She kept running. Her classmates filled the hall. The freshmen were tiny and clueless compared to everyone else. She remembered being one. Helpless, confused, but she had more serious problems than finding the right classroom. They were lucky that's all they had to worry about.

"Leo!" she shouted.

He stood down the hall at his locker. He perked up the moment he heard her voice. She ran to him. She couldn't slow down. She crashed against his skinny torso - he wasn't very stable or muscular - and they stumbled. He held her tight and grabbed the lockers to steady them both. They balanced each other but swayed a little from the sudden collision.

He laughed. "Hey, B. What's up?"

Bobby held up her test. It had a big, red A+ on the top corner. She hopped up and down, curls bouncing over her shoulders, as her earrings jingled. She squealed. "First big math test of the year and I aced it."

"I knew you could do it," Leo said.

Her face warmed. She knew he meant it. She put the test in her backpack. "What'd you get?"

"C+. Math isn't my greatest subject. At least it wasn't an F or a D," he shrugged. He didn't seem upset. He didn't get upset often. He had a calm, slightly boring presence, which Bobby appreciated. She had plenty of chaos for the both of them.

She nudged his shoulder. "For the next test, we'll study together. English too, I suck at that but you're great at it and by 'it', I mean English. You're great at English."

Unlike Johnny, who treated her like dirt, Leo showed how much he cared about her. He remembered her favorite snacks and brought them over. He listened to her stories and smiled when she got excited. He kept her steady but he also needed her for her support. She liked being needed.

"Deal." He nudged her back.

She bumped him with her hip. He smiled. He had a great smile. She loved how good she felt around him, butterflies fluttering in her stomach and heat rising in her cheeks. She never questioned if Leo cared about her and the time spent with him was always enjoyable. She loved every minute they were together.

"Slut and geek really found each other," Cindy said, standing beside Brittany.

Brittany leaned against the lockers and crossed her arms. Her tone was uneven as if she weren't committed to the insults. "Guess there is a lid for every pot."

"Ignore them." Leo rubbed Bobby's shoulder. She nodded. She hated that Cindy and Brittany could still make her feel worthless.

Every phone in the hall rang at the same time. Songs like "Shut Up and Dance" by Walk the Moon and "Shake It Off" by Taylor Swift played over each other, and beeps and bells clashed against each other. *What the hell?*

It was a mass email with a link. Bobby clicked it. The website had several articles about Height City and photos of its famous buildings; the Adler Building, before and after the fire, Cruise Industries, Vance Technologies, Key Hotel, City Hall, and many others. The font used was classy and bold spelling the blog's name: HEIGHT CITY ANONYMOUS.

"The one thing that truly separates us is our failure to empathize with another's situation," Cindy read out loud. "Our judgments blind us to the many similarities we all share."

The article was titled *Honeycombers vs Burrowers*. Bobby glanced it over. She and Brittany looked at each other but neither said a word.

"This was sent to everyone in the school, plus Baltic and St.Hariot's. Look at the comments," Leo held out his phone. "It was sent to every high school and college in the city."

"I wonder who it is," Bobby said. She scrolled through the different articles. They featured gossip about the Honeycombs and revealed rumors about the Burrows, most of which were accurate.

Whoever Height City Anonymous was, they did their research.

Jess walked up wearing an adorable plaid mini-skirt with white tights, a matching tank top, and a cropped, light blue sweater. Her hair was in two braids and her pearl earrings shone in the fluorescent light.

Bobby liked Jess's style. It was very chic and simple. She could never pull it off.

"Did you get the link too?" Leo asked.

"Yeah, I did. Cool, right?" Jess said. She held tightly to the sleeves of her sweater. Why was she hiding her hands? Was she trying to hide her fingers? Her face signaled there was more to her answer.

Bobby narrowed her gaze. What was Jess hiding?

"Why are you looking at me like that?"

"Looking at you like what?" Bobby asked.

"I don't know," Jess crinkled her eyebrows. "Suspicious. What is it?"

It didn't take long for Bobby to put the pieces together. Jess was the only one who didn't have her phone out. She wasn't as excited or fascinated as everyone else. She was hiding her hands, probably because she didn't want anyone to see her peeled cuticles.

Bobby gasped. She slapped a hand over her mouth and laughed. She couldn't believe it. It was awesome, such a bold move. She squeezed Jess's shoulders and shook her like a maraca. "You-"

"You?" Leo's eyes widened.

Jess gripped Bobby's elbows. She stood still for a few seconds, then cleared her throat. The shaking must've made her dizzy. She glanced between them. "Don't tell anyone, okay? I want to see how people respond first."

"This is amazing. Totally awesome!" Bobby squealed. She pictured Jess in a Sherlock Holmes-styled outfit but instead of a magnifying glass, she held a fancy, feathered pen. "Who else knows?"

Bobby didn't want to spill the secret. Since they were whispering, it seemed Cindy and Brittany didn't know, which meant for once they couldn't act superior.

Bobby heard giggling in her head.

"Just Alice and Tommy. I needed his help building the website and hacking the schools' emails, so I could send out the link," Jess smiled, proud of herself. She wasn't what Bobby originally expected. She wasn't a bitch like her Honeycomber friends and she was a great tutor.

Bobby threw her arms around Jess's neck. She couldn't help it. This was amazing. They were the same height, thanks to Bobby's heels.

Jess chuckled - a bright, relaxed chuckle - against her shoulder. Leo stood beside them until they both looped into him into the hug.

"This is gonna be huge," he said.

"I hope so," Jess said.

***

Alice

Lying to Mister Scotts made Alice feel terrible. Her stomach was tight and knotted when she was in his presence but she couldn't tell him the truth. She couldn't tell him she was going to the Burrows to fight criminals for the first time.

Bobby was at a job interview, so Alice used her as a cover story. Officially, they were out to lunch together.

Alice wanted to test herself. Why keep putting it off? She wasn't a perfect fighter yet but some real-life experience couldn't hurt. She was shaking with anticipation. Her nerves tingled as vibrations crept up her arms. She kept herself from sparking. Would she have to use hand-to-hand combat? Would she have to use her powers? Part of her hoped so. Her hair was tied in a bun and hidden under her hood. She cut holes in one of Leo's beanies and wore it as a mask.

Some kids in worn, ragged clothes stood around a flaming trash can at the edge of an alley across the street. Runaways, street kids like her friends. Their expressions were distant, lonely, like they knew the world didn't care about them. One boy wearing a jean jacket, shuffling a deck of playing cards made eye contact with Alice. Why did he look familiar?

A homeless man sat at the corner. His lips were blue and he was shivering, muttering random words to himself, as he played with a loose thread on his jacket. Alice felt a little uncomfortable, slightly afraid of him, like she should cross the street instead of passing by him. Maybe she should run past him, fast enough so he couldn't grab her.

She fought the fear. He seemed harmless.

Her olive-green sweatshirt was baggy on her body, it was two sizes bigger than what she needed and fleece lined the inside. Her mom bought it for her. They went grocery shopping after one of Alice's basketball practices and she found it while Susan was deciding whether or not she should get Mason a twelve-pack of new socks or a five-pack.

The sweatshirt was the last thing Susan ever bought for Alice.

She took it off and pulled off the beanie to show the man her face. Her bun was falling apart. She pushed her hair behind her ears, it was long and thick over her shoulders.

She crouched down. The homeless man didn't realize she was there until she brushed her hand over his knee. Their eyes met. His gaze was exhausted and defeated. He didn't have any physical scars but it looked like something had broken inside him.

He smiled. Did he have a family? Did he have a favorite animal or a favorite color? How long had he been alone on the streets? Was he hungry? He was cold, she could tell.

Alice handed him her sweatshirt. His fingers trembled as he took it. He wrapped it around himself and played with the drawstrings. His laugh was gentle and timid.

She wished she could do more for him.

Grunting echoed from another alley.

Alice yanked the beanie over her face and ran toward it. No hesitation, no fear. Vibrations bubbled in her belly and lightning sparked in her eyes. She was ready for action. Her sneakers squeaked against the pavement as she slid, turning into the alley.

An older man, a few years older than her dad, bled on the ground. Was he breathing? Younger men who looked to be in their twenties surrounded him. They had identical, red heart tattoos on different sections of their bodies. The edges were sharp and the color was faded. They must've belonged to the Hearts, one of the lower gangs.

A billion vibrations soared through Alice's arm and lightning shot from her fingertips. It hit one man and he flew into the air, screaming. He slammed against the ground. The others were shocked by the interruption, it took them a minute to understand the situation.

Alice ran toward them.

She swung her fist at one but he ducked. He punched her belly, fist rock solid against her torso, knocking the wind out of her. She stumbled. Another guy slammed his foot into her right knee but before she could fall, a third man snatched her up and swung her against the brick wall.

Pain shook her spine and blood spit from her head.

She ended up on the ground with thick, heavy boots beating her body. Hard. She scrunched up, knees bent against her chest while her arms protected her head. The men didn't stop. Were they laughing?

She couldn't scream. She couldn't fight. Agony, so much agony and pain, so much pain. Her vision started to blur. Was she crying? She couldn't tell. Her head throbbed. Was it possible for bruises to make your body numb?

Their laughter echoed.

Her thoughts were broken and unclear.

"Hey!" a familiar voice yelled. A silhouette ran up. *Cole?*

He didn't cower. He started yelling at the men who sounded annoyed as they yelled back at him. Their voices were blurred. It felt like Alice was underwater. She couldn't move.

The men left. How did Cole get them to leave?

Cole crouched down and yanked Leo's beanie off her head. Every part of her body hurt but she didn't care as she turned to look at the man she had tried to save. He was beaten, bruised, and bloody. Was he breathing?

"Is.. is he..?" she tried.

Cole shook his head. "He's dead."

"How did... Why did they..." Her thoughts were a thick, quiet fog. Her head was pulsing. She tried to take a deep breath and whimpered. It hurt to breathe. It hurt to move.

Cole yanked her up and set her against the wall. She stumbled but he kept her steady. Was the ground tilting?

"Leo texted. Thought you might need some backup, and..." When he touched her cheek, she winced. The concern on his face was frightening. "These are bad, it's okay, we've got medical supplies at the apartment," he stuffed Leo's beanie in his pocket. "Be glad I'm a known friend of Cece. People don't mess with us."

His image - blondish hair, kind eyes, a white T-shirt, and jeans - faded in and out. Alice couldn't focus. Even the bruises and gashes on her arms were blurry, far away. Was that blood on her shirt? She couldn't feel her feet. Her knees buckled.

Cole tossed her over his shoulder and carried her away.

Chapter 19

Alice

HER FACE WAS STILL bruised. The bruises were faint and mostly healed. Thank God, Cole had been there. Alice wouldn't have made it without him. Her limbs were sore and her ribs felt cracked but she was determined to power through. She didn't have time to be hurt.

Leo leaned next to Alice and they watched the crowds of students as they herded themselves through the halls, yelling and laughing. Their footsteps squeaked and lockers slammed. A banner above the front door advertised the school's latest book fair and posters decorated with glitter told everyone about the next school dance, which Jess was the head planner of.

Alice checked her phone again. "I don't get it," she turned it off and shoved it in her pocket. "Cece hasn't answered any of my calls or texts. It's been months-"

"Maybe something happened." Leo shifted his casual stance and leaned his shoulder on the lockers, backpack hanging off his wrist. His gray shirt had black writing that said: I WAS ADDICTED TO THE HOKEY POKEY BUT THEN I TURNED MYSELF AROUND. It was one of his favorites.

Alice didn't know what to think. Their friends weren't in the safest line of work, so why did any of them think it was a good idea to disappear? Was Cece hurt? Was she dead? Alice hated not knowing. She kept imagining Cece needed her help. "I'm worried."

Leo shrugged. "You're meeting Dave and Cole after school, right?" he yanked his backpack onto his shoulder and held the strap. "Ask them what's going on."

"Good idea." Her phone beeped. Mister Scotts's contact photo was of his reflection. He was fixing his bowtie - it looked like a monarch butterfly - and he was smiling at the camera through the glass. "Your dad just asked which lamp your grandma hates," Alice said. "Why's he asking me that?"

"I blocked his number," Leo said. "At least till Grandma gets here."

They headed down the hall.

The Scotts boys told Alice stories about Leo's grandmother. The woman sounded nice, a little intense but other than that, Alice didn't see the issue. Her impending visit had Mister Scotts on edge. He was completely freaked out.

"What's the big deal about her coming to visit?"

Leo shifted his backpack. "She's judgy. Neither of us can do anything right when it comes to her, so Dad hides anything that will set her off. It's less worrisome for me 'cause I get cash."

"Cash?"

"Yeah, birthdays, holidays, every time she visits. I've saved every penny from her since I was nine." Leo had a big, blue pinkie bank on one of the shelves above his bed. It had his name written on it and held over five hundred dollars. "Figured it was smarter that way."

"I can't picture a kid saving money instead of spending it," Alice said. She tried to picture Leo as a nine-year-old but the image wouldn't form. "Have you found a way to use it yet or are you going to keep it in your bank account or what?"

"Adding in the money I get for mowing lawns every summer and doing odd jobs for the super in our building, I've got enough to do some traveling," he said. "I thought about college but I don't think it's right for me."

Mister Scotts had a collection of college pamphlets and articles about the educational system. He thought school was the best future for his son and for

Alice. She couldn't remember the last time someone cared about her future. She hadn't planned that far ahead.

"Where are you gonna travel?" she asked. "When?"

"Wherever the wind takes me," Leo smiled with a dramatic gesture. He shook his head. "No, I don't have a plan yet but I'd like to leave sometime after graduation."

Alice didn't know he had a plan. She never thought about an "after" graduation. She was focused on being a hero, on fighting crime, and figuring out how to be the next Glisin. She didn't like the idea of Leo leaving. She could picture him in Poland or Germany, maybe in an Irish coffee bar. If this was his dream, he needed to do it. She'd support him.

He must've read her mind because he rubbed her shoulder and stepped in front of her. "This is months away, okay?"

"I know. I'm just," she sighed. "I'll miss you."

"I'll send tons of postcards, I promise," he said. "Come on, we're gonna be late for class."

She didn't know what it was like to have a brother but she figured Leo was hers. She loved him. She loved bickering with him. She loved fighting over the remote. She loved taking his picture. She loved watching him blush when Bobby was around.

Alice and Leo weren't blood but they were family.

"That sounds perfect," she said.

He nodded once. "Good."

After school, Alice told Mister Scotts she was going to Bobby's, which was a lie. Bobby had to work.

Alice went to Dave and Cole's apartment instead. They invited her over for a reason they wouldn't tell her. Buddy was talking to his pet rock when she got there. He gave a friendly wave and continued the conversation, whatever he was talking about, it seemed the rock disagreed with him.

Alice went into the building. 8B. She knocked on the door.

Cole opened it and dramatically gestured inside.

She smiled. Their place was always messy with chips or pretzels on the counter, scattered clothes on the floor, random crafting supplies in the fish tank, and weapons in the dishwasher. Alice liked the trampoline they used as a coffee table, it was cool.

Dave was lying on the plain couch with his feet up on the armrest, arms folded behind his head.

Cole checked Alice's bruises. He was happy with how well they were healing. "We talked it over and we want to help you, so you don't get hurt again like a few weeks ago."

"And so you don't end up dead," Dave said.

"That too," Cole agreed.

"I thought you guys were against it. You're technically criminals and well," she paused. "And I'm trying to stop crime, so." She didn't want to compromise her principles, her morals, or the mission. She wouldn't agree to screwed-up terms.

"I'm an independent, a racer," Cole shrugged. "The only illegal thing about what I do is the bets, ish," he smiled. He was purposely being vague. He gestured to Dave. "He works for Betty like Tommy and Cece do but nobody needs to know we're helping, right?"

"I guess," Alice said. It would be helpful. She didn't know the underworld like they did. She barely knew anything about it. She'd probably have to learn if she was going to fight crime. "Um, how are you gonna help, exactly?"

Dave tossed her a crinkled paper. She caught it, unfolded it, and read the chicken scratch written on it. The handwriting was terrible. "Sixth and Bullock?"

"Billy's zone?" Cole asked.

Dave shrugged. "He owes me money. Anyway, there's a handoff, coke probably."

Coke. Cocaine. Alice smiled. This was her next mission. There wouldn't be a group. It was a simple drug deal, how hard could it be? She grabbed her messenger bag, which now, instead of camera supplies, held her makeshift super suit, at least until Bobby and Karen finished the official one. "Can I change my clothes somewhere?"

"In there," Dave pointed down the hall.

Alice headed to the bathroom but when she reached for the door, it opened and a girl stepped out.

The girl wore one of Dave's T-shirts and a really short skirt. Her long, pale legs were basically naked. Her hair was wet and a freshly used towel hung on her arm. She was pretty.

She gave Alice a dirty look.

"Oh my God," Alice shook her head. "No-"

"Shut it, skank." She grabbed her shoes, purse, and a lamp off the counter. She rushed past the boys and slammed the door behind her.

Cole frowned. "That was our..." he waved, annoyed. "Bye, Samantha!"

Dave sat up, taking his feet off the armrest. He chuckled. "Sorry, I forgot-"

"That was my favorite lamp!" Cole yelled. The lamp was a monkey statue holding a light bulb. "Stop dating girls who steal from us!"

"They're Burrowers. They all steal!" Dave said like it was obvious.

"Stereotyping," Cole shook his head. "You're better than that."

Alice couldn't believe this. She knew Dave and Jess broke up but it was weird to see him with other girls, almost wrong. She had to tell Jess, right? It was the girl code or something, Alice wasn't sure.

She went into the bathroom.

***

Casey

The sky, blending in beautiful shades of orange and yellow, made the distant skyscrapers look like sharp spikes against the soft clouds. Casey would've let herself stare at the colors for hours but she couldn't because she had orders to follow. Her black, leather boots with silver buckles clanked on the sidewalk, each step was a warning, a threat. Whoever heard it needed to beware. She was close.

She turned into the alley and leaned her shoulder on the wall, hands in her jacket pockets.

Billy, wearing his signature gray trench coat, ripped winter gloves, and cargo pants, stood by the fire escape, smoking a joint. The holster on his waist was barely visible and the few other weapons he had hidden were strapped to the inside of his coat.

He looked at the blood on her jeans, eyebrows raised in question.

She smirked. It'd been a messy kill.

"You didn't tell anyone about this, right?" she asked.

"I told whoever asked that I'm selling to some idiot Nesters," Billy said. "Why does she trust me with this?"

Casey didn't answer. She didn't have to. Billy came from a long line of Betty Loyalists. His father, his grandfather, and his uncles' survival relied on Betty being in power. She made sure of it.

Casey wasn't sure where Billy's loyalties were, if anything he was most loyal to himself, but if Betty wanted him to do something, he'd do it. He knew who wore the crown.

Casey kept her posture fluid and tough. She twirled a sharp knife made of pure silver between her fingers. It was engraved with words Betty chose herself, specifically for her champion. Casey also wore an expression she perfected when she was twelve: a devilishly confident smirk, a playfully raised eyebrow, and a fierce yet chilling gaze. She was a cat with claws and she was eager to use them. "Did you bring it?"

Billy took an empty, black bag out of his jacket. He gave it to her. "Where'd this mole theory come from anyway?"

She clicked her tongue. "A new up-and-coming blog showed up about two months ago-"

"Height City Anonymous," he guessed.

She nodded.

Hobbs, Betty's right-hand and a certified computer wiz, found the blog. It had articles about the underworld, gossip about the Honeycombs, security footage from the Burrows' docks, and several other criminal-related places. It told about the lower gangs, The Arena, the drug deals, the dirty cops, and lawyers. It wasn't a ton of information, mostly old news and fresh rumors, but one article had Betty on edge.

"Right. It posted an article about Ted Marson and explained how he was connected to the Adler Building Fire, including how he really got out of Steel Prison. It even used Betty's little nickname, Crime Queen."

Casey had to find the wannabe journalist and the mole. She was under orders to kill them. How would she do it? A bullet to the brain? A knife to the throat? A blade to the heart? She couldn't wait to find out. Maybe they'd fight back, that'd be fun. She loved a good tussle.

Billy's task was to spread the word, scare people into giving up any and all information about the blog and its sources.

A thunderous crackle approached the alley, a sound Casey knew as well as the scars mapping her body. Her skin tightened and her throat went dry. She could almost pinpoint the exact moment someone started watching them. The guilt made her shiver.

Why now? Why couldn't she keep avoiding this? Why couldn't she keep avoiding the girl with the purple hair? If they didn't talk about it, if they didn't face each other, it didn't exist. She could pretend everything was fine between them.

Billy was oblivious. He nodded toward the empty bag. "What's it for?"

"Their heads." Casey pushed down her nerves and straightened her stance. She clicked her tongue and twirled the knife, so the blade was face up in her palm. She smirked. "Whoever Height City Anonymous is, I'll make them suffer until they're begging me to kill them."

Casey didn't need to see Alice to know she was there. It was stupid to think they could ever be friends. Glisin's daughter and Betty Beater's prodigy. They were born to be enemies. Why did she let herself get attached? Why didn't she blackmail Alice or tell Betty about her when they first met?

Casey knew the answer.

The day they met Alice risked her entire life, her safety, her secrets, her mother's identity, for a little boy who needed help and she didn't hesitate or second guess herself, she just did it.

Casey thrived in the darkness but she never wanted it to consume her and she didn't want it to consume the city either. If she had delivered Alice to Betty, then Casey would've proven once and for all, she didn't have a soul.

"Tell Bobby I say hello," Billy said.

Casey rolled her eyes. "Not likely."

He saluted her with two fingers and headed out of the alley. Once his shadow vanished from the sidewalk and she knew he was gone, Casey went to the alley's edge and waited. She couldn't run from this. She needed to face it and end it.

Her phone beeped. Tommy had to cancel their plans. The sixth time in two weeks. Was he avoiding her? Was something wrong?

***

Alice

Alice hurried down the fire escape, mind racing with questions. She thought this was a drug deal. What in the world was Cece doing there? Why was she promising to kill Height City Anonymous? To kill Jess. She didn't know it was Jess she was threatening.

She stood at the end of the alley. She put her phone in her pocket and adjusted her leather jacket. What was she waiting for?

"Cece?" Alice stopped a few feet behind her. She knew this was coming, the moment she decided to become a hero, Alice lost Cece forever. She hoped if they didn't face it, maybe the problem would magically disappear but it wouldn't.

Alice was the next Glisin and Cece was Betty Beater's champion. It should've been simple but it wasn't, it was never going to be.

Cece turned, tears making her green eyes sparkle. "My name isn't Cece," her voice was uneven. "At least to my friends, it's not but," she looked Alice in the eye, hiding her grief through a tired frown and vague stare. "We aren't friends, are we? We've always been on borrowed time."

Alice stood stiff while hot, salty tears trickled down her face. She couldn't hide her emotions like Cece could, she couldn't pretend this didn't hurt. Alice loved their friendship, she relied on it. They'd been through so much together, fought together, inspired each other. How could it end like this? Why did it have to end at all?

"I don't want to fight you," Alice sniffled, trying to sound strong. "I won't."

"You wouldn't win anyway."

Was this it? Was this their goodbye?

Cece shoved the knife she'd been holding in her boot and backed out of the alley. She looked at Alice with love and regret until she turned her back and walked away.

Alice stood alone, frozen, in the alley. She whimpered, she couldn't help it. She cried. It was the same despair she felt after her mom's ashes fell like no hope was left in the world, like the universe wanted her to be miserable. Alice hated that she and Cece were on different sides. She hated that she had to lose her best friend to honor Glisin. It wasn't fair but were sacrifices ever fair?

Cece chose her path. Now, Alice had to follow hers.

Her phone beeped. The text was from Leo saying his grandma had arrived.

Alice cursed under her breath and stuffed the beanie in her pocket. She'd have to mourn her friendship later. Small vibrations became larger. Sparks flashed across her body and she leaped off the ground.

Lightning flew over the city.

***

Leo

Leo put his phone in his pocket, watching his grandma look around the loft. She had her "deciding" face on, which made his dad sweat. It'd been a stressful three minutes. Leo wondered what her metal hip felt like. Her eager stride was terrifying for a woman of her age.

"You always had an *interesting* style," she said. "Frilly but comfortable."

Leo glanced at his dad, who tried not to roll his eyes. These visits weren't fun for him. He gave up his bedroom and bit his tongue. If he argued with her, she'd dig her heels in deeper. The woman never backed down. She was tough as nails.

"Wanna see my room?" Leo gestured to the metal staircase. His bedroom was a bridge-like area above the den. Floor-to-ceiling shelves held books - mostly graphic novels - knickknacks, old toys, action figures, and family photos of him and his dad. His bed, with superhero-themed sheets and pillowcases, sat on top of several drawers that held clothing and board games. Leo liked looking out the large window that connected his room with Alice's, staring out at the city at night made him feel humble, relaxed.

His grandma laughed. "Oh, honey, that's not a bedroom. It's a storage area. I never understood why you didn't get an actual apartment," she looked at her son. "Maybe because you decided to be a teacher. It's a noble cause but can hardly support a family."

"I'm fed," Leo whispered.

His dad sighed. "Okay, Mom." His fake smile was almost convincing.

She cupped Leo's face in her hands. Why were old people's hands always cold? Her wedding ring poked him in the cheek. "Now, grandson, how are your grades? You're not *still* getting Cs in math, are you?"

He didn't answer. What lie hadn't he used yet?

The door opened, slapping Leo with a sense of relief. His dad looked pleased too.

Alice came inside. Her purple hair was a little messy, probably from wearing his beanie like a mask. She wore a black, v-neck T-shirt, jeans, and the sneakers Leo's dad bought for her.

She smiled. "Hi, sorry, I'm la-"

***

Alice

Alice froze when a strange, elderly woman hugged her. She looked at Leo. He shrugged and smiled. Was he enjoying this? She rolled her eyes.

He never liked much attention. He preferred to stay in the background.

His grandma smelled like coconut oil.

"Mom, this is Alice," Mister Scotts said. "My.. our.. Well-"

"Your ward!" She squished Alice's face between her hands. "It's so nice to meet you. You can call me Grandma Scotts."

Alice smiled, cheeks squashing her eyelids. This woman had cold hands. Her voice was cheerful and her eyes were kind. She wore long, corduroy shorts and a loose, floral top. Her earrings were giant hoops and she wore a thin, gold chain around her neck.

"Okay," Alice mumbled.

Grandma Scotts patted her shoulders and turned to the boys. Leo laughed under his breath. Alice shot him an annoyed look but he didn't stop smiling.

"She's gorgeous! Absolutely gorgeous!" Grandma Scotts wrapped her arm around Alice. "I always wanted a grandchild."

"Thanks?" Leo asked, more confused than offended.

Grandma Scotts yanked Alice onto the couch. She was shockingly strong for an old woman. She grabbed her big, floral purse and held it above her head. "I have gifts! None for you, son, you're too old for presents."

"I'm her grandchild," Leo whispered.

Mister Scotts sighed and tried to comfort his son with a shoulder pat. "Two days... two days, it's only for two days." He sounded exhausted.

Alice smiled for encouragement. She wanted to understand his stress but Grandma Scotts seemed fine, a little much but nothing they couldn't handle. She raised a great son. A kind man who gave a grieving, lonely girl a good home.

Grandma Scotts handed Leo a card. It had a cartoon elephant on it and said something happy and positive. He opened it and held up a one-hundred-dollar bill. He smiled. "Thanks, Grandma, you're the best!"

"You're welcome, Booboo, you'll put it toward your college fund," she tapped the card. "You're gonna be the first successful man in the family."

Mister Scotts rolled his eyes. He muttered "two days" over and over again.

Grandma Scotts handed Alice a small, velvet box and a card with a cartoon donkey on it. Was this standard grandmother behavior? What was Susan's mom like?

She put the card on her lap and opened the velvet box, which contained a silver ring with a small, centered, dark green emerald. It was beautiful, sparkling in the sunlight shining through the windows. Alice had never held anything so expensive, so precious. "I don't know what to say."

Grandma Scotts showed them the thin, gold chain around her neck. It had four different gems; a garnet, a sapphire, an aquamarine, and an emerald. They were beautiful. She smiled. "It's a little tradition of mine. When my grandchildren are born, I give them their birthstones and put copies on my necklace here," she brushed her fingers over Alice's cheek. "Obviously, I couldn't do that with you but you're part of the family now, and so the tradition lives on."

"Mine's a brooch," Leo said. "A man's brooch."

"There's a hundred dollars in your card too," Grandma Scotts said.

Alice smiled. She looked at Mister Scotts with his yellow and orange striped bowtie and his suede elbow patches. He took her in when she had nobody else. He reminded her what a parent should be. And Leo showed her what a sibling was. She loved this family. They were amazing people. They made her feel welcome and loved.

She held the box and the emerald ring close to her heart.

"Best grandma ever," Leo said.

Grandma Scotts laughed. "Remember that. Now, present time is over, so what's for dinner?"

"I thought we'd order takeout from our favorite diner or maybe Chinese," Mister Scotts said. "I know how much you love Chinese food."

"That's good too," she turned to Alice. "He never was the master chef but his sweet potato casserole is fantastic. I could eat it all day."

"I think all of his cooking is great. He even taught me," Alice said.

Mister Scotts smiled. He enjoyed cooking with her as much as she enjoyed cooking with him. He rubbed her shoulder.

Grandma Scotts clapped. "Oh! You're gonna be a great wife to some lucky man someday, aren't you? Look at you!" she curled her fingers under Alice's chin and tipped her head up. "You're gorgeous, you can cook. You can already do more than I could when I married Booboo's grandfather."

Alice chuckled at the nickname. Leo mouthed *shut up* so his grandmother wouldn't see.

Alice could imagine herself as a wife someday. Marriage was a sweet idea. Her parents made it seem profound. Her vows just wouldn't be to a man.

"Dad's homemade cream puffs are really good," Leo said, changing the subject.

Grandma Scotts slapped her hands against her chest. "Those were your grandfather's favorite recipe!" she smiled. "He'd be so proud to hear you say that. Of course, your dad isn't the cook your grandfather was. Oh, I remember the first time he made his creampuffs. It was our seventh date and after we had dessert... We had *dessert-*"

"Hey!" Leo pointed to the den. "Wanna see Alice's room?"

She looked at it. "That isn't a bedroom! That's the place under the stairs," she grabbed Alice's chin, squishing her cheeks, and scanned her face. "You don't look like Harry Potter to me."

"Thanks?" Alice and Leo shared an awkward smile.

Mister Scotts closed his eyes. "Two days... Two days... Two days..."

Bobby

Bobby hopped from one foot to the other, trying to steady herself with the lockers, as she slipped on her high heels. She lost her balance and slammed against the cold, metal doors. Pain pinched her shoulder. She rubbed the wound and adjusted her white, button-up vest.

Key Hotel was a great place to work. She'd only been there a little while. The guests weren't high maintenance and her co-workers minded their own business. She loved the uniform because she got to wear heels. It was the best part. Plus, the paycheck.

Sally was proud Bobby got a job and kept up in school. She was proud of herself too. Her life did a complete one-eighty. She lived in a safe, loving home with an incredible roommate. Sally was teaching her to mix drinks and sometimes, Bobby helped out behind the bar. She had a stable job at the hotel and got good grades in school. When she needed help, she asked Leo or Jess.

She clocked in. Her hair was a mess. She used her fingers to brush and fluff her curls, checking to be sure her black collared top and clip-on bowtie were still adorable. She hurried up to her boss. "Sorry!" she said, panting. "Sorry, I'm a little late, I had some car trouble and-"

"Whatever," he said. Hamilton was a stiff man in a three-piece suit. He pointed to one of the room service carts, covered by a white tablecloth with a silver tray sitting on it. The dome-like lid hid the food. "Take that to the penthouse. They ordered it over fifteen minutes ago, which means Missus Mikes is going to be very angry."

Bobby wanted to protest but it'd be unprofessional. She pushed the cart into the elevator and pressed the button. Her reflection rippled in the silver doors.

Her fiery hair and sparkly, smokey eye makeup were beautiful. For a second, her pretty reflection distracted her from how much she hated going up to the penthouse.

The media painted the Mikes as a royal family but Brittany wasn't a princess. She was a witch. The girl who insulted or made fun of or bullied Bobby every day for three years. It wasn't fair. Their feud was ridiculous. One stupid mistake created their rivalry.

The elevator stopped at the top floor and the doors opened, revealing newly vacuumed green carpet, white walls, and gorgeous paintings. Large, floor-length vases held giant flowers with red petals and yellow centers while silver and gold sconces lit the quiet hallway. Whoever Lisa Key's decorator was, he or she had expensive taste.

Bobby pushed the cart toward a dark wood door with a brass knob. Instead of a room number, it said THE MIKES on a fancy, gold plaque.

The door swung open. Brittany stomped out, looking angrier than ever, and screamed, "I hate you! You're a horrible person-"

"Come back when you learn how to mind your own business!" Missus Mikes, Brittany's mom and the wife of Height City's mayor, wore a silk robe over lace panties and a ruffled top. She slammed the door shut and the lock clicked.

Brittany scoffed, furious and looking ready to scream at the wood, then her shoulders slumped and she leaned on the wall. Sobbing, she slid to the floor.

Bobby stood there awkwardly, glancing around. Could she hide behind the cart? Maybe she should run? She'd be seen. It was too late. Bobby was stuck. *Son of a bitch.* "Are you okay?" she asked.

Brittany shook her head. "My mother is a whore! She should get a reward. A gold penis or something. God, I hope she gets an STD," she chuckled through her tears. "I wanted to take a tour of the Eiffel Tower, take a selfie of her and me, and when I went to tell her the plan, I found her under the sheets with a French bellhop."

Bobby didn't know what to say. She was uncomfortable. She pushed the cart next to the wall and sat against it. She didn't want to feel bad for Brittany, of all people, but she wasn't heartless. Bobby wouldn't leave her to cry alone.

Brittany wiped her tears. "I can't tell my dad," she sniffled. "Now that I know, she brings lovers," she made a face. "Whenever he's gone and Stacy's at school or a friend's house. She's finishing a blowjob for the towel boy right now," her scowl was bitter and bitchy. "You know, a Christmas bonus."

She buried her face in her lap.

Bobby put the silver tray between them and lifted the lid, revealing a slice of fudge-covered chocolate cake with two forks. She took a bite. It was really good. "My mom left when I was a baby," Bobby said. "Guess I wasn't good enough for her."

She didn't think about her mom much. Out of sight, out of mind, she guessed. Vincent didn't talk about her often when he was alive. The woman ripped out his heart and stomped on it. Bobby wasn't sure why she left. She doubted Vincent knew. *Oh well*, Bobby thought.

Brittany looked at her, hurt and sympathetic. She grabbed the second fork and bit the cake. She paused, hand hanging in the air, as thoughts swirled past her eyes. She ran a hand through her hair. "I'm horrible to you. You should be laughing or posting a picture of my misery," she gestured to her red, puffy eyes and wet cheeks. "I'll give you a free go at it."

Bobby had never seen Brittany as a person before. She always saw Brittany as someone to blame or hate. A 2D psycho tornado from hell. It was nice to see her like this.

"I'm sorry." Bobby realized she never said it. She never apologized for kissing Tony in the hall in front of everyone at Morgan High. She couldn't remember why she was mad at Johnny that day, maybe they had argued or maybe he had hit her, she wasn't sure. But Tony noticed her. It was an easy way to get revenge. It wasn't right. It was stupid and petty. "For my part in our, whatever we've been doing these past couple years," Bobby finished. It felt good to say. A weight was lifted off her shoulders.

Brittany dropped her fork. She leaned on the wall and stared at the floor. For once, she seemed defeated, lonely. "I didn't want people talking about it, so I started the rumors," she sniffled, lost in the memories of their hatred toward each other. "Then you never seemed phased. Everyone thought you were a slut and it didn't bother you. You wore your ridiculous outfits, you didn't have friends, the teachers liked you. You were so... Happy with your life.." she frowned, a simple, tired frown. She sighed. "I don't think I ever was."

"You have everything," Bobby whispered. Wasn't it true? Brittany had money, parents, a sister. She was good in school. She was respected. Her friends adored her. She was the girl everyone wanted to be. The Honeycomber Queen.

"My parents hate each other, my boyfriend kissed another girl, then cheated on me with a different one. My best friend hasn't been around," Brittany shrugged, misery in her eyes. She clasped her hands between her knees, frown deepening. "I wish... I wasn't me anymore."

Chapter 20

Jess

JESS DROPPED HER BACKPACK in the booth and waved to Linda. She loved her weekly lessons with Tommy. She loved learning about computers. She read almost every book on computer science and cyber security. She was almost an expert. Her blog was doing well too. People started sending in tips and theories for her to write about, some of them were crazy, like the one about a monstrous shadow - which only one person had supposedly seen - stealing from several banks around the city, but most of the tips were helpful and fascinating.

She set her laptop on the table and opened a book titled *How to Build a Computer.* She was on chapter six.

Jess wanted to see if she could build a working computer from scratch. Two more books were in her backpack, the first of which was titled *Guide to Wounds and Lacerations* and the other taught how to clean, bandage, stitch, and fix those wounds and lacerations. After she saw the bruises on Alice's face, Jess decided she wanted to be prepared for the worst.

The bell jingled, and Tommy stomped into the diner. He sat across from her and leaned forward, arms folded on the table. The concern in his eyes was intense but his anger shined through his tough frown and furrowed brow. He had a large bruise on his cheek. Jess wondered who gave it to him.

"You posted the article about Betty and Ted," he whispered. "What the hell were you thinking?"

Jess expected this reaction. She never said she wasn't going to post the article. She considered every pro and con. She could cover her tracks now, thanks to Tommy's teachings. She could protect her identity. Why shouldn't people know the truth about their home? Height City deserved to understand who ran things.

"You named her the Crime Queen. You said, and I quote 'Ted Marson was released upon falsified evidence fabricated by her demand'," he said. His level tone sent eerie shivers through her bones. "You put a giant bullseye on your family's back."

"As far as anyone is concerned Height City Anonymous wrote, verified, and posted that article. I made sure the website is unhackable. My identity can't be found," she said. "Besides, people are commenting and emailing me about rumors they've heard and people they know who work for her, it's a perfect setup."

It would help Alice in the long run. An entire community wanted to help save their city. It was a powerful tool. Jess's best friend was a super-powered hero-in-training. She had Alice on speed dial. If she needed help, she pressed one.

Tommy seemed more worried than angry, stuck between a rock and a hard place. Why? She couldn't figure it out. What wasn't he telling her?

"Tommy." Her tone shook more than she intended. "What is it?"

He sighed, shoulders slumped in defeat. "Cece has orders to assassinate you."

Jess's throat went dry and her blood froze. She'd heard that word in movies but it was a lot scarier in real life.

She picked her cuticles.

"You and your source, which is my best friend," Tommy said. "Luckily, Cas," he paused. "Cece doesn't know who Height City Anonymous is or that Dave is the mole."

"He's not a mole," she whispered. Everything she wrote was said in private moments during their relationship, said by him and Cole. She used their stories and explanations because technically, it wasn't off the record. She didn't think it'd matter. This was horrible. The Crime Queen wanted her to be executed. Tears threatened to fall but Jess held them back, nerves making her shake.

The diner's other customers, old couples and families, sat in the different booths, chatting, laughing, and eating, oblivious to her fear. A few kids were at the jukebox trying to pick a song.

"You have to tell her, don't you? Betty Beater, that it's me. You're her hacker." Jess couldn't breathe under her panic, her racing heart threatened to break her ribs, and the cuticle on her right index finger was starting to bleed.

"I can lie. I'll protect you guys but she has other resources. Betty will find you eventually and Cas," he rolled his eyes at himself. "*Cece* is gonna have to kill you." Tommy didn't seem hesitant about lying to Betty. His low voice was calm, controlled, and his face was plain, purposeful. It was impossible to tell if he was afraid or not. Had he ever been in a similar situation? Why wasn't he more panicked or upset?

"Would she?" Jess asked. "Would Cece kill me?"

He shrugged. "I wish I knew."

"What about my parents? I didn't name them but I did implicate them." Jess tried to keep Layla and Bennett as far from this as possible. Despite the anger she felt toward them, she didn't want them to die. They were still her parents and she loved them.

"Betty still needs them 'cause she took care of it," Tommy said. "They won't go to jail or get suspended. They'll be fine."

Jess sighed, relieved.

The bell chimed as Martha Cruise and her son walked in.

Timothy wore a light blue polo shirt and tan corduroy pants. A Bearly uniform. Jess's old middle school, grades six through eight. He had the same color hair as Tommy. They shared other similar features too. They looked somewhat alike. She never noticed before, then again, she'd never been in the same room with both of them.

Timothy came to their booth and smiled. "Hi," he focused on Tommy but he nodded in Jess's direction to include her in the greeting.

She returned it with a polite wave.

Tommy's face softened when the young boy appeared. The weight on his shoulders and the haunted look in his eyes vanished.

Jess glanced between them. What was the connection?

Martha waved. She and Brad were friends with Layla and Bennett. They went to the same Honeycomber events and parties, and Layla had been trying to get into Martha' good graces for years in hopes she'd finally be accepted onto the Board of Pearls.

"What are you doing here?" Tommy asked.

"You talked about this place a lot, so I wanted to come see it for myself," Timothy said. "When are you coming over next? I'm reading this new book and I want to show it to you."

"That'd be great. I can come over whenever you want me to."

"Today?"

"If it's okay with your mom."

Martha put her hands on Timothy's shoulders. "It is. Any time. Jessica, how are you?"

"I'm good, and you?"

"I'm good," she smiled. Her posture was stiff, proper. She wore a simple dress, pantyhose, and heels. Her pearl necklace was long and fashionably knotted. "Brad says hello. I didn't know you two were friends," she gestured between Jess and Tommy.

Tommy didn't look Jess in the eye. He kept his cool but he seemed stiff. Was he uncomfortable? His behavior signaled he'd been caught doing something he wasn't supposed to but caught doing what, Jess had no idea.

"The Cruises are clients of my mom's law firm," she informed him.

Tommy wasn't surprised. He was amused, a little annoyed. "Ah."

"I watched that show you recommended. The black and white made my eyes hurt," Timothy said. He had good posture like his mom.

"It's not for everybody," Tommy shrugged. "How was school?"

"Jeremy beat me in a race and I got an A on my history test." He stood with pride. He had the same prideful stance as his dad. Whenever Brad gave a speech on television or at one of his parties, he stood the exact same way, like he owned the world, except Timothy had a humbling presence and a timid smile.

"You'll beat Jeremy next time," Tommy said.

"Yeah. Do you," Timothy paused. He glanced at Jess, remembering his manners. "And you, would you both like to come join us?" he gestured to an empty booth.

"I'd love to," Tommy said, glancing at Jess. He didn't want her to join.

Something was up. Jess wanted to know what. Why would one of Height City's richest families know a Burrower? Not only a Burrower but Betty Beater's tech support? Where would they have met? Was it some sort of trick?

Tommy smiled, a convincing, everything-is-fine smile. "I'll meet you over there."

"Lovely seeing you, hon," Martha waved to Jess. "Say hi to your mom for me." She led Timothy away from the booth. He waved. They sat on the other side of the diner and opened their menus.

Jess liked the Cruises and Tommy, separately. Whatever was going on, she hoped it wouldn't incriminate either of them, specifically Tommy. Was he spying on them, maybe, for Betty?

"How do you know them?" she asked.

His face fell. He looked more like himself. "Just Dave knows, okay?" he kept his voice low. "I haven't told anyone else. I really like them. They're good people."

"I know they are. What does Dave know? What aren't you telling everyone?" Jess was protective of the Cruises. She gifted Timothy books for his birthday every year and they played board games at her parents' Christmas parties. He was a good kid. Martha was a nice woman and a good mother. Brad was a successful, kind man. What the hell was going on?

"The night I killed Mick, Paisley told me something," Tommy whispered. "She told me who my biological father was. I found the DNA test later, it adds up. Brad is-"

"Your dad," Jess leaned back, and a wave of shock overwhelmed her.

Brad and Martha always seemed happy. It was hard to believe there was such a large crack in their marriage. If they got divorced, it'd be all over the news. Did Martha know?

"Don't tell anyone," Tommy said. "And don't post it on your blog."

"I won't." She meant it. It wasn't her business. "But... okay, far be it from me to butt into your relationship," she said. Jess didn't know Tommy or Cece very well. She doubted she'd ever know either of them completely. Cece annoyed her. But Jess cared about both of them and from what she saw, they made each other really happy. "But shouldn't you, at least, tell Cece? She's your girlfriend, right? She deserves to know."

***

Tommy

Martha and Timothy sat in another booth. Their quiet conversation and laughter made Tommy feel at ease. He wouldn't have thought it before he met them but they were amazing people. Timothy liked to read and he liked video games.

He loved this racing game, and he beat Tommy at it every time they played together. They had similar body gestures and looked alike. He was a great kid. He was innocent and Martha was kind. Neither of them deserved to be dragged into Tommy's mess, his darkness.

Tommy preferred the separation. He needed both parts of his life, the paradise and the reality.

"Not yet," he said. He wasn't ready to tell anyone, not even Casey.

"It's your relationship," Jess said. She scooted out of the booth, stuffing her laptop and her books into her backpack, she swung it over her shoulder. "Thank you for the warning."

"Call me if something happens, I'll be there," he said. He wanted her to see how serious he was. Because of their lessons, Tommy considered Jess a friend.

His favorite lesson was when he challenged her to hack the street cameras outside Linda's Diner. She did it in under five minutes. Two minutes faster than he anticipated. She lit up, proud and fascinated, the same reaction he imagined himself having when Hobbs challenged him to do something similar. He bought her a milkshake to celebrate.

Tommy went to the Cruises' booth and sat beside Timothy.

The boy blew through a straw and the paper-thin wrapper slapped Tommy's face. He laughed. He playfully bonked Timothy on the head with his menu, then opened it.

Timothy started throwing jelly packets and Tommy attempted to block them. Somehow, it became a game, a competition, in which any packets that made it past Tommy meant Timothy gained a point. Tommy pretended to have slow reflexes, so Timothy would win easier.

Martha smiled.

***

Bobby

Bobby held the silver tray up to her face and winked at her reflection. Her hair was in a short, fluffy ponytail and glitter sparkled on her eyelashes. Her makeup took an hour to do but it was worth it; a perfect smokey eye and fantastic red lipstick.

She put the tray on the cart, and set a plate, which held a stack of waffles drizzled in chocolate sauce and whipped cream, on the doily decorating it. She sighed, envious. The waffles looked too good to eat.

"Penthouse order?" Donna asked. She wore the hotel uniform too.

Bobby nodded. "Would it be weird if I took a tiny little bite?"

Donna whined. "I wish! Man, these rich people have no idea how good they have it," she crossed her arms and shook her head. "Jerks."

Bobby pushed the cart away. She put her earbuds in and pressed play on her phone. She hummed along to the lead singer whose voice was British and beautiful. Bobby loved the Renegades. Her favorite part was the bass player because she could still picture his smile while he was teaching himself to play. She always believed the boy across the street, the youngest Hale brother, would follow his dreams of being a musician.

The elevator doors slid shut, and Bobby was alone with the music. She punched her fists into the air and sang out the chorus. Her voice sailed in perfect pitch, harmonizing with the singer. Bobby danced in her own world, nothing existed except her voice, the band, and happiness.

She twirled, chuckling. She opened her eyes.

An old man stared. When did the doors open? Her pose probably looked ridiculous. Arms stretched above her head. Her calf bent against her thigh.

The old man raised an eyebrow.

Bobby cleared her throat and rushed past him.

"You have got to stop singing and dancing in public," she whispered. "Now you're talking to yourself. Jesus, B, seriously? You're so weird," she smiled, turning off the music. She'd go home later, to Sally's Place, and jam to her favorite songs.

She knocked on the penthouse door.

Brittany yanked it open wearing a blue, Cinderella-like ball gown with her hair casually pinned in pigtails. Her eyes darted to the chocolate-drizzled waffle stack. She smiled. "Thank God!"

"Hi?" Bobby crinkled her eyebrows. She shoved the cart into the three-floor apartment. The main level was an open-concept kitchen, living room, and dining area, all spread fifty feet apart, it seemed.

A spiral staircase leading upstairs hid the dining room from view but it seemed to house eight cushioned chairs around a long table decorated with candles, flowers, and doily-like placemats. Next to it, the kitchen had granite countertops and silver appliances, the fridge was huge with two doors and an ice maker, and everything was so clean like it had been power washed.

And the living room, at its center, were two antique couches with gold trim, each facing an expensive glass coffee table, near a marble, automatic fireplace. The mantle was decorated with newspaper articles and pictures from magazines, all featuring Mayor Mikes, his wife, and their daughters. In every photo, they were waving to the public or posing for the paparazzi.

Bobby couldn't tell if their photographed smiles were real or fake.

Dresses were everywhere; silk dresses, floral dresses, velvet dresses, backless dresses, strapless dresses, ones with long sleeves, short dresses, long dresses, ones with thin skirts or layered skirts, others were decorated with beads or sparkles or sequins or gold buttons. Any dress anyone could imagine.

This is incredible. Bobby wanted to wear them all.

"It's a mess." Brittany soaked a waffle in chocolate sauce. "Prom is a few months away and I want to start my campaign for prom queen. It's taking forever to pick the perfect dress." She stuffed the chocolate-soaked waffle in her mouth.

"This is heaven. It just needs a pegasus and a giant chocolate castle with a hot tub," Bobby laughed. "But yeah, this is it."

"Sugar is the best thing ever." Brittany licked the chocolate off her fingers. Her dress's puffy skirt was squished between the counter and a chair. She grabbed a jar of maraschino cherries and tossed three in her mouth. "I want to take a bath in it."

Bobby grabbed a dark blue, velvet gown with a beaded chest and loose sleeves. It was something a queen would wear. She wondered if it would fit her. "Where's your family?"

Brittany swallowed another waffle. "Daddy is at work, Mother is shopping or having a threesome," she shrugged, annoyed with the mention of her mom. "And Stacy is somewhere. The nanny took her somewhere, a movie probably."

Boy, did that sound weird. What would it be like to be rich for a day?

"What do you think? What do you think other people will think?" Brittany gestured to the dress she was wearing, then pointed to a silk one with a ruffled sash and sequin straps. "Or would that one be better?"

"They're both beautiful. Which one do you like?" Bobby asked.

Brittany shook her head. "I don't know. Does it matter? What if someone else is wearing a certain shade of green or I look fat in ruffles or I look bad in blue-" Insecurities and doubts flew out of her mouth. It was borderline pathetic. It made Bobby feel bad for her, which was weird. Feeling bad for Brittany Mikes, who would've thought?

She crossed her arms and listened to Brittany's rant. She sounded like Bobby but more crazy.

"What are you wearing?" Brittany asked. "To prom."

"I'm making my dress and my best friend's," Bobby said. "'Cause I'm dragging her there even if she throws a knife at my head."

"You have friends?"

"Quite a few but thanks for that."

"Sorry. I just meant that I never see you with anybody, really, except Jess and Ally, sometimes, or that boy with the beanie," Brittany said. "What's his name?"

"Leo," Bobby smiled. Her heart fluttered at the mention of his name. She cleared her throat. "Why are you afraid of what people think?"

"I'm not afraid. I'm just... People tend to judge me and my family, they have opinions and I want people to think well of me. I don't want them to think I'm awkward or weird, or horrible," Brittany shrugged. Being famous meant living under a microscope, it seemed. "I started the rumor about you freshman year and people still call you a slut."

"It's also written on the bathroom wall," Bobby pointed out.

Brittany plopped onto a stool, making her gown puff against her chest. She almost lost her balance. "You puked on the teacher's desk sophomore year and everyone laughed. You ran out of the room crying," she said. "I've never done anything to make myself look embarrassing."

"To be fair, my breakfast that day was a Twinkie and half a beer." Bobby held a little black dress with striped sleeves and a plunging neckline up to her chest. She wished she had a mirror. "Look, if you like yourself, then it doesn't matter what other people think," she dropped the dress on the couch. "After Johnny... I, he didn't love me, I know that now, but I didn't love me either. Now, I do. Now, I can feel how much other people care about me."

At first, Brittany didn't say anything as she absorbed Bobby's words. She smiled. "You're pretty smart."

It was a moment of understanding between them. A simple silence that made a world of difference. Maybe they could be frenemies.

***

Alice

The cheap comm irritated Alice's ear. Dave got it from Billy, so it'd probably give her a rash. She took note of her surroundings; buildings, a stray cat, trash on the sidewalk. Nothing abnormal. Was a gun pointed at her head? No. Of course not. It was a stupid fear. Height City only knew her as a high school student.

Static screeched, threatening to give her permanent hearing damage, so she adjusted the comm and the boys' voices became clear. She could tell who was who by the way they sounded, each of their voices had unique features, which somehow, she memorized without meaning to.

"You got the mask from Vicky?" Cole asked, annoyed.

Dave answered. "I told you, she had a collection of them. She brought one over and left it here."

Vicky. That name was familiar. Alice gasped. "Wait! I'm wearing a mask that belonged to one of your booty calls?"

It was a sparkly masquerade mask with beaded strings hanging over her nose and mouth. She had ripped the feather off the side before she put it on but because it hid her face, it was okay for now.

"You needed something other than Leo's crappy beanie to hide your identity," Dave said.

Leo scoffed. "Hey! My beanies are awesome."

"You have four," he said. "Wait, two. Did B ever give you the gray one back?"

"No," Leo chuckled. Every time Bobby's name was mentioned, he blushed and smiled, unable to control himself or his excitement.

"Who has that many beanies? You don't own a skateboard, so stop," Dave said.

Leo was defensive. "My head gets cold! Shut up."

"You shut up."

Cole sighed, interrupting the argument. "Alice, are you there yet?"

"I think so." She stopped outside a building made of chipped bricks and crappy metal doors, each one was bolted shut. She found a rusted ladder attached to the wall in the alley. She didn't dare glance at the manhole cover a couple of feet away. She wouldn't think about the sewers running beneath Height City, about what or who was down there, like Mick. His rotted, melted corpse was below the city somewhere, under her feet, and it made her sick. "Eighth and Belford, right?"

"That's the one," Cole said.

"Now, remember," Dave paused. Was he trying to be dramatic or annoying? "They have guns and aren't afraid to kill."

"You're not helping," Leo said. "Alice, you can do this."

"That's good," Dave said. "You be the fantasy and I'll be reality."

"You mean I'll be positive and you'll be negative," Leo said.

"Positive? Are you kidding me? False hope isn't positive, she could-"

"Thank you!" Alice shouted. She didn't need to be reminded of the dangers. For some reason, she was making a list of what could go wrong in her head and the list was getting longer by the second.

She glanced at her pulse tracker, the number was steady, as she tried to keep her nerves in check. She ignored the gnawing pit in her stomach and started up the ladder. The rust was rough on her skin and the metal clanked against her weight.

"The doors are locked, so you have to go through the skylight," Cole said.

"Good luck," Leo sounded more nervous than her if that was possible.

"I have nine and one dialed on my phone," Dave said.

Alice crawled onto the roof. She wore a Kevlar vest over one of Cole's shirts and black yoga pants. Her hair was piled under a baseball cap.

She went to the skylight. Muscular men with gnarly-looking scars passed by the glass wearing plastic aprons and goggles. Beakers and vials were strategically placed on different tables and a large pile of bottles was in the corner. *Cold medicine.* The entire place smelled terrible like rotten eggs.

This was a Markinson meth lab. And Alice was going to shut it down.

"Okay," she took a deep breath. "I'm going in."

"That's what he said," Dave laughed.

Cole groaned. "Shut up, Davey!"

"Don't call me that!"

Alice rolled her eyes. Her palms were sweating, which made her fingers slippery. She was more scared than she wanted to admit. She was better in her lessons with Rodrick. He was a good teacher. And Karen had helped her gain better tolerance of her powers. Her limits weren't as short. But none of that changed the fact, she was still an amateur. She wasn't her mother. *I can do this.*

"Shut up, I need to focus," she said.

"You're right. Okay, you got this," Leo agreed.

"Watch your back," Dave said.

Cole screamed, "something about saving kittens!"

She was starting to regret asking them to be backup.

Alice blasted the window and jumped through its frame. A thousand glass shards, reflective and sharp, rained down around her, shimmering in her lightning. For the slightest moment, she was in mid-air. She couldn't control anything. All she could do was fall until her sneakers hit the table.

Her knees bent too far and she slipped, slamming against the metal. Pain punched her shoulder.

She wasn't off to a good start.

Bullets thundered. She held in a scream as she flipped the table and crouched behind it. She felt the bullets on her back, making dents in the metal, sailing over her head, loud and terrible.

Maybe she should've worn a helmet.

Would she make it out alive? She didn't have a choice. It was survival or nothing. *I can do this.*

Alice jumped up and shoved her hand out. Vibrations squeezed her muscles and lightning clashed with the bullets. A blinding wall of sparks exploded between her and the enemy. The men wearing plastic aprons and gloves, guns in hand, covered their eyes. But the light didn't bother her.

She ran around the table.

She slammed into one and knocked him off balance. Another swung his gun at her head but she ducked and blasted him, lightning shoving him into the wall.

She turned. Her eyes met a gun's barrel. Fear hit her like a bag of bricks and reflex took control. She sidestepped and thunder erupted. She flinched. She grabbed the gun and yanked it from his hand, then shot him in the ankle and shot another man in the shoulder.

They dropped. Blood splattered everywhere but the wounds weren't deadly.

A hand grabbed her wrist. The man swung her and slammed her body into a table. The gun slipped from her fingers and a beaker shattered. Laying on the table, she kicked him in the stomach, sat up, and punched him right in the nose, leaving blood on her knuckles.

She felt the gash on her ribs, which were probably bruised, if not broken. She slid off the table, panting, with blood dripping down her face. She wasn't sure where it was coming from.

A man grabbed her shirt and turned her around, pushing her tailbone against the table's edge. His thick fingers clutched her throat, stealing her breath, as he pointed a gun at her forehead.

She couldn't even whimper.

Angry vibrations sang through her veins and electricity pulsed from her skin. Her heart hammered protectively. The man's hair fizzled and smoked, he looked confused. Eyes wide, he loosened his grip. Alice slapped his arm with her own and kicked him in the stomach, hard. He stumbled and the gun went off.

The bullet was fast. It dug through her skin, tore her muscles, and flew out the back of her shoulder. She hit the floor and blood spurted from the wound. Pain swelled. White noise buzzed in her head as Alice stared at the ceiling, lying flat on her back.

"What happened!" Leo yelled in her ear. "Are you okay?"

She balanced on her elbows. It'd leave a scar but it wasn't bad, only a graze although it felt a lot worse. She needed a bigger Kevlar vest. She stood up, holding pressure on the wound. "Getting shot sucks."

"Yeah, been there," Dave chuckled.

Leo gasped. "You got shot! I'm calling an ambulance-"

"We have a first-aid kit in the bathroom," Dave said.

"It's a gunshot wound, not a paper cut."

"Have you ever been shot?"

Leo answered, "no."

"Then shut up," Dave mocked.

Cole yelled, "shove a piece of broccoli in your mouths!"

"You are an idiom," Dave said.

Cole's anger diminished. It almost sounded like he was smiling. "No, you're an idiom."

"What are you talking about!" Leo asked.

Alice rolled her eyes. "Guys! What do I do now?" She looked around the lab. Glass shards littered the floor, and a few pieces crunched under her sneakers. Four men lay still, unconscious and covered in their own blood. "They're all down. Wait, six guns, four guys. What does that mean?"

"We've got some runners!" Cole sounded excited, entertained. Was he enjoying this?

Leo was concerned. "That's not good, is it?"

"They're gonna tell Markinson what happened," Dave said. His tone had a calculative edge like he was trying to solve a complex problem. "You're screwed."

She gulped. What else could go wrong? First Cece, now this. The problems were piling up. The thrill of the fight died down. The beakers, vials, and meth ingredients still had to be disposed of.

She checked her shoulder. The bleeding stopped. "How do I get rid of this stuff?"

Dave screamed, "don't use your powers!"

"What!" Her eyes widened. "Why?"

"Meth labs blow up," he said. Was he serious?

She scoffed. "You couldn't have told me that before I came in here!"

"You didn't ask."

She rolled her eyes. "You suck."

"You didn't get hit in the face, did you? We can't use 'a dog bit me' or 'I tripped on a rusty nail' again," Leo paused. "How the hell are we gonna explain a gunshot wound?"

"Your dad believed a stab wound to the thigh was 'I tripped on a rusty nail'"?" Dave asked. "I always knew teachers weren't smart."

"Shut up," Leo said, ready to defend his father.

"You shut up."

Alice was getting a headache. When she shifted her shoulder, a dull pain crept through her muscles. She groaned.

She checked each man's pulse to make sure they were alive, which they were. *Thank goodness.* None of them were conscious. Two were shot.

Alice was proud. She took them all down by herself. How badass was that? She adjusted her baseball cap and sighed. "Seriously, what do I do?"

"Every secret drug factory run by Markinson and Betty dump the extra crap into the sewers," Dave said.

Alice wondered what other horrible, disgusting things were underneath the city.

Leo groaned. "Ew, that's gross."

"Have you ever thought about what people really flush down their toilets?" Cole asked. "Like baby alligators and stuff?"

"I'm gonna call the police, they'll clean up the meth," Leo said.

Dave laughed. "You mean the pigs who are owned by Betty Beater and Markinson? Why do you think Alice or whatever her superhero name is, is needed in this crap town?" His voice rose. "'Cause it sucks and nobody cares!"

"We are working on the name," Cole yelled. "It's not that easy! Shut up-"

"All of you shut up!" Alice screamed. "You're like the *Three Stooges* but way more annoying!"

"The *Three Stooges* are amazing!"

Dave huffed. "Yeah, bitch!"

"They're legends," Leo agreed.

She pulled the comm out of her ear. She'd had enough. She put it in her pocket and debated whether or not she should look up *How to dispose of meth* on the internet.

Chapter 21

Casey

THE HALF-BROKEN DOOR OPENED to a metal staircase covered in rust, graffiti, and gum. At the bottom were ripped and stained layered curtains hiding a cell door, which led into an abandoned, public pool with stone walls and rotten wood. Dusty couches and crappy chairs were in the hourglass-shaped hole.

Different stereos played different music: metal, classic rock, and country.

Casey used to spend her free time at the Burrows' hideaway for criminals and runaways. She'd hang out with Bobby and the boys. They'd play games like Candyland - which Cole ruled at - checkers, War, poker, and Go Fish when they didn't want to argue, which was usually Tommy's suggestion. They'd chat about whatever topic came up; Dave and El's flirtatious friendship, Cole and Dave's many ridiculous disagreements, the latest jobs Betty assigned Tommy and Casey, and their training sessions with her.

But Casey wasn't there to relive fond memories. She had business.

She wanted to find the street kid and thief called Red.

"Cece." Verdant, a top fence, passed by her. He had a longstanding alliance with Markinson but still respected Betty's rules. He never messed with her because he knew his place. If he didn't, Betty would've made him disappear.

"There's the champion," Billy smiled. He opened his trench coat. Fidget spinners, foldable shot glasses, lighters, pocket knives, and concert tickets hung from the fabric. He gestured to the items. "Can I interest you in something?"

"Cowboy and the Chicks?" she asked.

"They're a really terrible band," he winked. "And I've sold twenty-five tickets so far."

Casey couldn't believe people were dumb enough to fall for his tricks. She fist-bumped him, then put her hands in her jacket pockets. "I'm looking for somebody. Rumors say she goes by the name Red. Have you seen her?"

"Is this about Height City Anonymous? You still haven't found the person behind it?" He was surprised, which was good. It meant he didn't doubt her abilities, if anything he feared her.

She tortured most of the independents - waterboarded, stabbed, ripped, skinned, and choked - but none of them knew anything.

Tommy hadn't made any progress either. He hadn't been around lately. Something was going on with him but Casey couldn't figure out what. She was trying to trust him but it was hard. He never acted so distant. *He'll tell me when he's ready*, she kept thinking.

Sally hadn't heard anything from her sources. Every lead seemed to be a dead end.

"She's around here somewhere," Billy shrugged. "Good luck," he smiled. The flirty smile that made Casey want to smack him. "And hey," he said. "Say hi to Bobby for me."

"Go take a cold shower." Casey knocked her shoulder against his.

He rolled his eyes as she walked away.

Fences sold stolen items while drug dealers met with their best customers and prostitutes sold information for expensive prices. Men and women with black Spade tattoos, red Diamond tattoos, or red Heart tattoos sat around, chatting, making deals, and playing cards. These were Casey's people, the ones with rotten morals and ruthless survival instincts. Height City's underworld.

"Anything I can help with, Cece?" Morey, a Burrows' businessman, asked.

She nodded once. "Yeah, you know Red?"

"Oh yeah, she's the one with the red hair." He pointed to a group of young teenagers on a ripped, blue loveseat and a couple of plastic lawn chairs. They were all about thirteen or fourteen, possibly younger.

Street kids like Casey used to be.

She headed toward them, thinking whoever thought of the nickname Red didn't seem to have a lot of creative potential.

A girl with shoulder-length, maraschino cherry red hair lay on the blue loveseat, feet up on the armrest, blowing bubbles from a plastic bottle. Every bubble shimmered in the dingy light, floating above her, twirling in serene little spirals. She wore black combat boots, ripped leggings, and a faded T-shirt under a black, raggedy hoodie and her matching beanie had holes in it.

Her bright blue eyes were noticeable and pretty.

"Hey, kid. Are you Red?" Casey didn't need to ask. She knew the answer but she needed an opening line.

The girl sat up when she saw who was speaking to her. She set the bottle of bubbles down on the cement floor. "You're Cece the Champion," she said in awe. "Why are you looking for me?" Fear hinted in her brave tone. Her calm, cool manner was impressive. She hid her nerves well.

Casey nodded toward the others in the group. They got the message and quickly left. Nobody denied an order from Cece, which she loved. It was good to be in charge, respected, and feared. She sat on a ripped ottoman and leaned forward, elbows on her knees. "I'm looking for some information."

"So go to that club on fifth. The bartender knows everything."

Casey chuckled. "Actually, she's the owner. I've been there already."

Red wasn't scared, only nervous. She didn't squirm or move but her eyes tended to drift, taking note of the exits. She also could've been searching for enemy backup. Smart but too obvious. "What's in it for me?"

"I won't slit your throat," Casey said.

A rookie acting superior was insulting. Either earn a place or get the hell out of dodge.

Red frowned. "Stupid question."

"I'd say so."

"Okay, what do you want to know?"

"There's this blog called Height City Anonymous and they posted an article about Betty, named her the official Crime Queen, and told some secrets she wanted to keep under wraps," Casey said. "I need to know who runs the blog and who their source is."

"You're gonna kill them, aren't you?" Red asked a little too boldly. Too forward. Was she concerned or curious?

Casey didn't say anything. Of course, she'd kill them. It wasn't up for debate. It was an order. She didn't question it or protest it. She just made it fun.

"I'll need a few days," Red gulped. "If that's okay."

"Sooner rather than later." Casey wanted it to sound like an order, possibly a threat. She adjusted her jacket and put her hands in her jeans pockets. "Meet me here in a week, tell me what you find."

"I can just find you," Red said. "So, you won't have to wait."

Casey didn't doubt Red would be able to find her. She turned to leave but couldn't, not until her curiosity was satisfied. She glanced over her shoulder. "You got a name? An actual name."

This kid stole from the Spades, the Hearts, and from Lorenzo Wilson. She had Sally's respect. She was a survivor, which reminded Casey of herself.

"Ruby. Ruby St.James," Red tilted her head to the side, looking like a curious puppy. Her gaze narrowed accusingly and a challenge rose in her tone. "What's your real name, Cece?"

Brave question, Casey thought. She didn't react. Instead, she walked away.

The soft breeze whistled in her ears. Height City was brighter today. Mayor Mikes started a program to repaint the oldest buildings vibrant reds, blues, oranges, yellows, greens, purples, and pinks. It was like a rainbow puked all over the place.

She climbed the fire escape and went to the roof's ledge. The Burrows looked as bright as any other part of the city but it held more shadows. Skyscrapers, both near and far, reached toward the sky while empty storefronts were either boarded up or broken into. Some shops were still standing like Sid's Beauty Parlor and a pawnshop called Moira's Merchandise. Half-abandoned apartment complexes and crappy, one-floor houses lined the streets, and warehouses were crowded next to the river.

The Honeycombs and the Nests were in the distance, roaring with activity.

Casey backed away from the ledge until she was standing in the center of the roof. Once there, she ran without hesitating, then launched herself off the ledge. She soared. Her body hung in mid-air, arms stretched at her sides. No fear, no worry, no anger. Nothing existed except her and the clouds.

Sometimes, she wondered if she'd sprout wings and fly away. Although, the idea crumbled when she realized she had no idea where she'd fly. Height City was her home.

When her feet were off the ground, nothing mattered. It didn't matter that she burned the bridge between her and Alice, someone she dearly missed.

She chose Betty. She chose her future as the next Crime Queen. What could be better? She'd rule the underworld with a sharp smirk and a silver blade.

Alice probably gave up on her. Was it a relief or a betrayal? Either way, it was better.

Alice was going to be a great hero. The next Glisin. The rumors about her were already spreading through the underworld like wildfire. Burrowers whispered about how powerful her lightning was and how clumsy she fought. She shut down a Markinson meth lab and stopped three minor drug deals in one week.

Casey tried not to be proud.

Tommy was acting weird. He canceled plans and barely came to the basement. He even kissed her differently, less sincere. He was hiding something. He was a good liar, maybe better than Casey, but she knew him better than anyone. He couldn't lie to her. Was he struggling with Paisley's absence? Maybe it was

Mick's death? His role as Betty's second enforcer? No. He would've told her. This was something he didn't trust her with, but what was it?

Her boots hit the roof. Knees bent, she tucked herself into a somersault and landed on one knee. Her heartbeat thundered almost as fast as the first time she jumped across an alley. A few strands of her blue hair fell in her face, messy and wild. She laughed.

She needed that.

Casey decided to go somewhere familiar, somewhere she was safe. All her friends were either at school, with a girl, or something else. She could be alone. She needed to think, maybe wallow a bit, mourn a friendship, and worry about her relationship.

She went to Linda's Diner.

She sat at the counter and fiddled with her necklace.

Linda, with her sugary smile and plain gaze, set down a beer mug; root beer and vanilla ice cream drizzled with caramel sauce. Casey's favorite. The first time she ordered it was with Betty. The Crime Queen wasn't a diner chick but she let Casey, at eleven years old and before she was champion, choose where they'd talk. Betty let her order whatever she wanted, which ended up being french fries and a root beer float with caramel sauce. As an orphan, she never had caramel sauce before.

"You look like you need a pick-me-up," Linda said. Her thick southern accent made Casey smile.

"I'm gonna need something stronger than soda." She sipped the rootbeer. Cold, fizzy, and sweet. She wouldn't admit it but it helped brighten her mood a little.

"What's the problem, sugarpie?"

"I made a choice. I'm gonna follow the path laid out for me." She stared into the soda. Her reflection rippled in the carbonation. She saw in her face disappointment, which she wasn't sure she felt. "I've never wanted anything different, so why go back on it?"

"You're a strong girl," Linda said. True and unhelpful. "Things will work out, you'll see."

Casey pinched the tips of her blue hair, pulling a strand in front of her face. She dyed it after her first fight. When she became the champion. A shift in her reflection to show the changes in her person. It was Cece's signature. A way to recognize her in the crowd. People respected the color. They feared it.

She slid off the stool and headed to the bathroom.

***

Tommy

Tommy opened the door for Martha and Timothy. They all waved to Linda, who stood at the counter in front of what looked like a root beer float. Her apron was stained with tomato sauce and flour. She must've been helping her cook in the kitchen before they came in.

Timothy slid into a booth and put a small, gold-painted trophy on the table. It had his name on it.

Martha chuckled. "My boy's a genius."

"It was just a spelling bee," he blushed. He was smart, he did well in school, but Tommy wasn't sure he enjoyed it. Timothy seemed happier when he was studying by himself.

Martha nodded. "Yes, and you won. It's an achievement that you should be proud of."

The only reason Tommy was invited to the spelling bee was because Brad had to work and the ticket would've gone to waste. He loved to see his little brother succeed. He loved to cheer for Timothy, encourage him, and be proud of him. It was almost unsettling how much he'd grown to care about Timothy in such a short amount of time.

"Thanks for coming," Timothy said.

"I wouldn't have missed it."

"I think we deserve a round of ice cream," Martha said. "What do you think?"

"Mint chip!" Timothy hopped in his seat.

Tommy smiled. "With whipped cream and chocolate sauce."

He waved Linda over and froze. Casey stood at the counter, staring at him. The betrayal, confusion, and anger written across her face hurt his heart. She never looked at him that way before. He never wanted her to find out this way, maybe he never wanted her to find out at all.

How could he not have told her? The one person he trusted and cared about more than anyone. The girl who kicked his ass when they sparred. The girl who never took crap from anyone. The girl who protected her friends with a warrior spirit. The girl who sat with him on his mother's porch, listening to the screams of his past, as she held his hand and said *You're not alone.*

How could he have lied to her? And for so long? His compartmentalization rule shattered. Was this the part where he lost her? Tommy couldn't let that happen.

She rushed out of the diner. He excused himself and ran after her.

***

Casey

All the canceled plans, the stupid excuses, avoiding her, she knew he'd been lying but to see him with a rich, Honeycomber family was just confusing. It didn't make any sense. What lie could involve them? What was so horrible that he couldn't tell her?

A hand grabbed her wrist. Casey knew his touch before she saw his face. He pulled her back and made her face him but she broke his grip and shoved him away. She swung her fist at his nose but he ducked, then blocked her kick. She punched and he caught her knuckles, holding her hand against his chest.

"Let me explain!"

"Liar!" She wanted to bruise his face. She wanted to knock out his teeth and break his kneecaps. She wanted to yell at him. But what would she be yelling about? Casey deserved to hear the truth and Tommy deserved a chance to tell it. She could yell at him, and possibly kill him, after he explained himself.

She crossed her arms. "Better bring a damn tear to my eye or I'm gonna smash your nuts with a sledgehammer."

"Shut up and listen to me." Tommy wasn't afraid of her or her threats. Sometimes, she hated it and sometimes, she loved it. "When I took Paisley to the bus station that night," he paused for emphasis. "I asked her about the shell company." He hadn't spoken much about his and Paisley's goodbye, which didn't seem weird because he never liked to talk about his mother. "It belongs to Brad Cruise. He's been paying her to keep me a secret. I'm his... he's my..."

"You're a Cruise?" she finished for him.

She looked in the window. Martha and Timothy looked exactly like they did in the magazines and the newspapers. Timothy Cruise, Height City's golden boy, was Tommy's brother. Of course, he wanted to know him. Why wouldn't he? Tommy never had a good family, maybe this was his chance at a better one.

"Why didn't you tell me?" Casey asked. Her anger seemed to have vanished, replaced by a hollow worry in the pit of her stomach. A worry she hadn't had since Alice came to The Arena for the first time. The fear of being abandoned but this time it was a million times worse. It made her nauseous.

"I wanted to get to know him by myself without putting a target on his back, without the murder or the hacking or the criminal aspect and I didn't want Betty to find out." The apology was in Tommy's eyes, the perfect brown eyes Casey loved to lose herself in, but it was the raw sincerity of his voice that convinced her. He was begging her to believe him. "I didn't know if they were going to like me," he shrugged. "It seemed more peaceful."

She understood. She hid her demons and her darkness from Alice because it was easier. Alice was her escape from the shadows. Casey felt more human around her. How could she blame Tommy for doing the same thing she did?

"Who else knows?" she asked.

"I told Dave," he said. "And Jess kind of found out. Purely by accident, I swear, so, don't bite my head off."

She rolled her eyes, arms dangling at her sides.

He'd lied for months about how he found a piece of himself and was happy about it. Why couldn't he have shared that with her? What was the problem?

Casey prayed, wished, and begged to meet her family when she was a kid. Before they met. She'd stay up at night and wonder why whoever she came from left her in a basket on the porch of St.Marian's Orphanage. She used to come up with possible scenarios, maybe they were astronauts lost in space or spies on a secret mission. As she got older, she accepted that her family left because they didn't care, she wasn't good enough for them, for anyone, it seemed. Her parents didn't even give her a name, neither did the nuns.

How could she be angry with Tommy for any of this? Tommy deserved to get to know his brother. How could she not forgive him?

"Timothy is a good kid and Martha is a good mom," he said.

"You really care about them, huh?" It was a rhetorical question. She didn't need him to say it.

Tommy stared at her. He didn't touch or move near her. He was waiting for her to say something. Anything. Her silence was making him nervous. She could tell by how his jaw was set.

She took a breath. "Does this change anything with us?"

She needed to know. She couldn't lose him.

"Never," he said. The definiteness in his voice made her fears disappear.

Tommy tugged her jacket collar and pulled her closer to him. She reached her arms around his neck and buried her face against his shoulder. His hoodie smelled faintly of gunpowder and soap. He held her against him, gentle and strong. She could've stayed in his arms forever.

He kissed her head.

"You wanna come meet my family?" he whispered, warm breath tickling her ear. "They don't know that they're my family but you get the gist."

"What the hell?" she smiled. "Let's go meet the parents."

They went inside.

Martha and Timothy had obviously been watching them. The mother and son glanced between the couple with curious smiles. Four bowls of mint chip ice cream with whipped cream and chocolate chips were sitting on the table.

Tommy held Casey's waist, keeping her close. She bent her elbow on his shoulder.

"Who's this?" Martha asked, seemingly delighted.

"I'm Ce," Casey clicked her tongue. "I'm Casey Cavalier."

It'd been ages since she said her real name, the name she chose for herself, not the one Betty gave her.

Tommy proudly smiled at her.

Martha scooted over and Casey sat beside her. Tommy and Timothy sat together on the other side. They shared the same shy smile and reserved gaze as if they were both hiding tragedies flowing through their blood. An interesting similarity Casey wouldn't have predicted.

Timothy introduced himself with a polite handshake, then he grabbed the whipped cream bottle and sprayed Tommy with it. Fattening, white fluff covered his face.

Martha gasped. "Timothy!"

"Nicely done," Casey said.

They high-fived.

He laughed. "Thanks."

***

Bobby

Bobby sat on Cole's kitchen counter, doodling ideas in her design binder. She needed to make two beautiful prom dresses and needed to think of a plan to get

Casey there. So far, the plan involved handcuffs and the hood of her mom's old sports car. Casey would never fit in the trunk.

Cole dropped a can of beans and two cans of chicken noodle soup into a box labeled AWAY IT GOES. He pointed to a cabinet. "Can you look in there for non-perishables?"

She nodded. She found a bag of uncooked pasta shells and handed it to him.

He dropped it in the box. There was a good amount of food in it.

"What's all that for?" Bobby asked.

He smiled. "A homeless shelter in the Nests. I'm giving them whatever we don't eat." Cole talked about his good deeds as if they were no big deal, which was impressive. He never asked for praise or a "thank you" either. "How's designing?"

She shook her head. "I want my dress to be amazing and it will be, as soon as I know what it's gonna look like," she pointed her sparkly, feathered pen at his nose. "I'll figure it out," she said, determined, then dropped her hand in her lap. "I'm excited to bring Casey. She's never been to a school dance with me."

"Can I go too? It sounds super fun. I can pick out a really cool tux," Cole said. "Is Leo going?"

Bobby wondered the same thing. She never asked him. Prom wasn't Leo's scene. He probably wouldn't enjoy it and he hadn't mentioned anything about it.

A pretty, brunette girl came out of Dave's bedroom. She was carrying a bra and her shirt was inside out. She glanced at Bobby and Cole, slightly embarrassed, as Dave led her to the front door. He'd sure gotten around lately. Bobby knew three different girls he'd slept with, not counting Jess or El.

"Wait!" Cole grabbed a tiny metal detector and went over to the girl. He politely searched her clothing, randomly waving the device. Did he know how weird this looked? Did he care?

"Dude, what the hell?" Dave asked.

Cole stepped away. "You're good. Have a wonderful rest of your day."

The girl ran. They probably wouldn't see her again.

Dave shut the door and threw his arms in the air. "You're so weird!"

"Your dates steal from us!" Cole tossed the metal detector on the couch. "The last one took my flip-flops! So, don't act like I'm the nutter butter here!"

Before Dave could respond, Cole's phone beeped and he held up a finger, taking it from his pocket. He smiled. He showed them the screen. "Have you heard of this blog? Height City Anonymous?"

"Yeah. Word on the street is Betty wants whoever it is dead," Dave said.

Bobby's heart stopped, a cold dread seized her bones and tensed her muscles. Was she having a heart attack? She slid off the counter and set down her binder. She couldn't feel her toes. Could she ever feel her toes? If Betty wanted Height City Anonymous dead, then Casey would be the one holding the knife. This was bad. This was really bad.

"No, no, no, no, no, no. No!" Bobby waved her hands to get their attention. The boys looked at her like she was shouting about losing a limb. "Oh my God, no!" she said. "Jess is the blogger! She's Height City Anonymous!"

"His Jess?" Cole pointed to Dave.

They wore the same dumbfounded expression. Dave yanked the door open, slamming it against the wall, which made Bobby flinch. He left.

***

Dave

Dave drove to the Honeycombs. He used the same routine he did when he and Jess were dating. He parked his motorcycle down the street, out of sight from anyone who might call the cops, and snuck into her backyard. He climbed his favorite sycamore tree onto the roof and crawled to her window. It was locked. Why the hell was it locked?

Jess sat on her bed. She was chewing on a red pen, staring at a bunch of papers on her bed. Her hair was draped over her shoulder. She wore gray, silk shorts and a white tank top.

She saw him and crinkled her eyebrows, questioning why he was there. He knocked on the glass, urging her to let him in, but she shook her head. He wouldn't take no for an answer. He knocked again.

Dave couldn't believe she used the things he told her in private for her blog. Stories about the Burrows, about his friends, about his world. She used it all. How could she betray him?

Jess closed the bedroom door, put the chair under the knob, and came to the window. The lock clicked.

Dave opened it and crawled through.

Her bedroom was so familiar. The smell of her rose-y perfume, the chaotically organized books and pictures, her bed, the sheets and pillows. Her beautiful caramel eyes, her soft lips, her pink streaks, her delicate curves, and her peeled fingertips.

"You're Height City Anonymous," he accused her. "You used everything I told you in your damn article! Do you realize how stupid that was?" he couldn't contain his anger. She completely betrayed his trust. How could she be so reckless? He couldn't believe it. "You put a damn target on my back! Casey is going to kill us!" he yelled. "I'm gonna have to go in The Arena! You-"

"Stop screaming!" she shouted. "You can't come in here and scream at me!" she huffed. "Who the hell is Casey!"

"Cece! Cece is... It doesn't matter!" Dave was sick of double names. He couldn't keep track of who knew what about whom. He wanted to grab Jess and shake some sense into her. Was she that naive? Wasn't she supposed to be sensible? Did she lose her mind?

"I know what I did! I feel horrible enough, okay? But you can't come in here and yell at me, it doesn't work that way," she said. "We're broken up!"

"Who's fault is that?" He'd been so angry at her for breaking up with him. He hated the way they left things. He hated not being with her or being able to talk to her. He missed listening to her talk about the latest book she read. He missed watching her work. He missed telling her about his day. He missed having her in his bed, holding her while she slept. It was probably for the best. Did they really fit as a couple? The princess and the criminal. Maybe they never should've gotten together.

"You're the one who's been sleeping around like some unpaid gigolo," Jess crossed her arms. Her glare reminded him of Layla's, rageful and mean. He was tempted to tell her that but he didn't.

"How do you even know that!"

"Bobby and Alice told me!"

"Well," he paused. He couldn't think of a comeback. "We're not together, so it's none of your business."

Maybe he was being petty but Dave didn't care. She was pissing him off.

She nodded. Shoulders tense, she went to her closet. Usually, when she was tense, he'd rub her shoulders or kiss her, distract her, to keep from going over the edge. He couldn't do that now.

She came out holding a simple, round hat box with a fancy, curly ribbon attached to the lid. She shoved it against his chest, hard enough to make him grunt. She had bags under her eyes. Her silence spoke volumes. She wouldn't look him in the eye. She crossed her arms. "Get out."

What was Jess giving him?

He dropped the box on the bed and yanked off the lid. The box was filled with CDs, a wrinkly T-shirt, a DVD, a cigar, and a copy of *Romeo and Juliet*. He bought it. He wrote his random thoughts and jokes in the margins, then gave it to her as a gift. She read the first few pages and laughed at his comments, which was the first time he realized how much he liked making her laugh.

"So, first you break up with me, then you basically sign my death certificate and now you're doing this?" Dave was more heartbroken than he wanted to admit. "You know what? Doesn't matter," he said. "It's all rebellion, right? You'll forget about it later. Like it never happened."

"Excuse me?" Jess asked, offended.

He held up the book. "Journalism, me, it's all in the same boat. You'll throw it away when you're done with it. You'll go back to that stupid plan of your whackjob mother's and forget it all."

He wanted to hurt her. She hurt him. These items weren't his. The T-shirt used to be. It was black with a white, female silhouette playing guitar. Block letters above her head spelled RENEGADES. One of his favorite bands.

Bobby's too, she knew the bass player.

Jess wore the T-shirt the first time she spent the night at his and Cole's apartment. The first time she lay in his bed. Dave could still see her in it. It was big on her, hung just above her knees. Her hair was down, a little messy, which never happened. She was thrilled with herself for sneaking out. He remembered how easy it was to let her in. He figured she already knew his scars, his traumas. She met his father and if Ted didn't scare her away, nothing would.

***

Jess

"Don't act like I don't care. I love journalism and I love-" Jess stopped herself. She couldn't do this right now. It hurt to be near him. She hated herself for putting Dave in danger, for risking his life but she couldn't take it back. She wished she could because the way Dave was looking at her, like she was the enemy, tore her apart.

"Just go," she said. She had to get back to work. She was Miss Z's teaching assistant this semester. She had to correct the rest of the students' papers.

Dave dropped the crinkled T-shirt and the copy of *Romeo and Juliet* on the bed. He slapped the lid on the box and took it to the window, tossing it outside. It hit a couple of twigs on the way down. He was about to leave but he stopped. He turned to her. "I thought you were supposed to be the sensible one but you've just killed us both."

"Go back to your cocotte castle." Jess couldn't disagree but she was too angry to apologize.

Once he left, she slammed the window shut and locked it. She watched him climb down the sycamore tree and disappear, back to the Burrows.

Why did heartbreak have to be so hard? She couldn't even blame him for sleeping with other girls. They were broken up.

She sat on the bed, tears threatening to seep down her cheeks. She held the Renegades T-shirt against her chest and buried her face in the fabric. It smelled like Dave.

She remembered the first time she wore it. She was so excited about sneaking out of her house and going to his apartment that she forgot to bring pajamas. Dave let her pick whatever shirt she wanted. When she came into the bedroom, he was lying on the bed in nothing but his race car pajama pants, playing with his dad's old lighter. His focus immediately went to her.

She liked how fearless he made her feel. She never wanted to lose that.

***

Alice

"That was really good." Mister Scotts leaned back in his seat. The kitchen table was a medium-sized circle with four dented, crayon-covered chairs. He bought them when Leo was two and was going through an artistic phase.

"Eh," Leo shrugged. "The chicken was dry."

Alice playfully punched his arm. He rubbed the wound. He ate two pieces of chicken and all his sides, so she knew it was a joke. Along with the breaded chicken, she made mashed potatoes, green beans, asparagus, and garlic bread. Simple but delicious. She cooked everything herself because Mister Scotts had to grade papers.

"Help me with the dishes." He gathered the plates and put them in the sink.

Leo licked the potatoes off his fork and grabbed the silverware.

Alice threw her napkin away, rolling her lips. "Is it okay if I go over to Jess's for a bit?"

"Did you finish your homework?"

"Yep. All done."

"What about you?" he looked at his son.

Leo considered the question. "Uh... define 'finished'?"

Alice smiled. He rolled his eyes.

Mister Scotts turned on the faucet. "Do you need a ride?"

"No, thanks." She grabbed her messenger bag and went to the door.

"Home by eleven."

"Don't die!" Leo whispered-yelled. He hid his mouth as if it'd keep his dad from hearing.

"What!" Mister Scotts asked, freaked.

"What?" Leo turned to him, wide-eyed.

"Bye!" Alice decided to let him handle this by himself.

She went into the hall, closed the door, and headed to the stairwell. Did she have everything? Keys, phone, lip balm, camera, Kevlar, baseball cap, and a booty call's masquerade mask. She stuffed what she didn't need under a loose baseboard on one of the steps. Her bag and belongings could fit. She only needed her temporary uniform.

She got dressed - the stairwell didn't have any security cameras - and opened the window. Cole helped her steal the key from Bowman, the super, and she copied it. Within three hours, the key was back on Bowman's belt like nothing ever happened but now, she had a secret way to leave the building.

Lightning zoomed across the twilight sky.

Headlights, city lights, and street lamps flashed on. One by one, they illuminated the city. Every building had someone inside it. A janitor cleaned a lobby's floors while he listened to his favorite podcast; a single mother wrangled her three kids, trying to get them to bed; some college students set up a keg for their midnight party; newlyweds had an Italian dinner; and an old man napped in front of the TV. So many lives and Glisin used to protect them all.

The Burrows seemed dim even with the bright colors on every building. A gorgeous spotlight on a sickly depression. Sally's Place didn't have new paint. The two-story building looked rundown, unnoticeable, with its chipping bricks and fogged windows. The neon sign flickered on and off, screaming OPEN with all its might. A group of laughing twenty-year-olds went into the club. By the looks of it, the party was just getting started.

A woman in a gold, sequined cocktail dress stood next to the dumpster. Her heels were about six inches high. How was she still standing? She thrust two full trash bags into the garbage and turned to the door, heading inside. She was pretty. Kenna, the part-time bartender.

Alice met her the summer she lived with Cece in Eddie's basement. They used to go to Sally's Place a lot.

A man with a red heart tattooed on his neck came out of the club, stumbling toward Kenna. She seemed to know him. She pushed him away but he wouldn't leave her alone. He shoved her against the brick wall and pressed himself on her.

Alice tackled him. The force of crashing into him made her body reappear. They both slammed against the ground and rolled away from each other. She ended up on her belly with the wind knocked out of her. It took her a few seconds to breathe. The baseball cap lay beside her. Her long, purple hair trickled out of its bun, falling in her face.

Kenna ran inside the club.

The man stood up.

Alice grabbed her hat and put it on, jumping to her feet. Her hair was in unbrushed loops, half under the cap and half hung over her shoulders. She was a little dizzy and disoriented from tackling him in her lightning form. She didn't realize it could affect her so much.

She stumbled a bit but caught herself. She tried to blast him but he grabbed her arm before she could.

He shoved her against the wall, making pain shoot through her waist, and her head slapped the jagged bricks. His fingers tightened around her neck, one hand held her arm above her head, and his legs held hers still.

"You'll do," he whispered, lips tickling her cheek. His breath stung her bare skin.

Alice couldn't breathe. She couldn't move. Her heartbeat, thundering against her ribs, echoed in her ears but her pulse tracker was silent. Now would be a great time for instinct to kick in.

He smiled at her chest. *Ew,* she thought. Giant vibrations erupted throughout her body. Tiny earthquakes tensed her muscles, coursed in her veins, and shook her bones. An incredible euphoria washed over her. Lightning sparked from her body and flickered in her eyes.

The man screamed in terror but he didn't let go, he couldn't let go. His fingers started smoking and his skin started to char. What the hell was happening? He stumbled backward, shaking, trembling, and smoking as if he were being set on fire. His face was burned. He yelled in horror and agony, begging for mercy, begging for the pain to end. THUD.

Alice stood still, back against the wall. She stared at the man lying on the ground. Did she kill him? She wasn't sure. She counted to ten, trying to keep herself calm. She didn't feel excited or upset, maybe a little uncomfortable, and terrified. Definitely terrified. She didn't want to be a murderer. She wasn't a killer. She couldn't come back from that. She couldn't handle it.

She crouched down and checked his pulse. He had one.

The burns covering his face and arms were bad, at least third-degree. It was like her powers cooked him from the inside, then surfaced on his skin. Alice didn't know she could do that.

After she called an ambulance, Alice went home. She didn't want to be on the streets anymore. She couldn't remember what lie she told Mister Scotts about why she came back early. The night was a blur. Her bed felt good, soft and firm. The sheets were warm. The Scotts boys' snores rocked her to sleep but she dreamt of the man she almost burned to death. What would her mom think?

She woke up to sunshine fluttering through the window. The pale blue sky seemed confused. The clouds couldn't choose which direction to roll in. She got dressed, ate breakfast, bickered with Leo, and got in the car. They went to school.

Mister Scotts carried a messy stack of graded papers, trying to organize them, as he muttered to himself about the decline of education. He didn't like giving his students Ds and Cs but very few earned an A. He headed to his classroom and Alice followed Leo to his locker.

She couldn't get used to being part of the early bird group. School wouldn't technically start for another twenty minutes.

"I think I almost killed a guy last night," she said. She couldn't stop thinking about it.

Leo raised his eyebrows, shocked. "What! How?"

"I burned him. I called every hospital in the city last night. He was admitted and he's gonna live but I," she paused. Alice couldn't stop picturing him, the smell of burned flesh, his charred skin. She was lucky he didn't die. She gulped. "I could've been a murderer," she shook her head. "He's yucky and horrible but I don't know, I hated it."

"Well, you're not a killer. You're not built that way," Leo said. "It's a good thing."

"Maybe I should make a rule." She hugged her books. "Thou shall never kill, or what's Shakespeare for I?"

"You'd have to ask the man himself but hey, I like it. You shall never kill." He nudged her shoulder, trying to comfort her.

She nodded. It was good to say out loud. Alice needed rules. She wanted to draw lines in the sand and never cross them. There was a right side and a wrong side. Or was it more complicated than that?

Jess walked up, carrying a big binder labeled MISS Z.

Leo pointed to it. "Are those our tests? Did I get an A?"

"Yes, it's our tests and you'll have to find out when Miss Z gives it to you." She wore a fitted pink tank top under a black and gold striped blouse, both paired with a pleated skirt. Her hair was down and looked the same, perfect with pink streaks.

"You didn't give me an A?" Leo asked. "When you're a teacher's assistant, you're supposed to help out your friends and give them good grades."

"I'm not giving up my integrity so you don't have to study."

"Fair enough."

She handed Alice the binder and took out her phone. She scrolled through what looked like emails to Height City Anonymous.

Leo tried to sneak a peek at the graded papers. Alice slapped his hand. He pulled her hair. She kicked his shin.

"Hey!" He hopped, holding the leg she kicked.

Jess took the binder and handed Alice the phone. "Read this, please."

Alice wasn't sure if she should be worried. She looked at the screen. It was an email from the woman she saved the night before. It pleaded for Height City Anonymous to write an article about the lightning who could transform into a woman. Alice had never been called a woman before, not in the adult sense. She was always considered a kid. "This is from Kenna."

"Who?" Leo asked.

"She works at Sally's Place sometimes. I saved her last night," Alice said.

Jess nodded. "Yeah. She's calling you the 'Woman in Lightning'," she smiled. "There are a bunch of chat rooms created by people who have seen you in the past year. There's even a photo of you, or, well, the lightning going into the Adler Building."

"That's freaking awesome!" Leo laughed.

Alice couldn't believe the city was talking about her. People noticed her. She was still a rookie but the attention was nice. She laughed, shaking Leo's arm. Why wasn't he more excited? He smiled. For some reason, they started jumping up and down. Alice didn't care if they looked ridiculous, this news needed to be celebrated.

"It's a good thing barely anybody sees that outfit you wear," he said. "When's the real super suit supposed to be ready?"

Alice shrugged. Bobby and Karen were working round the clock to finish Alice's super suit. They bickered about certain things like whether or not they should add Glisin's symbol to it. Alice wasn't sure if she deserved to wear her mom's navy blue thunderbolt. "Bobby and Karen want it to be perfect, so I have absolutely no idea."

"Who knew they were more into perfectionism than Jess," Leo said.

Jess rolled her eyes. "Can we not talk about this again?"

"You vacuumed your room twice in an hour while we were still eating the chips!" he said. "I was halfway through when you took the bag and banned crumbs."

Jess crossed her arms. She'd been more stressed than usual because of the sword hanging over her head. Betty Beater wanted her champion to kill Jess and Dave. Jess hadn't been able to focus on anything else. She asked Alice to stay over a lot in case someone tried to break in and murder her in her sleep. Sometimes, Leo tagged along.

"Okay," Jess stood a little more proper. "I searched all night and no major news outlets have done an article on the 'Woman in Lightning.' You're not up to their standards yet, I guess," she shrugged. "Anyway, since I'm your best friend and it'd be great for my blog, I wanted to do an article about you, coin you, as they say."

"Does that mean you get to name her," Leo paused, glancing at Alice. "I mean, name the 'Woman in Lightning'?"

"Ideally," Jess said. "I have to move fast. I have some ideas and you can have final approval-"

"Cole and I have a list of names," Leo said quickly, holding up a bossy finger. "You can only pick from that, got it?"

"Fine," she gestured for him to be quiet. She looked at Alice. "What do you say?"

Alice knew the press and media were part of becoming a hero. Her mom dealt with the cameras all the time. Glisin gave a few rushed interviews in her day. Alice couldn't control what people would say but at least with Jess writing the first article about her, she could control her introduction.

"Of course," she chuckled.

Jess quietly squealed, "Thank you."

Bobby, in a zebra-striped skirt and a fitted, black T-shirt with a big orange on it, looked exhausted. Her books were piled in her arms, ready to slip out of her grip at any moment. She leaned on the lockers and hummed a polite "hello." Her panda purse hung next to her hip.

Leo smiled. He drifted toward her. A magnetic force seemed to pull them together. Alice wondered why Bobby was early. She was never early.

"What are you doing here?" Leo asked.

"I had a really late, early," Bobby yawned, eyes half closed. Faint, light blue eyeshadow and sparkly pink lip gloss decorated her face. "Shift at the hotel. I got about thirty minutes of sleep and threw my alarm clock out the window."

"You did what?" Leo asked, perplexed.

"Something I picked up from Case," she crinkled her eyebrows. "Cece, I mean, Cece. Yep, that's her name." She nodded decidedly. "Anyway, what's up?"

She stumbled a bit but Leo steadied her. She leaned on him for support without realizing what she was doing. He put his arm around her, stiff and a little sweaty. He swallowed his nerves and his face turned red.

Alice took out her camera to snap a photo. It captured how much Leo liked Bobby and how nervous she made him. It also showed how comfortable Bobby seemed to be in his arms.

Her temple was level with his shoulder. They were adorable.

"Hey, I was wondering when my super suit is gonna be ready," Alice said. She was too excited not to ask. If Height City had its eyes on her, she wanted to look epic. "I want to wear it to save people."

"Karen and I are busy," Bobby rubbed her eyes. "We're going as fast as we can but soon, I promise you that," she yawned. "It'll be amaze-some."

Leo chuckled. "Amaze-some?"

"You heard me," she said. She leaned her cheek on his shoulder and tilted her head back. She looked at him like he was Prince Charming but he didn't seem to notice. She glanced at his T-shirt and crinkled her eyebrows. "Why does your shirt say 'Talk nerdy to me'?"

"It was on sale," Leo looked down. "You're one to judge." He pointed at the giant orange printed on her chest. "You're wearing fruit."

"How do you even talk nerdy?" Bobby asked, genuinely curious. "Do you whisper the periodic elements to each other while you make out?"

Jess chuckled at the joke.

Leo rolled his eyes. "If it bothers you guys that much, I'll take it off," he glanced between them and held out his hand. "But it'll cost you to see the show."

"Oh, I'm not sure you have anything I want to see," Jess said.

Bobby laughed. She seemed much more awake now. She high-fived Jess, then wrapped her arms around Leo's torso. His cheeks turned pink. If she noticed, she didn't say anything.

Alice leaned on the lockers. She liked listening to her friends tease each other. She liked how comfortable they were together. She was tempted to ask Bobby how Cece was but she didn't. She wasn't sure she wanted to know. Cece probably never wanted to see her again.

"Hey," Brittany waved, a little awkward, wearing her cheer uniform. Her hair was in a braided ponytail and her little pearl earrings were shaped like unicorns. She smiled at Jess and Bobby, then turned to Leo and Alice. Her forehead wrinkled. Was it guilt or embarrassment?

"Ally and Leon," Brittany guessed.

"Close," Leo shrugged. "Lose the 'N'."

"Leo," she said, chuckling. "Okay, Leo and Ally." She started to insert herself into the group after she and Bobby agreed to give each other a chance. Supposedly, Cindy started dating Tony, which pissed Brittany off. She and Cindy weren't speaking, so she had no one else to hang out with. She still couldn't remember Alice or Leo's names. It was hard to tell if she was really clueless or didn't bother to pay attention.

"Her name is Alice," Jess said.

"Alice... Alice," Brittany nodded. "Okay, got it."

"Ally Scotts," Leo whispered. An inside joke. A nickname and another life. Alice pictured Ally Scotts as someone different, a girl without powers, a regular high school student who wasn't the daughter of a superhero or abandoned by her father, but Leo saw her as a character in a comic book. His inspiration came from coming up with her hero name.

Jess slapped his shoulder. "Don't confuse her."

"Is Bobby okay?" Brittany asked.

Bobby was still hanging onto Leo for support, falling asleep on her feet.

His protectiveness over her was almost blinding as he narrowed his glare at Brittany. "Now you know her name? You've been calling her slut and whore for four years and now you know her name?"

Bobby blushed. She touched his arm and his focus shifted to her, gaze softening. She smiled. "We're getting a new start."

"Yeah, Loki," Brittany said to make him mad, crossing her arms.

"I wanted to tell you guys," Jess said, determined to change the subject. "We have a pop quiz in Miss Z's class. It's on the most recent chapters we've read."

"Thanks for the tip," Leo smiled. "See? That's what being a teacher's assistant is all about."

She shifted the binder and the folders of extra credit work in her arms. "I love being Miss Z's teacher's assistant. It's fun," she chuckled. Leave it to Jess to be excited about schoolwork. "I've eaten in the teacher's lounge so often, Principal Penez and I started playing online chess together."

"You're friends with the principal," Leo paused. "That's weird."

Alice didn't personally know Principal Penez but he and Mister Scotts were friends.

She wrapped her arm around Jess's shoulders, trying to make her feel less like a nerd, not that Jess minded being one. Alice loved her more for it.

Brittany took a half-filled bottle of water out of her backpack, untwisted the cap, and chucked the water into Bobby's face.

Leo's jaw dropped. His entire right side was soaked but he didn't move away.

Bobby gasped and wiped her eyes. Her lip gloss smeared and mascara leaked down her cheeks. "Bitch!" she screamed.

"I was trying to wake you up," Brittany said. "We have a test today."

Bobby cursed under her breath and rushed away. She may have been on the verge of tears but the way she flipped Brittany off signaled she was more angry than embarrassed. Jess followed her, dragging Brittany close behind in an effort to make her apologize.

Leo squeezed the water out of his T-shirt and leaned against the lockers.

Alice leaned beside him. "You like her, don't you?"

She knew the answer but she wanted the confession.

Leo chuckled, face as red as a tomato. He shrugged, trying to act nonchalant. He didn't answer her question out loud but it was obvious that he had fallen head over heels for Bobby Jones.

Alice nudged his shoulder, nodding. "I thought so."

***

Tommy

Dave was lying in his bed next to Kenna. The sheets covered their legs and they each had one pillow. Her clothes were scrunched on the floor and she wasn't wearing a bra. A muffler shop flier hung from the doorknob, which was Dave's version of a sock on the door. Tommy couldn't believe it. How dumb could Dave be? Sleeping with Kenna from the club was such a stupid move.

He and Cole stood across from each other, both leaning against the door-frame.

"She got saved by Alice or, well, she doesn't know it was Alice," Cole whispered. "Anyway, he came up with some story and told her that he fought a mugger like a ninja, backflipped, the whole deal and I guess the 'Woman in Lightning' came and stopped a bullet. It was confusing." He rolled his eyes.

"He did a backflip?" Tommy asked.

They burst out laughing. The lie was somewhat believable. Dave could handle himself in a fight but he wasn't a gymnast. Tommy wished he'd been there to watch the disastrous flirting but he had to do a job for Betty. He punished a man by using a rusty cleaver to chop his hand off. Blood went everywhere, squirting onto the floor like a hose. It made his stomach twist and bubble but he didn't throw up, which was progress.

Dave saw them staring and rolled his eyes. He grumbled a couple of curse words as he grabbed a T-shirt and yanked it over his head. He was wearing plain, navy blue boxers. He slapped their heads.

Tommy shoved him forward, closed the door, and followed him to the kitchen.

"We're never gonna be able to go back to Sally's again." Cole leaned on the counter. He wore a plain T-shirt, gray sweatpants, and Easter bunny-themed socks. He crossed his arms, annoyed, and seemed ready to give Dave a lecture.

Dave sniffed the fresh pot in the coffee maker. He grabbed a mug from one of the cabinets - it was shaped like a T-rex's head - and poured himself a cup. "Sally's is our turf. We'll be fine. Plus, we've got Casey on our side and she's the most terrifying person ever." He added some milk and sugar to his coffee.

"That's my girlfriend." Tommy liked to say it.

"Dude, I know, I'm as shocked as you are," Dave sipped his drink. "What the hell were you thinking?"

"I'm gonna tell her you said that," he smiled. He grabbed a mug and poured himself a cup of coffee. It wasn't his first choice in beverages but it was good all the same.

The trampoline in the living room was covered in scrapped newspaper, different types of glue, paints, brushes, and a big, bendy-wire statue. Another one of Cole's projects. He was over sock puppets.

"Why?" Dave asked when he saw the mess.

"I'm making a piñata," Cole said.

"Again, why?"

"I want to and it's awesome and fun and cool," Cole said. His tone mocked Dave's annoyance. "It's gonna be an elephant wearing a top hat. Next, I wanna make a camel wearing a cape and tap shoes."

"This place is gonna be filled with weird-ass piñatas, isn't it?" Dave asked.

"Yes, sir," Cole said proudly.

Tommy admired Cole's creativity. He remembered watching Cole decorate his bedroom ceiling with the constellations. He used glow-in-the-dark stars and white paint, and he could name almost every single one. Tommy was sure Dave and Cole's apartment would be filled with piñatas shaped like zebras, goats, and chickens, all wearing bowties and witch hats. Cole would probably give them to a charity or a school or St.Marian's Orphanage.

Casey walked in. She slipped her toolkit into her jacket and kicked the door closed. Her hair had grown past her shoulders and her roots were blonde. Usually, she would've redyed it by now but she hadn't yet. Tommy wondered why but decided it was better not to ask.

"Hi, Casey," Cole paused. "Or is it Cece?"

She ignored him. She showed them a small, white box with a red bow.

"What's that?" Dave asked.

"A bomb." She tossed it to Tommy.

He caught it and rolled it around in his palms. It looked like a box you might find a pair of expensive earrings in. He shook it by his ear as a joke. "One with a timer or a remote control?"

Casey smiled. "Happy birthday, T." Her excitement made the green in her eyes brighter. She gestured to the box. "Open it."

He lifted the lid. The gift was a silver keychain with the word GUARDIAN clumsily carved in it. Tommy recognized it from the first time they met.

He went into a store that laundered money for Betty. He'd been training with her for a while but he still lived with Paisley. He couldn't remember what he'd been looking for, maybe clothes since Paisley hadn't bothered to buy him any.

He wandered over to a miscellaneous section - the shelves were full of knickknacks - and found a girl about his age. She had blonde hair and curious green eyes. She looked like any other street kid in the Burrows, tired and paranoid, except she was wearing a baggy cardigan and a khaki skirt. The St.Marian's Orphanage uniform.

She didn't notice him. She was too busy stealing. She took the keychain and stuffed it in her pocket but the store owner saw her do it. He yelled and she froze. Eyes wide, she didn't move, as he threatened to cut off her fingers. Tommy grabbed her hand - which was trembling and bruised. His touch seemed to snap her back to reality - and they ran. He guided her down several alleys until he was sure they were safe.

He wasn't sure why he helped her. Dave probably would've advised against it. But Tommy couldn't abandon her. When they stopped, both panting and sweating, he realized she was laughing. Who laughed at a near-torturous experience? She wasn't fearful, she was exhilarated.

He couldn't believe her reaction. *Why are you laughing?*

Because we got away, she said. They introduced themselves. She showed him the keychain and thanked him for having her back. He decided she was worth learning more about.

He took her to Sally's Place and they'd been side by side ever since.

"You kept it," Tommy chuckled. The memory reflected off the clumsily carved letters. He wondered who sketched the word into the metal. GUARDIAN.

Casey shrugged. "Figured I'd find some use for it." She was trying not to smile. Her casual stance was too relaxed. She was more excited than she wanted to show. "Like it?"

He grabbed his key ring. He had a key to his apartment, to Dave and Cole's, to Eddie's basement, one to Sally's Place, and one to Sally's jeep. He really needed his own ride. He clipped the keychain to the ring and jiggled it. He set the box on the counter.

"Who knew you were such a girl," Dave teased.

Casey frowned. "Shut up."

Tommy tugged at her jacket and pulled her close, bodies pressed together. He wrapped his arms around her waist while she rested her hands near his elbows. He loved the thrilled skip in her heartbeat as he kissed her. Her lip gloss - probably borrowed from Bobby - tasted like green apples. Her arms looped around his neck and she hung off him a bit, so he had to hold her tighter, which might've been her intention.

Her T-shirt lifted a bit as she stretched, so his fingers touched her bare skin. Tommy became very aware of his friends in the room. Casey smiled against his lips. Did she sense his hesitation? He could've kissed her a lot better and probably forever but PDA made him self-conscious. She kissed him harder, fervent and loving. Her careful, calloused hands drifted down his torso and gripped his hoodie, pulling him against her. He lost himself in her eager touch.

His fingers lightly cupped her face. He yanked himself away from her.

"Aw," Cole smiled.

Dave shrugged. "Eh, you've seen it once, you've seen it a thousand times."

Tommy pinched the angel wing necklace hanging from Casey's neck, exactly where it always was.

He remembered wanting to get her something special for her birthday. He considered flowers, gag gifts, chocolates, a specialty-made knife - which he would've gotten but Betty gave her one already - Nothing was good enough. Tommy saw the necklace on display at a Burrows' pawnshop. Its unique design and silvery finish were like one of her knives but it wasn't dangerous, it was celestial. He hoped it'd remind her that she had a soul and one of the best hearts he'd ever known. He couldn't afford it but he could steal it. Dave acted as his lookout. Like taking candy from a baby, Tommy took the necklace from the glass case and went to meet Casey on their rooftop.

"Have you talked to Alice?" He let the necklace go.

She clicked her tongue, unhappy with the question. "Nope."

"Have you found the blogger?" Dave sipped his coffee. His face revealed his nerves.

Tommy understood the fear. He hated lying to Casey but if she found out about Jess being the blogger and Dave being the mole, she'd be given a choice, a choice she couldn't come back from, and he didn't want her to be forced to make it. Hopefully, Betty would get pissed at something else soon and forget about Height City Anonymous.

"The kid, Red, hasn't gotten back to me yet," Casey shrugged. "Why do you care?"

"Just curious," Dave said, tapping one side of his mug. "You know the rule, nobody betrays Betty."

If anyone broke the rule, they'd end up dead, tortured, or thrown in The Arena where they'd be forced to face Cece. Whoever fought Cece usually died or wished they were dead.

"Hey," Tommy wanted to change the subject before Dave lost his cool. He hugged her, back against his chest. He kissed her head. "I told Timothy it was my birthday and he told his mom, so Martha invited me for dinner," his cheek brushed against her hair. "Wanna come?"

Casey held his hands, arms lying on his. "Am I invited?"

"Yeah, she wants you there. I want you there."

"I'm in."

Kenna came out of Dave's bedroom. Her dress was on backward and her hair was tied in a messy bun. She held her jacket in one hand and her shoes in the other. She stiffened when she saw everyone.

Tommy could feel how hard Casey was trying not to laugh. He hid his smile behind her head.

"Oh," Kenna frowned. "I didn't know Dave's crew was here."

"We should name ourselves that," Dave said.

"Over your dead body," Casey said. It was most likely a joke.

"Coffee?" Cole offered a mug to Kenna. "We have Pop-Tarts too."

"I'll take a Pop-Tart." Casey went to the snack cabinet, grabbed a box of s'mores-flavored Pop-Tarts, and reached inside.

"Uh, okay," Kenna chuckled, obviously uncomfortable. "Dave, call me." She grabbed her purse and hurried out of the apartment.

Cole waved.

As soon as the door closed, Dave rushed to lock it. He turned to the others. "Don't judge me."

"You're not gonna call her," Tommy said.

"No, but-"

Cole flicked his forehead. "Stop being a whore!"

"I'm not a whore!" Dave rubbed the wound.

"You're acting like one, so stop it. Idiom." Cole put his hands on his hips.

"You need a boyfriend," Dave frowned, more annoyed than angry.

Tommy plucked the Pop-Tart out of Casey's hand and set it on the counter. "We should go."

He wanted to get to the Cruise Estate early for his birthday dinner. He never really celebrated his birthday before. Paisley didn't buy him gifts or have parties for him. Sometimes, she'd bring him a slice of vanilla cake home from the diner. She'd light a candle and tell him to make a wish. He knew by the time he was five that birthday wishes didn't come true but he played along to keep his mom happy.

"I wasn't done eating that," Casey said.

"The sooner we leave, the sooner we get cake," Tommy said.

She chuckled. "Cake. Alright, let's go." She gestured to Dave and Cole. "Give the lovebirds their privacy."

"I am way out of his league," Cole said, almost offended.

Dave scoffed. "*You're* out of *my* league?"

He did not agree.

***

Cole

Cole hugged a stuffed dinosaur while he slept upside down on the couch. He'd fallen asleep watching *Friends* after he ate an entire bag of chocolate chips and a peanut butter and jelly sandwich. He dreamt of a purple eagle born in fire and a blue panther with a devilish grin racing through a colorful jungle. The sky was black and white checkers. Where were they going?

He wanted to follow them but a loud knock woke him.

He slurped the drool back into his mouth and shifted into a sitting position. He was a little dizzy from lying upside down. He wondered who was at the door. Probably Kenna. She must have come to yell at Dave for sleeping with other girls or maybe it was another girl ready to yell at him for sleeping with Kenna. People were exhausting.

Cole considered getting a complaint box to hang on their door but he doubted Dave would let him.

He opened the door. *Oh crap.* Shock and fear seized him like an electric shock. Lorenzo stood in front of him, looking angry, with a buff man behind him. He looked mean.

The little girl, Red, must've learned who the blogger and mole were but she didn't tell Casey, instead, she went straight to Betty with the information. Cole was worried she might do that but nobody ever listened to him.

He screamed, "DAVEY-"

Lorenzo punched him, knuckles cracking against Cole's cheek. The hit left a bell ringing in his head. Lorenzo shoved him against the wall and a frigid shake went up his spine. Gunshot. A bullet dug into his skin and tore his shoulder. Blood splattered, and Cole slid onto the floor.

The buff man went to Dave's bedroom. There were some muffled screams, then he came out, carrying Dave's unconscious body over his shoulder. How'd they drug him? Or did they hit him hard enough to knock him out?

Lorenzo laughed, slamming the door as they left.

Cole's breath overlapped. His heartbeat echoed alongside the rushing water in his ears and panic filled his chest. He pushed his back against the wall, getting to his feet. It took all his strength and focus to stay steady. Was one leg shorter than the other?

He put pressure on his wound, blood trickling down his torso and pooling on the floor, but he didn't care. He stumbled to the kitchen. He needed the first-aid kit and his phone. Where in the world was his freaking phone?

Chapter 22

Casey

THE BASEMENT WAS PITCH black. Car horns and truck engines echoed from outside. The mattress sagged from the weight of their bodies but it was still comfortable. Casey was curled perfectly against Tommy's torso. She felt him breathe - steady and constant - and his arm was draped over her body, warm and protective. Her fingers were lazily laced with his.

They had a great time at Martha's. She and Fernanda, the Cruises' maid, made Tommy a big, vanilla sheet cake with chocolate frosting. He blushed when the two women insisted on singing him "Happy Birthday." Martha lit the candles and Timothy helped him blow them out. Tommy didn't notice how much Timothy looked up to him but Casey did. They acted more like brothers than Tommy would let himself see.

He rubbed frosting on Casey's nose. In return, she grabbed a chunk of cake and smashed it in his face. Timothy laughed so hard he spit water out his nose. Martha took a picture and Fernanda lovingly lectured them about wasting good cake.

To see Tommy with them was incredible. He was unburdened, weightless. They helped him forget his guilt and darkness. It was a version of heaven that

Casey couldn't have. Being with Tommy made her feel loved, darkness included, but being around Alice made her feel like maybe she could be better than what she was. A feeling she didn't completely believe. She didn't regret choosing Betty but thinking about the decision gave her a stomachache.

Her phone buzzed. The screen lit up with an address and the red dress emoji. Casey groaned. Why couldn't Betty have the decency to let her sleep in? Whatever it was, it had to be important.

She slowly slid out of bed, careful not to wake Tommy. He wore plaid boxers and his brown hair was in disarray, he'd likely have a bedhead in the morning. He wasn't tense or wide awake like other nights. His job as Betty's enforcer kept his nightmares fresh.

Casey yanked her leather jacket over her baggy T-shirt - it was Tommy's T-shirt - and grabbed her boots. She checked the pockets to make sure each one held a knife. She slid on some jeans, stuffed her phone in her pocket, and left the basement.

Eddie's Bar was empty, the black sky reflecting in the front window's glass. The stars were starting to disappear as the sun rose over the city. It was too early to care how beautiful it was.

The address Betty texted was one of her little prisons. This particular prison was near the Trenches, Destroyer's territory, the worst part of Height City. Supposedly, only Destroyer and her gang lived there. Everyone else never dared venture across the border.

The first room was barely lit. The walls were drenched in dry blood and the floors had a layer of grime and loose teeth. It smelled like copper. A rusted, metal door led to the back area where pained, muffled grunts were echoing.

She could almost see the first time she tortured someone. Her victim's puffy, bruised face, bloody clothes, hair, cut skin, and tear-filled eyes. Her fists were raw, trembling, and her blue hair was drenched in blood. Tears stained her face. She remembered her reflection in the blade. Clear as day. Betty rewarded her with a pat on the back and a proud snicker. *Well done, Cece*, she had said.

Lorenzo walked in, wiping his bloody hands on an even bloodier rag. He had fresh bruises on his knuckles. He nodded toward the door. "Your next fight is tonight, your victim's in there."

She never saw her victims - opponents - before they faced each other in The Arena. What made this one any different? Who was the next name on Betty Beater's Most Wanted list?

The rusted door creaked open.

His wrists were raw under the ties. Half his nails were torn off and his fingers were bruised, most likely smashed with a hammer. His right eye was huge, red, and puffy, punched repeatedly. His cheek had a giant, black and blue gash. Was his jaw crooked? His nose and everything below his neck were drenched in dark red blood. Was he breathing?

The puzzle put itself together. If Dave was the mole, then Jess was the blogger. Little Miss Journalist and Marson Junior, such a pair of dumbasses.

"He hasn't told us who Height City Anonymous is." Lorenzo finished wiping his fingers. He took a sharp, rusted ax from his torture toolkit - a large briefcase filled with weapons and surgical tools - and blew on the edges. He stood behind her, forcing her to stay and stare at her injured friend. "Betty knows you two are friends. She needs to know it doesn't matter. She knows you'll kill him."

Casey never thought Dave would be her victim. He was smarter than this. He knew how to survive in Height City, in the Burrows, as well as she did, maybe better than she did.

Jess was supposed to be smart too but this had to be her mistake.

Now, Casey would have to slice Tommy and Alice's best friends' throats. She gulped at the thought. It was enough to make her skin tighten.

She squeezed his broken nose. Dave tried to scream but he couldn't. He started coughing. The blue in his eyes was hidden by misery, blood trickling onto his lip. He whispered something but it was lost in his weakness. It didn't matter what it was.

"Nobody betrays Betty Beater." Casey could taste her ruthlessness.

She let him go and his head fell forward.

This was the job description. Kill whoever broke the rules. She was the champion, the enforcer, the prodigy. This is what she lived for.

"See you tonight, Cece," Lorenzo said.

She smirked. "Can't wait."

***

Alice

Vibrations soured through her arm and white lightning blasted the door off its hinges, snapping it in half, and the two pieces hit the floor like giant toothpicks. She'd worry about the property damage later.

A trail of blood led from the door to the kitchen. Cole lay in the puddle, his fingers loosely wrapped around his phone. He was comatose.

Her sneakers squeaked on the blood. Alice knelt beside him and put her ear to his chest. His heartbeat seemed silent but when she checked his pulse, it was a faint whisper. She didn't know CPR and she wasn't a surgeon. What could she possibly do? Was she going to have to watch another loved one die? She couldn't handle that. There had to be a way.

"Please don't die," Alice whispered.

She took a deep breath. The number on her pulse tracker rose but it didn't beep. She counted to ten in her head. What happened to him? The first-aid kit was lying open on the floor. Its contents - bandages, tweezers, needles, thread, and several other things - were scattered across the kitchen, and so was the blood-covered bullet. He must've patched himself up.

But why wasn't he waking up?

"Don't you dare." Alice didn't know what to do. Her pulse tracker beeped. The number was high. She was panicking. She started panting, wanting to cry. Her lightning flickered. Wait, her powers. Energy. Electricity. *That's it.*

454

She ripped his shirt and slapped her hands against his bare chest. His belly was solid, brawny, not too much but nothing to be ashamed of. Her fingers sparked. Vibrations coursed through her body, squeezed her muscles, and raced to her palms. Like a wicked punch to the gut, electricity crashed between them.

Alice fell on her butt.

Cole gasped. He sat up, darty-eyed and panicked. He reached out and grabbed Alice's arm. His entire body was shaking.

Alice chuckled. Her powers were better than she thought. She squeezed his shoulder. He looked at her, seemingly confused, which was understandable.

"Are you okay?" she asked.

His forehead wrinkled. He glanced at his ripped T-shirt and patted himself down. "I... I think so?"

"Good enough." Alice got to her feet and yanked him up. He stumbled forward but she steadied him.

Cole held onto her for support, using her as a crutch. "He got taken. He's gonna have to fight... The Arena... he might be dead."

His knees buckled. Alice helped him to the floor, feet splashing in the puddle of blood. He leaned against the cabinets and rubbed his forehead, panting. He felt the bandage on his shoulder as if he hadn't realized it'd been there until now.

"Who?" Alice clutched his wrist. Whatever he had to say was urgent but the pieces weren't all there. She needed to know everything if she was going to do something about it.

He met her gaze with a serious stare. "Dave."

"Dave?" she paused. "The Arena," she covered a gasp. "He's gonna have to fight Cece?"

"Yeah-huh!" Cole pressed his hand against his chest. Was he having a heart attack?

She needed to stop recklessly testing her powers. Though to be fair, she had limited options at the time.

"Tell me where he is. I'll grab him," she said.

Cole shook his head. "No. He would be hunted. He has to die or win against the champion," he looked at the floor with a mournful, thoughtful expression. "He's doomed, and so is Jess as soon as they find out she's the blogger." He never looked less like himself. "Cece has to kill them."

Alice wasn't willing to accept that. She could find a way out of this. She had to. What option had a good outcome? She felt like screaming. She twirled the emerald ring on her finger - the one Grandma Scotts had given her - using the movement to help her focus, to help her think. It had some of Cole's blood on it but the emerald still sparkled. What was she supposed to do? How was Alice supposed to fight Cece?

She called Jess.

"Hello?"

"Dave got taken," Alice blurted out. It probably wasn't the best way to break the news. "They know he's the mole." She counted the ring's rotations in her head. *One, two, three, four, five.* She twirled it fast. The blood stained her fingers.

Jess didn't say anything for twelve rotations. She was holding back tears. "What?"

A quiet rustling came from the speaker. "Hey, it's me," Leo said. "What's going on?"

"Dave got taken. He's gonna have to fight in The Arena against Cece, then she'll probably come for Jess. I have an idea but I'm not sure I'm capable." Alice could fight Cece. They could battle for their friends but one would have to lose. The loss would most likely end in death. Alice couldn't be a killer. Cece was one. The odds weren't in her favor.

"This is all my fault," Jess said. "I shouldn't have-"

"Do you think she'd really hurt them? Would she actually kill her friends?" Leo asked. "Our friends. She's better than that."

Alice couldn't answer his questions. She didn't know what Cece was capable of or what she'd do. To her, the Crime Queen didn't seem to be a villain. Cece had mixed emotions about Betty Beater. She couldn't see through her own twisted loyalties.

Cole yanked himself to his feet. He wobbled but when Alice offered him a hand, he shook his head. He never looked so serious. He never seemed more solemn or focused. It was almost creepy. "I think there's something you should know," he said. "It's a long story and Case," he paused. "Cece won't like that I told you."

"Jess? Leo? Stay safe, okay? I have to go." She hung up. Alice knew Cece had secrets. This was the moment she learned them. "What don't I know?"

***

Cole

Cole hated betrayal but the truth could only help now. There were too many lies. He wouldn't let his friends die. He couldn't let Casey become the monster she considered herself to be. He loved them all too much, he wouldn't let them fall apart.

"What don't I know?" Alice asked.

"Her real name for starters," he said. He groaned. His shoulder hurt. He couldn't remember taking the bullet out but he knew he did it. He wasn't sure where it was either. "We grew up at St.Marian's. We weren't really friends. I was the runt of the litter and she was... Alone... Angry..."

When Cole was a kid, a boy twice his size pushed him into a wall so hard that his arm broke. He still had the scar. The bigger boy didn't care. He beat Cole. Every orphan felt unloved and unwanted. The more aggressive ones ran the show. Before the boy could hurt Cole any worse, a girl whacked him in the head with an umbrella.

The boy fell and yelled out, whimpering in pain.

He rolled onto his back and the girl raised the umbrella above her head, ready to hit him again. The girl had long, blonde hair and piercing green eyes. She

457

didn't have many friends in the orphanage. Cole knew the stories about her; The way she stole food for the younger kids or snuck onto the roof to walk the ledge or watch the sky. A few kids were spreading rumors about her somehow leaving the orphanage altogether.

You okay? she asked. Cole nodded despite the raging pain in his broken arm.

Before she could bring the umbrella down on the other boy's head, a nun grabbed her wrist, making her drop the umbrella. The horror of getting caught - which lit up her face - didn't stop her from struggling. The nun took her into a room and locked the door. Her agonizing screams echoed from inside it, unmuffled and terrified.

The next day, Cole saw the fresh, bloody belt marks on her lower back. The nuns at St.Marian's liked to punish the kids they deemed rebellious or bad listeners. Casey was both.

She saw him through the full-length mirror the girls all shared. She didn't smile or frown. Her face didn't show any emotion but the bags under her eyes signaled she'd been up all night, probably in pain, maybe in tears.

"We called her Jane for Jane Doe or blondie back then," Cole told Alice. "The nuns didn't care about what we called ourselves unless we already had names, they knew us by our bed numbers. Casey came up with her name after one of the nuns died. Some kids said she stole the name." He couldn't help but wonder if Casey really did steal her name. She never confirmed or denied the rumor. "And Cavalier is the last name she created for herself."

"Casey Cavalier," Alice said for the first time.

He nodded. "Betty gave her the name Cece and helped create the whole champion persona. She put Casey and Tommy through things, made them-" he broke off.

He heard stories about Dave and Tommy's childhoods, not only the things Ted and Paisley put them through but the things Betty and Hobbs taught them, forced them to take part in, it was why Cole didn't join her too. Then Casey became her student. Betty wanted to mold them into monstrous soldiers.

Sometimes it was harder to be an independent but Cole didn't care. He didn't want to kill. He didn't want blood on his hands or to know how to torture someone. He'd been through his fair share of trauma and he wouldn't wish his childhood on anyone but he didn't escape one nightmare just to enter another.

"I am going to save her," Alice said, determined. Her gaze was serious, more serious than she probably realized. She squeezed his hand. Was she trying to comfort herself or him?

Cole didn't want her to make a promise she couldn't keep. If she tried, that was enough. He just needed her to try.

"Can I borrow your phone?"

***

Casey

Casey couldn't get Dave's bruises out of her head. What did he try to tell her? Was he begging her to let him live? Was he begging her to let Jess live? She unlocked the basement door and went inside where she found Tommy sitting on the couch's armrest, phone in hand.

She figured he lied about his inability to hack Height City Anonymous. He knew all along and never said a word. What, didn't he trust her?

"I lied," he said. "I shouldn't have but I'm terrified you're gonna kill him."

At least he didn't waste any time. The concern in his eyes made her heart sink. It wasn't concern for Dave or Jess's lives, it was concern for Casey's soul. He didn't know if she'd kill his best friend or not. She couldn't blame him for lying. He wanted to protect her and their friends. How could she be angry at him for that?

She had bigger problems.

"He's the mole. Jess is the blogger and I'm the champion," she said. It was simple in theory. She needed to do her job. Murder was her middle name. Wait, she didn't have a middle name. Murder was her purpose. Simple.

"These are people we care about. Jess is Alice's best friend. Dave is mine. You can't kill them, you can't do this," Tommy said. "This isn't who you are."

She couldn't picture herself hurting Dave or Jess but that didn't mean she couldn't do it. If she chose to save them, it meant betraying Betty. It meant hurting the woman who made her. Betty made her strong, skilled. She was the reason Casey was alive. She loved her. She owed her. But it was more than that.

Casey Cavalier was an orphaned little girl left in a basket. Abused by nuns, unloved, alone, and punished for taking extra scraps of food, not for herself but for the younger kids at St.Marian's Orphanage. She was beaten down for standing up until she snuck out. She didn't want to be helpless again.

Cece was Betty's champion. A strong, feared, respected warrior. She had a future. She was going to be the next Crime Queen. She'd own Height City someday. Betty gave her that. Betty trained her for it. She liked that future. She liked the power.

"I can't do this for you." Tommy kept himself still, waiting. He wanted to tell her what the right decision was but he didn't, which she appreciated.

She stepped closer to him, feeling the need for a little support. She put her hands on his shoulders. His hoodie was soft, worn, under her fingers. She could feel his muscles. She liked how his body wasn't bulky or too showy but if he needed to, he could carry her to safety or beat her in an arm wrestling competition.

He held her waist. With him sitting on the armrest, he was shorter than her, which was weird.

She needed help. She didn't know what to do.

"I don't know who I want to be," she admitted. "Cece or Casey. I feel like two different people and I don't know which one is real anymore." She wouldn't have told anyone else, not even Alice. Tommy was the only person who knew both sides of who she was. Cece or Casey. The champion or the survivor. "I don't know which version of me is better. Cece is-"

"Cece is a bitch," Tommy said so bluntly it almost made her laugh. He cupped her face in his hands and forced her to focus on him. He whispered in a firm, honest tone, "Bobby, Alice, Cole, Dave," he paused as if choosing the right words. "We don't love Cece the Champion. That's just a mask you wear but Casey Cavalier," he smiled. His bright, perfect smile. "You're freaking incredible."

His thumbs brushed her cheeks as he wiped away her tears. She found comfort in his embrace.

She sat on his thigh and laid her head on his shoulder. He kissed her forehead and played with her hair, his fingers tickling her neck. She let him hold her. She let him protect her from what she had to do.

She closed her eyes. What person did she want to be?

Chapter 23

Jess

GUILT MADE JESS'S HEART ache. One stupid mistake and her entire life was over. Dave was out there right now, hurt and alone. He was going to die and it was her fault. Height City deserved the truth but not at the cost of their lives.

"Where do you think we go when we die?" Leo was lying on her bed, staring at the ceiling, hands folded on his belly. He seemed too calm. Why wasn't he freaking out more?

Jess needed to do something. Her cuticles were bleeding so much, she couldn't pick them anymore. She grabbed the taser off her dresser - the one Cole had gifted her - and dropped it in her purse. She headed to the door but Leo beat her there.

He spread his arms to block her way. "This is a really bad idea!"

She didn't care. She tried to push past him but he grabbed her. He swung her toward the bed and made her sit down. She stood up. She wasn't going to sit and wait to hear whether or not Dave was alive. She wanted to help save him.

"What are you gonna do? Trade yourself for him?" Leo asked.

"Maybe." It took everything she had not to cry. "I have to help him somehow. He shouldn't die because of what I did. I... I don't want him to die," she paused. The tears escaped her eyes. "I don't want to die."

Jess wasn't ready to die. She hadn't lived yet. She wondered how her parents would handle her death. Would they be able to move on? Would they be okay? Would they get divorced? Would they stay together? Would their lives be completely ruined because of her choices? Why, even after all she did to move past their plans for her, was she still thinking about how they would be affected by how she lived?

"Alice is gonna save him," Leo said without a trace of doubt. "You have to trust her."

Jess wanted to argue. She wanted to race out the door, drive to The Arena, and save her ex-boyfriend. Her stupid, frustrating ex-boyfriend who taught her how to be fearless and take risks. She couldn't save him. She dropped her purse and sunk onto the bed, biting her cuticles. Picking them wasn't enough. "I don't trust Casey."

"Who?" Leo asked.

"Cece." Jess pulled her knees against her chest. "Casey is her real name. Dave told me by accident." When she tried searching for Casey on the internet, nothing came up. When she searched Cece the Champion, only rumors and chats from the dark web came up. "What if she kills us?"

Leo wrapped his arm around her. He rubbed her back, trying to comfort her, but it didn't help. She laid her head on his shoulder. Having him there made her feel less alone, at least.

They sat in silence.

Jess thought about Dave. The careful, strong way he touched her, the passionate way he kissed her, the blue in his eyes, the charm of his smile. He could lift her up and carry her. He taught her how to pick a lock. On their first date, at Eddie's Bar, he wanted to teach her to play pool but she already knew how to play. She learned on Tony's pool table but Dave was excited to teach her, so she let him. She loved his arms around her and how he whispered in her ear. She wore a leather skirt she knew he'd like. After a few games, she started to win.

Someone learns fast, Dave had said, suspicious.

Beginner's luck? She didn't want him to know she faked it but when he called her out about knowing how to play, she reluctantly admitted it.

He laughed, impressed, and pulled her against him. He kissed her.

Jess wasn't sure if she felt it then or later, but at some point, she had fallen in love with him. And she never got to tell him.

"I wonder if any of the religions have it right." She had read about certain religions and their beliefs. She wasn't sure which one she agreed with. "Maybe some version of heaven or hell is real or maybe we become energy for some other form of matter." The logical scientist in her wanted to believe that. No heaven, no hell, but a transformation instead. "We wouldn't feel anything but we'd still contribute to the circle of life."

"I like that," Leo said. "But I think I prefer the version where you're with your loved ones. When I, you know," he paused for emphasis. "I'll see my mom and my grandpa. Everyone I've ever loved and lost will be there and I'll be at peace," he shrugged. "Or I'll be happy or whatever."

"You're not gonna die, Leo." Jess wondered what Layla would have written on her headstone, maybe something like *RIP Jessica Peace, the daughter who never achieved my dream.* Layla would probably be relieved to see Jess go. She wouldn't have to deal with her daughter's rebellion and everyone would have sympathy for her. Jess sighed. "You'll grow old, have kids, have a life."

She wasn't sure what she pictured Leo's future as, maybe he'd be a teacher like his dad or maybe he'd be a movie director. He liked movies. Did he want kids? Did he believe in marriage? She couldn't answer those questions for herself, how could she expect him to know?

"You're not gonna die either. You guys are gonna live," he said. "I know it."

Jess wished she believed him.

***

Cole

Cole couldn't breathe. His emotional stress was giving him a headache. His injured shoulder hurt with every movement. He could barely keep up with Alice's determined strides. Her long, purple ponytail bounced behind her head, sneakers clapping against the sidewalk. Was his heartbeat shaking?

He wished they could've taken a cab. "How are you so fast?"

"I'm going slow for you!" she said.

"That's just not fair," he huffed. Was it possible for lungs to ache? The Arena didn't seem so far on other days but now it seemed a million miles away. They couldn't get there fast enough.

The Arena was packed with every Burrower in town. Their cheers and screams were like sirens. Why was everyone so excited? As far as they knew, this was just another fight, nothing special.

"I heard the opponent tonight is David, the Marson boy," Liam Hale laughed, standing next to Billy. Both boys were watching the empty cage, which wouldn't be empty for long.

"Really?" Billy asked, uninterested in the conversation.

Cole stood still as the crowd moved and weaved around him. He held tight to Alice's wrist, so they wouldn't lose each other in the chaos. He forgot all about Liam and Billy when he saw red and orange curls through everyone's scars and tattoos.

Bobby and Tommy were together.

"Thomas!" Cole shouted.

"Who?" Alice asked.

Bobby was playing with the tulle of her tutu. As a Burrower, she could understand why everyone was so excited. Cole used to love Cece's fights. She kicked ass every single time, sometimes it got to be repetitive, her unwavering winning streak. This was different. This wasn't entertaining or fun. He couldn't stand in the crowd, eat popcorn, and root for her. They wouldn't go to Sally's Place later, sit in the corner booth, and talk about the highlights of the fight. This was a lose-lose situation. Either Dave would die or the champion would. Neither option was good.

"She's gonna fight," Tommy said, unnervingly calm.

Cole swore he heard wrong. "You couldn't talk her out of it?"

"I didn't try."

"What are you doing here?" Alice asked. The edge in her voice showed how worried she was. Her eyes searched the crowd for any sign of Casey but it was pointless. The champion wouldn't be brought out until the fight was about to start.

"Two of my best friends in the entire world are about to fight to the death," Bobby said. "I wouldn't miss it. I have to be here."

Cole looked around. The vibrating thrill of the crowds' shouts and whispers made him want to scream. Why were these people taking bets without Dave? Why were they excited and eager when Cole was about to lose his friends? His family.

***

Dave

Beads of blood dripped down his face. The excited cheers blurred against his ears as if he were floating underwater. The ties on his wrists made his skin raw and itchy. His eye was swollen and his cheek hurt like hell. The fluorescent spotlight burned his vision. Was he breathing? He couldn't tell.

Dave tried to picture how he looked but all that came to mind was his mother's beaten corpse on a broken Lego set. He'd probably see her soon.

Blue hair and devilish green eyes blurred in his blackening sight. Part of him was ready to die. He always thought he would've moved up in the world before it happened. He'd make something of himself. Instead, he was just a Marson. Less than nothing. He wished he could've lived.

***

Casey

They cheered her name. They cheered for their champion. Their voices drowned out her heartbeat, which was slamming against her chest, bruising her bones. She had a choice to make.

She looked beyond the cage's isolation. *Purple hair? Alice?*

Tommy, Cole, and Bobby stood behind her, staring at the cage. Each of their faces was different; Cole looked terrified and worried, almost as worried as Alice. She was shifting on her feet, desperate to do something. Bobby had her hands in a ball like she was praying but she didn't look scared. She had a hopeful gleam in her eye. Tommy had his unreadable expression, no worry, doubt or fear until he pointed to the other side of the cage.

Casey turned her head. A long, red dress surrounded by cigar smoke glimmered in the dark corner. The beautiful Asian woman wearing it had an elegant frown and a calculated, devilish stare. Anyone who noticed her quickly turned to get out of her way. *Betty's here. Betty's watching.*

Casey grabbed Dave's chin, nails digging into his skin with bruising pressure. He could barely stand on his own, let alone fight. This would be boring, easy, which was disappointing. The crowd wanted some excitement. "Cece! Cece! Cece!"

Did he reveal Jess's identity? No. He would've died to keep her safe.

Casey jammed a syringe into his thigh. He gasped, eyes widening, adrenaline returning. Their fight had to be fair. She wouldn't fight him if he couldn't defend himself.

She punched him, knuckles slamming against his broken nose. His blood splattered across her face and he stumbled, shaking off the hit. He turned to her, wide awake, a question in his eyes.

She didn't answer.

She swung her arm but he blocked it. He ducked two punches. Dave knew how she fought better than most people. They sparred enough times for him to know how she thought in battle. She had to throw him off track, mix it up. She kicked him in the stomach and he staggered back. She attacked again. He dodged her fists, then ducked under her foot.

He moved fast despite his bruises.

Who did Casey want to be? What path did she want to take? What name was really hers? Did her loyalties lie with her friends or with the woman who made her?

She caught Dave's fist. He almost punched her throat but she knew how he fought too. She swung herself around his body.

The Arena whirled in her vision until the entire room was upside down. She squeezed Dave's throat between her thighs. He stumbled forward from her weight and they hit the floor. The cement was cold and hard against her body. She stretched his arm against her torso, ready to break it. Her legs still around his neck, she felt his windpipe close. His body stiffened. He tried to struggle but she had him locked. He slapped her boots, trying to breathe.

The Burrowers' cheers swirled around her. The echoes of her two names made her dizzy.

If she did this, if she chose to kill him, she'd be giving up the girl with the purple hair. She'd be giving up her best friend and the guy she loved. She'd be choosing to be a villain. She'd be choosing Betty, instead of loyalty. She wasn't sure when her loyalties shifted but at some point, they did. She didn't want to fight for the Crime Queen. She wanted to fight for the people who made her better.

She let Dave go.

He gasped and coughed, panting.

Casey jumped to her feet and pulled a knife from her boot, twirling it between her fingers, one foot on either side of him. Dave lay still. She held the knife above her head, the silver reflecting in the spotlight.

The cheers got louder, more excited and desperate.

Anger and betrayal twitched in Dave's stone-cold expression. What was he thinking? Was he expecting her to stab him?

They both knew he couldn't beat her.

***

Bobby

Bobby couldn't look away. Her grip tightened around Tommy and Cole's fingers. They kept her from running to the cage and screaming Casey's name. Was this the moment Casey lost her soul?

She knelt on Dave's stomach, blade against his throat. His blood seeped down her knuckles and pooled beside them both, making a mess on the cement. He held still, ready for death. He couldn't do anything to stop it.

The crowd screamed in Cece's favor. Their champion. She leaned forward and put her face over Dave's. Was she going to kiss his cheek?

Their bodies glowed in the spotlight. Ted Marson's son and Cece the Champion. Bobby doubted anyone could've predicted this match-up.

In one swift motion, Dave snatched a knife from Casey's boot and jammed it into her side. He twisted the blade, digging it deeper into her skin, and blood splattered across his bruises.

Casey dropped her knife. The silver blade splashed in the pool of Dave's blood as hers mixed with it. She grabbed her wound but the blood wouldn't stop. Dave cradled her head and laid her down, kind and respectful. He scrambled to his knees and dropped his blade beside hers. Both knives shined in their shared blood.

Casey was still, serene. *She's not breathing.*

Chapter 24

Alice

"NOOO!!!!" Bobby screamed. Tommy held her in his arms. He kept her from falling to her knees or running to the cage. She squirmed and cried, trying to loosen his grip. She tried to push him away but he wouldn't let her go. He hugged her, back against his chest. His face, his emotion, was unreadable. How could he not react to his girlfriend's death?

Alice didn't understand. How did Casey lose? She was lying on the floor, drenched in her own blood, next to Dave. His neck was bleeding. He'd have several new scars but he'd live. He stood on his knees, panting and wide-eyed. He probably couldn't believe what he did.

Nobody seemed to believe it.

The Arena was silent, staring at their champion. Casey looked dead. She wasn't moving. Her skin was pale, her blood was dark and her eyes were closed.

Alice's heart sank into her belly. She felt nauseous. Hot tears stung her eyes. How was this happening again? How was she losing someone she loved again? Her best friend. Her sidekick. The girl with the blue hair, the first person to know Alice's secrets, was gone. How? Wasn't Casey supposed to be invincible? She acted like she was.

The Arena erupted into shocked whispers.

"Get her to Jess!" Tommy whispered-yelled.

A muscular, African-American man with long, blond dreadlocks and many peaceful tattoos stepped into the cage. He blew a loud, annoying horn and all the Burrowers went silent. He looked at Dave, who was about to pass out, then at Casey's body. He took both blood-covered knives and raised them above his head in honor of the fallen champion, in honor of Cece.

Alice decided to do exactly what Tommy ordered. She ran out of The Arena. Giant vibrations twisted her insides and she launched off the ground. Into the sky she went, then right back down into the building, zooming through the bars, she grabbed Casey and flew across the city.

Over rooftops, streets, cars, people. There was no time to enjoy it.

When she arrived at Jess's house, Alice crashed through the window, making glass shards sprinkle the carpet, as she transformed back into herself. Both their bodies became physical.

Casey lay on the carpet, panting and sweating. The blood leaked through her clothes - a white tank top under a black, cropped T-shirt - and drenched the carpet.

Leo and Jess hopped off the bed and stared in disbelief. What were they waiting for? A giant banner that said "help"?

Jess knelt next to Casey, putting pressure on the wound. Leo stood behind her, wide-eyed and panicked. Jess used her sheets as a giant gauze and pointed to the bathroom. "First-aid kit!"

Alice was glad they decided to put a specialty-made first-aid kit in Jess's house. Like the one at Cole and Dave's apartment, it included items that could be used for bullet wounds and other near-fatal injuries.

Leo went to get it. He came back and gave it to Jess with a trembling hand.

Alice squeezed Casey's hand so hard she could feel her pulse. She couldn't let go. How was Casey alive right now? How was she breathing? It looked like Dave had killed her.

"What was that? What did you do?" Alice asked. She tried to go over the events, the fight, the stab, the cheers but she couldn't figure it out. None of it was really clear.

Casey's pulse was steady and her breathing was fine, a little heavy. She was the calmest one in the room. "I'll tell you when I'm done bleeding."

Alice nodded once. "Right, yeah, good idea."

"No vital organs were hit. She seems fine, just a lot of blood." Jess pushed gauze on Casey's wound. Her hands worked skillfully and carefully on Casey's body. She cleaned the wound with alcohol pads and a warm wash rag. "Who did this?"

"Your ex-boyfriend," Casey leaned her head back. She hid her pain well. "T and I weren't the only ones who learned a thing or two from the Crime Queen." She chuckled, a dry, tired chuckle. Her nails dug into Alice's shoulder as she bit her lip to keep from screaming.

"Dave's alive?" Jess asked, surprised and trying to stay focused.

"Yeah, he's alive," Casey said without a trace of regret.

Leo laughed. He bent over his knees, finally able to breathe.

Jess kept her relief quiet but her smile revealed how happy she was to hear Dave was okay. She muttered the tips from her books as she sewed Casey's wound closed. Her hands didn't shake or tremble and her focus never wavered. She had practiced stitching on her stuffed animals. She bandaged Casey's skin. Her fingers were stained in blood and sweat dripped from her forehead. When she finished, she sighed. "It'll leave a scar but you'll be okay."

Bloody sheets, bandages, alcohol pads, and thread were scattered across her bedroom floor.

Casey lay flat on her back, breathing evenly, as she closed her eyes and smiled. She looked as relieved as Alice felt.

Leo patted Jess's shoulder, fist-bumped Casey, and hugged Alice.

She needed a hug more than she realized. She started crying. She couldn't help it. She wiped the tears with her wrist, taking a few deep breaths. Relief, happiness, stress, and anxiety mixed together, forming a brick in her belly, but she was able to laugh. She wasn't sure why she laughed, it just happened.

The doorbell rang, so Jess and Leo went to answer it, which was good because Alice needed to talk to Casey alone. It'd been months since they were in the same room. They hadn't spoken to each other in just as long. Alice wasn't sure what to say first.

She missed Casey so much. Casey, Cece, whichever was her real name, she was one of the most important people in Alice's life.

Alice handed her Jess's robe to cover up, then helped her stand. Casey's shirt was balled up on the floor drenched in her and Dave's blood. The girls sat side by side on the edge of Jess's bed.

"You didn't kill him," Alice said. She wasn't sure if she was surprised or not. She was afraid that Casey would kill Dave, then Jess. Seeing her become Height City's Crime Queen would've been a real life nightmare. Alice knew about The Arena but she didn't know about Casey's time at St.Marian's or how much she'd actually done for Betty Beater. Cole filled her in on a lot but there were probably things he didn't even know. Casey kept the darkest parts of herself away from prying eyes. Alice was ready to listen. She wanted to understand. She wanted to repair the damage between them.

"I couldn't," Casey stared at the bloodstains on the carpet, fiddling with her angel wing necklace. "I thought I would but when it came down to it, I couldn't." The memory of the fight pushed tears from her eyes. For once, she didn't look like the invincible badass she portrayed herself to be. She was scared, worried, and stuck in disbelief. She held tight to her necklace, squeezing the charm like she needed it to breathe. "She's gonna kill me."

Alice knew who she meant. The Crime Queen. Casey broke the rules. Betty would hunt her down through the streets and kill her as soon as she slipped up. Alice wasn't going to let that happen. She wasn't going to let Casey fight alone.

"Do you trust me?" Alice asked. She wanted to hear it. She needed to know Casey wasn't going to turn her back again. She needed to know they were in this together.

Casey looked her in the eye, considering her answer. "Yeah, Al," she paused. "I trust you."

"Then we'll beat her together," Alice said.

Casey chuckled, amused but appreciative. "We, huh?"

Alice hugged her, arms wrapped around Casey's shoulders. She needed the hug too. She liked feeling Casey breathe, knowing she was alive. Casey leaned her head against Alice's. She couldn't move very well, thanks to her wound, but she didn't tense or pull away. She seemed comfortable, even grateful for the embrace. Nothing could ever tear them apart again, Alice wouldn't let it.

***

Jess

Jess smiled at Alice and Casey sitting together on her bed. She was proud of how well she handled the patchwork. The wound wasn't deep, it'd barely leave a scar, but Jess was glad to know she could be useful. All the medical books she read came in handy.

She leaned against the wall across from Bobby.

Leo and Cole stood by their sides.

"Bring it in," Leo spread out his arms. Cole hugged him. They patted each other's backs and made room for the girls. Jess wrapped her arm around Cole while Bobby hugged Leo. The night finally seemed calm. A peaceful ending.

"You got chicken wings?" Cole asked. Layla and Bennett were at an event for the children's hospital. They'd be gone for another two hours, maybe longer, so the group had the house to themselves.

"We have chicken but it isn't in wing form," Jess said.

They headed down the stairs.

***

Bobby

Bobby and Leo followed behind Jess and Cole. When they realized their arms were still around each other, they pulled apart, feeling awkward. Bobby hated this weird limbo they were in. Part of her wanted to jump in and take the risk. The other part was terrified, what if she was wrong about him?

He gently nudged her - his smile made her happy - and went to the bottom of the staircase.

Bobby listened to Casey admit trust. Why couldn't she? Leo was a good guy. He cared about her. He was sweet. He was smart and funny. She needed to trust her gut. She knew who he was. He wouldn't harm her. Leo wasn't Johnny.

She met him at the last step and grabbed his hand. He looked at her, fingers starting to sweat, clammy but in the best way ever. All she felt was safety, love, and butterflies. She wanted to take a chance.

They both deserved that.

Bobby leaned in closer. Leo didn't move. He wasn't tense but he wasn't relaxed either. He didn't pull away. She touched his cheek and her other hand held his shoulder. He chuckled, unable to stop himself. His nervous heart hammered against his chest. She loved how excited he was to be so close to her. Arms dangling at his sides, he didn't know what to do.

She kissed him. At first, it was light, careful, then she dived in. She pulled him closer and explored the idea of them together. He wasn't an experienced kisser, so she had to guide him. She took his hands and put them on her waist. She kissed him again, deeper, sweeter.

His hands drifted curiously up her shoulders and lingered in her curls. He smiled. He looked at her like she was a dream coming true. Nobody had ever looked at her like that before. Leo kissed her again with a little more confidence. His lips were excited. He couldn't hide his happiness. It was adorable.

It wasn't Bobby's first kiss but it was definitely her best.

***

Cole

Cole flipped through the giant envelopes all addressed to Jessica Peace. Each one held an acceptance letter. Journalism schools, law schools, and scholarships. It was amazing. He always knew Jess was smart but this was plain impressive. "Why aren't you excited?"

She handed him a paper plate with some cold chicken strips.

He smiled, starved, and ate one. It'd been a long, stressful night. He hadn't eaten anything all day. He was glad everything worked out. It'd be weird to see Dave as champion but at least Casey and Alice were back together.

"My parents are over the moon that I got into Zak City Law but I'm just not," Jess shrugged. She never got excited about her future but when she looked at the envelopes, she seemed void, depressed. "I don't want to be a lawyer. I want to be a journalist."

"So go to journalism school," he said. Cole never thought too seriously about his future. People in the Burrows didn't live long, safe lives. He figured it was best to focus on the present.

"My mom would hate me. I'd probably kill her with the news and," Jess paused. She leaned on the counter and cupped her hands together, picking her cuticles. "What about my blog?"

Bobby and Leo came into the kitchen. Leo was blushing. He had lipstick on his lips. And Bobby looked happier than she had ever been. They were holding hands, which was good. Cole wondered when they'd finally get together.

He held up the college envelopes. "Our girl got into college." He didn't want to embarrass the new couple by asking uninvited questions. "Woohoo!"

"Wow, that's a lot of acceptances," Leo chuckled. He hugged Jess in congratulations.

Bobby grabbed a piece of chicken, tossed it in her mouth, and looked over the envelopes. She smiled. "Which one are you gonna go to?"

"I don't know." Jess wasn't excited. The conversation made her hesitant, unsure. "I don't want to disappoint my parents but I don't want to be a lawyer." Her serious frown matched the confused crinkle between her eyebrows. "I feel stuck."

"All that matters is you're happy," Bobby said with a serious expression, more serious than Cole thought she was capable of being. "The people, the situation, the feeling that makes you happy. It shouldn't matter what your mom wants for you, it isn't her life. What do you want?"

Who knew Bobby could be so wise? Cole was a little proud. He elbowed her, trying to show her how much he liked her advice. She giggled.

Jess didn't answer. She stared at the envelopes, deep in consideration. Whatever her future looked like, Cole knew she'd accomplish amazing things. She worked harder than anyone he'd ever met. She also had a thirst for knowledge and an undying curiosity. He was interested to see where those traits would take her.

Cole ate another chicken piece. He felt better having food in his stomach.

"Hey, B," Leo said. He'd been unusually quiet. His stare was glued to her but his body jittered, revealing his nerves. "Do you wanna go to prom with me?"

A giant smile spread across her face. Bobby clapped. "Yes!"

***

Dave

Whatever drug Casey dosed Dave with was wearing off. His entire body felt sluggish and defeated. His face hurt. Was his nose throbbing? He couldn't tell because one of his eyes was swollen shut. His vision wasn't clear but he was pretty sure his tears had blood in them. Seriously, torture sucked.

His muscles tensed and ached with every movement. He needed a nap and a cheeseburger. But the burger would have to be made into a smoothie because he was pretty sure his jaw was broken.

The pain, the fists, the blood, the screams, his screams; it all would've stopped if he had told them who Height City Anonymous was. He didn't. He'd never send Jess to her death, even if she did stupidly do it to him.

Casey beat him up pretty well too. Her knife would leave a permanent scar on his throat and he'd never forget the feeling of her knuckles on his face. He couldn't believe she let him win.

Tommy bandaged Dave's wrists, arms, legs, and jaw. He worked expertly, making sure Dave didn't have any broken ribs or internal bleeding. He checked Dave's pulse, vision, and reflexes, then dosed him with some sort of pain relief drug. Tommy came prepared. "Congrats, you'll live."

Dave swallowed the blood in his throat. "Never thought I'd be champion."

"None of us did," Tommy said, a little too bluntly. "Guess the impossible can come true." He handed Dave a lollipop. "You did well with the stab placement."

Dave put the lollipop in his pocket. He remembered learning to fake a stab wound. Moira, one of Betty's inner circle members, taught him how to do it when he first joined the Crime Queen's ranks. He never thought he'd need the skill. He was happy he and Casey both survived but the new problem was that if Casey wasn't dead, Betty would come after her. *Nobody betrays Betty Beater.*

Her being alive also made Dave's title hollow. The rule was if you killed the champion, you became the champion and Dave didn't kill the champion. He'd have to be extra careful. If the underworld learned Cece was alive, her loyalists might come after him. Either way, every Burrower in Height City was watching his every move.

"I've been thinking," Tommy gathered the rest of the bandages and shoved them in his laptop bag. "With Casey out and I've got Martha and Timothy to think about now, maybe it's time for me to get out too."

He was always the Crime Queen's most reluctant student. He had the potential to be the best, the most skilled and ruthless, but he never seemed dedicated in Betty's lessons. He knew how to ignore his darkness and it'd be nice to see him escape it.

"Good luck," Dave said. In a way, they all won. They all lived, Tommy had his family, Casey got her friends back, and Dave had a higher rank. He wouldn't only be known as Ted Marson's son anymore. He'd keep his friends one way or another. Cole was still his roommate.

"Tell your girlfriend she owes me one," he tried to smile but it hurt.

Tommy finished setting Dave's nose. He bandaged metal against the bone so it could heal correctly. He yanked Dave to his feet and kept him from stumbling or tipping over.

The Arena was empty. After the lightning - or Alice to those in the know - took Casey, everyone was in shock. Hobbs announced Dave as the winner of the fight and the Burrowers cheered for him. They'd mourn Cece for a few days, then he'd have his first fight as David, Betty Beater's new champion.

High-heeled footsteps echoed against the cement floor. The familiar sound sent a fearful shiver down Dave's spine. While he was growing up, Ted told him stories about the Crime Queen, describing her as a Greek Goddess but with a more devilish flare. She wore a crown made of skulls and a dress the color of blood. The stories were what made Dave go to her when Ted was arrested. She only agreed to take him in after he set one of her henchmen on fire using his dad's old lighter. The guy survived, a little singed but he was fine. Betty accepted Dave as her first student because he used Ted's psychotic methods to earn her respect. He hated himself for doing it but at the time, he didn't have a second option.

A beautiful, slender, Asian woman stepped into the fluorescent spotlight. Her stiff, queen-like posture showed how ready she was for a fight. Her smile was cunning, wicked, with an invisible threat painted on her lips. Her calculated stare had a murderous gleam and it was impossible to tell what she was thinking.

Her black hair was twirled in a bun hanging low on the side of her head while sparkling strands of diamonds hung down from the back of her neck like a cape. Her fitted, red gown kept her back bare and her weapons hidden. A long, thin cigar was placed between her fingertips. "Quite a shocking end to the night, boys." Her tone was sinister and smooth. "Congratulations, David."

Dave tried to stand straighter but pain shot up his back, making him wince.

Tommy was still, solid as a rock, as he kept Dave steady. He looked at Betty without fear or defiance. His unreadable calmness and seriousness could be creepy and very intimidating.

"As my new champion," Betty focused on Dave. "You'll take up Cece's last mission. You'll find the person behind Height City Anonymous and kill her."

Dave planned for this. He reached into his pocket and smoothed out a crumpled check. It wasn't the one Layla signed but it was the same money. He didn't want Jess to be hurt. She made a mistake but that didn't mean she deserved to die. Besides, if she did, he wasn't sure how he'd handle it.

Betty took the check. She raised an eyebrow. "Five thousand dollars." She wasn't impressed. She seemed insulted. "Cheap. What is it for?"

"I'm buying the blogger's freedom. Whoever it is won't step foot in The Arena. She won't be hunted and she'll be set free," he took a deep, shaky breath. "You can kill me if you want."

She folded the check and slipped it into her bra. She took a long drag from her cigar and blew the smoke out in three perfect circles. She was in control. She could kill him with one swift motion, using one of her blades or maybe the gun she kept strapped to her thigh. Betty smiled. "I accept but I suggest you tell your ex-girlfriend to keep her blog posts focused on anything besides my organization."

She knew? Of course, she knew. She was the Crime Queen. She was Betty Beater. She had eyes all over Height City. She made it her business to know everything. There was a reason she was top brass.

"Can we go?" Tommy asked. His tone was respectful, level. No fear or nerves or hesitation.

They'd been raised by this woman, trained by her. Dave had never been able to look her in the eye. If he did, she might steal his soul and trap it in a jar or something. He wasn't sure what Betty could do to him.

Tommy didn't cower in her presence but he did stiffen a bit.

"Of course," Betty gestured to the door. "Be sure to tell Cece that I expect an explanation for her treachery."

Dave couldn't believe it. How did she know! The boys left as fast as they could, Dave limping beside Tommy. They shared the same look. The same thought: *We need a plan.*

Chapter 25

Jess

"Honey! Are you ready?" Bennett called from the living room.

Jess turned the corner, heading down the stairs. She smiled. It felt good to know tonight could be fun and light-hearted. No stress or threats were hanging over her head. Tonight was extra special for her because Jess helped organize the Morgan High Senior Prom.

Her parents stood at the bottom of the stairs. They looked at her with pride and love. For once they seemed to agree on something; their daughter looked beautiful.

She wore a pale pink, slender gown layered with long tulle. It had some glitter, a sweetheart neckline, and no sleeves. Her hair, long and wavy, was loose over her back with a thin braid, decorated in gold leaf barrettes, clipped behind her head.

Bennett took a picture. "Gorgeous as always."

"I liked the other dress better. It'd make your eyes pop-" Layla stopped when Bennett gave a loud, warning sigh.

Jess appreciated the back up. She posed for a few more photos, then grabbed her purse and left the house.

Alice

Alice was a little surprised about how excited she was for senior prom. She never went to school dances. She barely took an interest in socializing her freshman year and the past few years had kept her busy. Part of her wished Mason could be there to send her off. She wondered if he was okay.

A car horn interrupted her thoughts.

"That's our ride!" Leo hurried down the metal staircase. He rushed past the den and went to his dad.

Mister Scotts was fiddling with his brand-new camera, trying to understand how he was supposed to take a picture with it. "I can't figure this out."

Leo took the camera and handed his dad a tie. It was orange, probably to match Bobby's dress.

Alice stood behind the room divider, which acted as a bedroom wall. She never noticed how much the father and son looked alike. Their eyes were the same shape. They stood the same way. They had the same build and the same nose. Everything else Leo seemed to have inherited from his mom.

Mister Scotts tied the tie while Leo fixed the camera.

He pressed a couple of buttons and slapped it. "What did you do to this thing?"

"I pressed a button," Mister Scotts said. "I was trying to turn off the flash."

"Don't press it again, okay? It almost had a heart attack."

Mister Scotts finished the tie. He patted his son's shoulders and smiled with pride. Leo wore one of his dad's old suits. It was a bit big on him but he looked handsome.

Alice smiled. She came into the living room, twirling the emerald ring on her middle finger. She liked wearing it, she liked being part of their family. Her dress was a soft pastel green. It had spaghetti strap sleeves and a fitted waist. She also wore her favorite sneakers - the ones Mister Scotts bought her - and her hair was in a ponytail. She had just redyed it.

"Beautiful," Mister Scotts gestured to her and patted Leo's shoulder. "And dashing. Okay, it's picture time. We can't keep your friend or your date waiting."

Leo and Alice put their backs together and crossed their arms. She couldn't help but laugh. She had no idea why she agreed to this pose but Leo had begged her. Mister Scotts took the photo, then took one of Leo by himself and Alice by herself.

She liked being in her mom's dress. She could almost hear Susan's voice telling her to have a good time but not too good of a time. Alice chuckled as she imagined the memory she'd never get to have.

"Do you want me to send this photo to your dad?" Mister Scotts asked.

Alice hadn't seen or spoken to Mason in what seemed like forever. Eddie stopped sending her updates, he was busy with the bar but he'd let her know if Mason was hurt or if something was wrong. She couldn't see any reason to send a prom photo to her father but at the same time, why couldn't he care?

"Yeah. Yeah, go for it." She hugged Mister Scotts and left with Leo.

***

Bobby

"Nervous?" Sally asked.

Bobby wanted to answer but her throat was dry. The sweat on her palms was making her fingers sticky. She couldn't believe she was there. She couldn't believe she had a date. She and Leo hadn't been on any actual dates or even kissed again. Were they a couple? Were they starting to be? Bobby only knew his existence made her smile.

"If he hurts you, I'll get my shotgun." Sally smiled but it wasn't a joke.

Bobby appreciated it but she wasn't worried about Leo breaking her heart. She didn't need to protect herself from him. He'd never harm her or even think about harming her. She couldn't wait to see him.

She couldn't wait to go to prom.

"Did you ever go to your prom?" she asked.

"I'll dig out my old yearbooks and you can see," Sally shook her head. "I looked horrible, big hair, even bigger dress," she chuckled, waving away the memory. "It was a long time ago. Right now, you go dance your face off, okay?"

"X is SOS." Bobby hopped out of the jeep.

She remembered when she dreaded going to school. When she was hungover with a pounding headache, when she didn't know what mood Johnny would be in, and when she had mean girls to deal with but now, she couldn't wait to go inside.

Colorful streamers hanging from the ceiling created a vibrant rainbow above the tile floor, which was covered in orange, pink, blue, and purple confetti. A black and white spiraling balloon arch decorated the double doors leading into the gym.

Her classmates, wearing tuxedos and fancy gowns, filled the gym, chatting at round tables scattered by the walls, dancing in the center of the room to upbeat pop songs, and eating at the refreshment table, which had all kinds of cookies, chicken wings, a big bowl of cherry punch, a vegetable plate, several pizzas, chocolates and other candies, and tiny bottles of water.

The decorations were incredible. Layered fabrics of all different colors hung from the walls, ruffled and sparkling, creating wondrous caves and hiding places, while lights shaped like triangles, circles, and squares twirled and blinked over everyone's faces and bodies.

Miss Z and some other teachers who volunteered to chaperone stood by the photo booth, monitoring it to make sure none of the kids did anything they weren't supposed to. Principal Penez walked around the dance floor, hands folded behind his back, as he searched for any inappropriate behavior or PDA he needed to stop.

Bobby's confidence in her homemade outfit grew once she saw what everyone else was wearing. If there was a reward for best dressed, she'd win for sure.

Her fitted, dark orange gown had a detailed beaded design on the chest. One long sleeve hung over her right arm and the other arm was bare except for a leather bracelet Vincent made. The pleated skirt was cut above her knees, revealing black tights with a faint glitter decoration. Her fiery hair was curly as usual but with a simple, yellow carnation tucked behind her ear. She also wore her sparkly, four-inch heels.

Leo looked really good in his black suit. He looked nervous, glancing around, waiting to spot her. When he saw her, he smiled. His smile made her heart jump. Alice and Jess were with him, each holding a red, plastic cup. They were both beautiful in their dresses.

"What are we talking about?" Bobby asked.

Jess smiled. "I was about to tell you guys that I finished the article on the 'Woman in Lightning'." Her excitement couldn't be contained, she was practically squealing. "It just needs final approval."

"What was the name you guys decided on?" Alice was jumping out of her skin, too excited to stand still.

Bobby couldn't wait to reveal the super suit. She and Karen had a few things to add but it was definitely fit for a hero. Hopefully, it would've made Glisin proud.

"Okay, Cole and I did a lot of debating. It took forever," Leo chuckled. He was excited, fidgeting with his suit jacket. Was he pausing for dramatic effect? Very impressive.

Jess and Alice shared a slightly annoyed, curious glance. It was the same look Bobby would've shared with Casey.

Where was Casey? She promised she'd show up. Bobby made her pinky swear. She knew it wasn't a big deal to pinky swear but she liked the idea of it being a big, binding promise and Casey knew that.

"Tell us!" Bobby hopped, heels clicking on the floor. She grabbed Leo's arm and tried to shake the name out of him.

He laughed. "Okay!" he said. "Okay. We went through our list and we crossed off a lot of options until we picked the perfect name." He rolled his tongue as a drumroll. "Eidolon!"

He gestured like a showman, proud of himself and the name.

Bobby loved it. It sounded mysterious and epic. She could picture it being in the headlines and on the front page of every newspaper in the city.

"What do you think?" Jess asked.

Alice had a beautiful smile. It showed how much she appreciated the things that made her happy. Her purple hair was long, straight, and pretty. It would've looked better down. The ponytail made her hair less noticeable but she still looked great. Tall with a thin, toned body and faint blue eyes.

After the longest minute ever, she nodded. "Post it."

"Don't you want to read it first?" Jess asked.

"I trust you completely," Alice said. "I love your writing, I love the name, so yeah," she smiled. "Do it."

"I'll go post it now," Jess hugged Alice, quick and appreciative, then hurried away. Her pink dress went well with her pink streaks. She looked like a princess but a pretty one who was poised and elegant, not an obnoxious bitch.

Bobby turned her focus to Leo. She fixed his tie as an excuse to stand closer to him. It was orange like her hair and dress. Her favorite color. "Why'd you pick this tie?"

"What?" he glanced down at it. "Oh, uh," he started blushing. His entire face turned red. "I thought it looked good. I like orange."

Bobby smiled. She intertwined their fingers and squeezed his hand. She wasn't sure which one of them was more nervous. Could he hear how loud her heartbeat was? She could barely hear herself think. Her nerves were making her nauseous. She didn't eat anything before she came. Maybe food would help her feel better, less awkward.

Leo stared in awe at their interlocked fingers.

She tugged his arm to get his attention. "You wanna get something to eat?"

She nodded toward the snack table.

"Sure," he said.

They headed to the refreshments.

***

Jess

Thrill, pride, and excitement coursed through Jess's body every time she finished an article. She felt accomplished and creative. She debated giving it up but she couldn't. Her blog's following had grown. Her purpose, at least for the foreseeable future, was clear. This was her calling.

She posted the article about the 'Woman in Lightning'. She did a pretty great job on the writing and hoped to get more attention from it. She wanted to see how far she could take Height City Anonymous. Maybe she'd build a media empire someday. She knew one thing, she wasn't going to be a lawyer and her mom would have to accept that.

"Isn't the party in there?" Dave asked. His voice was a bit hoarse, probably from all his injuries. He wore a gray suit without a tie and his hair was messy. His nose was healing well. Some small bandages were on his face and his black eye had faded. He was standing a little better too, less shaky and unstable.

Jess put her phone in her purse. "What are you doing here?"

"Bobby and Cole wouldn't give up," he said. "What are you doing?"

"Posting an article." She wasn't sure what to do. She didn't want to pick her cuticles, it'd reveal how weird she felt. Why was this weird? They weren't strangers. They'd been through a lot together. He showed her an entirely new world and protected her from its dangers. She'd never be able to thank him enough for everything he'd done for her. She wondered if other people had such an intense connection to their first love.

"Thank you again," she said. "For whatever it is you did or said to Betty. It means a lot to me that I don't have a target on my back." Jess asked him several times to tell her how he saved her life but Dave wouldn't budge. She gave up. She'd be more careful from now on. She'd stay away from Betty's organization and report on other crimes in the city. She was curious to see what else was happening in Height City's shadows.

Dave tried to shrug but winced instead. "You're welcome."

What else was there to say? The conversation seemed to be over.

She turned toward the gym but she couldn't walk away yet. What if this was the last time they saw each other? What if this was the end of their era? Was getting back together an option after everything? Whatever they used to have was over, she ruined it. Her mistakes were unforgivable. But Jess couldn't imagine her life without him.

She turned to him. He was staring at her. His loving, regretful expression surprised her. Could she have imagined it? In less than a second, his face changed back to his unreadable blue eyes and charming smile. No emotion, no regret. Nothing.

"Friends?" Jess asked.

Dave took a shaky breath in. "Sounds good, princess."

She smiled. The first time he called her 'princess', it was a rude insult meant to hurt her because she was a Honeycomber, now it was a sign of affection. She felt better. Maybe they wouldn't completely lose each other after all.

"Enjoy the party," she said, going into the gym.

***

Dave

Dave sighed. His face, body, and his heart hurt. He wanted to tell Jess how beautiful she looked, how she didn't need to thank him for saving her because he'd do it again, no matter what. But he couldn't. He watched her go into the gym. He let her slip away, too far for him to reach her or find a way to repair whatever happened between them. It was time to let go. They had different futures and his new title would only put her in danger.

Dave was Betty Beater's champion.

He already felt the respect that came with the title. Now, he needed to keep it. He asked Tommy to help him train. People didn't know his win against Cece was a lie but Dave did and it didn't sit well with him. He promised himself he'd win his next fight fair and square.

"Hey, buddy!" Cole wrapped his arm around Dave. He wore a powder-blue tux with ruffles and sparkles. Believe it or not, he bought it.

"Still sore," Dave pushed him off.

They walked into the gym. Neither had ever been to a school dance before or attended high school at all. What was the big deal? These were the same people Bobby and the others saw every day, except now they wore overpriced clothing and costume jewelry.

Alice and Jess were together at the edge of the crowd, dancing and being goofy, doing dance moves from the eighties and nineties, and laughing at themselves. Cole patted Dave's shoulder and moonwalked over to the girls. They started a three-person conga line.

Dave went to the snack table because he was too sore to dance.

Leo and Bobby were huddled together, blushing and chuckling, as they ate chocolate chip cookies. Bobby looked cute. She looked happy. She pointed excitedly toward their friends, took Leo's hand, and yanked him over to others. She twirled him and he stumbled into Alice.

She steadied him while Jess admired Bobby's dress.

Cole took a yellow flower from Bobby's hair and gave it to a boy wearing an expensive, plaid suit, which was an interesting fashion choice, almost as interesting as Cole's tux.

What was it about these people that made Dave so damn happy?

He pulled a flask from his jacket, flipped open the cap, and poured some bourbon into the punch bowl. He always wanted to spike the punch like in the movies.

"I saw that." Brittany Mikes held out her hand and gestured for the bottle. Should he hate her? Didn't Bobby say they were frenemies? Dave wasn't totally sure what 'frenemies' meant.

The peacock feathers in Brittany's long, curly hair matched the ones decorating her greenish-blue dress. Her makeup seemed to be professionally done with gold sparkles in her eyelashes and dark red lipstick. She also wore heels and held a little black purse.

Dave hated to admit it but she was hot.

He handed her the flask. "Are you gonna tell the principal on me?"

It'd be entertaining to see the Morgan High principal try to tell him what to do.

Brittany put the tip of the flask against her lips and threw her head back. It seemed she could hold her liquor. Impressive since she was a Honeycomber.

She closed the bottle and sighed, refreshed. "Good stuff."

"I know a guy," he said.

Casey broke into some Honeycomber guy's fancy mansion on a job for Betty. While she was inside, she stole a bottle of old, expensive bourbon from his wine cellar. Maybe it was from the O'Hares? Dave wasn't sure but he liked it.

Brittany handed him the flask. Her eyes floated over his body. She smiled, a cute, flirty smile, but something in her eyes was cold, confident. "Where'd you get the bruises?"

"Oh, you know, I wrestled a bear," Dave said. He tried to smile but his face hurt. His vision was clear and the pounding in his head had stopped but he was still sore. He didn't have the energy to come up with a lie, so he made a joke.

Brittany didn't laugh but her smile didn't fade either. Maybe she did have a sense of humor.

"I'm sure," she rolled her eyes. "I'm Brittany, by the way."

"Dave," he said.

"I know. Bobby's mentioned you, so has Jess," Brittany said. He could only imagine the kinds of things Bobby told her. The stories from their everyday lives would make him look like an idiot. He wondered what Jess said about him, especially while they were together. Good things, he hoped.

"You know, I've always wanted to ride a motorcycle. Maybe sometime you could take me out," Brittany said. Was she flirting with him? She walked away as if she knew he'd watch, as if people would fall at her feet and beg for her autograph.

***

Tommy

Tommy never imagined himself at a school. He'd been to Baltic but it was for business, not learning. He studied on his own with the help of Betty and her inner circle. Part of him felt guilty for wanting to leave her. Betty saved his life, taught him, trained him but Tommy knew he could live without her. He wasn't sure he could live without Casey or his friends or the Cruises.

Alice, Jess, Leo, and Bobby were all doing the robot, trying to see which one of them had the most accurate moves. Dave wasn't far from where they were dancing. He must've been acting as the judge because he was too bruised to join in. The idiot could've been killed. Tommy didn't know how Dave possibly survived his torture. Lorenzo and Moira did thorough work.

Cole was dancing with some guy in a plaid suit who had a yellow flower in his jacket pocket, wearing it like a boutonniere. Were they flirting? They seemed fascinated with each other.

The gym looked amazing with top-notch decorations, layered fabrics creating caves and hiding places, flashing lights, and hundreds of balloons. The music was upbeat and energetic, perfect for dancing, which was what everyone was doing, including the teachers.

"Puts *Footloose* to shame." Casey stood beside him. Her dress was black. It had a halter top and a fitted, knee-high skirt. Her shoulders were bare. Unlike him, she was never embarrassed about her scars, which showed prominently on her skin. A leather choker was around her neck alongside her angel wing necklace and her earrings were shaped like little, silver stars. Her blue and blonde hair was styled in a braided crown with a few loose strands framing her face.

Bobby probably had some input on the outfit.

Casey had a leather holster, which held a knife, strapped to her thigh. To the untrained eye, it wasn't noticeable but Tommy could spot every single hidden weapon Casey had on her.

He didn't put much thought into his appearance. He wore a nice, button-up shirt with jeans under his black, leather, racer jacket. It had two sewn-in holsters and hid the gun on his hip.

"We should prank the principal. Maybe glue his desk to the ceiling," he smiled. He saw it in a movie once. He knew it wasn't realistic or easy but he always wanted to do it to someone.

She chuckled, a light-hearted chuckle she rarely used. "Or put a chicken in his car."

"Where could we get poultry on such short notice?" Tommy asked.

Earlier that night, he reluctantly agreed not to talk about her dire circumstances as Betty's ex-champion. Casey wanted to enjoy the party, so she made him promise not to worry about her the entire night.

She took his hand and pulled him forward. He took a few steps, then stopped when he realized where she was trying to take him. The dance floor. Both her hands were around his wrist, she tugged his arm. "Come on, let's go dance."

"I don't dance," he said. He didn't like to dance in public. In private, he was a master at Just Dance. Cole had a Wii and was obsessed with the game. But other than that, Tommy tried to refrain.

"Make an exception." Casey wasn't taking no for an answer.

She stepped closer to him, hands sliding up his arms, then loosely clasped behind his neck.

Bodies pressed together, all Tommy felt was heat and electricity. He traced the scars on Casey's arms and shoulders, each one a different tragic story. Her green eyes sparkled in the flashing lights, watching him with an expression only he could read.

At first, their bodies synchronized in a slow sway, then linked as one, they stepped into a waltz. The waltz was simple. The easiest dance Betty made them all learn. He had to count in his head to keep track of the steps but Casey didn't have any trouble. She liked to move. Dancing, gymnastics, fighting, it was all in her wheelhouse. But he matched her in most skills.

Shockingly, she let him lead.

Hand resting on the small of her back, Tommy guided her through each step. Her strong, eager heartbeat made him forget his dislike of dancing. She pulled away, fingers locked with his, but he pulled her back. He knew what she was thinking. She wanted to take him out of his comfort zone, so he beat her to it.

Tommy twirled her twice, fast and elegant, then brought her closer. He tucked one hand under her leg and lifted her up. She held him tight and he slowly spun around. She squeezed his shoulder, chuckling, excited and surprised.

He set her down, twirled her again, and guided her back into a simple waltz.

"Nice moves," Casey smiled. "Got any others?"

"I don't know if you can keep up," he said. Tommy knew she'd take it as a challenge.

Casey did a stylish, slightly sexy hop and twirled around him. She relocked their fingers and he twirled her again, then she stepped into his arms and let him hug her, arms around her torso. She smelled like sandalwood. She held his wrists and kept herself against him, leaning into him.

The entire room, all the noise and chaos, faded.

He guided her into the correct position, so they were facing each other. No distance between them, forehead to forehead, arms around each other. They swayed to the imaginary music in their heads because the real music was a bad techno song.

"After tonight, we should start looking for leverage on Betty," Tommy said. He couldn't help himself. He didn't want to waste any time. "Once we have something against her, it'll be that much harder for her to kill you."

"We're lucky she hasn't tried anything already," Casey said. Her gaze drifted to their shoes and the happy, blissful moment was broken. Something was wrong. She reached for her angel wing necklace but stopped herself. She held his shoulder, trying not to squirm. "Um, you said something interesting," she clicked her tongue. "Before my fight with Dave when I didn't know what side to pick." Her body tensed and she gulped. It was a privilege to see her nervous. "You said *we* love you, did you mean..."

She couldn't say it. He liked that she wanted to know. They never actually said the words but he was pretty sure they'd both felt it for a while, maybe since their first kiss.

Tommy was shocked when Casey kissed him on the ledge of their favorite rooftop. With the necklace dangling between them, sparkling under the moon, she kissed him and all the stars seemed brighter, better, the city too.

He wasn't sure how long he had liked her or when his crush developed but after the kiss, his feelings were clear. He didn't know what to do next and neither did she. The day he kissed her at Sally's Place, she had the same expression that she had now. The need to ask or say something but without the words to speak it. She needed him to take the lead.

"Casey." He gently cupped her face in his hands. He wanted to be clear. No jokes or miscommunication, no boundaries or walls they kept up to protect themselves. He smiled. "I love you."

It was the first time he ever said it to another person and was sure he meant it.

Casey chuckled, a relieved, happy chuckle that matched the brighter green in her eyes.

He assumed she wouldn't say it back. He didn't need to hear it. He knew how many walls she kept up, even when she trusted someone. She'd tell him how she felt when she was ready. He could wait.

"I love you too, Tommy Gleason." Casey kissed him, arms wrapped around his neck.

Tommy hadn't heard that phrase in a long time. It always sounded like a lie or a responsibility but this wasn't. This was honest, meaningful, and had been a long time coming. Casey loved him. He couldn't imagine wanting to be loved by anyone else.

His arms encircled her completely. He lifted her up - maybe in celebration - arms securing her torso. She bent her knees and held herself against him, hugging him.

He set her down.

Casey held his forearms, happier than he'd ever seen her. "Say it again."

"You first," he pulled her close and kissed her again, deep and sincere. He never wanted to let her go, maybe he'd never have to.

She chuckled. She cupped his face in her hands, palms lightly pressed against his cheeks. She teased him with her tongue and whispered that she loved him like it was a secret only he was allowed to know.

Tommy smiled. "So, should we revisit the ship name ideas?"

"Not this argument again," she rolled her eyes but her smile didn't fade. "Just kiss me."

He didn't get a chance to kiss her again because Brittany grabbed her arm and yanked her away from him.

Casey looked ready to jam a screwdriver in Brittany's eye.

Tommy's heart was racing. He didn't realize how fast it was. He cleared his throat and tried to come down from the "I love you" high.

"Criminal chick, I need your help," Brittany said in an urgent tone.

"With what?" Casey asked, wiggling her wrist out of Brittany's grip.

"Stuffing the ballot boxes," she said. "I'll explain on the way to Miss Z's classroom, come on." She wasn't leaving without Casey.

Tommy kissed her quickly. "I'll see you in a bit," he whispered. She nodded, then followed Brittany across the gym and into the hall.

Tommy smiled. He wasn't sure he'd ever been this happy before.

His phone buzzed. The red dress emoji. He clicked the video attached to the message. He recognized the furniture in the living room and the shadows in the kitchen. The counter where Fernanda made dinner, where Timothy did his homework. Tommy spent several evenings in the Cruises' kitchen, helping Timothy with his Latin and math.

A muscular, dark-skinned hand grabbed a stainless steel steak knife. *Hobbs.* He'd been in the Cruises' mansion. The camera moved up the grand staircase and through the halls. Decorative, modern art and antiques were on every surface. The windows looked out onto a wrap-around, stone balcony and a vast, green yard. Timothy was in his bedroom, asleep.

Tommy's heart dropped into his stomach. He felt nauseous, frozen. How did he not see this coming? Why didn't he figure it out?

Betty didn't move against Casey because she planned a move against him. This threat, this video, meant she wanted him. Why him? How was he more important than Cece?

Betty had a plan. Of course, she had a plan. The bitch was always thirty steps ahead.

***

Leo

Leo's legs were starting to ache. He needed to sit or lay down. His shoes were pinching his toes.

Bobby could move. She wasn't tired at all. Neither were Alice or Jess. They were all laughing and dancing, twirling each other and doing silly moves. Cole was flirting with Isaac Cohen, Cindy's brother. They seemed to hit it off.

The music stopped and the lights flickered on. Was the party over? Was it wrong if Leo wanted it to be? He'd rather be at home with his friends, on his couch, than at a prom but Bobby made it better. She made everything better.

Principal Penez stood on the stage wearing a simple suit. He had giant bags under his eyes. He seemed annoyed. He didn't want to be there either. At least Leo wasn't the only one.

"Let's get this over with, huh? Since you all voted, I figure you care who's prom king and queen, so," Principal Penez sighed, bored. "Here to announce the winner is, your junior prom queen, Brittany Mikes, give her a hand, people."

He stepped back. The students clapped, whistled, and cheered as Brittany came on stage. The cheerleaders started jumping, overly excited, as Brittany thanked the principal and grabbed the microphone. She owned the spotlight, holding an envelope decorated with yellow and blue scribbles and a drawing of a falcon.

What was the big deal? Why did they need a king and queen? To make other people feel bad or the winners feel good? Leo didn't get it but he enjoyed the perks of being a voter. Cindy's campaign for prom queen included chocolate-frosted, vanilla cupcakes, which tasted great, if not a little like desperation.

"Prom king... Leo Scotts!" Brittany yelled.

Wait, what? Leo wasn't sure he heard right. Was this a joke? Everyone clapped, following Brittany's lead. Half of these people ignored him for four years and the other half called him Leon. He didn't care. He didn't want to be known. Alice's camera flashed in his face, blinding him for a few seconds.

He loved her but he wanted to put her on a train headed to the other side of the country. Was that normal? Leo didn't know what the protocol was when you had a sister.

Bobby smiled, hopping up and down. She looked beautiful in her homemade dress. She shoved him toward the stage.

He stumbled up the steps and went to Brittany.

She handed him a wand or was it a scepter? It was a plastic stick with a cheap, reflective orb. The crown was covered in fake jewels. All eyes were on him, which made him want to shrink into oblivion. Was it too late to hide?

"Now for the important announcement," Brittany's voice boomed off the microphone. "Morgan High's newest prom queen is Bobby Jones!"

Colored lights flashed across Bobby's face. Her shock was visible from a distance. Her eyes were wide, her mouth hung open, and she was white as a sheet. All the false rumors, all the stupid insults, all the uneducated opinions proved that nobody voted for her. So, how was this possible?

Leo nodded for her to come up. *Might as well.*

She came on stage. Brittany placed the plastic, gold tiara covered in fake topaz, on Bobby's head.

She faced the crowd, standing tall. It reminded him of the freshman play except this time, nothing knocked her down. He never knew someone could be so vibrant and strong. Everything she did was amazing. She gave him his first kiss. Seeing her was the best part of his day.

Three years ago, Leo wouldn't have been able to imagine this scenario; he had an incredible group of friends, a girl who liked him, and a sister. He'd been part of some amazing adventures and one gruesome cover-up.

Mick's corpse and the vacant, hollow look in his eye still haunted Leo, keeping him up at night, torturing his mind. It was the worst, most horrible moment of his life but it was also the most thrilling, which left him feeling twisted and insane.

Their classmates clapped, cheering and shouting "Congratulations" but Leo swore he heard one guy yell "Recount!" While others looked confused, whispering questions like "Do you know him?" or "Isn't that the slutty girl?"

Bobby looped her arm with his and waved, ignoring the whispers.

He laughed, nervous. All Leo wanted to do was get off stage. Public attention was awful.

***

Casey

Bobby hugged Leo's torso and waved to the crowd. It was good to see her happy. Leo looked stiff and awkward. If Bobby hadn't been holding him, he would've jumped off the stage.

Alice was taking photos, Dave was using her as a crutch, and Jess was telling the deejay what song to play for the king and queen's big dance. Cole and the Honeycomber, who now seemed to be his date, stood a few feet from the group.

Tommy was nowhere to be found.

Casey snuck away to find him. She understood how someone could love an empty school. The halls felt haunted like the rooms at St.Marian's that were off-limits. She pushed open the front doors and found Tommy sitting on the steps. His eyes were on the sky. The stars weren't visible but the full moon was huge, hanging over the city, with a cold, lonely light.

"Hey, you okay?" she asked.

He looked entranced, lost in a chaotic thought process and dark memories. What happened? Not an hour ago, they were together, they were happy. Casey loved dancing with him. He was a good dancer, better than her, and he always made it fun.

Tommy told her he loved her. It was the best three words she'd ever heard. She told him she loved him too. Once she said it, she never wanted to stop saying it. She loved him more than she ever thought possible and she wanted him to know that.

She sat beside him on the steps. "T, talk to me."

He flipped his phone over in his palms, then shoved it in his jacket pocket. He looked her in the eye as if nothing was wrong. He leaned his shoulder against hers and kissed her forehead.

She loved the quick, attentive kisses he left on her forehead, cheeks, and fingers. She loved when his fingers traced her scars and when he held her in his arms, she was home.

He put his forehead gently against hers and played with one of the loose strands of her hair, tucking it behind her ear.

Bobby suggested the braided crown.

Casey stared at Tommy's half-closed eyes, waiting for him to say something. Anything. He was freaking her out, acting as if the world was about to end.

Their friends burst through the front doors, laughing and yelling at each other, the night's excitement radiating from them. Dave and Leo were arguing about who would win in a fight; Alice or Wonder Woman, which seemed like a pointless argument. Bobby had her arms locked with Cole's, they were whispering about the boy he'd been dancing with and he was blushing.

"I'm exhausted," Jess sighed.

"You guys wanna go to Linda's?" Alice asked.

"Yes, cheeseburgers," Leo practically licked his lips. He handed his cheap, plastic crown to Cole and tucked a beanie on his head.

Cole put the crown on and posed like a knight. "What do you think?"

"I like it," Bobby said.

"Who else is sick of the prom?" Dave lifted his flask. Casey took it and drank the last few drops of bourbon. The bourbon she stole and generously shared with him. He snatched the flask back, tipped it, and shook it. He slapped the bottom but nothing dripped out. "Not cool, Cavalier."

She enjoyed messing with him. "Relax, Davey, I'll steal you another bottle."

Leo changed the position of Bobby's tiara, so it was crooked, her curls fluffed underneath it. She looked good in a crown. It suited her. Her hand found its way into Leo's and he smiled. He was gentle with her, kind and caring, which Casey liked. She still needed to have the if-you-hurt-my-best-friend-I'll-kill-you-in-your-sleep conversation with him but he probably didn't need it. He was a good guy.

Casey's focus returned to Tommy. He walked beside the group, nodding along to the conversation and chuckling at the jokes like nothing was bothering him. But she knew better. Something happened, something he didn't want to talk about. She had to trust him. He'd tell her when he was ready.

He wrapped his arm around her, holding her close, so they were walking together. "You wanna split a brownie when we get there?" he asked.

"How about we split a brownie and some cake," she suggested.

"I'm never taking this off, my new official name is King Cole." Cole tapped the crown. His blondish hair was unbrushed and messy. He wore his fancy, powder-blue suit with pride but he looked ridiculous. He had the same goofy, sweet smile he did when they were kids. He was the only orphan she remembered who ever seemed to dream of a better life. He had hope, and when the others tried to beat it out of him, Casey didn't let them.

"I'm never gonna call you King Cole," Dave nodded toward the plastic crown. "I'm hiding that thing when we get home."

Leo pointed to an alley. "There's a dumpster back there."

"No!" Cole announced. "I'm never giving up my royal status!" He ran down the sidewalk, waving the crown above his head.

Dave shouted a couple of hilarious curse words and limped after him. His bruises slowed him down.

They yelled insults and pathetic trash talk at each other.

Leo hurried to join them. He attempted to tackle Cole but wasn't fast enough. Cole dodged him, jumped on a car's hood, and declared they couldn't get him because he had the high ground.

"Oh my god." Jess stood next to Casey. She was staring at her phone. "One thousand subscribers have read the 'Woman in Lightning' article."

"What?" Bobby laughed. She squealed, clapped, and elbowed Alice. "You're famous! Wait," she turned to Jess, excitement paused. "How many subscribers do you have?"

"Six thousand so far and growing every day." Jess showed them the screen. At the top of the article was a picture of several white lightning bolts twisting together to create a giant one shooting toward a large building engulfed in flames. It was Alice at the Adler Building Fire. Next to the picture, it said ONE THOUSAND VIEWS. Not even close to half the city.

"Damn," Casey whispered. "Guess it's official, you're Height City's new hero."

She was proud of the girl with the purple hair. The girl who saved that boy all those years ago. Had it really been three years since they met? Alice had come a long way, and so had Casey. She wasn't Betty's champion anymore. Cece wasn't the champion. It felt weird but right.

Jess's article would start rumors. Criminals liked to talk. They were cautious when it came to heroes. After Glisin died, everything changed. The underworld shifted. New rules were put in place and Destroyer crawled back into her hole. As long as everyone stayed away from the Trenches, nobody got hurt and she didn't come out. It was a solid system.

Alice stared at the screen, perplexed. This was what she wanted, wasn't it? She chose to become the next Glisin. She was pretty stubborn in her decision. Her hand dove into Dave's jacket pocket - which he gave her to hide one of her bruises when someone asked where she got it. She lied and said she tripped backward into a door. - she held up a small, buzzing device.

"What's that?" Bobby asked.

"Karen made it. It reads frequencies," Alice said.

"Police radios," Tommy said. He knew all about technology, so of course, he understood the logic. He could probably explain how it worked and what each individual piece did.

Alice nodded. Her purple hair was falling out of its ponytail in a stylish mess. Under Dave's brown, leather jacket, Alice wore her mom's pastel green gown, which suited her, she looked beautiful. The flickering street lamp above her created a dome of pale blue light, engulfing her in a euphoric sense of heavenly air. She put the device in her messenger bag, which was hanging across her torso, and brushed the hair away from her face. "I'll meet you at Linda's."

"Go save the day, Sparky," Casey smiled. "I'll order you a piece of pie."

Alice chuckled. White lightning flickered and glittered against her skin. It sparkled in her eyes, reflecting the powerful storm that raged inside her. Within seconds, her body vanished, replaced by pure electricity. An unstoppable entity. Twisting and looping together, always moving.

It cracked across the ink-black sky, illuminating the world and challenging the moon.

That will always be cool, Casey thought.

Chapter 26

Mason

COLD STRUCK. ICEY BRICKS slapped Mason in the face and ripped him out of a deep sleep. His lungs squeezed as he gasped and coughed, desperate to catch his breath. He sat up. He was soaking wet. He was lying on a cot in Eddie's office. Mason had slept there several times.

The wood desk had dark, metal hinges on each corner and a padlock where it opened. The window was square and tinted, the blinds were shut. The coat rack, buried beneath a sport coat, several hats, two scarves, and a holster meant for a gun, stood by the door. Framed black and white pictures taken from Eddie's army days decorated one wall.

The old man didn't like talking about his military days.

Mason couldn't remember anything from the past week. *Crap, not again.*

Eddie stood at the end of the cot, dressed in a button-up shirt and nice slacks. His gray hair was starting to turn white. He wore a wedding ring but he'd never been married. He dropped an empty, tin bucket on the floor and crossed his arms. "Five, two, eighteen."

"What?" Mason rubbed his head. What day was it? Why was he being asked a math question? He was way too hungover for math. He needed about six aspirin and more whiskey. Why was he in a suit? Did he get another job? Blood was splattered on his tie.

"It's been five years since your wife died and you fell off the wagon. Two years ago, your daughter moved in with her teacher," Eddie hissed in disappointment. "She's going to be eighteen and she's graduating high school today."

Mason remembered the list differently. Five years ago, the love of his life went into a fight she knew she couldn't win and was murdered by the most feared criminal in the entire city. He watched her body crumble from his TV screen. He wasn't there with her. He didn't get to say goodbye or have a funeral for her. He was forced to create and tell heinous lies about her.

He was afraid to be a single father. How could he raise such a perfect child alone? How could his wife have chosen all those strangers over her own family?

Two years ago, his daughter left him. He couldn't blame her. He failed her in too many ways. She deserved better than him. She found it.

Eddie slapped an envelope on the desk. It had Mason's name written on it. What was it? His tab? Because he didn't have enough money to pay it right now.

"The only reason I ever let you hang out here is because Susan was a friend and Alice deserved to know where you were every night but I'm done with your crap," Eddie's angry glare could've melted stone. "You need to be an adult again. You need to take responsibility for your actions and your choices and you need to go to your daughter's graduation or you'll lose her forever." He shook his head. "Maybe you deserve that but she doesn't."

"She's better off without me," Mason pointed to the envelope. "What's that?"

"A ticket to the graduation ceremony. Mine's on the bar. Alice invited me," Eddie yanked open the door. He grabbed his sport coat and a flat cap from the coat rack. "If you don't go and beg her to forgive you, and clean up your act, then you can forget about ever coming here again."

He left. The door's slam made Mason flinch.

***

Alice

A toddler, wearing tiny, purple overalls and adorable braided pigtails, walked by the window. Her parents held each of her hands, protecting her, comforting her, caring for her. She had nothing to worry about, nothing to fear or make her ache. The world was bright and waiting to be conquered.

Alice remembered that feeling. She remembered being innocent but she wasn't sure if she missed it.

She sat in her regular booth at Linda's Diner. It hadn't changed in thirteen years, maybe longer, neither had the owner except for a few added wrinkles. Linda set two plates on the table. Pie and cake. She smiled. "It's on the house. Happy graduation, darling."

"Thanks," Alice chuckled. So many memories were wrapped up in this place. The times she came with her parents, the times she came to study or stress eat, the time she met Casey - it was still weird to call her Casey, not Cece - and the times she and her friends spent there.

Prom night being one of them.

They all smashed into one booth and ordered french fries, cake, burgers, and pie. They talked about nothing, everything, and they laughed. They laughed a lot. Linda stayed open late, so they had the diner to themselves. Linda seemed to enjoy having them there. She knew all their names.

Casey walked in wearing her leather jacket, a gray T-shirt, ripped jeans, and her boots. Knives were hidden in various places on her body, a gun too, probably. Her angel wing necklace hung beside a leather choker. It was the first time Alice had seen her without a new bruise or scratch or bandages on her knuckles.

She looked the same as she did when they first met except for a few more scars and her hair was blonde. The blue had mostly faded. Casey hadn't said if she was going to redye it.

She sat across from Alice and dropped a big gift bag on the table.

"What is this?" Alice asked.

Casey clicked her tongue, "A gift, a present, a donation, an offering to the goddess of energy," she shrugged. "Whatever term you prefer. Open it." She leaned forward and smiled. Her excitement was unnerving.

Alice stood on her knees and reached into the bag. The leather was cold, brand-new. She pulled it out. The bomber-style leather jacket was a few shades brighter than her hair. She shoved her arms through the sleeves, feeling the warm fleece inside. She untucked her thick, long hair and spread it across her shoulders.

She smiled. *Perfect fit.*

"You love it?" Casey asked.

She nodded. She couldn't express how much she loved this jacket. The smell of the leather and the feel of the fleece was amazing. She felt like an instant badass. She always wanted one.

"Check the pocket," Casey said.

Alice obeyed. Her fingers felt around. Nice material. Was that rubber? What was it?

She took it out; Glisin's mask. "Is this real?"

If this was a joke, it wasn't funny.

Casey nodded once. "I did a little grave robbing last night," she smiled. "I figure Karen and B will finish your suit sometime in the next twenty years," she jokingly rolled her eyes. She was the one who kept assuring Alice that Bobby would finish the suit and it'd be perfect. "And when they do, you'll need the perfect mask. Like it?"

"I love it. I absolutely love it," Alice said. This was the greatest gift ever. Seeing it again, feeling it again, was incredible. She could picture her mom looking in the mirror, wearing the mask. She looked different behind it. Stronger. Alice never realized how much the mask changed Susan. When she put it on, she became someone else. To Alice, Glisin was her mom, a hero, but to Height City, to the world, Glisin was a memorialized entity who kept evil at bay. Maybe one day, they'd see Eidolon the same way.

The thought made Alice nervous. *Wait a minute.* "You robbed her grave?"

"Yeah," Casey chuckled. "It was fun." She laughed harder, amused by the memory. "I made one of the grave digger guys pee his pants. It was hilarious."

"You're unbelievable." Alice grabbed a fork and stabbed the pie.

Casey ate some cake. They switched plates multiple times until the two desserts were gone. They waved to Linda and went their separate ways. Alice had a graduation to get to.

The buildings were colorful, vibrant reds, blues, greens, yellows, oranges, and pinks. Some of them had vintage designs or were made of brick. Most had modern touches and new roofs. Every building stood solid and steady, reaching toward the clouds. Others were short, little gaps between the tall ones, almost funny how different they were. Midgets against giants.

A taxi and another car honked at each other, both stuck in traffic. The taxi driver leaned out his window and held up his middle finger. The other man screamed curse words at him.

Behind them was a billboard advertising the New Adler Building.

Cruise Industries, Vance Technologies, and several other major companies donated money for the reconstruction after the fire. Mayor Mikes announced that it'd be finished in a few months and the new design was dedicated to the 'Woman in Lightning'. Otherwise known as Eidolon. Secretly, Alice Johnson who still had trouble believing the dedication but she loved it.

She tied her hair into a ponytail and took a deep breath. She adjusted her leather jacket. The fleece felt great on her bare arms, soft and warm but not too warm. As soon as the light told her to go, she rushed off the sidewalk, sneakers slapping the pavement. Her heart was racing but her pulse tracker stayed silent.

She was so incredibly late.

People crowded the street, trying to find a parking spot. They shouted directions and frustrated insults, honked their horns, and tried to maneuver around each other. The crossing guard kept blowing his whistle while fifty turn signals flickered in different directions.

Alice shoved open the front door, making them burst open, and she stumbled into the hall. She almost face-planted into the tile but she caught herself. She headed to Mister Scotts's classroom, sneakers squealing on the freshly mopped floor.

The entire school had been cleaned from top to bottom. Everywhere you looked, there was a banner or poster shouting Congratulations seniors!

Mister Scotts stood by the door, looking at his watch. His hair was neatly combed and his bowtie had little, cartoon graduation hats on it.

"Sorry!" she shouted. "Sorry, I know I'm late. I ran, I swear, I-"

"No time." He handed her a plastic garment bag. It held a dark green graduation gown. Her graduation gown. Alice smiled. It was simple, understated, and probably cheap but it was one of the greatest things she'd ever seen.

Mister Scotts plopped the graduate cap on her head and patted it down, making sure it was secure. The pride he had for her shined through his smile, matching his kind eyes. "Go get changed. They're seating people, so you need to hurry."

She nodded and went into the classroom. She unzipped the bag. The gown was polyester. She shoved her arms through the loose sleeves. Her faint reflection on the whiteboard looked grown up, larger than life, tall and beautiful.

She wondered what her mom would've said to her today. Would Susan have had any advice to give? A pearl of wisdom? Mason might've made a joke about becoming an adult. They might've even taken the traditional photo of the parents with the graduate.

Alice would never know.

"There you are." Jess stood in the doorway. Her long brown hair - with its vibrant pink streaks - was in many delicate curls slightly squashed by the dark green graduate cap and spread across her shoulders. Their gowns matched. She held a stack of note cards, her valedictorian speech. She seemed more stressed than usual. Was she sweating? Her fingers weren't bleeding, which was a good sign.

"Nervous about your speech?" Alice asked. They headed down the hall.

"That's not what I'm nervous about," Jess flipped through the note cards too fast to read them. "I'm not nervous at all, I'm terrified. What if Layla has a heart attack? What if she kills me when I tell her?"

"It's too late, you missed the deadline. You have your plan, it's a solid plan," Alice said. "Just tell them like ripping off a Band-Aid."

Jess decided she didn't want to go to college, at least for a while. She was afraid going to college would distract her from her blog, which was getting more popular. Height City Anonymous had hundreds of emails and tips sent to it every day. Jess wrote articles using the information. Layla and Bennett had no idea she purposely missed the deadline for Zak City Law, they had no idea Jess started following her own plan and stopped following theirs. She picked one of her cuticles, then yanked her hands apart.

"I'm proud of us." Alice locked their arms. She meant it. She was proud of herself and Jess. They had both come a long way from who they used to be. And she was glad they stuck together. They were closer than they were before, less fragile. No more lies separated them.

Leo appeared at Jess's other side. He held his graduate cap on his head. His best hat yet. He twirled in front of them, walking backward. He looked grown up. His solid-colored bowtie matched the dark green color of the gown and his new dress shoes were shiny, clean. "We're graduating! Can you believe it?"

He laughed.

He talked about it all week. How it was the next chapter of their lives. A brand-new beginning. A horizon to be met and an adventure to be had. The cheesiness was outweighed by his excitement.

He high-fived both the girls. He flicked the tassel on Alice's hat. "Dad wants us to take us all out to Linda's Diner later, and by 'us', I mean everybody."

"Are you gonna introduce him to Bobby?" Alice asked.

Leo and Bobby spent time together over at Sally's Place but they weren't at the loft often. They were still learning to be together but there was no questioning how they felt about each other.

Leo chuckled, blushing. His nod was interrupted by girly giggling.

Brittany and Bobby were leaning against the lockers. They had become quite the chums. Apparently, all was forgiven. They both wore a graduation gown and cap.

Brittany waved and headed in the other direction while Leo took Bobby's hand and pulled her beside the group. She hugged him as they walked.

Bobby's big, teardrop earrings sparkled under her fiery curls. She wore the plastic, prom tiara on her graduate cap, and the tassel was covered in glitter.

"Are you really gonna wear a crown when you get your diploma?" Jess asked.

"Why not? I look good," Bobby shrugged, fingers interlaced with Leo's. Alice admired Bobby's total disregard for others' opinions. She was a stronger person than Alice expected.

"Hey, did you guys hear about Tony?" Leo asked.

"Ugh, Tony," Bobby rolled her eyes. "Whatever he did, I don't wanna know."

"Me neither. Hey, what do you think about this line?" Jess showed Alice one of her note cards. The neat, intricate handwriting was written in black ink.

"Oh! I totally forgot," Bobby pulled Leo to a stop. "Good luck with your speech, Jess, we'll see you guys out there."

The couple ran down the hall.

***

Bobby

Leo didn't resist Bobby's pull. She wouldn't have let him anyway. She was on a mission and she needed him as a partner. She wanted to commemorate the day. This amazing event neither her father nor her best friend would see. She gave Casey special permission to miss it.

She shouldered open the door, yanking Leo into the girls' bathroom, and they stumbled. Her heels slipped on the tile but he grabbed her. He held her waist and kept her steady.

She loved his arms around her.

"I'm pretty sure I'm not allowed in here." His curious glance meant he didn't mind.

She yanked him into a stall. They were close, so close she could hear his heartbeat. He gulped, staring at her, unsure of what to do next. Whatever he thought, it wasn't what she was doing. She pulled a permanent marker from her panda purse and held it between them. Bobby wanted to erase the rumors about her. Literally, she couldn't, but metaphorically, she could.

She drew a giant blob on the words BOBBY JONES IS A WHORE. Bobby scribbled over anything else rude or mean about her, then clicked the cap on the marker. She didn't want future generations to judge her on an idiot's opinion.

She faced Leo.

He chuckled. "Why didn't you do that before?"

"Brittany or Cindy would've done it again and besides, I didn't think of it until now," she laughed. It felt good to be here with him, giving herself a fresh start.

He gestured to an empty space on the wall. "Write something positive. Like, um, 'puppies' or something. It'll be your version of revenge."

She loved the idea. Something positive. Maybe something hopeful? Something that made her feel good, brave, and happy. There were too many options to pick from, so she settled on the subject at the very top of the list. Hers and Leo's initials in a clumsily drawn heart.

"Too cheesy?" she asked.

He smiled. "A little but... I like it."

"I can't believe I'm here. I can't believe I'm graduating."

She was determined not to cry. They'd be happy tears but still. It was a good day. She always pictured herself as a drop-out or worse, especially with the company she kept. She loved knowing Sally would be there to cheer her on, she loved knowing Leo would be there to hug her when the ceremony was done. This was the perfect surprise.

"Let's go graduate," he whispered, fingers drifting between hers.

She held his hand. She loved holding his hand. She wanted to kiss him but they were already leaving the bathroom.

The school set up a small stage in the parking lot. Parents, grandparents, siblings, aunts, uncles, and family friends were behind the dark green, polyester sea made of graduating seniors. Karen, Sally, Eddie, Layla, Bennett, Grandma Scotts, Dave, and Cole were scattered about, somewhere in the crowd.

Bobby and Leo split and went to their seats.

Principal Penez started the ceremony.

***

Casey

Casey needed to get leverage on Betty as soon as possible. She was fairly certain her friends could handle themselves but she preferred the insurance. Tommy texted her to meet him at their spot; the rooftop where they first kissed. The place where they watched the stars and stood above the city.

Maybe it was about a plan. Maybe he had some ideas.

The sky encased the world in a cloudy dome. Skyscrapers reached up and shorter buildings were squashed below. The road was a thick line of chalk. Horns echoed and pigeons flew by. It was quiet, protected, the perfect escape.

Tommy stood on the stone ledge wearing his gray hoodie under his leather jacket. His hands were in his pockets. The holsters were hidden well but she knew they were on his waist, ankle, and shoulder. There were probably a few other surprises hidden under his clothes.

His face was reserved, expressionless. He didn't look at her. Why wouldn't he look at her?

She stepped onto the ledge. Her balance was perfect but the possibility of death was so accurate that it gave her a slight thrill. Casey used to walk the ledge on St.Marian's roof. She taught herself how not to fall. Up here, she was invincible. Nothing could touch her.

"Betty wants you to come back," Tommy said. His tone was neutral, no emotion.

She didn't get it. Tommy already told her the Crime Queen knew she was alive and wanted an explanation. It was an invitation Casey declined. Why was he repeating himself? Unless the offer had been renewed.

Why wasn't one of Betty's lower henchmen telling her? Why Tommy? It didn't make sense. He was still technically part of the gang but Betty wouldn't have her favorite deliver a message. It was below his rank. This was meant to say something.

"How'd she get to you?" Casey asked.

He took a deep breath, staring at the road. He still wouldn't look at her. "Take the deal."

"Or what?" She knew the answer. If she didn't take her place as one of Betty's assassins or the champion again, she'd be hunted down and murdered. The Crime Queen always got her traitor.

"You know," he said.

Casey faced him, standing still, and she spread her arms like wings, making herself a willing target. It was a guess as much as a challenge. "Do it. Kill me."

Tommy finally met her gaze. If he felt anything, he didn't show it. He had to know what she was doing. If he didn't play along, he'd show weakness, not only his but Betty's. *You're only as strong as your weakest link*, she once said. She was right. That's why Betty never let anyone slip up.

He pulled out a gun. Glock twenty-seven. He built it himself. He could break and rebuild any gun within an hour or two, at most. A skill Betty taught him. He pointed the barrel at Casey's chest, finger steady on the trigger. One simple move and he'd end her life.

Neither of them broke eye contact.

Casey waited for him to do it. Part of her wanted him to kill her, prove that he was never on her side, prove that he was never in love with her, but he didn't.

Tommy stood there, frozen, pointing the gun at her heart.

She dropped her arms, slapping them against her sides. She chuckled. "No wonder she likes me best." It took all Casey's strength to keep herself in control. She wouldn't cry. It'd be weak. "Too bad I'd rather get eaten by a giant slug than be her bitch again."

He kept the gun between them. He could shoot her at any moment and end it all. He'd be the bringer of her death. He'd give Betty exactly what she wanted but Casey wasn't afraid. Thinking of death was like thinking of an old friend she wasn't ready to meet. Anger didn't begin to describe the way Casey felt; she wasn't just mad, she wanted to slice Betty's throat.

Her chest ached with the broken pieces of her heart. Tommy was the first person she ever truly trusted. He was the only person to ever say he loved her. Casey shared every insecurity, every hurt, every memory with him. All her darkness, all her weakness, the best and worst parts of who she was. She never would've guessed he'd be her worst betrayal.

"You're not invincible, Casey." He'd been saying that since she became the champion. She kept proving him wrong. She was trained in the art of torture and murder. She could use over fifty different kinds of weapons, could fight in almost every style, and knew Height City like she knew her own scars. She remembered how she got every single one. She learned from each experience.

She stepped closer, putting herself against the gun. "If Betty wants a war," she stared Tommy in the eye, cold as ice. She threw up every emotional shield she could, not allowing him to see her fear or heartache.

He didn't move or look away. He was still, unwavering, unemotional. They were both perfectly balanced above the city. Neither one was likely to break.

"I'll give her a war," Casey finished.

She turned and slowly tipped over the ledge, letting herself fall. The wind whistled against her ears as her hair whipped above her head. The Earth hurtled toward her, closer and closer and closer; She was in complete free fall. Free and unattached.

Her boots slammed against a window washer's scaffold. The force shot up her legs, making them shake, but she stayed standing. She grabbed the railing as the scaffold rocked back and forth.

Her overlapping breath shook and shuddered. Her heartbeat was fast, too fast, hammering inside her chest. Incredible thrill was overshadowed by unimaginable grief and horror. Not only did the Crime Queen want her dead but Tommy was now Casey's enemy.

Casey felt as if her heart had been torn from her skin and snapped in half right in front of her. She lowered herself to her knees, unable to stand by herself. Her legs felt weak, her knees felt like crumpled paper. She wanted to scream but a burning rage kept her quiet. Betty Beater's entire arsenal; her army and all her resources against Casey Cavalier.

Hardly seems fair, she smirked.

Chapter 27

Alice

ALICE STOOD IN MORGAN High's empty halls. She remembered being surrounded by other students, so many voices, so many lives but she was alone.
Unloved and alone. Nobody cared if she existed, not even her.

Today proved her life had changed. All those people she saw when she walked
on stage; Karen, Eddie, Grandma Scotts, Sally, Dave, and Cole cheering her on.
When Principal Penez handed her the diploma, they all stood up. Mister Scotts
clapped the loudest. It meant everything to her.

"You did great." Mason stood in the corner wearing a tan jacket and a simple,
blue tie. How did he get a ticket? She didn't get him one. She figured he wouldn't
care but here he was. Her dad saw her graduate but instead of congratulating her
or saying how proud he was, he looked ashamed and sad.

She knew those feelings weren't directed at her but it still hurt.

"I wish Mom were here," Alice said. What would Susan have said today?
What would she have worn or eaten or anything? Her mom didn't get to cheer
or be in the traditional graduation photo. Of course, when were the Johnsons
ever traditional?

Mason smiled. It'd been a long time since he smiled. "She'd be so-"

"Proud?" The familiar voice - delighted and entertained - made Alice's blood run cold.

The devil incarnate. Her black cocktail dress had tassels hanging from the hem and her colorful heels were covered in fur. Her hair was long, curling into vibrant, rainbow colors. She was beautiful in an evil, sinister sort of way, with no emotion on her face except a bloodthirsty smirk. And her hands were hidden inside red, leather gloves.

The sight of this woman made Alice want to vomit. Her entire body froze, stuck to the ground and stiff, unable to hear herself think. Her heart stopped, at least, she couldn't hear it anymore or could she? There was an intense thump echoing in her head but she couldn't tell what it was. She couldn't breathe. Everything felt distant and blurry. The lockers, the floor, the walls, and all the exits were a thousand miles away. Nothing was clear or made sense. She couldn't move. Was she having a heart attack?

"Destroyer," Mason said. He sounded far away but he was still standing next to her.

The woman laughed. She jumped and spun in the air, ankle slamming against his face. He hit the lockers. CLANG. His body and her heels clapped to the floor at the same time.

She flipped her hair. She pulled off her gloves, hooked them to her belt, and grabbed Alice's wrist.

Alice's skin tightened, suffocating her, stealing her breath. Her organs were being ripped apart piece by piece. Her ribs folded in on themselves, crushing her lungs, and her heart inflamed, burning inside her chest like agonizing fire. She couldn't break free. Her scream echoed, distant and hollow, but her voice wasn't connected to her body. Was this what Susan felt before she died?

Instinct kicked in and Alice's insides juddered, powerful and unfaltering. The vibrations fought against Destroyer's grip, against the pain and death. She couldn't control it. She didn't want to. As much as she wanted to hug Susan again, Alice wasn't ready to die.

Gunshot.

Destroyer twirled and reached out her other hand, grip firm on Alice's wrist. A bullet soared, zipping through the air, crashing into the villain's palm, and it became nothing but ashy pebbles, which slid between her fingers and sprinkled onto the tile.

"Oops," Destroyer chuckled and shoved Alice into the lockers.

She hit the rough metal and slid onto the floor, falling flat on her belly, arms stretched above her head. Her blurring vision was focused on her unconscious father. The unbearable pain became an enraged soreness throughout her muscles and bones. She could almost feel her mother reaching out to her, welcoming her into the abyss.

***

Jess

Rapid gunshots came from a few halls away. Jess knew it was one of her friends but which one? What were they shooting? If Cole and Dave decided to shoot pudding cups in the cafeteria, she'd be really pissed. Maybe the anger would overcome her guilt and uncertainty. She told Layla and Bennett about her plan. She was going to take a year off and figure out what she wanted. Her mother didn't take it well.

"I probably shouldn't have done that!" Dave screamed. He sounded afraid.

Cole yelled, "don't let her touch you!"

Panicked footsteps squeaked as the boys skidded around the corner and ran toward her, their faces filled with fear. What in the world? Why were they so freaked out? What happened?

Dave grabbed her arm, yanking her beside him, hand locked on her wrist. She stumbled a bit but caught her balance, running behind him. He didn't slow down. Cole ran by his side, eyes wide and panting. Neither said anything.

They kept going. They ran as fast as they could. They tried to turn the corner but slipped, bodies slamming against the lockers.

Pain shot up Jess's arm. *Seriously?* She whimpered. "What-"

"What's going on!" Bobby yelled. Leo stood beside her. They looked perplexed, which was good, it meant they were in the same boat as Jess was.

Dave's fingers shook on her wrist but he didn't let go. Was he using her to keep himself steady? Why? She'd never seen him so utterly terrified.

Cole looked the same way.

"So, our newest hero does have a team," Destroyer twirled around the corner, chuckling. Glisin's killer. The infamous leader of Height City's powered-people gang. The woman who scared everyone out of the Trenches and made it her fortress. She was here. Murderous delight in her eyes.

"You just had to write the article," Dave whispered.

Was he blaming Jess for this? She couldn't believe it. She wrote about Eidolon. A woman with lightning or energy powers seemingly connected to Glisin. Nothing about Alice's identity or anything about them. How dare he blame her unless could he be right? Terror struck.

Could they run? Could they hide? What were they supposed to do? Were they supposed to accept death? They were all frozen to the wall, fearful and powerless.

Bobby hid halfway behind Leo, who looked about ready to faint. His fists clenched at his sides.

Cole held onto the lockers for support. The panic in his eyes was bright and terrible. He shared a mournful glance with Dave who was white as a sheet. This was it, wasn't it? Jess faced death before but it still scared her.

"What do we do?" Leo asked.

Cole screamed, "ALICE!"

***

Alice

Her skin shredded against her bones like sandpaper. She wanted to cry or scream or wait for the pain to subside but it wasn't an option. They were in danger. She had to get to them.

She needed to save their lives.

Alice yanked herself up, stumbling, as she tried to stay on her feet. Her knees wanted to buckle but she resisted the urge. She ran. The tiniest movement sent fire through her bones. Her chest felt hollow but a heavy weight kept her from breathing.

All that mattered were her friends.

She passed a gun lying on the floor with piles of ashes surrounding it.

She faced her worst nightmare and survived; the woman who killed her mother. The woman who killed Glisin. Height City's first hero. The woman who gave her life for its people, its children, and its very soul.

The faded image of Susan's smile came into view. Her laugh echoed through Alice's head. The smell of her cooking, the way she moved, her mango perfume, the way she playfully bickered with Mason, the color of her eyes, the comfort of her touch, were all moments that helped turn Alice into who she was now. Her mom would be proud.

Her sneakers slid as she rounded the corner. Loose strands of long, purple hair fell into her face. She slammed against the lockers. Her chest rose and fell in rapid motion, matching the speed of her panting breath. Her pulse tracker beeped.

She heard heartbroken screams that weren't her own. A body crumbled, fingertips, eyes, skin, and bone became ash, which sprinkled from the air and fell into a pile at Destroyer's feet.

Her laugh was triumphant. Her smile was entertained as if it were all a game. She strutted away, confident and daring, chaotic and terrible. No one would stop her. No one could.

This wasn't the nightmare that started five years ago. This was a new hell, a new grief that wasn't for Glisin. This was a new responsibility for Height City's second savior.

The war had only just begun.

Thank You!

Thank you for reading the first installment of The Masks Series.

If you want updates about the series and the author's journey, please check out the author's bio page, follow Payton on social media, and join her newsletter. You can find links to her newsletter on her website and on her various social media accounts.

Don't forget to leave a review on Amazon, Goodreads, Fable, social media or anywhere else you enjoy leaving reviews.

The second book in The Masks Series

Available on various platforms, including Amazon, Kobo, and Bookshop.

Acknowledgements

Creating a book is a lot more work than I originally expected. Writing has been one of my favorite things to do since I was thirteen which is also when I began brainstorming the world of The Masks. These characters have been with me through thick and thin, and I am so excited to share them with everyone. What I didn't realize at thirteen was how many steps there are to the publishing process and how many people it takes to make a book great.

So, that said, I'd like to thank:

My very first reader. She supported my stories and my dream of being an author since I started writing. She's read each of my first drafts (there were many) and she's fangirled over the characters and their friendships with me for years.

And my beta readers, you're amazing. I loved working with all of you and appreciate your support and incredibly helpful feedback. Thank you.

My amazing baby brother whom I spent hours creating imaginary worlds for and who introduced me to the Arrowverse which is one of the many inspirations for The Masks series.

My mom who has supported my dreams no matter what they were, and never made me doubt myself or question what I wanted. You are the reason I was brave enough to start publishing my stories.

I am extremely grateful for everyone who helped make my author dreams come true.

Payton Balog is an author of speculative/superhero fiction with a little bit of everything. She enjoys writing fun banter, action-packed storylines, and emotionally depth characters. She is a proud big sister and a survivor of chronic kidney disease. When she's not writing, she's either reading with one of her adorable cats or relaxing with a TV show.

Connect with Payton:

Linktree: https://linktr.ee/authorpaytonbalog

Website: authorpaytonbalog.wixsite.com/authorpaytonbalog

Instagram: @paytonbalog.author

Threads: @paytonbalog.author

TikTok: https://www.tiktok.com/@authorpaytonbalog

YouTube: https://www.youtube.com/@paytonbalog.author

Pinterest: @authorpaytonbalog

Goodreads: https://www.goodreads.com/authorpaytonbalog